CRUEL ILLUSIONS

MARGIE FUSTON

HODDER &
STOUGHTON

First published in Great Britain in 2022 by Hodder & Stoughton
An Hachette UK company

2

Copyright © Margie Fuston 2022

Published by arrangement with Margaret K. McElderry Books, an imprint of Simon
& Schuster Children's Publishing Division. First published in the US in 2022.

A CIP catalogue record for this title is available from the British Library

Hardback ISBN 978 1 399 71136 4
Trade Paperback ISBN 978 1 399 71135 7
eBook ISBN 978 1 399 71137 1

Printed and bound in Great Britain by Clays Ltd, Elcograf S.p.A.

Hodder & Stoughton policy is to use papers that are natural, renewable
and recyclable products and made from wood grown in sustainable
forests. Theloggingandmanu   facturing processes are expected to
conform to the environmental regulations of the country of origin.

Hodder & Stoughton Ltd
Carmelite House
50 Victoria Embankment
London EC4Y 0DZ

www.hodder.co.uk

For Lucas, who's the best
storyteller I know.

CHAPTER 1

I always stop for lost-pet flyers. I can't stand the thought of animals out on the street when they have a home and a family waiting for them. This one's a cat, and even though the paper's yellowed from the sun and the ink's smeared from the rain, I memorize the gray stripes and the name: Suzy.

Maybe Suzy's already back home.

Still, I dig a pen out of my backpack and write the number on my wrist, where I'm less likely to wash it off. I've found a missing pet only once, but I remember the way the little dog squirmed in my arms when we reached his door and the way his owners almost cried and then hugged me like you would a long-lost relative—they gave me twenty bucks, too.

Sometimes I wish I could post a flyer and have a kind stranger show up at my door and give me back everything I've ever lost.

But most lost things never come back.

My hand drifts to the four quarters I always keep in my pocket. I pull them out and fan them between my fingers, blinking them away almost as quick. I give a bow to a watching squirrel. It turns and runs into the street, dodging a car just to escape my performance.

I smile. Magic reminds me of Mom and Dad. The good memories.

The bad one creeps in too. It never leaves, and this time of year, it's all I can think about.

Shoving my quarters out of sight, I speed the hundred yards down the sidewalk. I take the stairs to my foster house two at a time and fumble with the lock on the red door while the Rolling Stones' "Paint It Black" runs through my head.

The hardwood floor creaks as I enter. No matter where I go, this house speaks to me with every step. Even when I'm not moving, when I lie in bed staring at the notches in the wooden beam dividing the ceiling, it groans and whispers as it stretches its worn joints. It has too many stories to tell to stay silent. I love to listen to them, especially at night when everyone else is asleep.

I've been in new houses, all white and beige and clean. The silence of them eats me alive.

At least this house has one thing going for it.

"Dinner," I yell up the stairs. I head straight for the kitchen and pull out a bowl of leftover spaghetti from the refrigerator and plop it in the microwave. I tap my fingers on the tiled countertop as I wait.

It beeps, and I set three plates out, spooning spaghetti onto them in heaps.

I'm still alone in the kitchen.

"Guys," I yell again.

Parker and Jacob stomp down the stairs, drowning out any of the subtle creaks and groans with their chatter. They take the two seats next to each other. Figures. I end up alone on the other side, watching them.

Parker and Ava Perry. We share a last name. It should be me and him, with everyone else on the outside. Jacob's the bio-kid of the house. He doesn't need Parker the way I do. But I keep my feelings off my face these days. When we first got here, Parker and Jacob bonded instantly over video games and *Star Wars* and zombies. They acted like they'd been friends forever. Or brothers. But I noticed Parker cutting his laughs short when I was in the room and looking at me like I was a fragile thing his laughter might hurt. It did. It does. But I *want* this for him. I'm glad he loves it here.

I pull out two quarters. "Do you want to see a trick?" Mom did card tricks every night at the dinner table. I'd cheer, and Parker would too, but he doesn't remember it. I wish I could give him those memories to hold on to, but this is the best I can do. Mom gave me these quarters when I was five to practice sleight of hand because my fingers were too small for playing cards, and I've never used anything else. I tuck one quarter between my thumb and palm, hidden from my audience. The other quarter, I press into the back of my hand. "I can pass this coin through my skin."

Parker rolls his eyes. "I already know how you do that one, Ava."

"I don't," Jacob says.

"She's got two quarters." Parker blows the whole thing.

I let my hidden quarter clank to the table. For a second, I keep the other one pressed into my hand. Sometimes I get the urge to push it straight through my skin, like it would just go—no trick, just real magic. I dig it in a little and nothing happens except for an angry red line when I give up.

I used to try stuff like that a lot as a kid, especially after Mom died, when I needed a little magic that wasn't pretend. I don't know why I still do it.

Shoving my quarters back in my pocket, I pick up my fork and press it into the table, gone soft with age, scratching in another gouge.

Nobody will ever notice. This table looks like it's been through a lot of families.

But it feels like a small rebellion and it distracts me from Parker and Jacob on the other side, laughing about some prank their friend pulled at school yesterday.

I deepen my gouge, then smooth my finger over the gash, suddenly wishing I could magic it away. But scars don't work like that.

I drag my plate over the mark and grimace as Parker shovels luke-warm spaghetti into his mouth. He hangs his jaw open so the noodles drip down his chin and lets out a low death gurgle.

Jacob snorts, spraying flecks of milk almost to my plate.

Disgusting.

I glare, but they're too wrapped up in their zombie lovefest to notice.

Jacob turns serious, widening his dark brown eyes. "Dude, I would totally put you down if you got bit."

Parker nods. "Same." He swallows the spaghetti he's talking around. "No hesitation."

"I'm going to put you both down if you don't shut up and eat," I growl.

They laugh in the high-pitched, cracking sound of twelve-year-old boys and start debating who the best zombie-fighting badass is.

I twirl a bite of spaghetti on my fork and shove it into my mouth, chewing without tasting.

For the hundredth time, I glance at the hideous clock above the refrigerator. The hour hand settles on the faded drawing of the rooster by the number seven. Deb is late. She's almost never late. I actually like that about her. She's not the worst foster-whatever. I'm just supposed to get the boys dinner, and she makes sure it ends up in their mouths and not all over the floor like entrails.

"Ava, can we be done?" Parker and Jacob stare at me with wide,

MARGIE FUSTON

innocent eyes, their plates still half full. I'm sure they have a stash of cookies in their room.

"I don't care."

They bolt and leave me alone to clean up their mess.

Figures.

Pushing back my chair with a scrape, I start stacking the dishes, then dump them in the sink.

I look at the clock again. Seven p.m. on a Friday night. *Friday*. I let myself smile a little. Parker and I watch *The NeverEnding Story* together every Friday night no matter where we are. Even if we don't have a DVD player, we tell the story to each other. I can recite that movie scene by scene—but that's not something I usually brag about.

My steps lighten as I hurry from the kitchen and dart up the stairs, dusting the banister with my hand as I go.

I pause outside the bedroom with the yellow hazard sign nailed to the door. Inside, the pop, pop, pop of an automatic rifle mingles with the bloodthirsty cries of young boys.

I rap on the door and silence answers.

Parker opens with raised eyebrows. He doesn't remember what night it is.

I almost back away. Forget it. But I can't. It's tradition.

"It's movie night."

Realization crosses his face . . . but not excitement.

I fidget, scraping at a hangnail with my thumb.

Parker turns to Jacob, who's smiling as he sits on the lower level of their bunk, facing the TV across the room. I wish I could see whatever look Parker gives him. Or maybe I don't. The nothingness is already growing inside my chest, and I'm a helpless princess in a floating kingdom, waiting for a little boy to save her and give her a name.

Call my name, Parker.

On second thought, maybe it's better if I don't watch *The NeverEnding Story* one more time.

Parker turns back to me. "I kinda forgot."

We share a last name, and still he can't make me feel any less alone.

I shrug. No big deal. I can sit alone in my room and swap stories with this house.

"Why don't you play with us?"

Jacob's smile widens, inviting me as well, but it's too wide to be sincere. He brushes a lock of hair from his forehead and glances back at the screen of frozen men with assault rifles.

Parker's smile matches Jacob's. They could be twins.

My brother's hair is bitter chocolate. Mine is too, but only because I dye it. It's naturally an almost white blond, but I got tired of people thinking we weren't related. My brother has my mom's round face and soft features. You can see the resemblance in the photo he keeps of her—all three of us sitting outside our trailer, the forest tight around us, my brother squirming in her thin arms, and me with my too-big dark brown eyes that mirrored hers. Parker with his deep blue eyes that matched our dad's. Our mom died two weeks later.

Parker loves that photo, but I can't look at it without picturing the way I found her body. And it's already so ingrained in my mind that I don't need the extra help.

Besides, if I want to remember our parents, I just look at Parker.

People say he's handsome.

Parker's staring at me with something like pity in his eyes, and I lock down whatever emotion he's reading on my face.

"I'm good." I back away from the door as Parker shuts me out.

The nothingness in my chest grows cavernous and hungry. The floorboards creak.

I open my bedroom door and close it behind me, leaning against the comfort of the solid wood. My room is brighter than the rest of the house. Deb painted the wood panels a soft dove gray. A purple bedspread and floral prints above the headboard give everything a light, girly feel. Silver-shaded lamps sit on white shabby-chic night-stands. It's the kind of room meant to appeal to any foster girls passing through.

I hate it.

Deb can tell. I don't know how. I've never said anything, but she offered to take me shopping for a new bedspread more my style. I said no. I don't like gifts.

I cross the room and plop sideways on my bed.

Mom pushes into my mind again. I *needed* Parker tonight. I needed a distraction, but I don't want to tell him why. I doubt he knows that this week is the anniversary of her death. She died when I was eight, just before Parker turned three. Dad died not long before I turned six, and I only have blurry memories of him that blend together. Parker doesn't have any memories of them at all.

I focus on Dad anyway. It's weird that the safer parent to think about is the one who died in a mugging gone bad, but I was so little that I don't really remember that moment. I only remember the before and the after. *Before*, I would stand on the side of a small stage at a little club or community theater, holding the hand of a babysitter while I stared open-mouthed at Mom and Dad on the stage making rabbits and birds and cats appear from top hats or from behind sparkling curtains. Dad wore a red vest made of sequins over a billowy white shirt. Mom wore red silk over a rounded stomach that held Parker. She always wore fresh red roses in her hair. I don't really remember anything else about Dad besides those nights on the side of a stage.

After, we had a trailer, and we moved around even more, and Mom was a little bit different, like a fancy dress missing the sequins it once had. She didn't talk about Dad very much.

I learned more about my dad from his Wikipedia page than I ever learned from my mom. Joseph Perry wasn't a magician with a household name, but he was well respected for his teleportation illusions. Some people speculate that he was on the verge of being one of the greats when he disappeared from center stage and became known for doing small pop-up shows with a mysterious woman—my mom. It perhaps made him *more* famous because he became illusive. And then he died. I've read all kinds of theories that he disappeared because he was running from someone he owed money to or another magician whose trick he stole, and that his death wasn't random at all. I've been down every odd rabbit hole and theory, but all I know for sure is what Mom told me: he was in the wrong place at the wrong time, and Dad couldn't actually make himself disappear.

Mom's death was different. I know what happened to her. I found her. I saw the wounds.

I'm about to let myself dwell on it when the door opens downstairs. Deb's home. If I'm lucky, Deb will go to bed without checking on me.

I'm never lucky.

She knocks on my bedroom door but doesn't wait for me to answer. She knows I won't.

"Ava?" My name in her mouth is always a question that she doesn't know how to ask and I can't answer.

She smiles as she slides through the door, still wearing her scrubs and practical white sneakers. Her brown hair is piled back with a clip that went out of style ten years ago. Her eyes dart around the room before settling on me, out of place, in the center.

"I bought you some things."

I notice, with horror, the bags from department stores dangling from her forearm.

"You didn't have to do that." I mean this on two levels: (1) Foster-whatevers get money to feed and clothe us, but that doesn't mean they actually have to buy us shit; (2) Deb wears a nauseating amount of pink. Her scrubs right now boast pink kittens. *Pink kittens.* I don't want anything in that bag. It probably has sequins.

"I wanted to." Deb's smile stretches like a worn-out sweater. She smiles too much, and I don't trust it.

She ignores the fact that I'm looking at her like a monster from a horror film and walks toward the bed. Her bags rustle together, creating the creepy soundtrack of impending doom. I scoot over as she drops them on the bed, and they all crinkle together in the big crescendo that lets you know the main character is not going to live much longer. I try not to flinch. I hope she'll just leave the stuff and go, so I can slide the bags under the bed without looking, but she rifles through them.

She takes out a pair of dark-wash jeans, loose and baggy. I only wear them that way or tight and stretchy enough to feel like skin— both work for running in a pinch. She glances at my face and takes my silence as confirmation that they're okay.

She pulls out a red T-shirt, plain and V-necked with a small pocket on the breast. I try not to let my face show any surprise at it not being pink. She sets it aside and takes out another pair of jeans, a green racer-back tank, a blue plaid button-up, a gray hoodie with thumb holes in the sleeves, and finally, a black tank top printed with tiny vines of red roses. It's the only piece of black in the pile, and it's marred with flowers. None of it is pink though, and I might actually wear some of it even if my wardrobe is usually composed of black at multiple stages of fading.

Deb fusses with the pile, clearly stalling, waiting for me to speak.

I almost say thank you and accept the clothes. It's perhaps a small enough gift I can accept without any strings.

She clears her throat first. "Maybe we can get rid of some of your old stuff."

I stiffen. Any words of thanks freeze in my mouth. "What's wrong with my clothes?"

Her eyes drift to my frayed T-shirt. The stitching along the hem is gone and the material curls on the edges. The picture of palm trees in the sun on the chest is cracked and splintered. You can just make out EAGLES above it and HOTEL CALIFORNIA below. A few more washes and it'll be unrecognizable. My jeans have a hole in the knee. I say it adds character.

"I just thought—"

"They weren't good enough."

"No." She looks at the door, probably wishing she hadn't come in here at all. "No. I just thought that starting college in the fall would be easier on you with some new clothes."

"I don't care what anyone thinks of me." *Including you.*

And I don't really want to think about the fall. I'm signed up for basic classes at the community college, but even that feels like something you do when you have an end goal. I don't really have a plan. I've spent so much time looking back, I forgot to look forward. At what point in my life was I supposed to let go of the past and do that? I feel like I missed it, and nobody was there to help me find it.

Anger boils over into the nothingness that filled me only moments before. It feels good to be full of something, no matter what it is.

Deb stands up from the bed. I half expect her to take the clothes back as she leaves. She doesn't. She just pauses at the door with one hand resting on her waist, covering a kitten chasing a ball of yarn. "You can wear what you want. I just wanted to do something nice for you."

　　　　　　　　　　　　　　　　MARGIE FUSTON

I'm sure the words are supposed to make me cringe with guilt. They don't. When you're a foster kid, people expect you to be grateful for the smallest things, like getting to go out to McDonald's for some nuggets that taste like they were made from cardboard chickens—the kind of things that other kids don't think about, much less say thank you for, when it's their real parents who are paying for it. I stopped being grateful for shit a long time ago.

Deb stands by the door for a minute, but I'm not looking at her anymore. I stare in the full-length mirror of my closet without seeing my reflection. I wait until my door clicks shut and then brush the clothes and bags off my bed and fall backward.

Deb's footsteps move down the hall. She opens the door to the boys' room, and their laughter weaves together like magic—like family.

And I want to be a part of that. I do. Deb's house is the best place we've been by far, but it's not fair to Mom. I can't let myself be part of this until I can really put her to rest—until someone pays for what happened to her.

I consider curling up in my annoyingly lavender bed and distracting myself by watching Criss Angel pull a quarter from his bleeding arm for the millionth time: a personal favorite. But I crave the familiarity of the night air on my skin—one of the only constant things in my life. It always calms me down.

I grab my beanie and my backpack, checking to make sure my crude wooden stake is still tucked away at the bottom. I always check. When your mom was killed by a vampire, how can you not?

CHAPTER 2

I wander, letting the repetitive sound of tires on asphalt push stray thoughts from my head. I will not think about Parker and Jacob laughing together. I will not think of Deb's condescending gifts. My body wants to run, find a rhythm and focus on nothing but breathing, but I *never* run at night. Running's an invitation for something to chase you. I want to be the predator, not the prey. Besides, I already ran five miles this morning.

Out of habit, I head to J Street, where more people gather at night—a vampire might find warm, drunk bodies and easily accessible necks there. After fruitlessly hunting all these years, I don't really believe I'll find one, but I still peek down the occasional dark alley, looking for anything odd. And I'm ready if I do find one. I'm fast. I'm more comfortable with a stake in my hand than a pencil. I spent years watching vampire movies and mimicking the moves of vampire hunters until my muscles remembered every action. I've seen every vampire movie twenty times. Not because I like them. I hate them—the scenes that make them seem good or sexy make my stomach turn—but they're all I have.

Because nobody knows shit about vampires except that they're out there.

Vampires revealed themselves when I was eight—just two weeks before I found Mom with dripping wounds on her neck that looked like bite marks. The adults wrote it off as some type of animal attack. When she died, I didn't know vampires existed yet because we didn't have a television. But once I got placed in a temporary home where the television ran all day, I knew what really happened to Mom. I felt it in the way my skin froze watching that redheaded bastard on television brag about how he hadn't killed anyone in a long time. His name was Gerald. There were a few others, but his face was on the television every day for weeks. The foster-whatevers I lived with at the time were obsessed with it. They had the news on constantly even though I said it scared me. They made me sit with them in the living room, all our dinners on trays, and watch news story after news story until all I could picture was that vampire's smirking face. All I could imagine was his teeth on my mom's neck, even though it probably wasn't him. He lived in Paris, but it didn't matter. I stopped sleeping.

That's when I started hunting.

In one interview, they asked him if a wooden stake to the heart really killed vampires, and the bloodsucker didn't answer, but I saw the way his mouth tightened and knew it was true. That was the first night I snuck out after the foster-whatevers went to sleep. I armed myself with pencils and made it only a block before I turned around and went back, but it felt good to be out there in the night doing something instead of crying and remembering.

A vampire took Mom from me. Me and Parker. I wanted to kill one, just one, to pay them back. If I could do that, I thought, then maybe I had a shot of smiling again and finding a family, because families liked happy kids, not kids who woke up crying.

Then one of the vampires killed a child not long after they tried to live "peacefully" with humans, and they disappeared again. By now most people have chalked the whole thing up to a hoax.

I kept looking though. It became a ritual almost. I had to check the night before being able to sleep. Eventually, I replaced the pencils with real stakes I carved, but the only time I used one was to threaten some guy trying to follow me when I was fifteen. He wasn't a vampire, just a creep, but it turns out that stakes scare those, too.

The ten-year anniversary of vampires happened a couple of weeks ago, so every television station is still playing an endless stream of documentaries and movies. I came home the other day and found Parker and Jacob watching *The Lost Boys*. Laughing. Like creatures that killed people to survive could ever be funny. I wanted to run into the room, grab the remote, and throw it into the screen. But I didn't. I've never told Parker how Mom really died. So I let them keep watching it while I went to the bathroom and threw up, imagining that evil fanged face being the last thing Mom ever saw. She must have been scared.

This time of year makes me edgy. It makes me want to be a vampire hunter for real. I'm strong enough—that was one thing I *did* have control over. I started running and lifting weights at fourteen. I figured it would take a lot of endurance to catch a vampire and a lot of upper-body strength to drive a stake into its heart.

I know there are people actually trying to track them down again. If I didn't have Parker to take care of, I could travel—we still live in the same town Mom was murdered in, but surely I'd have found something by now if vampires were still here. I need to widen my search to bigger cities where there are rumors of sightings on vampire message boards. Sacramento hasn't had any spottings in years, so for now I walk the streets out of habit and sometimes imagine what I'd do if I found one.

I reach back and touch the bottom of my backpack, feeling the shape of the stake there.

I take a deep breath and try to relax into my routine. I'm distracted tonight. I force myself to focus on the familiar.

Each side of the street boasts several neon signs with burned-out lights. I pass Cooper's on the right, the *C* burned out months ago. Nobody cares. Certainly not the few patrons inside already teetering on their stools. I tuck my head down and keep moving.

The throaty and boyish sound of Def Leppard begging for sugar drifts from the next place along with high-pitched, forced laughter. I don't have to turn my head to know what I'll see—a short skirt riding high and groping hands. The night is nothing if not predictable. It may be why I love it now.

I keep moving, letting the familiarity fill and empty me at the same time.

I stop at a light pole on a corner and scan it. I may not be a vampire hunter, but I know how to hunt lost pets, and that's something at least. No sign of Suzy, though, so I guess I'm not good at that either.

All the other pets must be home and loved tonight since there are no other posters, but my gaze catches on something else. I pause in front of a thick green piece of cardstock with a picture of a dove erupting from a magician's hat. Gold letters loop across the top: LOSE YOURSELF. The date, time, and "J Street" are in fine print at the bottom. No address.

Someone's taken great care in attaching it to the pole without leaving any visible tape. I grab the edge and pull. Maybe the address is on the back, meant only for the most ambitious to find. I flip it over. Nothing. No tape, either. I run a hand over the cold metal it was stuck to, coming up empty.

I shiver in the late evening breeze, or maybe from the thrill of a tiny piece of magic in my hands. I could use a little bit of illusion right now. Tonight I need some extra help pushing the bad memories away. Plus, I'm on the right street, even if there's no address.

I keep walking, rolling and unrolling the green flyer, making the dove disappear and reappear. I still pause to glance down a dark alley or two, but for the first time in a long time, I have a different purpose.

There. A small flash of gold catches my attention, and I kneel in the middle of the sidewalk, running my finger along the gold-painted magician's hat no bigger than my fist. The tip of a bird's wing peeks out the top. A gold arrow beside it points forward. I grin, walking quickly, knowing what I'm looking for now.

I find the next one painted on the side of a trash can. The bird's wing is farther out of the hat this time. The arrow points across the street. I wait for the cars to clear before darting to the other side.

I find the next one and then the next one—the bird rises out of the hat a little more with each painting. Mom would love this. She was always planning scavenger hunts for me after school with a note taped to the front door and a plate of cookies hiding at the end. She made the best butterscotch chip cookies.

Finally, I reach a navy door painted with the same small hat and a dove flying free above it. A Black girl sits perched on a stool beside the door. She wears a green sequined dress that pops against her dark brown skin and falls around her knees in points. Miniature silk flowers in an array of colors line the hem. Her black hair curls down to her waist, and as she shifts to look at me, the gold glitter sprinkled into her hair flashes in the light. She reminds me of Tinker Bell.

"This is what you're looking for." Her words jar me. Her voice is deep and smooth, like she's a breath away from singing, and it feels like a kind of magic already. Her warm brown, gold-rimmed eyes stare right into mine like she's reading my mind.

"How do you know?"

A soft smile spreads across her face, and she slumps a little on her stool like she's breaking character. She nods to the flyer in my hand.

"Oh. Right." I twist the paper again before tucking it away and pulling money from my pocket. I hold it out, but she doesn't take it.

"Are you sure?" she asks instead.

I just stare at her. She's the one who told me this was what I was looking for.

"You can't go back, you know," she says.

She must be in character, trying to unsettle me before the show even starts, but there's an earnestness in her eyes that almost makes me step away from her.

But then she smiles again and waves my money away. "The first show's on us."

She hops from the stool in a swirl of flashing green, pulls open the door, and gestures toward the dark. I step into a heady mix of perfume, cologne, sweat, and alcohol. Underneath, the dank, old smell of the building bides its time, waiting to take control when the room empties. Old buildings always have that same mustiness at their base. It's comforting. Something I can count on.

I step around the hipsters heading toward the booze. The gleaming metal stools contrast with the tired oak of the bar.

Unfortunately, there's no music, and noisy shouts and drunk laughter grate on my nerves.

Someone bumps my shoulder. The crowd swells, and I let myself flow with it toward the seats set up in front of a metal stage draped with plain and simple twinkle lights, the kind I get sick of seeing around the holidays. They aren't magical. If anything, they're tacky.

I plop down on one of the black folding chairs near the front. I take the edge seat and regret it immediately as I shift my knees to the side every time someone needs to move past me. My toes still end up bruised. Drunkenness has no grace.

A blond boy with spiked hair sits down beside me. He stares at the side of my face as I focus on the stage, willing him not to speak to me.

The lights fade and the noise fades with them. Only jarred lights dangling above continue to flutter, barely illuminating everyone's heads. Any remaining whispers die as a spotlight flickers on.

A girl stands with her chin tilted slightly down so her black ringlets fall against her cheekbones. She glows under the harsh light, and her strapless purple dress shimmers even with her stillness. The dress ends above her knees, leaving just inches of bare white skin between the hem and the top of her lace-up black boots.

She stays frozen long enough for the audience to fidget in their seats. Everyone holds their breath, and I realize I'm doing the same. I let mine go the second before the loud thrum of a violin bursts through the speakers. With the sound, one of her palms twitches upward, and a ball of flame shoots to life. There's a moment of silence, aside from the low murmurs of a few assholes in front of me, and then her other palm opens with a surge of flame, accompanied by the violin.

This time the music continues, drifting away until the violin whispers just on the edge of our hearing before slowly growing as she finally raises her head. She stares out at us, face stoic, until the music hits a loud and frenzied high, and she jerks her hands toward the audience, sending harmless sparks above the heads of the first two rows.

Her palms close, and she smiles, taking in the few whistles and claps.

I don't clap. I've seen similar tricks online with people shooting sparks from their hands and using hand sanitizer to light their palms on fire. It's a cheap party trick used by drunk frat boys. I've never seen anyone maintain it as long as she did, but I crave more. I want the rush of seeing a new trick and believing for one glorious second that the magic is real and anything is possible. I want those childhood moments of wonder while standing at the edge of the stage watching Dad make Mom disappear and then reappear across the stage. Or those times at the dinner table with Mom when she made a card appear underneath my dinner plate while she was across the table. My parents were magic—even if Mom told me again and again that it was only illusion.

The music dies, and so does the little applause. Her boots click as she turns and walks to a table set up on the side of the stage.

She picks up three red balls and holds them out for us as if she's asking for our approval before launching them in a couple of lazy arcs.

Some jerk boos and the crowd snickers.

She gives a small, mocking bow while raising her eyebrows. Her smile is back, but it's different now, sharper.

Twisting and grabbing two more balls off the table, she launches all five in the air as she takes a few steps toward the center of the stage.

She's flawless. The balls rise and fall in a pattern that looks effortless but can't be. But it's not enough to lose myself. It's not enough to forget about Parker and Jacob laughing back at Deb's without me.

And then, as if she can read the audience's growing boredom, a single ball catches fire as it passes from her hand and back above her head, and then another and another until they all burn.

The audience applauds, finally satisfied.

They rise and fall like fireworks, the kind that explode downward like a wilted daisy.

I catch myself leaning forward in my seat before pulling back. The rest of the crowd is in awe with me. The boy next to me has his jaw ajar.

She completes a spin. The balls fly effortlessly like she never moved. She spins again, leaving two flaming balls in her hands and three flying through the air. Her purple dress blossoms like a flower.

Only this time, when she faces the crowd again, one ball slips below her grasp, and she catches it with the tip of her boot, kicking it out above the audience, where it erupts into ash like it was nothing more than a runaway wisp of paper from a bonfire. Before the audience can react, she lets ball after ball connect with her boot and soar above our heads only to become nothing.

She's left with two flaming balls she tosses up and down in each hand. She stares at us impassively as she lops each one to the side, into one of the stage curtains.

The curtains blaze to life in green fire as she turns and stalks off the stage. People in the front row rise to their feet. My face heats in the second row. The fire is real.

Some people shout and others clap—the green flames don't touch anything but the curtains.

Spike-hair turns toward me. "Amazing," he breathes into my face, along with the overpowering stench of beer.

I wave him away, leaning into the heat wafting off the unnatural flames. This. *This* is what I was waiting for.

The audience is beginning to squirm when a white boy with green hair saunters onto the stage. In his hands, he bounces a deck of cards back and forth. They thwack as they gently hit one another. He glances at the burning curtains and snaps his fingers.

The flames go out, and the curtains remain whole, with no trace of burns.

"She's so dramatic," he says, grinning.

The crowd roars, and he just waits there, smiling like the world will always be on his side, and with a face like his, he's probably right.

It's the kind of face I hate.

Except his hair is the bright, deep green of forest ferns, almost shaved on the sides, longer and flopped over on the top. The hair of someone who doesn't give a shit.

He wears fitted slacks that crease perfectly to his polished black shoes. His bottom half could be headed for a business meeting at any one of the sky-high office buildings down the street. His top half tells a different story. He has a vest, sure, black and pinstriped with green to match his hair, but he wears no shirt underneath.

I try not to notice the way his muscles flex slightly as he passes the cards between his two hands. It's a ridiculous thought.

He paces at center stage. "I'm going to need a volunteer for this one."

Hands dart up. I catch my own hand in the air and drag it back down before he can notice. Memory made me do it. I don't really want to be up there, but for a split second, I was a little girl again, sitting on the couch in our living room, watching my mom in her best red dress ask for volunteers as she twirled a top hat in her hands. I'd dart my hand up, and she'd pretend to scan the invisible audience before calling me to the stage.

Maybe I *do* want to be up there. But the thought of standing next to him in his crisp black clothes while I'm dressed in my faded black tee turns my stomach. I definitely don't have Mom's grace and style, and I might enjoy my coin tricks, but I've trained myself to be a killer, not a performer. I clasp my betraying hands together in my lap.

His eyes narrow as he scans the faces in front of him. He pauses the movement of the cards long enough to lift a finger in the air and do a spinning motion. The spotlights shift off the stage and into the crowd.

People groan. I wince and lift a hand to shield myself from the glare. Turning slightly, I look down and away from the light. Black, shining shoes pause in front of me.

CHAPTER 3

Shit.

I don't look up.

He clears his throat rather loudly, and the people next to me snicker.

One of his shoes taps lightly on the ground, keeping time with my accelerated heartbeat.

I'm stuck like a freaking rabbit in a hat, except I can't make myself disappear, so I drop my hand and glare up at him.

He gives me a wicked grin, catching the cards dancing between his lithe fingers in one hand. Holding out his other hand to me, he says, "Give a round of applause for my lovely assistant."

I force myself from my chair, ignoring his outstretched palm as I step around him into the aisle.

He lets out a roaring laugh and leans down to spike-hair. "Pleasant company, isn't she?"

Spike-hair laughs at my expense with the rest of the audience.

My skin tingles from embarrassment, and my pulse beats too hard in my throat, like all my blood's trying to make a run for it, and I can't tell if it's begging me to turn and leave or begging me to take the stage. I choose the latter.

At least a couple of people give me a jealous glare as I pass.

When we reach the steps, he holds out his hand for me again. Probably because he knows I won't take it. I don't. He gives a soft chuckle only I can hear—a joke between us and not the audience.

I hope I get to throw knives at him.

The spotlights shift and follow us to center stage. Squinting, I tug at the hem of my T-shirt, wishing I'd worn some of my new clothes.

The boy gives me an exaggerated bow as the audience laughs.

Rising, he splits the deck between both hands and flicks his thumbs at the same moment, creating two perfect fans of cards. Bringing them together, he flaps them toward the audience like a childish butterfly. One clearly drunk girl in the front row giggles. He raises an eyebrow at the rest of the crowd. "No?"

Someone boos, but the boy only chuckles in response before turning back to me. A red stone in a brown leather cuff on his wrist blinks in the light as he angles the cards for only me to see.

"Choose your fate."

Not my card. He's awfully dramatic, yet the words pause my hand. I glance up at his face, relaxed and amused, but his eyes don't match— green and burning like an unnatural fire on damp spring grass. They narrow at my hesitation.

I focus back on the cards and raise my hand, plucking the queen of spades from directly under his thumb and pulling it back against my chest. Mom's favorite card.

A sly smile crosses his face, like he already knows what I chose. It changes from sly to dazzling as he turns back to the audience.

"Show these lovely people your card, please. Don't let me see it."

He winks at me, then turns slightly for effect as I lift my card out to the shadowed faces before me. The orbs of light above them highlight their foreheads and cheeks, leaving their eyes darkened and hollow—a crowd of skeletons. My hand shakes only a little as I pull the card back toward me.

The magician turns to me again, the cards in one fan now, held facedown in front of him.

I slip my card back into the deck without being told.

He laughs toward the audience. "She's a natural." He slides the deck together and places it in my hand. "Mix them," he commands.

I do as I'm told, shifting the cold cards until I don't know where my queen has gone.

I hand them back to him, and our fingers touch. I jolt. My pulse throbs in my fingertips, and he smiles at me, eyes laughing now. What the hell is wrong with me? My face flushes, and I hope nobody notices in the bright lights.

Taking the smallest step away from me, he fans the cards out and flicks them back together in the same breath. And then they're just gone. He holds out his empty hands for the audience and gets a few claps in return.

He sighs. "You're a tough crowd."

Rolling up the sleeves of his jacket, he takes another quick step back. The spotlight on him shifts to a greenish hue as he raises both arms out into the air, palms facing the audience. He snaps, and the nine of diamonds blinks to life in his fingers. He raises his eyebrows. "Is this your card?"

I shake my head, and he frowns. The audience cackles.

He snaps the fingers of his other hand as the nine disappears, and a jack of spades takes its place.

He glances at the card and then at me. "Not it," he says without even asking. "Shoot." The card disappears, and he flips his hands back and forth in front of him, then pulls at his sleeves and glances up them. "I think I lost it."

The audience murmurs. Some laugh, unsure if they're in on a joke or not.

I shuffle my feet.

He lifts his arms again, palms forward, and the cards begin pouring from the cracks between his fingers.

The crowd gasps and applauds, and the cards just keep coming. An impossible number—more than the single deck he held in his hand at the start. Just as they begin to pile around his feet, he drops his hands to his sides, staring down at his mess.

He closes his eyes for a moment, stepping back slightly from the pile. Only his chest moves up and down.

Someone coughs.

My muscles tense with something like anticipation, and I take the smallest step back.

His eyes snap open, and he jumps forward, landing in his pile of cards, making them bounce off the ground. Only they don't come back down. They float upward toward his splayed fingers as his hands rise, pulling them with invisible strings until they fly over his head like a gambler's personal storm cloud. Lifting his face toward them, he blows, and they shift with his breath, taking shape, forming wings.

Building a butterfly. Spades and clubs, hearts and diamonds, separate to create patterned wings.

Now I move forward, holding a hand out underneath it, feeling for the gusts of air that must be keeping it afloat. Nothing. My hair blows gently from the beating wings.

The magician gives me a cocky grin.

Strings, then. I look for the hundreds of wisp-thin threads you'd need to pull this off.

He shakes his head, still grinning. He pushes his lips together and blows again, and it moves, drifting out and over the heads of the audience. Some of them grasp for it, but it flies just out of reach. Their mouths gape, but I turn from their faces to watch him.

With the audience's focus on the butterfly, his smile vanishes like one of his cards. His lips are set, and his eyes narrow like those of something feral, a cat kicked one too many times. I recognize the look as one of my own.

"Do you like me now?" he asks them. There's a sharpness in the question. He turns to me and the look disappears, replaced in an instant with bland amusement.

The audience claps. He bows for them a few times before raising a hand for silence. They obey his every command. He has them now, and the smile on his face turns genuine as he brings his hands together in one loud clap. The butterfly explodes. Cards rain on upturned faces, and the people roar, rising to their feet with applause. My skin vibrates with the noise. My hands sweat, and I wipe them against my jeans. He's done it—given me that moment when every wild thought feels possible. It feels like home.

Forgotten by the audience, I back toward the stairs of the stage, but he sees me and straightens, lifting one hand out to me. "My lovely assistant," he croons. "I'm not done with you quite yet." The audience stills and settles back. He glides toward me, and I struggle to stop myself from stumbling down the stairs before he gets to me.

Facing me, he holds out a hand, and when I don't reach for it, he takes my hand from my side and pulls me a step back toward the center.

And then he starts coughing, wheezing so hard he bends over at the waist, and I'm not sure if I should slap his back or let him go. He stops, finally, and holds a hand in front of his mouth, spitting into it.

He opens his fist and lifts out the queen of spades. Holding it delicately between his middle and pointer fingers, he shows it to the audience. "Found it."

He hands it to me, and I take it, grimacing at the dampness.

"That's your card, is it not?"

"Mine was drier."

The crowd laughs, and this time it belongs to me, not him. They're in my hand. I meet his stare to make sure he knows it. He does. He gives me the tiniest nod of respect, then joins their laughter, turning back to them. "Quite a character, eh?"

They clap and roar for me, and I swear the blood in my veins is carbonated, bubbling against the skin containing it. I feel sick and powerful all at once—like I could explode and have everything I've ever wanted. I bend slightly at the waist. The magician observes me for a moment, and I know he recognizes what I'm feeling—maybe this is what everyone feels onstage. Maybe this is why everyone wants to be a singer or an actor as a kid—to feel like this.

The magician shakes his head slightly, almost like he's breaking his own trance. He reaches forward and grips my hand in his, raising our joined fists above our heads as he spins us to face the audience. He bows, and I awkwardly follow his lead, a second behind, as he pulls our hands down together. When we rise, his fingers slide from my palm to my elbow as he leads me to the stairs. I expect him to let me go then, but he takes me all the way to my seat as people clap and watch.

He lets me go when we reach my chair, and I slump down on the cold plastic, ignoring the gaping mouth of the guy next to me. The green-haired magician leans down until his lips almost touch my ear. "You've been lovely. See you later."

He walks away and disappears behind the scenes. My heart pounds fast enough to impair my breathing, and I'm not sure if it's from the rush of applause or so much contact with another human being. My face already heats from the memory of his lips so close to my skin.

I try to control my breathing and fail. Part of me wants to vomit and part of me wants to run back onstage and never get off again.

A tall girl with long black hair takes the stage, and I'm sure whatever she's about to do will be amazing.

But I can't stay any longer. The rush I feel doesn't belong to me. It's like wearing expensive hand-me-down clothes. Right now the world is magical and full of promises, but what about tomorrow when the show is over? The memory will haunt me with all the magic I'll never really have in my life. If Dad and Mom had lived . . . if even one of them had lived, it would have been me onstage, pulling someone from the audience and making them feel alive for a moment. They would have trained me. We could've been a family act. But none of that is possible, and this magic is almost too good. It makes me want, and that's never wise. Better to leave now before I make it worse.

I slip from my seat, and in a moment, I'm through the door and on the now-empty street. It's colder than earlier, and I curse myself for not bringing a jacket. I pull my beanie down almost to my eyes and bury my fists in my pockets like that will help.

The cool security of my coins greets me. I pull one out and flip it into the air, holding my palm open to catch it.

But it doesn't land in my palm.

I stare down at the sidewalk, thinking I missed it. Nothing.

I can't leave without it. I've had the same four quarters forever.

I dig the other three coins out of my pocket like they can help me find their missing sibling.

But I'm holding all four. I stare at them, counting them again and again like one will disappear.

A slow clap almost makes me drop them all.

I jerk toward the sound, hungry for it. Addicted. I bite the inside of my lip and draw blood, distracting myself from the desire.

The green-haired boy leans against the brick wall in a narrow alleyway that must have a side entrance into the building.

"Nice trick," he says.

I open my mouth to say I didn't do a trick, but I did. I must have done it without thinking—on instinct, high on the rush of being onstage.

"Thanks." My voice is casual. I slide my coins back into my pocket, resisting the urge to count them one more time just to be sure.

"You're leaving. Did you not like it?" His arms are folded across his chest, which is still covered in only his performance vest.

"Do you not like clothes?"

He looks at me hard for a moment and then bursts out in laughter.

A breeze hits me, and I shiver.

He sees it. "I'm not the one who's cold. I'd offer you a jacket, but . . ." He lets his arms drop, and he holds his palms out toward me in case I needed extra evidence that he doesn't have an extra scrap to give me.

I don't. I'm already way too aware, and it's an uneasy, unfamiliar feeling.

"I have to go." I turn away, hoping I can outrun whatever draw he has on me.

"Ava," he calls after me.

I freeze before turning back slowly. "How'd you know my name?"

His eyes pinch like I've caught him at something. "You gave it to me. Onstage."

"I didn't." I never give my name out easily.

He shrugs, and a charming, easy grin spreads across his face. "Well, maybe I'm a mentalist." He winks.

"But you're not." I say it like a statement, but it's more of a question. Mentalists freak me out a little.

"No." He chuckles. "Pretty sure you gave it to me onstage. You haven't asked for my name, though. Are *you* a mentalist?"

"No. I just didn't want it."

"Ouch." His smile's too bright to be hurt. "I'm Xander."

"Sure." I step away again, taking his name with me and leaving mine behind.

"Aren't you going to answer my question?" he calls after me.

"What?" I glance back.

"Did you like it?"

I hesitate. "I loved the show."

He grins as I start to turn away again. "It's more than just a show. Come again tomorrow, and maybe you'll see."

His words almost pull me back, but I shake my head and start walking. The boy's chuckling follows me, nipping at my heels. He's only joking. Magicians always want you to believe they're more. Except Mom. She always scolded me when I called what she did magic. *It's just a trick, Ava. Nothing more. It's never more.*

Her voice is so clear in my head that I stop walking.

My chest tightens. I can't stop myself from thinking about it any longer. I wish it weren't so easy to remember, but all the details, every little one, are hungry to rise to the surface—and not just what I saw but what I *felt*.

The day my mother was murdered is imprinted in my memory.

That morning, I woke up and headed to the kitchen, where Mom should have been making breakfast. She wasn't.

Something felt wrong, like the air was too heavy. I wish I could forget that feeling—that sinking dread before you even realize something is *really* wrong.

I moved to the back of the trailer to check her bed, just in case she was sleeping in, even though she always woke up early. Nothing.

Mom had decided the day before that we needed to move again, so we were parked in an empty campground on the road toward who knows where. I wasn't supposed to leave our trailer without telling Mom, but I pushed open the door into the cold morning air and shivered as I stepped out onto the metal step.

Mom was sitting against a tree on the edge of our campground. I didn't want to walk across the dirt or go back inside and get my shoes, so I called her name twice. She didn't move.

As I picked my way across the rock-covered ground, I laughed like it was a trick. But she wasn't just sitting against a tree. One leg was bent awkwardly to the side, not broken, but not how anyone would ever sit. Her arms were splayed beside her in the pine needles, holding nothing, doing nothing. Her head was tilted to the side, one cheek against the bark. Her eyes were open, looking at me but not.

Then I got close enough to see the blood on her neck: two wounds with a little stream running from each one.

I got on my knees and grabbed her wrist. It twitched like something releasing, and for a second, I thought she'd get up. That her eyes would flash with that bit of excitement when she knows she's pulled off something marvelous, and then we'd laugh.

But she never laughed again.

I didn't laugh again for a long time either.

I still don't. My laugh is a surprisingly deep chuckle. It sounds so much like Mom's that every time I laugh, I feel like I'm stuck in that moment again, waiting for her to smile.

I'm still half in the memory when I start walking again and crash into something hard and unyielding. I stumble back.

A cold hand grips my arm and keeps me upright.

My glare meets a crisp white button-up shirt, and I assume I've stumbled into one of the many corporate workaholics heading home after reliving their tired day over multiple beers, but then I look up.

He's not a businessman. Sure, he's got the black slacks and white button-up, but it's rolled to the elbows and unbuttoned at the top in a way that looks like it *never* gets buttoned, and he wears black suspenders that most businessmen probably wouldn't be caught dead in. And he's young, not much older than me, with sharp features softened by curly dark auburn hair that falls at every angle around his face. If he were smiling, he might look chaotic and charming, but his mouth is tight, and his dark brown eyes are hard.

All of it doesn't quite add up, like something about him is just *off*.

And his hand is still gripping my arm way too hard.

I step back, and he lets go.

"My apologies." His voice is a low, soft rumble.

"I wasn't looking," I answer as I take another step back.

He puts his hands behind his back, but he doesn't move away or walk on.

"You didn't do that trick on purpose, did you?" His eyes bore into mine with a seriousness that doesn't match the question. It's unnerving, and I can't get my feet to move, even though my skin is prickling with unease.

"What trick?" My mind's still half in the past.

"With your little coins."

I bristle at the way he says "little coins." Who is this guy? And how would he know anything about what magic I can and cannot do, and why the hell is he watching me in the first place? I'm not the one putting on a show.

"I don't know what you're talking about." I finally get my legs to move and step around him. "If you're looking for some cool magic, try

in there." I gesture to the door I came from as I walk around him, trying to get him to glance away from me. He doesn't. He stays still, but
he doesn't stop watching me until I'm past him.

"Don't come back here," he says when I'm almost out of earshot.

I think about yelling a retort, but when I turn, he's facing away
from me. So I keep going, glancing back multiple times just to be sure
he isn't following, but he's still just standing there, hands folded behind
his back, staring at the doorway to the club.

CHAPTER 4

My eyes blur from lack of sleep. I stayed up all night researching floating card tricks, but I didn't find anything that rivaled Xander's butterfly. There are plenty of tutorials on how to levitate a single card or object or even yourself, but nothing that comes close to touching what Xander seems to be capable of.

What I did find was a familiar video. When Joseph Perry left the flashier stages of magic for dark and dingy little clubs where people rarely knew his name, he was careful about making sure nobody knew exactly where he was or what he was doing, so all his shows had "no recording" rules. It's easy to find videos of him performing *before* Mom, but there's only one of him onstage *with* Mom. Of course it would come up while I'm searching for butterfly magic tricks.

I've already watched it more times than is probably good for me.

The clip shows Dad in his red vest, smiling as he runs a hand through his slicked-back blond hair. He stands beside a small golden table with a top hat on it, and he's watching Mom wave her hands underneath the table and then tip the hat up, shaking it out to prove there's nothing there. This is my favorite part, not the trick—the way Dad looks at Mom like *she's* the magic, like nothing that comes next will compare to her. It makes my chest ache to know that Mom had someone look at her like that, and it got taken from her. I understand why she didn't talk about Dad that much.

Mom puts the hat back on the table, and Dad steps up behind it, but before anything can happen, a white-haired kid runs onto the stage. Mom and Dad both move to catch me as I reach the hat and nudge it with my hand. Butterflies explode from behind the rim in a burst of color that drifts upward and then spreads as the audience goes wild. It's a basic trick except for the amount of butterflies, just like Xander's trick would be basic except he floated more cards than should be possible. But the part of the video that I always rewind to watch again and again is the expression on my parents' faces: shock. And then something that doesn't make sense: fear. It'd make more sense if they were performing an ax-throwing act or something, but it was only butterflies. Mom rushes me offstage. Dad stands there for a moment and scans the audience like there's some type of threat, and then he gives them a dazzling smile and bows before striding off the stage. I'm not the only one who's noticed how oddly they reacted. I know the comments below the video by heart.

> **magicianX:** am I the only one who noticed their
> expressions?
> **Debby B:** Clearly they didn't expect the butterflies.
> **Ryan464:** The kid obviously just tripped the release
> switch early.
> **georgeblack:** they looked afraid.
> **magicfreak:** That's Joseph Perry. He died like a week later.
> **georgeblack:** how'd he die?

magicfreak: They say it was a mugging.

georgeblack: they say?

magicfreak: It was all really weird. This is the only video of him in a four-year span before he died. People wondered if someone was after him—money or rivalry or something.

georgeblack: weird

Vampire Biter: I recognize the woman. She died right before vampires came out. They said it was an animal attack, but she was only wounded on the neck.

magicfreak: You're kidding me.

Vampire Biter: Nope. Did you see the way he looked out at the audience? Maybe they were afraid of something else.

It doesn't really surprise me that someone recognized Mom. During the frenzy of the vampire reveal, people searched for anything that might have been an attack. Someone found a news report of her death and latched onto it as possible evidence of vampire violence. So plenty of people believe what really happened to her and know the police just wanted to cover it up to avoid mass panic, but Mom didn't go by the last name Perry. This is the only comment that connects her to Dad, and it's haunted me for years. What if the vampire attack wasn't random? What if Mom knew there were vampires before one killed her?

I just don't want to believe she'd keep that from me. But we were always moving, and Mom said it was so she could find fresh audiences. She was still a performer, but she only did birthday parties and private gatherings. When I think back, I wonder if we were running.

But I know a vampire didn't kill Dad. The details of his death are easy to find: stabbed three times in the chest. That sounds like an evil *person*, not an evil monster.

I replay the video one more time and focus on the butterflies—too many to count.

My mind wants to wander to a place I haven't let it go in a long, long time, because it's a fantasy world meant for children. It doesn't make sense. But that trick made no sense, so here I am dreaming of the impossible again.

I reach under my bed and pull out a worn red shoebox. It's not anywhere near as pretty as the pink one full of treasures that Mom kept. I always used to pull hers out from under her bed and dig through it. It was full of journals—some brand-new with crisp white pages, some so old-looking that the pages were eroding at the edges and the ink was browning, but Mom's big looping letters covered all of them. And then there were the pictures of Mom on all kinds of stages: sometimes holding a top hat, sometimes in a sequined dress fanning a deck of cards, sometimes with her head and feet sticking out of a box that seemed to be cut in two. Some were in vivid color, and some were sepia or black-and-white—probably promo shots for vintage-style advertisements. Those were my favorite, but I loved every single one of them. I loved imagining Mom as the magnificent stage magician with her wide smiles instead of the tired ones she had when performing at children's parties. Because before Dad, Mom performed with a troupe of magicians and carnival performers. She actually talked about her time performing with them more than she talked about Dad.

And then there was the jewelry: gold rings, dangling earrings, silk chokers—but my favorite was a gold choker studded with big red gems that she wore in almost every photo.

The shoebox was empty when she died, and I never knew if she'd packed the stuff away or if the vampire that killed her took it. The jewelry had to be worth something.

But they didn't get everything.

As soon as I was old enough to read, Mom started hiding the box. It became a game. I'd find it, and she'd catch me before I could get very far. But what she didn't know was that each time I found it, I took a little something: a page from a journal or a photo. Never the jewelry, because she would have noticed that.

I've kept them all these years, but it's been a long time since I looked at them. The pages were always gibberish to me, like maybe she was writing a novel or something. But they're nagging at me now—enough that I open the shoebox and pull them out.

I pause over the pictures because I haven't seen them in a while. The first one's in color, with Mom in a deep-purple corset and miniature top hat on the crown of her head. She holds a white dove in her hand, and she looks about thirty years old. Next to her stands a man in a solid white suit with blond hair slicked behind his ears. It's not Dad, though. The man stares at her instead of the camera. The other one is a black-and-white image of a man with a broad forehead and a slender, pointed nose. Chains drape across his body. Beside him, dressed in a huge, flowing skirt and a button-up jacket, is Mom. Her face is grim. It's not a very good promotion shot, but that's all it can be. I didn't recognize the man when I was a little kid, but later on I did: Houdini.

My heart aches with the desire to ask her about the photo. I want to know all about the shows she used to do—did she copy Houdini's tricks? Was that why she had this photoshopped? Why isn't she smiling?

But those aren't the answers I'm looking for right now. I shuffle through the four journal pages I have. I'm looking for the oldest one. The one with ink that looks like rust. I pull it out and read.

> There's nothing quite like the thrill of discovering
> a new talent and watching it morph into something
> stronger—something that takes their tricks and
> pushes them just beyond what's humanly possible
> and watching the audience's eyes widen as they try to
> figure out the secrets, and all the while, we're smiling
> backstage, knowing they never will.

I was that audience last night, even though I was on the stage. I craved their secrets, and even after spending all night on websites explaining magicians' tricks, I've got nothing. *Beyond what's humanly possible* rings in my ears. That's why I always thought what I held was a piece of a fantasy. A story Mom was writing that blended fiction into her life. Mom always showed me how she did her tricks if I asked. There was *always* an explanation. I move to the other one I'm looking for. The page is white and crisp, from one of the newer-looking journals.

> The craving to use it is so intense sometimes. Even
> doing silly little birthday parties, it builds up until my
> blood is boiling and I think I might explode from it.
> I want to let it loose—do something truly impossible
> for those screaming children, even if it's just disappear
> the family cat and make it reappear in a tree and then
> back again. I need that rush of true awe, but not more
> than I need my family. I can't risk it. No matter how
> miserable I feel.

Nonsense. That's all it was to me, but now my skin tingles with unease. *Blood boiling.* Didn't I feel that last night on the stage? Vampires exist, so why not magic? I used to ask myself that question a lot after she died because I needed to believe in something besides horrible creatures that could kill you in the night.

But when she was alive, Mom always made sure I didn't believe in it.

She even got mad at me once when I said I wanted real magic. She told me I couldn't have it—not that it didn't exist, but that *I* couldn't have it.

My skin tingles as I pull a quarter from my pocket and hold it against the tender flesh of my palm. Maybe I could push it through. I shake my head and drop the quarter on the bed. I'm being ridiculous. There's a reason I stopped looking at these journal entries—I always let myself get carried away.

What I really want is illusion. I want what should have been my birthright: a place on a stage with the best magicians in the world. I want the buzz I felt last night—that's where the magic is. I need to go back. Xander told me to come back.

Deb hollers from downstairs that breakfast is ready. I was so lost in what was and what might be that I forgot what day it is.

Saturday mornings are for pancakes.

The better foster places all have something—taco Tuesday, Friday pizza night, Saturday game night. But in some places, every night is take-care-of-yourself night.

Deb does pancakes.

I can deal with pancakes. I like them with cheap maple syrup—none of that hundred-percent-pure crap. Deb buys both kinds even though she loves all that organic stuff. I almost like that about her.

I smell the batter as the floorboards at the bottom of the stairs creak good morning to me.

Deb must hear them too.

"Pancakes," she hollers, just in case I'm thinking of slipping out the front door without eating.

I squeak into the kitchen, past Parker and Jacob, already scarfing down their chocolate chip pancakes, and pull up a seat at the table. My finger drifts automatically to the scratch I made in it last night. It'll stay here long after I'm gone. Every place I've been I could probably go back to and find some piece of myself I left behind—my name scrawled on the inside of a closet door, an inconspicuous gouge out of the back deck, a drawing on the underside of a table. Pieces of me are always with them, even if some of my foster-whatevers don't remember my name.

Deb will have this scratch. She'll maybe have Parker, too.

Once, I dreamed of turning eighteen, finding a good job, and getting custody of Parker—finally building our own home together. But I'm already eighteen, I don't have a good job, and Parker . . . he's happy here.

I've only actually seen him really happy somewhere once before. The first year we were in the system, we weren't together. They had to place us quickly, and two kids are harder to place than one, but they put us back together in a place that was okay. Nobody was mean, but it felt more like we were furniture than kids. But then they placed us with a couple that wanted a foster-to-adopt situation. He loved it there. But it didn't last. There was no happy adoption story in the end. Then we got placed in our last home, where we were two of six kids. It felt more like trying to survive at a summer camp than a home. But those foster-whatevers decided to move, and I wasn't eighteen yet, so they found us a new place.

And after just six months, this is home to him. I can see it in the way he sits there with syrup dripping on his shirt without worrying whether Deb will yell at him for it. She won't.

I know what home looks like. When Mom died, I was already old enough to understand what home means—that natural and instinctual belonging. Even when that home wasn't perfect, it was mine in a way that Deb and Jacob can never be, but they could be home for Parker.

Sometimes I worry I'm standing in his way. I know I'm a type of home for him like he is for me—no matter where we are physically—but I can't ignore that he's never had a physical place to call home. It's not the same. I know it. I'm sure he knows he's missing that too. Like a little kid who has never had candy before. They don't know exactly what they're missing, but when they see another kid with a lollipop, they just know it's something to be desired.

Deb's humming, and I'm pretty sure it's the theme song from *The Andy Griffith Show*. Parker used to like that show. I never did. I couldn't decide whether to feel bad for Opie because he had only one parent or jealous because he had one parent.

Deb's a single parent. Jacob's dad died in a car accident when he was only a baby. But Deb's a good one, and she has enough money from her late husband's insurance to work only one job that she loves. Parker would be lucky to have her. But it doesn't stop me from dreaming.

She stops humming and turns off the stove.

"Anyone want bacon?" She turns and flips her hair from her eyes. On weekends she wears it long and loose and slightly out of control.

"Yeah," Parker and Jacob mumble in sync. She drops some on their plates and looks to me.

"No, thanks." I smile, and it's not for Deb or for me, but for Parker. Because even though I may not feel at home here, he does, and I will smile all day, every day, if it means he can be happy.

She grins back, taking my smile at face value. Most people do. But smiles are my greatest illusions.

Her eyes go to the top of my new green racer-back tank peeking out the neck of my sweatshirt. I pull the zipper higher. I shouldn't have worn it. I've given her some kind of victory now, and that is too much. I don't like to give foster-whatevers a victory unless it serves my larger goal—whatever trick I happen to be playing on them. Although I'm not actually playing any tricks on Deb. I can see that she cares about my brother. All I have to do is not be an annoyance. But I won't do any more than that.

At least she doesn't mention it. She turns back and moves more pancakes from the grill to a large plate and brings them to the table.

We eat in silence for a while. She put fresh blueberries in the pancakes that she probably woke up early to get. They're my favorite, even though everyone else likes chocolate chip. I like that she remembers that—it feels like one of those little things parents do to make their kid feel loved. Sitting here, like this, I can pretend that I belong here, that this is any other family enjoying a Saturday breakfast together.

My chest aches when I snap myself out of it.

"Parker's birthday is tomorrow," I say. I'm surprised she hasn't mentioned it. She remembered mine a couple of months ago, but I insisted on no presents. I did accept a chocolate cake, though. But you never know, so I'm measuring Deb's reaction. This is an easy test for whether you have a good foster-whatever or a bad one. Part of me hopes she fails, and Parker will realize I love him more, but I hate myself the minute I think it. I hope she passes—for his sake.

"I know," Deb says.

Good. Parker will almost certainly get a gift from her. I already bought him a Star Wars movie, but I can't afford much else.

But then Deb continues. "I actually wanted to talk to you about his party."

I freeze with a piece of pancake halfway to my mouth. A drop of syrup slides off the bite and onto the table, pooling in my ugly gouge. I always plan Parker's party: We do the same thing every year. I save up and take him out for a slice of pie if I can. Then I perform coin tricks for him and any other kids in our current foster house.

"I meant to tell you sooner . . . work's just been so busy, but I invited some of his class over for a *Star Wars* party."

I drop my fork on my plate. It clangs louder than I mean it too. "We usually do something else, just the two of us."

I turn to Parker and regret it immediately. He winces and shoves another bite of pancake into his mouth, chewing with a slowness he rarely possesses. Swallowing, he meets my stare but says nothing.

"Do you want a big party?" I ask.

I should let this go, but I need for him to say it. Part of me doesn't quite believe he'd break another one of our traditions. Another, better part of me wants whatever he wants.

"I thought it might be cool," he mumbles, not looking at anyone. "We could do our thing after."

"Right. Yeah. No big deal." I take another bite. I can barely swallow it. "You can't beat *Star Wars*."

I laugh, but it sounds wrong.

Jacob stares at his plate. Deb stares at the side of my face.

"You could do the magic tricks for all my friends this year," Parker says. His blue eyes are wide and earnest and too much like Dad's.

"Even better." I force a smile, and I work my magic so it looks real. He falls for it.

Deb doesn't. I feel her glancing at me as I choke down the rest of my pancakes as quick as possible so I can bolt. The stairs welcome me back as I climb them. I need to lose myself, but the magic show's not until tonight. I settle for a book.

Books, like any good illusion, pull you in, and for a moment there is only Gatsby, Daisy, Tom and Nick, and you, and sometimes, if the writer's a master, you're not even there anymore—you've disappeared and pieces of you take root in each character. I find myself in Nick and his desire to peek behind the curtain, but also in Gatsby and his ability to create the grandest of illusions, even if the stage collapses in the end. For just a moment, he had his audience in his palm. He got the applause I crave.

I read the whole thing in one sitting, but all I can think about is going back to the show, and I need backup. I need someone to ground me in the real world so my imagination can't float away like one of Xander's cards.

I dig out my phone and call my friend Stacie. We met sophomore year when she stopped some jerk from bullying me about my coin tricks. It definitely wasn't friends at first sight. I'd even say I didn't really like her that much, but she just kind of kept hanging around. I didn't let her in until she admitted that she was in the system too.

She picks up on the first ring. "I was wondering when you'd call me back."

Keeping in touch is not my strong suit.

"Want to go to a magic show tonight?"

The line's quiet for a moment, but then she laughs. "You're never going to be into small talk, are you?"

"It's at eight." At least I hope it is—that's the same time as last night.

"You know I'm always up for an adventure."

I breathe a little sigh of relief. She's not wrong—if it weren't for her inviting me places, I'd leave the house only for runs and nighttime prowling. I tell her what time to pick me up.

Stacie picks me up twenty minutes late, because her reliability for an adventure doesn't cover punctuality, so by the time we find a parking spot on the street, the show's been going on for at least thirty minutes.

I turn to tell Stacie about my weird encounter with the boy on the street yesterday, but she's got her visor mirror pulled down and is dabbing at her peach lip gloss. I want to tell her to hurry, but I don't. I'm used to it. I grab my backpack and push my door open.

"Ava, you're not seriously going to lug your ratty backpack into a club."

I shrug. "I took it last night."

"You came without me?"

"It was spur-of-the-moment. I found a flyer on the street."

Her eyes narrow. "Weird."

I don't know what she's referring to—how I found the show or me doing something without roping her in first.

She shakes her head. "I cannot be seen with you carrying that thing."

I tighten my grip on the straps.

"Ava," she says softly. "We're not going to be attacked in the middle of a crowded place."

I bristle. She knows what happened to my mom. She knows I carry a stake in my bag. I told her a long time ago, shortly after we met, actually. I usually don't tell people, because once vampires went back into hiding, a lot of people decided it was a hoax. Ten years later, most people don't believe they exist. But when we first met, Stacie wouldn't shut up about how good she'd look with sparkly skin. I think she could tell how on edge I got whenever she brought up vampires, so she started peppering me with questions about my past until I finally caved.

She believed me. She was the first person in my life who really believed me, so when she gently tugs my bag away from me, I let her. I trust her.

Stacie finishes her makeup and finally rises from the car, strutting around it like we have all the time in the world. I link arms with her, and she laughs because it's the type of thing she'd do, but really I just want to make her match my own pace.

The same girl sits on the stool outside. Her black hair is piled in curls on top of her head, and she wears a silky green dress tonight that hugs her plump curves. She looks like she should be onstage instead of watching the door.

"You're late," she says. "I didn't think you'd be late."

My stomach clenches. She might not let us in. But more important, how could she have known I was coming?

Stacie raises one brow as she glances at me. "My bad. I took too long getting ready."

The girl frowns slightly at her, then turns back to me.

"I'm supposed to let you in for free," she says. "He didn't say anything about a plus-one."

My chest tightens. She can only be talking about Xander.

Stacie pulls out some cash. "How much?"

The girl eyes the money, then waves her away. "On the house."

Stacie nods and pulls me away, opening the black door.

"That was weird," she mutters.

She stares at me for a moment like I might give an explanation. I nod as I step inside.

The people in the club cheer as we walk in, and for one bizarre moment it feels like it's for me. My heart pounds in my throat again— every nerve ending in my skin suddenly, painfully alive.

Stacie brushes my arm, and I jump at her chilly fingers. She leans close to my ear. "I think we're going to have to stand. Oh, wait. I see a spot in the back." She grabs my hand and pulls me in the direction of a single seat at the end of the back row.

"There's only one," I whisper, trying to pull her to a stop. She's always been surprisingly strong though, and in a second, we're there, and she's bending down to talk to the man in the next seat over.

He looks her up and down in an obvious way that probably deserves a drink in the face, but her smile never wavers.

"Would you be so kind as to give me your seat?" she asks.

The man starts but gets up, smiling like she's done him a favor. He nods in my direction, even though I'm sure he doesn't even see me, and goes to sit at the bar in the back.

Stacie slides into her stolen seat and then pats the empty seat next to her. I take it.

"I really don't know how you do that." I've seen it a million times before. She's gotten us a lot of free stuff in the last few years just by flipping her hair.

She pauses like she doesn't know what I'm talking about, then turns in her chair to give a little wave to the guy, who still watches her. She grins as she looks back at me. "Magic."

I nod at her joke, but she's not wrong. It may not be magic, but it's certainly power.

I tug at the strap of my tank as the lights dim.

The spotlight glares, capturing the appearance of an Asian girl onstage.

Her sleek black hair falls all the way to her waist in uneven strands like she's never cut it in her life. The dress she wears is old-fashioned on the top, with billowing white sleeves poking out of a dove-gray corset. Good sleeves for a magician. Her skirt is something else altogether. A cascade of white feathers drops from her hips, flowing down into uneven edges that drift around her knees as she walks to center stage.

She sets an empty, ornate wooden pedestal next to her and stands smiling at us. Her round eyes twinkle. Music whispers out of the speakers, soft and delicate against the heavy, impatient breathing of the audience as she pulls out a silver handkerchief from nowhere. Placing it flat on the pedestal, she pinches the center and lifts, leaving behind the tiniest of finches in its wake. It takes off and flies circles above her head.

We give her a smattering of applause as she folds and unfolds her handkerchief, doubling it to the size of a placemat before repeating the trick and giving us two blue parakeets.

Again, she folds and unfolds and brings to life four doves.

Then she gives us a parrot. The crowd goes wild for the bright red plumes and flashy yellow accents as it launches and dips out above our heads before joining the strange array still circling just above her head.

The handkerchief is the size of a cape now as she drops it over the pedestal, and this time she uses three fingers to pinch the cloth, raising it in the air two feet before twirling it away and revealing an elegant swan.

The swan stays perched on the pedestal, watching us with a keen grace that cares nothing for our clapping.

The girl smiles though.

She shakes out her magic cloth and it doubles again, growing to the size of a bedsheet. Pinching the two longer ends in her hands, she gives us a demure smile before flinging it up and over the flying birds above her head. It dances in the air, like they're struggling under the weight, before it drifts to the floor and lies there in folds that could or couldn't have live birds underneath them. She bends over and grabs the sheet, shaking it out like she's making her bed on a lazy Sunday morning. Smoothing out one last wrinkle with her toe, she steps onto the sheet as everyone applauds. I bring my hands together. For a moment, I think she looks right at me and smiles.

A silly thought, of course—she'd never be able to see me all the way back here.

I almost miss the finale.

She has the sheet off the floor now and is shaking it in front of us. Only the swan stays, sitting on its pedestal, waiting. The sheet drifts over its head, and it's gone.

The audience sits in silence for a moment and then we all clap. Some stand.

The girl waits patiently for us to stop. We do, leaning forward as one, waiting for what she will give us. She leaves us hanging there for a full twenty seconds before her soft voice caresses the room. "I seem to have lost my birds." Her gaze slides over the room. "Will you please check your purses?"

I don't have a purse. I nudge Stacie. She's so focused on the stage that I have to shake her arm to get her attention.

I point to her gold clutch sitting on her lap. "Open it."

"Okay. Okay." She releases the clasp, pulling it open. Nothing happens for a moment, and she sighs, moving to close it again. "She's just—"

A small blue parakeet soars out, and Stacie jumps back.

All around the audience, birds break free of purses. A chorus of chirping fills the stunned silence as they flit above our heads. The bird girl whistles, and the birds follow the sound, sailing past her and out of sight backstage. She gives us a small wave, no bow, and follows behind them, still whistling softly to herself.

The applause tops anything from the night before. It vibrates against my skin until I feel like an instrument being played.

It's almost like my blood's boiling.

But it could be nothing. The adrenaline. The thrill. Maybe that was all Mom meant in her journals—she was talking about big stage productions with technology and props that helped you do the impossible. She said she stopped putting on big productions because of our family. It takes a lot of time to put on that level of performance. She let go of those dreams for me. It hurts to know how much she missed this.

I glance at Stacie. She's not clapping, but her mouth is open, and she stares at the stage like she's hungry for more. I can relate.

She seems to shake herself and snap out of it. "Wow," she says, eyeing the inside of her purse. "I hope it didn't poop in here."

I gape at her. *That's* what she's wondering about?

"Can I see it?" I point toward her purse, and she hands it over.

A wallet. Lipstick. Keys. Tampon. Nothing out of the ordinary. Still, I don't want to hand it back to her—this small piece of the show.

The lights come on, but I barely notice. People walk past us on their way to the bar.

It's a good trick. A great trick. It's the kind that draws you in so deep you forget to look for the little flaws and giveaways until afterward, when your brain runs every moment together into one beautiful blur of awe, and there's nothing to do but accept what you've seen and move on.

Unless it's not a trick. The thought keeps needling in, forcing me to talk some sense into myself over and over again.

Mom always told me my imagination ran away with me sometimes. It's just been a long time since that happened. The excitement of it felt good.

They may not be real, but I still want to do more than just watch these illusions. I want to live in them with my good memories of Dad and Mom and forget about vampires for once. Magic could help me forget.

"Umm, can I get my purse back?"

I didn't even realize I still held it. I'm clutching it to my chest in a weird way, so I force myself to give it back.

Stacie chuckles. "I forgot how much you love this stuff."

I nod.

A small blue feather teeters on my knee, and I reach out and pluck it up, twisting it back and forth between my thumb and finger. It would be easy enough to manipulate a single feather—even I could do that—but an entire bird? My thoughts try to pull me back into my conspiracies. *It's always a trick, Ava. Find the strings.* Mom's voice brings me back. If you hid a bunch of birds around the room and released them at the right moment, people would believe some of them came from their purses. The power of suggestion. None of us saw what we thought we saw.

"Hey, look."

I glance up to where Stacie points. Xander and the bird girl walk among the audience, shaking hands with people.

"Let's meet them," I say, jumping out of my chair. I don't mention I already met Xander.

Stacie glances between me and Xander, and a knowing look crosses her face. "That one's all yours," she says.

"I'm not—"

She glances at her phone. "Actually, something came up. Do you think you could get a ride home from here?"

I sigh. I'm pretty sure she's just trying to make me look more available, but I don't really want to argue. "Yeah. I need to get my bag though." I follow her out of the club and wait as she grabs my backpack from the car and holds it out to me. I grab the strap, but she doesn't let go.

"Go get him," she says with a grin.

I frown. "That's not why I'm here."

She leans in and air-kisses my cheek. "Whatever you say, babe." She winks before darting around to get in her car.

My resolve wavers as she drives off. It was nice to have a friend to back me up.

But I still crave more magic. My feet carry me back into the club and toward Xander like they know what I want, even though my head and heart don't want the chance to be rejected, but then I think of the words of the girl at the door. Xander was expecting me to come back. That puts too much pressure on the encounter.

I veer off course and make my way to the bird girl. Up close, I see that two identical blue parakeets sit on her shoulder, nestled in her hair.

I wait patiently in line, and when I finally reach her, I stand staring at those birds like they hold all the magic, and if I look at them long enough, they might give it to me. All of me buzzes with excitement.

Her smile is warm, reaching her angled brown eyes, even though I stand there without words.

"You were great," I say, and wince. It hardly seems adequate.

"So were you."

I start.

"You were onstage last night with Xander." She brushes a strand of hair from her face, and the birds nestle farther into it.

"That was nothing."

"It *was* something. Not everyone can hold their own with him."

I follow her gaze across the room to the only guy with green hair. A brunette girl in a gold dress clings to his side.

My throat tightens in an unpleasant way.

"I don't know," I say. "It looks like assistants are an easy thing to come by for him."

The girl laughs, soft but sharp as chimes. "True—but good assistants are hard to find."

I twist the feather still pinched between my fingertips. The girl watches the movement, and I'm vaguely embarrassed to be holding on to it like some little kid saving a memento to tuck away in her diary, but I can't let it go.

"He'd want you to go say hi," the girl says.

I nod and take a step back from her, even though half of me wants to stay there and ask her a million questions about the strings behind her tricks. The other half of me wants to follow the string leading me back to Xander. He has more than one trick I need to figure out.

His smile widens as I stop in front of him. I may be imagining it, but gold-dress girl's smile shrinks the smallest bit.

"You matched me," he says.

"What?"

He waves a hand at my green tank and then points to his hair.

My face heats. He's right—a perfect match.

My mouth opens and closes in a way that can't be attractive while he watches my discomfort with what can only be described as delight.

"I wanted to be prepared in case you pulled me up onstage against my will again," I finally say.

I try to sound snarky to cover up the lie. He catches it.

"Don't pretend you didn't raise your hand." He leans in a little closer to me, like he'll tell me a secret. The girl awkwardly follows so she can keep a hand on his arm. "Don't pretend you didn't love it up there."

He stares intently at me, smile gone.

My face must be as hot as those green, smoldering curtains from the night before.

I swallow, and his eyes dip to my throat. I take a quick step back.

"You two know each other?" the girl asks.

Xander glances at her like he's surprised she's still there.

"I helped with one trick," I say. "It was nothing."

"She's a natural," Xander says. "Practically one of us."

His words make me flush in a new way, not with embarrassment but with something else harder to understand.

"Hey, do you two want to meet the rest of the troupe backstage?"

Backstage, where all the magic can be picked apart and I can puzzle out how he does what he does. I doubt I'll find anything while the show's not going on, but I can hope.

"I'd love to," the other girl blurts out as she shoots me a look I'm not sure how to read.

Xander smiles at the girl, but it seems tight. Then again, maybe I'm seeing what I want to see.

I don't want to go backstage with her. I don't even want to go backstage with Xander. Not without the show going on. What I want is to be right on the sidelines again. I want to be part of the tricks, not the one being tricked.

There's a twinkle in Xander's eyes that says he'd love nothing more than to trick me.

"I'm actually not feeling well," I say.

"Do you need a ride or anything?" Xander glances at the black watch on his wrist. "There's another act coming up, but they don't need me."

I ignore the little thrill in my belly. Now I really do feel sick.

"I'm good," I say.

He looks disappointed.

My heart's beating way too fast as I head for the door, but I don't push my way out into the familiar night. I'm tired of the familiar. All the magic and all the good memories of my parents that it brings has me bursting with want. I turn back around. The bird girl and Xander are both still talking to their fans. But Xander's watching me like he hasn't taken his eyes off me since I walked away. His expression is odd, like he's relieved to see me coming back, and then his lips quirk at the corners in a way that makes my stomach flip, and I glance behind me like he must be looking at someone else. His grin widens when I look back at him. I nod in response and take a seat like I'm staying for the rest of the show. I stay there until he looks back at whoever he's talking to. When I'm sure he's not tracking me anymore, I get up and stroll through the crowd until I'm at the door that leads backstage. I slide it open and step into a dingy hallway with a naked bulb lighting it. The hallway leads to a back room, and to my left are stairs that head to the side of the stage. I take them two at a time until I'm standing just behind the side curtains. In the center of the stage is a giant tank of water. Maybe the next trick's an escape artist like Houdini.

It's different standing back here, where I can see the way the stage curtains are frayed at the bottom, or the gouges in the stage floor, or the bare, dusty beams above. It's less glamorous than sitting in the audience, but it's more real. It feels like home.

Muffled laughter and conversation drift under the curtain. I imagine the chairs filling with skeptical people waiting to be lifted out of their daily disenchantment, and those who come enchanted already and want validation that they are right, that the world is magical at its core. You only have to find it.

Being able to give them what they want is where true power lies.

Lights flicker beyond the crack in the curtain, telling the audience the show will go on soon, and I can't just stand here on the side of the stage where the performers can see me, so I tuck myself behind some boxes that seem to be overflowing with costumes. They're so dusty I have to hold my breath to stop a sneeze right as the curtain begins to pull open.

Twin girls who look a couple years younger than Parker come out onto the stage in white dresses tied with ocean-blue ribbons. Their blond hair is pulled back in high pigtails. I'm surprised to see kids doing a trick in water, but maybe they were raised by magician parents. Maybe that would've been me at age ten in a different life. When I was ten, I was trying to figure out how to make my stakes sharper with the limited tools in my foster-whatever's garage.

But I don't want to focus on the past right now. I want to see what's right in front of me.

The girls don't speak before climbing the two ladders onto the makeshift platforms beside the tanks. The girl in green who greeted me at the door walks onto the stage and places a hand on a black velvet drape that's set up to the side of the tank.

A hush falls over the audience.

Twin lights illuminate the girls as they step off into the water. Their dresses rise as they sink, revealing old-fashioned white bloomers. They twirl, bringing their arms down and the dresses with them so only the long ribbons float out above them.

The crowd applauds. Nothing has happened, but crowds are more generous with children.

The girl in green, walking quickly and gracefully, pulls the curtain to the other side of the tank, blocking the girls from the audience's view.

I wait to snatch up their secrets and store them away, even though I probably won't ever do this type of trick.

The second the curtain closes, their white dresses turn to black gowns.

They *turn* black—no quick maneuvering, no wet puddles of discarded clothing hidden behind the tank. That was going to be my guess.

I must have blinked.

The girl in green yanks back the curtain to reveal the new dresses billowing around the entire bottom of the tank. The twins do a slow twirl so they look like giant inkblots spreading in the water, and then the girl pulls the curtain again while I keep my eyes narrowed in on the tanks. The second the curtain closes, the dresses turn blue, with long, flowing sleeves.

I did not blink. The dresses shifted right in front of my eyes. My heart beats in my throat, and I might throw up. I force a breath in and out of my nose, trying to calm myself. This is no trick.

The curtain is pulled, and they blink into orange.

Then white sequins.

Then white covered in an array of multicolored flowers.

Then they explode into flowers. The tank fills with daisies, carnations, and roses all pressing against the glass.

My head jerks upward, looking for where they must have dropped from without my seeing.

Nothing.

I grip a dusty skirt spilling from the box I'm hiding behind and press it against my mouth to stop myself from screaming. My brain's a jumbled mess of thoughts. *All* their tricks defy possibility—not because they're the best magicians I've ever seen, but because the tricks are not tricks at all. The thought hits me hard in the way only an impossible truth can. The type of truth that tilts your world and leaves it spinning forever off-balance. Like finding out vampires exist. They may not be vampires, but they're something. Something my mom *might* have been as well. Her journal entries were the fantastical things I imagined they were as a kid. But if she had real magic, wasn't she always warning me away from it? Why?

The tank's so packed full of flowers that I can't see the twins anymore.

Until their hands slap against the sides of the glass. The crowd quiets. Unsure.

I don't know whether this is part of the trick or if I should run onstage and fish them out—human or not, they're kids. They haven't been up for a breath this whole time. How long has it been? I can't be sure. It feels like I've been hiding here in shock forever.

The twins erupt from the top of the tank at the exact same time, lifting their small hands and waving at the audience. Wet flowers dangle in their hair.

The crowd gets on their feet, giving them more love than Xander got for his butterfly. I'm not sure what to do. I can sneak away and pretend I never saw this, or I can dive into the water and maybe drown, because one thing I know for sure is that if Mom had magic like this, she hid it from me. But what if she was just waiting until I was older to let me in on her secrets?

She's not here to ask. These people feel like the closest thing I have to her lost journals. If I miss this moment, if I walk away and they pack up and leave tomorrow, I'll spend the rest of my life wondering, and I've already spent too much of my life wondering why both my parents are dead.

My legs wobble as I stand up and head down the steps, turning away from the door leading to the audience and heading back to where the answers are. I expect to step out into a room and have them all turn dramatically to look at me, but there are rows and rows of boxes, like every show that's ever performed here has left something behind that's never gotten tossed out.

Cold seeps from the cement floor, and I shiver.

A voice rises and drifts off.

I move around several rows of boxes until the conversation grows louder.

"She left," a girl practically shrieks.

"What did you want me to do, drag her backstage?" Xander. There's an edge to his voice.

I scoot around another row of junk and duck. The next row is shorter. Cages of birds sit balanced on top of the boxes. I'm creeping forward like some kind of awkward spy. I pull my hood over my head.

I want their secrets, after all. This is one way to get them.

"We need her. She's the only one who'd even have a fighting chance this late in the game. You have to go all in."

"You know I hate doing that," Xander says. His voice is softer, suddenly more like a caress than the blade it was a second ago.

"Think of Sarah." Another girl's voice is feather light—perhaps the bird girl.

"I always am," Xander snaps. "I'm just not convinced this is the right move."

"It's our *only* move," the feather voice says.

Unease creeps up my spine. There's a desperation in their voices that doesn't make sense.

I grip one of the boxes, rising up to peek through the bars of the birdcage. All the magicians sit around a huge wooden table. No one seems happy.

"Then it's settled," the original voice says.

I lean forward to see her face, and the box teeters under my grip. I pull away too fast, and the birdcage crashes forward.

CHAPTER 5

I hope the birds are okay.

I slink down to the floor, breathing hard.

Boots stomp toward me. Instinct propels me to my hands and knees, and I scramble back the way I came, but a hand grabs my sweatshirt and yanks until I backpedal onto my butt. I'm dragged around the last wall of boxes and into the light.

The bird girl looks up from where she's bent next to her cage of spilled birds. Her eyes widen in recognition, but she says nothing, going back to cooing softly at her riled doves.

The fire girl looms above me, flames twisting in one of her palms, but it's her face that scares the shit out of me. I scoot away from her snarl, but she's faster. Her free hand snatches my upper arm and pulls me to my feet. Even though she's not much taller than me, her grip is iron. But it releases me the second she makes eye contact. Her hand darts out and yanks the hood off my head.

"Hey," I say. I feel more vulnerable without my face half hidden.

"You," the fire girl grumbles. "What are you sneaking around for?

I almost roasted you like a bug." She turns her glare on Xander, who's leaning against the edge of the long wooden table with his arms folded across his chest, watching us with a smirk on his face. "You told me you lost her," she says.

Lost me?

"And now I found her, darling." Xander's voice is practically a purr, like he's talking to a wildcat.

I'm *not* here for him, but my stomach drops a little at the way he calls her darling.

"No. She found us." Her expression could set him on fire. Maybe they just have history. Turning back to me, she gives me a once-over. "Come on in. I'm Aristelle. We have a lot to talk about." She propels me toward the table.

"I . . ." My mouth opens and closes. I glance around the room. It's nothing much—just as dingy and chaotic as you'd expect backstage to be, with clothes piled on the floor and boxes with props overflowing. The long, worn wooden table sits in the center, surrounded by an array of mismatched folding chairs. It's the kind of room I'd be comfortable in—if not for the people.

My stare settles on the twins. Their clothes drip even though their hair is bone-dry. Their breath falls and rises like any other human, except for the fact that they never seem to breathe out of sync with each other.

In and out, in and out. They turn their heads toward me and stare back.

I grab a full cup of water that's definitely not mine from the table and lift it to my lips, eyeing them over the rim. Holding their breath that long isn't even the weird part. David Blaine held his breath for seventeen minutes. No illusions either. He explained the lengths he went to, to be able to do it. The first time he tried to break the record on television, he ended up convulsing underwater as the overwhelming urge to breathe took over. He was pulled out, but he kept trying. The only strings behind his trick were sheer determination and will.

The twins weren't under that long.

I'm still struggling to find another explanation—one that's easier, one that lets me go back to just wanting impressive illusions.

But their clothes changed right in front of me.

I can't remember if I blinked. I didn't. But I was trying so hard not to, maybe I did, like when you're playing the blinking game as a kid and knowing you can't blink makes the urge almost impossible to fight.

I blinked. I must have.

But no. I didn't.

I place the cup back on the table. My hand trembles, sloshing water over the side.

"She already knows," Aristelle says.

"She must have snuck onto the stage," the bird girl says.

"I suppose that gets rid of the awkward bit," Aristelle says.

"Ava." I don't like the soft, slow way Xander says my name. He sounds like a predator trying to keep me from running. "Why don't you sit down, and we'll talk about what you just saw."

"I didn't see a thing." My damn voice cracks. I don't know why I deny it. I came back here for answers. It must be the basic instinct to pretend everything is the way you'd thought. It's probably why so many people refuse to accept that vampires are real. But I'm not one of those people. I can make leaps that others won't.

Aristelle's head snaps in my direction. "She's going to bolt."

Xander takes a step closer to me.

Aristelle rises slowly from the table and stalks toward me.

I consider fleeing like prey. I'm standing in a room with people who aren't quite human. I feel that truth in the tremble in my limbs that screams at me to go, go, go. Maybe they *are* vampires. Maybe vampires have magic, and that's why Mom didn't want me asking about the real stuff. Maybe she knew a lot about vampires, and that's why they killed her. I don't know. The real vampires didn't give up a lot of details during their ten minutes of fame, so all I know are myths and legends and movies. Maybe vampires walk in sunlight and play with cards.

But I don't think so. If they were vampires, they had plenty of time to rip my throat out.

This is something else.

This is what Mom wrote about. It wasn't hyperbole or fantasy. She was talking about *this*.

I need to know. The bird girl slides into a seat at the table next to the girl dressed in green. Both give me small smiles, so I take the open end of the bench next to them while Xander and Aristelle sit across from me. I sit down a little too hard.

"Okay, then," Aristelle says.

Xander puts a hand on her arm. "Let's give her a minute to settle in."

"We don't have a minute." Aristelle jerks her arm away from him.

"Yes, we do." Xander turns a tight smile on me and then waves a hand at the girl in the green dress. "This is Diantha."

Her green dress shimmers as she twists slightly toward me and smiles, warm and inviting even though she says nothing. She's gorgeous as always. I pull at the hem of my sweatshirt.

"Briar and Bridgette." Twin girls with white-blond hair shift their sky-blue eyes on me. They don't smile. They seem disappointed that Aristelle didn't burn me.

"Reina." The bird girl reaches across Diantha and pats me on the arm.

"Sorry about your birds," I mumble.

"They're fine." She winks.

"And, of course, Aristelle." Xander gives her a dramatic little bow, like he's introducing her onstage. She looks as if she could burst into flames again at any moment.

But I'm with her. I'm burning with my need for answers—not pleasant introductions. I decide to just blurt it out before Xander can decide to talk about the weather. "So, you have magic . . . like, real magic. No strings. No tricks. *Magic*."

"Well, I'm actually quite good at sleight of hand," Xander says. He snaps his finger, and the queen of spades appears in his hand. He winks at me. "That was all skill. No magic, but this . . ." He opens his palm and the queen of spades floats into the air and then explodes into all four suits of queens. He blows them in my direction, and they drift around my head like a crown. He waits, like he expects me to clap or something.

I give him nothing. I already know *what* he can do. I need answers about *how* he's doing it.

Diantha clears her throat. "Maybe now's not the time for that."

"Sorry," he says as the cards drop around me. "You've heard of the Society of American Magicians?"

I nod. They were formed in the early 1900s. Houdini was the well-known president for a while, until he died.

He takes a deep breath. "Well, we're part of an older society with secrets that go beyond how we pull off illusions. We call ourselves the Society of *True* Magicians, and yes, we have real power in our blood that lets us perform tricks way beyond what an ordinary magician could do."

I open my mouth, but he holds up a hand with a tight smile. "Save the questions until the end, please."

I scowl but stay silent.

"The Society formed in Rome around fifty AD with some sleight-of-hand magicians called the Acetabularii. They practiced the ball-and-three-cup trick we still see today. Anyone with real skill at sleight of hand could do it. I bet you can do it?" He raises an eyebrow in question.

I don't bother answering. Of course I can.

He smirks. "Thought so. Anyway, the story goes, one of the magicians was gambling big on her own tricks, confident she could move the ball where she wanted with skill and misdirection. She was the best. The crowds loved her. But one day a very wealthy man wanted to play, and the magician bet her entire worth on that single game, but the wealthy man guessed correctly, and no amount of misdirection was going to save the magician from destitution. She knew the ball was under the guessed cup, but in desperation, she *willed* it to move to another one. And it did. It didn't make sense. She went home with her newfound wealth and tried to make it move with only her mind again, and it worked at first, but only for a day or two. So she tried again with an audience, and it worked again."

"The audience *gives* you magic?" I ask. It's actually easy to believe when I think about the way I felt onstage with Xander, when the audience was enthralled and half believing he had real magic. It felt like I did too. It felt like I could do anything at all.

"Yes and no. The audience feeds the magic already in us. Magicians stuck together even back then, so they started experimenting. They found that more than one of them could move the ball only with their minds, but the conditions had to be right. They needed an audience to watch. Though now we've realized it's more than the watching; it's the *believing*. The magic's strongest when your audience believes your tricks are real, and then you *can* make them real. Not everyone could do it, though. The ones who could do real magic described the feeling of being in front of an audience as a bubbling or humming in their blood. They passed it off as adrenaline, but it was something much more." Xander pauses, and his eyes focus in on me, waiting.

Bubbling blood. *I* know that feeling. *I* passed it off as the rush of being onstage.

Mom knew the feeling too. Craved it.

"I'm one of you," I say.

"I wouldn't go that far," Aristelle says. "You're not one of us until you're one of us. You've got magic in your blood, but that doesn't make you special. Everyone does."

I turn to Xander like I'm expecting him to rebut her and tell me I am special, but then I feel a little silly about it.

Xander sees my look. "We think everyone has a little bit of power in them, but for most people, it's so insignificant that they'll never feel it, and for those who feel it, they explain it as something else. Very few people have enough of it to use it."

"But you think I do." I narrow my eyes at Aristelle before shifting my stare to Xander. "You were talking about me before I sent the birds flying." It was either me or the girl in gold, and technically he directed that invitation backstage to me. "You told me to come back after the first show. Did you already know who I was?"

"Aren't you a sneaky little rat," Aristelle says.

"You clearly want something from me, so I'd rethink insulting me."

Aristelle looks like she's choking on her tongue. Xander chuckles, but his eyes stay locked on mine like he's trying to read me.

"You knew my name," I press. "Did you already know who I was?" My skin prickles. I'm starting to feel like this was a trap set just for me. If they already know who my parents are, then maybe it was.

"I told you that you gave me your name. I didn't use any manipulation on you."

I don't believe him, but it's not impossible. I was in a bit of a daze from the high of being onstage.

"*Should* we know who you are?" Aristelle raises her eyebrows.

I could drop my last name. I could tell them about Mom and what she wrote in her journals, but I don't. There wasn't just a desire for her old life in Mom's journal entries. There was fear, too. And there was one page I'd written off before, but it digs into my mind now.

> I don't know if he's coming after her or me. Probably both.

I always wondered who the *he* was in the entry. And if I was the *her*. It could have been written before I was born. Mom could have written it about one of the members of her troupe, but *who* was after her? We did move around a lot. What if it was about another magician chasing us? A rivalry? What if the vampire who killed her was involved?

I think of the tall, creepy dude who warned me away from here.

My uncertainty keeps me from sharing.

I also don't like the way they keep stealing glances at each other. But I notice things like that—probably more than most. When you don't have stability in your life, reading people can be the only way to see what's coming.

I don't have their whole story yet, so I'm not going to give them mine.

"Are you somebody?" Aristelle asks. I don't like the way she phrases the question.

"No," I say.

They sit silently for a moment, like I'm going to change my answer.

"You're not answering my question. Tell me why you were waiting for me."

Xander nods like he's made up his mind about something. "We travel in troupes because if we perform together, we *all* get that boost of magic in our blood. We can also feel other magicians when their powers are being used or sometimes if we're just close by them. People who don't know any better pass the feeling off as attraction."

I work hard to keep my face straight, because I definitely felt that pull to be close to him, to be close to all of them, really, and I wrote it off as wanting the illusions or, in Xander's case, being attracted to him. I'm almost relieved to know it's not real.

"So when you were on the stage with me, I could feel the power building in you." He pauses. "A lot of power, actually, and then I watched your coin trick on the street. You're a natural. That's why I told you to come again, and that's why I invited you backstage. You clearly have the ability to be one of us with the right training."

He thinks I did that coin trick on purpose. I open my mouth to correct him but change my mind. I want them to think I belong with them. "But you said *you* needed *me*—not that *I* need *you*. You're forgetting I heard all of that, so why don't you stop dancing around and tell me everything."

Reina's been quiet for so long that I almost forgot she and Diantha were beside me. "We were looking for a new apprentice, so we were watching for anyone to respond to the magic." Her warm smile soothes some of my instinct that's telling me to get out of here. "Obviously you caught our attention."

"But you sounded desperate."

"We are," Diantha says.

I wait for her to say more, but she looks at the table.

They all stare at each other like they don't know how to explain whatever's coming next. Xander looks like he's working himself up to speaking, but then he freezes and tilts his head like a voice is speaking just to him. Another look passes between Xander and Aristelle.

"We have a quick thing to take care of. Wait here." Xander stands up.

"What?" I rise from my seat.

"Now doesn't seem like the time for this," Reina says.

"There's always time for this," Aristelle says.

Aristelle and Xander practically run out the door.

Reina turns a painfully cheerful smile on me. "They'll be back in a jiffy."

"Do you want to play dice?" the twins ask in unison.

I shake my head and step back. "I think I need some fresh air." Diantha and Reina share a look. "I'm not going to run," I add, but my own voice doesn't sound sure.

They let me walk away, but I'm barely out on the street when Diantha comes up beside me.

"You should follow them," she says. "I don't know how much they're planning to tell you, but whatever they say, it's not the same as seeing." She points to the left. "They went that way."

I have no idea how she can tell where they disappeared to. I don't see them, but I don't hesitate. I need to know what they're not saying. What someone's not telling you is always more important than what they are telling you.

I give Diantha a nod and then run. I hate running at night, but it's fairly busy, so I'm not too worried about getting jumped.

Before long I spot Xander's green hair and slow. I follow, keeping to the other side of the street. I try to stay behind other people walking to their evening plans, but Xander and Aristelle keep stopping. Each time they do, they shift their heads in the same direction before moving on. We're drifting out of the heart of downtown. There are fewer people, and I worry they'll turn and spot me, but they don't. They only pause and wait, like they're deciding which way to go, but they don't talk to each other before striding on. It's like they know where they're going but don't at the same time.

The hairs on my neck prickle.

It feels like I'm hunting them, but it feels like they're hunting too.

They pause beside a bar with nobody outside. Xander reaches out and grabs Aristelle's hand, interlocking their fingers. He flashes a smile at her as he does, and then they move around the side of the bar.

My stomach feels like it's in my toes, making my feet too heavy to move.

That's not what I expected, but I force myself forward.

Just before I reach the dark alley they disappeared down, a young man runs out of it.

I take a step back. His wide eyes roam over me like he doesn't even see me. His fingers hold his neck. He runs in the other direction.

My heart starts pumping so fast I let out an unsteady gasp. *Breathe*, I tell myself as I reach into my backpack for my stake.

I've practiced for this.

I watched *30 Days of Night* a dozen times, even though the scenes where vampires killed people made me sick. I wanted to cry and hyperventilate each time, but I taught myself to breathe through the pain and the fear and the memory.

Focus.

They've obviously tricked me. Of course real vampires would have powers I don't know about. Mom must have gotten tangled up with them somehow. Maybe she even knew they were vampires. Maybe she even knew Xander and Aristelle. For all I know, they're the ones who killed her.

My breathing is calm. Perfect.

The stake in my hand is rough, and my grip is solid even though my palms sweat.

I take the last few steps to the mouth of the alley.

Xander pushes a girl against the side of the bar. His forearm presses into her throat. Aristelle stands in front of the girl, her nose just inches from the girl's neck. They're only a few feet from me, so I don't wait, I don't think, I just charge.

Xander's closest, with his back slightly to me, so I hit him and send him stumbling into Aristelle, who gets knocked onto her ass. She snarls, but then her eyes widen a fraction when she realizes it's me. As Xander stumbles, he grabs onto one of my biceps and carries me with him, and *I* end up slammed against the wall.

There's a wicked curl to his lips when he looks down at me, but then it fades. "Ava?"

"Saying my name won't help you," I say.

His eyes widen as he feels it: my stake pressed against his skin, ready to take his heart.

CHAPTER 6

The one thing I've drilled into my head with all my training is to always get the stake lined up right where you want it to go. Don't lose the stake.

I'm a little surprised I actually did it. It's one thing to practice that, and it's another to do it while you're tangled up in a flailing vampire you kind of had the beginnings of a crush on. I feel nauseous about that last part.

My hand shakes, leaving tiny red lines across Xander's chest, like I'm marking the spot for later, but I won't wait for later. All I need is confirmation that he is what I think, and then he's dust—or whatever actually happens to them when you put a stake through their heart.

He stares down at my shaking hand.

I hope he doesn't think it's weakness. It's not.

"You believe in vampires," Xander says, his voice even and calm.

"My mom was killed by one, so, yeah." I don't bother looking up to see his reaction to that, but he's silent for a beat.

"You think *we're* bloodsuckers?" He loses his calm and half spits, half chuckles the last word.

I look up to see his lips twisted with disgust that would be hard to fake, but I don't move my stake away.

"You were about to eat that girl."

Xander sighs. "*We're* not leeches. The girl was." He reaches up and closes a hand over my fingers that grip the stake and slowly pulls the point away from his chest as he looks me in the eyes. "We're hunters. Vampire hunters." He turns around and glances at Aristelle, who's dusting off her pants. "We were getting to that part if you'd just waited." He looks down the alley, at me, and then back to Aristelle. "I've got this. See if you can find her."

Aristelle puts her hand on her hip like she'll argue, but all she does is glare at me as she gives her pants another brush before sprinting away without looking back.

Xander steps back from me, raising his hands. "Seriously, you can put that away."

"I want to hear the rest of the story first."

"Fair enough." He glances around the dark alley, at the bags of trash near the back and the few scattered cans and bottles, and shrugs like this is as good a place as any. He steps a few paces back from me so he can lean against the other wall, making it impossible to see his expression as he begins. "The Society of True Magicians isn't just a bunch of people who love magic and want to cultivate it. That might be how it started, but I only gave you half the story."

I don't say anything, just wait. I want all the answers to everything right now. I want to know why my mom died. I want to know what Xander and his troupe are. I want to understand the power in my veins.

Because I want to know how it can help me kill a vampire.

The thought of actually doing it, actually getting revenge, has my heart pounding. My arms tremble, not from magic or fear, but from being closer to something I've wanted for so long. Something I'd all but given up on, pushing it down until it became a dark, festering hole of hopelessness inside me. Who would I be if I could fill that hole up?

"Just tell me everything," I say. "I believe you. I can handle it."

"The original vampires were magicians gone bad."

Didn't see that one coming, but I wait quietly.

"Some of the Acetabularii were happy enough with their powers. They couldn't lose, but a little taste of power is never enough for some people. They wanted to test it. They wanted more, and the power boost from a performance only lasted so long. As you well know, we can *feel* the power in our veins, so someone had the idea to go directly to the source, and it worked. Prick a finger and you could send a ball across the room. Slice a palm and you could send it across town. But even that wasn't enough. The more power you have, the more you want to *keep* it, and the only way to do that is to never die. So they pushed themselves closer and closer to the brink of death with their bloodletting. And finally it worked. Someone went too far and used enough blood and power for the magic to grant the request, but the spell sucked dry every bit of their magician blood to do it and left them with an insatiable hunger for more blood to keep the spell going. All spells need to be fed to last, so if a vampire doesn't drink, their immortality is gone. They hurt others to save themselves."

"So my mom was killed by a magician gone wrong." My blood goes cold. It doesn't feel like magic in my veins at all. It feels like death.

"Not necessarily. The magic's not supposed to leave the body. Blood magic is harder to control—a ball sent across the room with a pricked finger might appear in someone's throat, for example. The immortality spell was a lot of magic let loose. It became what it wanted, not what the caster intended. Now anytime a vampire drains the last drop on anyone, human or magician, the spell gets activated in that person. They become a vampire too, and many of them don't know why or how—only that they're a creature of myth and legend."

"My mom was drained, and she's just dead," I say.

"She probably wasn't completely drained and still died from blood loss," he says.

His words are gentle, but they clench around my throat and drag me into the memory. He's right. She wasn't dead. I grabbed her wrist when I found her. Her hand was limp, but then I felt that twitch under her skin. It gave me this ridiculous hope, and I kept shaking her and saying her name, but the twitch wasn't hope. It was the last bit of life leaving her body. I was the one there when she died. The vampire was long gone.

"Hey." Xander's voice is soft. "We don't have to finish this right now."

But I need to. It feels urgent. Being a vampire is a curse. One some people accept but others have forced upon them. It doesn't really matter which of these categories a vampire falls into—it's not an excuse. They still hurt people. They're monsters that need to be snuffed out.

Xander begins to step toward me, but I shake my head. I don't need comfort. I need the truth I've been desperate for since I first saw Gerald on television and knew in my bones that he was a lying killer. "I still don't see how you all have a chance against literal vampires. Aristelle, maybe, but you?" I point at Xander. "What are you going to do with a deck of cards? Death by a thousand paper cuts? Are Reina's birds going to peck them to death?"

"I have many other talents, Ava." He pauses, holding my questioning stare. "Plus, we're immortal."

I'd take a step back if I weren't already against a wall. He just got done telling me the cost of immortality. My fingers clench around the stake I'm still holding.

Xander notices. "Wait. Don't go all Buffy on me again. Although, the Buffy Xander certainly deserved to get stabbed." He cracks a grin, but I don't. I'm not in the mood for vampire jokes on a good day.

He darts forward so quickly that he's a blur of green, and then he's back against the wall with my stake in his hands.

My mouth gapes. "You're not helping your case."

He gives the stake a twirl. "You were making me nervous with this thing."

"Give it back."

"If a vampire sneaks up on us, you're safer if I have the stake."

With the speed he just moved at, I should probably believe him, but I don't trust him. "Give it back."

"We're still not vampires," he continues, ignoring my outstretched hand. "Once vampires were created, some of the Acetabularii wanted to wipe their hands of it, but others felt an obligation to do something. But the curse makes the vampires strong and fast, and they can heal instantly from almost any wound because the curse wants to be fed, so it made them superior hunters. Nobody knew how to stand a chance against them without ending up cursed in the exact same way." He twists his face up in such pure disgust that I find myself nodding with the sentiment.

"The Acetabularii started experimenting with natural ways to up their power, like more elaborate tricks to draw a bigger reaction from the audience and performing more often so the power lasted longer. But eventually two of the most powerful Acetabularii realized we'd never be strong enough without using blood magic, so they did. One of them sacrificed every drop of her magician blood, but she didn't create her own immortality—she gave her life so the other magician could make these." He holds up the leather cuff with the jagged red jewel in its center. "These hold the spell for immortality, but because we didn't sacrifice our own blood, we don't have to feed to sustain it. We still have to feed the spell, but it's not fed with blood—it's fed with performance."

I eye his cuff. "So I need one of those to kill a vampire?"

"No, but it evens the playing field. It doesn't just let us live forever, which in turn helps build the magic in our blood—the older we get, the more powerful we get. It also helps us store extra magic, like an amplifier. We're stronger, faster, and we can heal wounds that aren't severe. But even someone with no power at all can get lucky and bring down a vamp. A stake to the heart will work just fine. It's the easiest. They can't heal from wounds made by wood because it's a natural thing in an unnatural body." He grins down at my stake like a long-lost friend. "But they can't heal from decapitation or burning to ashes either."

There's a viciousness behind his grin, and I know you don't get that way without a reason. I thought he was all charm and flirting, but when I think back, I saw it in him last night when I was onstage with him.

I can think of only two reasons you join a secret magic society of vampire hunters: you love magic or you hate vampires. I do both.

And I can guess which category Xander belongs in.

"You lost someone."

His smile crashes in an instant. "My brother. I was seventeen, and he was only fifteen." A ghost of a smile crosses his lips, and it's so different from his usual too-easy grin that I hardly recognize him. "He begged me to take him to this party. It was just supposed to be your regular old high school party . . . a bunch of teens and too much alcohol. It was getting late—we'd already missed curfew, so I went searching for him. I saw him in the woods behind the house." He lets out a harsh chuckle that sounds more like choking. "I thought he was getting lucky. A girl had her face buried in his neck. I almost left him alone, but our parents liked to ground me one hour for every minute I broke curfew, so I called his name. The girl ran, and he just . . . dropped. I thought he was drunk, but I ran to him and tried to pull his face up to me, and his neck . . ." Xander pauses and runs his hand over his face.

"You don't have to keep going," I tell him. I know the moment he's in. For me, it was the last little pull of life leaving my mom's body. For him, it's this.

His breathing now is tight and heavy, but he shakes his head and keeps going. "There was a lot of blood. It wasn't like those dainty little pinprick bites." He swallows. "Some vamps are more vicious than others. She ripped him open. He was already gone . . . I tried to put him back together for a moment. It was the first time I used my power. I'd been doing some little cup-and-ball tricks at the party, experiencing that little buzz of power that we can feel even if we don't know how to use it. Aristelle said the shock probably made me shove the power from my body and try to heal him. Didn't work, of course. The police came. Everyone called it an animal attack. You know how people are. Bloodsuckers have literally shown their faces to us, but most don't believe in them. But Aristelle felt my power being used and found me, and she believed me, and they needed an apprentice." He shrugs.

"Aristelle felt your power? Was she there?"

"No. The more power that's used, the greater the distance that other magicians can feel it. Think of it like a bomb going off. There's an initial burst that draws everyone's attention, and then you're smoldering for a bit afterward."

"You felt that vampire. Earlier, you both acted like you heard something."

"Yes. It's how we find vampires too. When they feed, they're using magic to stay alive. It's how we hunt them."

He tosses my stake in the air and catches it. "There's something else you should know," he says way too casually. "Vampires can feel us too when we use magic. Magic feels the same no matter what type is being used, so it's like we're constantly calling to each other, but you don't know who is doing the calling: a magician or a vamp. Vamps will eat anything, though, even each other, but they prefer to eat us."

Fear prickles on the back of my neck. "Why?"

"Drinking our blood lets them do magic again, for a little while at least. It lets them walk in the sun again too. Burning in the sun was another side effect of the curse. They also get cold when they haven't fed recently—not enough blood circulating. But with magician blood in their system, they can pretend they're one of us."

I swallow. "So every time you build your magic to hunt vampires, you're drawing them to you."

"Does that scare you?"

"No." I've been looking for them my whole life, and now he's telling me I can bring them right to me.

The fierceness in his answering grin takes away my uneasiness.

We sit in silence for a minute.

"So you said you did magic before this?" I like that it might not be just about hunting vampires for him, too, because while I want that, I also want the magic.

"Not really. I was into charming the ladies with little tricks, so nothing's changed." A weak version of his smile comes back.

I can tell he doesn't want to dive into his memories again, so I do my best to make my tone light and joking, even though my throat aches with pain for him—for both of us. "So exactly how long ago did you become immortal?"

None of this has freaked me out, but the immortal thing is a looming question in my mind, and if he tells me this was forty years ago, well, that might change things.

"Four years. I've been seventeen for four years now." His grin comes out in full force. "So now you know everything." He clears his throat and runs a hand through his hair, flopping the green strands to the other side. "I guess you were following us for a while . . ."

"Yes." I'm not sure where he's going with this.

He gives a forced little chuckle. "It's not what you think. It's just part of our cover. A couple stumbling into a vampire and their meal in a dark alley is a lot less suspicious than the two of us just charging forward. It gets us closer. We have a better chance of staking it."

"Right," I mutter. I'm glad it's dark so he doesn't see my cheeks flush. I guess he *is* flirting—it wasn't just the zing of magic.

"It's true." I jump at Aristelle's voice behind me. I didn't hear a single step of her approach. "There's not enough money in the world to make me hold his hand," she continues, "but I'll do it for a single dead vampire."

Her face hardens, and I know she's like Xander. She's not in this for the magic. She's in this for the blood.

"What happened to you?" I ask. It's a horrible way to say it, but it's what pops out. *What happened to make you as hard as me?*

Her cold eyes meet mine, and she's silent for so long I don't think she'll answer, but she does.

"It was 1969." She pauses and watches me.

I try not to give a reaction.

She seems satisfied when I don't. "I went to Woodstock. I was all peace and love back then." She scowls like she wishes she could reach out and smack her past self. "It was crowded. It was so packed that a vampire came up behind me and drained me to the point of unconsciousness, and nobody noticed until I was left on the ground. I woke up in the hospital, but I remembered what happened to me. I remembered the fangs. I started hunting vampires before I ever tapped into my magic. That's how a troupe found me."

I don't tell her I'm sorry or anything. I have a feeling she'd hate that.

Instead I say, "So you're like, what? Seventy years old?"

She gives me a hard smile. "I wish." She looks uncomfortable, like she didn't mean to say it out loud.

"You wish you weren't immortal?"

She shifts like she'll turn away from me and shares a look with Xander before answering. "The spell doesn't just freeze our bodies—it freezes our minds too. In most ways, I feel like I did the day I became immortal. I still feel those little hopes and dreams I had before, and I still feel all the anger and pain of what happened like it was yesterday, but then I also have a bunch of memories that don't fit from the past fifty-three years—it's almost like I'm two people that shouldn't exist in this world."

I can tell she's being more vulnerable than she likes, but she holds my stare as she talks, and then after, waiting for my reaction. "How do you live like that?"

She shrugs. "It's a struggle every day. A lot of us just sort of shut down . . . give up on feeling human." She hesitates. "Some of us become like vampires in that way."

I glance between them. "But not you."

"Never," she spits.

I swallow. "Is it worth it?"

"I've killed three hundred and fourteen vampires. Wait . . ." A sharp grin lights up her face, and she looks more like herself. "Make that three hundred and fifteen."

My mouth pops open. Over three hundred vampires.

But it doesn't seem to have given her any kind of closure. She didn't answer my question.

Xander bites his lip as he watches my expression. "Are you with us?"

"Take me hunting now." I need to know what it's like. I need to know if it fills the hole inside me—it's been all I've wanted for so long that I can't imagine it wouldn't.

Aristelle laughs. "Somehow I like you both more and less every minute."

Xander shakes his head. "You need more training."

"I've been training most of my life for this."

"It's better if we get you one of these first." He holds up his cuff. The bloodred jewel looks black in the dark.

"Fine. I'm in. I'll take one."

"Are you with us?" he asks again.

"Is there anything else you're not telling me?"

Xander and Aristelle share a look I don't like—one that leaves me on the outside without some key information.

"He hasn't told you everything yet," Aristelle says.

Xander glances at his toes, and I focus on Aristelle. This has to be bad news, and she seems like the type of person who loves being the messenger of disappointment. "You tell me, then."

She smiles. "The Society doesn't have unlimited power." She holds up her wristband. "One of these only becomes available when one of us dies, and we don't hand them out like five-cent candy. We're not the only troupe. *All* the troupes train an apprentice, and then we meet once a year. If we've lost someone, we hold a competition where you show you have the skill to control the magic in your veins. You need to be the best of the best to join us. You'll have to fight if you want to be a part of this."

"How often does someone die? Is there a spot this year?"

"Not every year, and we don't know until we arrive," Aristelle says. "But if there's not an opening, we'll keep training you for the next year."

So it could be years before I get what I want, and I've already waited long enough, but I feel a little guilty about hoping someone's dead.

"Almost every year," Xander adds, reading the disappointment on my face. "Hunting is dangerous. Vampire bodies use blood magic without them even having to think about it. They heal faster than us and move faster than us because their entire body is a spell in action. Our powers take more focus and don't always work. But that's why we collaborate, and that's why we hold the competition. We're not going to let you hunt without making sure you're the best."

My stomach sinks. "But I can't do what you do."

"Don't worry," Xander adds a little too eagerly. "We have time to train you."

His reassurance is too quick. "What happens if I lose?"

"You go back to your old life—stripped of your memory of this."

But what am I going back to? Sometimes I feel like there are a million different lives behind me. I don't want to go back. The only time of my life I've ever wanted to go back to isn't even possible. You can't go back to the dead. Some horrible part of me wishes that vampire had drained my mom completely, so at least a version of her existed, but that thought makes my stomach squeeze.

I'll just be back to wandering the streets at night searching for something that might kill me if I find it, all while trying not to think about the fact that my brother has a home that I'm only a fixture in.

I shake my head. I can't be consumed with what I have to lose. People who only think of what they might lose never win anything, and I want this more than ever.

I feel like I'm walking forward into a dark night, but I have people with me for the first time. Hell, I even have a girl who can light the way with fire, even if she might singe me once or twice.

And they *want* me. Mom talked so much about the big troupe she used to travel with that they felt like distant relatives to me. Her face would light up with stories about Edgar, who swallowed fire; Angela, who could contort herself into impossible spaces; Samuel, who did daring, dangerous acts; and my personal favorite, Julia, who made whole lions disappear with just a wink. The way Mom talked about them . . . they sounded like family. Even as a kid, I had a craving for that—for a big family that went beyond our small trailer, but instead, what little I had was taken from me.

Sitting around the room earlier with Xander's troupe felt like a glimpse of a big family. Reina and Diantha leaned against each other. Xander and Aristelle kept sharing looks that seemed to carry secrets. The twins . . . well, they were staring straight ahead like dolls who'd been set down, but when one of them sneezed, Diantha had pulled a tissue from her sleeve the second *before* it happened. Even in the small amount of time I sat with them, I could tell they were family.

Mom always said that one day we would perform together. She never let me help with the birthday parties, but she always said one day it would be my turn, and I used to do little drawings of what our mother-daughter outfits would look like.

I'll never be onstage with Mom, but here, right in front of me, is the chance to join my own troupe—to take back one of the dreams I thought died with her.

"So are you with us?" Xander asks again.

I weigh his words for a moment. But the only thing in my life I really love is Parker, and as much as it kills me to say it, sometimes he's just not enough. I need this, and it's not just about revenge. I want the power to create my own life, one I can share with him, and it's standing right in front of me. I can hunt vampires until I feel whole again and then get a residency in Vegas with tricks the world's never seen before. This could help me escape . . . everything.

"She's with us," Aristelle says. "We leave the day after tomorrow. Five a.m. sharp. The competition is in Santa Cruz."

"What?" My voice squeaks. "You said I had time to train."

"You do. We have to check in, though, and then we're granted time to train at our compound."

"So that's why you needed me. What happens to you if I don't go?" Something bad. Something to make the desperation I heard in their voices earlier make sense.

They share a look, and there's true fear in it.

"The Society takes the competition very seriously," Aristelle says. "With a limited number of immortality spells, we need the best of the best to keep vampires from overrunning the world. If we don't bring someone to the competition, our troupe gets split up."

My stomach bottoms out. I know what it's like to be afraid of that. Parker and I were separated at first, and I'll never forget how desperate I was to get back to him. And then after, how afraid I was that we'd be separated again—that someone would want a sweet little boy with big smiles and not an older girl who cried in her sleep.

They both look like they want me to stop asking questions, but I have one more. I'm not going to let my sympathy override my common sense.

"Who's Sarah?" I ask.

Aristelle grimaces.

Xander's the one who answers. "She did a trick she wasn't ready for and got hurt. She's fine now, but she left the troupe. This life's not for everyone. There is danger, but you have us to help you navigate it."

I've been looking for danger. It doesn't scare me.

"We can start training you tomorrow morning," Aristelle says.

"No," I say, and hate the scared look they share before I continue. "I want something from you before I accept."

Aristelle frowns.

The corner of Xander's mouth quirks. "What would that be?"

"I want you to perform at my brother's birthday party." It's perfect. I'll be able to give Parker something truly magical before I leave, and it'll be way better than anything Deb's planned.

Aristelle laughs again. "Do we look like we do party tricks?"

I stare at her elaborate carnivalesque outfit, with her thigh-high boots and red brocade corset laced over a billowing black shirt, and then Xander's open vest over his bare chest. "Yeah, you do."

Xander snorts as Aristelle glares at me.

"You need to start training," Aristelle says.

"It's my brother's birthday, and I'm spending the day with him."

"What time's the party?" Xander asks.

"Two."

"I'll be there." He presses buttons on a phone and then passes it to me. I expect to put my number in, but it's my phone with his number added.

"How did you . . . ?"

He winks. I don't need to ask that question anymore . . . or at least not for much longer.

We walk back to the club in silence. I catch Xander and Aristelle both glancing at me like they're still waiting for me to run, but I'm not going to. They're offering me too much. They could tell me I had to fight my way through a cage of tigers and I might do it just to feel closer to Mom. And to get closer to revenge.

When we reach the club, Aristelle walks in without saying bye, but Xander lingers. "See you tomorrow," he says, but there's a question in his voice.

I nod, but he still takes a moment before turning away, as if he's afraid I'll disappear into smoke. I wait until he's inside before gulping in the night air, like I haven't been breathing for the past twenty minutes.

I turn my feet toward Deb's, feeling the need to walk for a little while. I need my routine. I fall into it, taking steady steps, checking down one dark alley and then the next.

Shit.

There's actually someone down there. It's hard to tell in the dark, but a man hunches slightly as he leans against the wall. I think he's alone for second before a flash of blond hair moves away from him.

My heart stalls and then kicks into high gear. My limbs turn to jelly. Not all creepy men in the dark are vampires, but I reach for my backpack to fish out my stake.

Shit. Xander never gave it back to me.

My adrenaline turns to absolute dread. If he is a vampire, I'm toast, and if he isn't, I could still end up dead, but I can't just turn around and leave. If I go back to the club for help, this girl could be dead by the time I return. I stalk forward until I'm at the lip of the alley. They're arguing in whispers—his is so low it's barely audible, and hers is soft and high. Not a vampire, then, but that doesn't mean he's not dangerous.

I creep closer and cringe as glass scrapes under my boots.

The man whirls around so fast I don't have time to be startled. He takes two long strides and is in front of me in an instant.

I'm surprised I hold my ground, but I think it's more that I've frozen than any type of bravery at this point.

"You're scaring her!" The girl runs up beside him. Her long yellow hair catches the streetlight from the road and glows like a torch in the gloomy alley. Even in the dim light, her cheeks are somehow rosy against her white skin. She smiles at me, and it's so wide and sincere that I don't know how to make it fit in this scenario. She keeps it planted on her face until some of the tension in me starts to leak out.

"Are you okay?" she asks.

"I thought *you* were in trouble. I heard you arguing." My voice comes out strong—as if I can handle the situation.

"Oh." She laughs and straightens the baby-blue sweater she's got on over her soft-pink sundress. "I just want to get an ice cream cone before all the shops close, and this grump won't leave his post."

I finally look at the guy, who's been only a blur of threat on my radar. He's scowling at the girl.

I take a step back. "You." It's the weird guy I ran into last night.

He stares at me for a second through the flop of curls dangling in his eyes and sighs. "I was hoping I wouldn't see you again."

"That feeling was mutual."

"Then why didn't you listen?" He folds his arms over his chest like a father scolding his child.

I bristle. "I don't know who you think you are."

The girl behind him sighs dramatically. "You'd think you'd be better at this." She turns to me. "He's only looking out for you."

"Are you one of the other troupes?"

The boy sighs. "You know, then. They got you. Did you already agree to be their apprentice?"

"Why wouldn't I?"

"It's dangerous." His face is tight and cold, like a vault of secrets I'll never open.

The girl claps her hands. "I'm an apprentice too."

I look between them. "If it's so dangerous, why do you have one?"

Something dark flickers across the boy's face.

The girl's face falls a tiny bit, like she really hadn't considered it. "Maybe we could talk over ice cream?"

"I don't—"

She grabs my arm and starts pulling me back onto the street before I can even protest. "It couldn't hurt to have a friend, right? If we're going to be in the same competition?"

"Willow," the boy growls.

"Ignore Roman," Willow says. "He doesn't do friends." She lowers her voice like she's sharing a secret. "I'm pretty sure even *I'm* not his friend." There's sarcasm in her voice, but also a little bit of hurt. I relax into her grip on my arm. I don't trust people who are too bright and too happy, but there's something underneath her that feels more truthful.

And while I'm not really looking for a friend, I am always open to more information. I can go along with this.

"I'm Ava," I tell her, surprised that I give her my name without even being asked, but I like the way she's just talking to me like she doesn't even need it.

The walk to the ice cream parlor takes an eternity, but maybe it's because Roman trails behind me, and I can't help feeling his stare on my back.

I have to fight the urge to glance over my shoulder at him.

We come to a halt outside a busy ice cream parlor with a chalkboard full of bizarre flavors like lavender and green tea. I've passed this place multiple times, but I've never been. Parker and Jacob always want Blizzards at Dairy Queen.

Willow puts herself in line behind a pair of young men, who gawk at her before coming to their senses and turning back to the counter. They don't glance at me. I can hardly blame them. Willow's long blond hair swings almost to her waist and is tangled in a way that makes you imagine her running through the forest in her bare feet while branches snag her hair. She turns bark-colored eyes toward me.

"Do you have a favorite flavor?"

"Vanilla, I guess." Based on the sign I saw outside, vanilla is off the table.

She hums, twisting around the boys in front of her to eye the multicolored tubs. "You should try the green tea."

I don't know how vanilla led her to green tea, but I nod, and she grins like this is some spectacular moment for us. If this were a movie, this would be the moment we realize we are destined to be friends forever. We get to the counter, and she orders me one scoop of honey vanilla and one scoop of green tea. She orders lavender and peanut butter for herself—just the thought of the combination makes me gag, and I try not to show it. She pays for our cones before I can even reach for my pocket.

"You don't need to—"

"I want to. It's what friends do."

"You're not friends," Roman grumbles behind me.

I glare at him like I wasn't thinking the exact same thing. We can't be friends.

She ignores Roman and leads me to a chrome table surrounded by metal chairs with wooden seats and backs. The chairs shriek in protest as she rearranges them.

"I guess we have to include him," she says, and sighs.

"I guess." I glance at Roman, who sits next to Willow with a single cup of honey vanilla. He seems to be pretending not to hear us.

Willow licks a drip of cream running down her cone and eyes him. "He doesn't know how to do ice cream." She grins at me.

"It's sad, really," I answer with a stiff smile, but I can feel myself melting a little bit ,like the ice cream in my hand. In this bright place, Willow's energy bounces all around, filling me with a buoyancy I don't often feel in social situations. I take a lick of my vanilla ice cream. It's sweet and thick, with the slightest tang of honey. "That's amazing."

"I knew you'd like it," Willow says, and just like that we've known each other forever again. I don't actually know her at all, but something about her demeanor makes me feel like I do, and I *never* get that feeling—that feeling like we're friends.

I try to shake the feeling. It's not why I'm here.

Roman glances between us and sighs. "This was a bad idea. I told you. No friends."

Willow pouts. "I need friends."

"Why?" I ask. I'm genuinely curious. Friendship is not something I've ever felt like I need, even if I sometimes want it. Even if I want it now.

"Look at who I'm stuck with all day. He's the only member in his troupe." Her smile drops just a hair—it'd be unnoticeable if I weren't so used to reading people. "I miss my big family."

"You're competitors, not friends. You can't be both," Roman says darkly. "Only one of you will stay."

"But we could be friends for now," Willow says. "What do you think, Ava? Friends for now?"

I can't remember the last time someone just flat-out asked me to be friends with them. It's the kind of innocent phrase you hear only on a playground next to the tetherball. Even as a little kid, I can't remember anyone saying the words to me. I was the kid in secondhand clothes, sitting on the stone wall in front of the swings without the nerve to get up and wait in line. Part of me must have wished someone would throw those words in my direction, and now I have to resist the urge to shout yes and grin like a fool.

For now. I latch on to the one negative part of her statement, using it to pull me down and back into myself where I belong. Only one of us can win and join. Our new friendship already has a short life span. But I'm used to things not lasting.

I stare at Willow across the table, assessing her with new interest, evaluating her long and lithe limbs. She's beautiful but probably not quick. I don't know what the contest will be, but I file away the information like a skilled warrior.

A slow smile spreads across her face as she does the same to me.

I smile back, enjoying my ice cream just as much as her honesty.

"Friends?" She holds out a hand across the table.

"And competitors," I answer, grasping her hand in mine.

She nods and laughs, letting go and leaning back in her chair. Her eyes are a warm, liquid amber. "What's your specialty?" she asks, licking a drip of ice cream from her finger.

Roman's vanilla ice cream melts in his cup. He hasn't taken a single bite.

"Oh, umm . . . I do coin tricks," I say, and wince.

"Nice." Willow smiles like I've given the perfect answer.

"That's not good enough," Roman growls. His spoon snaps in his clenched fist.

I jerk back. I know it's not as cool as what the rest of the troupe can do, but they haven't started training me yet. Roman's anger is not really directed at me, though. He's glaring into his cup.

"I'm sure I'll learn other stuff," I add.

"With what time?" He drops his broken spoon on the table.

I thought we had time to practice—not a lot of time, but enough. I turn to Willow. "How long have you been practicing?"

Willow hesitates. "Ten months."

My mouth goes dry. My ice cream runs down my hand in sobbing streams now, and if I had any sense left, I would try to stop it. I don't.

Absently, I'm aware that I'm nodding like this is all okay, like I haven't just learned I don't stand a chance at this dream that I only just stumbled into. I'm surprised at how much that hurts.

It's Roman's fury that pulls me back. I focus on his fist on top of the table, his long fingers clenched tight enough for the veins to pop out. I don't know why he cares so much. He should be glad his apprentice has the better chance.

"That's why I warned you away," Roman says. "They *never* train their apprentices enough."

"Why do you care?" I ask, then turn to Willow. "And doesn't it give you a better chance?"

"I like a fair fight," she says.

Roman doesn't answer.

"Well, I'm still planning to give you one." Xander said he felt a lot of power in me—that I would be a natural. I have to believe that.

We eat in silence for a few minutes. When I'm certain they're not going to give me anything else, I stand up. "It was nice meeting you." I direct my words to Willow alone, because even though I'm not ready to call her my friend or anything, I *know* Roman's not.

"See you soon." Willow waves.

I push out into the night air.

"Ava." His deep voice says my name with hesitation, like he's not sure he has a right to use it.

I turn around and look into Roman's serious eyes.

"Why'd you do that?" he asks.

I shrug. "It's a long story." I try to sum it up for him. "I want something different. Xander's troupe offers me that."

"No," he says, his brow furrowed. "Why did you step into that dark alley with me and Willow? You clearly thought I was a threat, but you stepped in anyway. Most people would have ignored it or gotten help." He says the last bit like that would have been the smart thing to do.

"Instinct."

His face is grim.

I start to turn away.

"It was brave," he says.

"Thanks," I say. I don't know what this is, so I start walking.

"I'm not sure it's a compliment," he says so softly I barely hear him.

It sounds like another warning.

CHAPTER 7

One of the kids snorts and spews orange soda out of their nose as Parker shoves another hot dog in his mouth with a single bite. Jacob does the same, battling it out for the title of most disgusting eater of hot dogs. They're on to their fifth or sixth. Another boy and one girl keep pace with them. I admire the girl. She looks ready to puke, but she's reaching for another when Deb calls time. Everyone cheers, and Jacob lifts Parker's hand in the air as champion, even though I'm sure Jacob was one ahead of him. I actually like that kid, I have to admit.

Stacie pulls a face beside me. "Tell me again why I'm here?"

"I invited you to hang out because I'm leaving tomorrow for a while."

"You're leaving and you can't tell me where exactly you're going."

"I did tell you. Santa Cruz."

"That's not an actual address. Text me where you are when you get there, at least. I know you're terrible at communication, but I don't want the next time I see you to be your terrible junior yearbook picture on *Dateline*."

I sigh. We've been through this ten times already. I told her I was going to travel with the magicians as their apprentice. I left out the magic-being-real part. Stacie believes in vampires, but that's still a big jump to people moving stuff with their minds. She's certain I'll end up murdered in a ditch.

"I'll try," I tell her, but we both know I'll probably forget.

She wrinkles her nose as she looks around the room again. "As much as I love preteen shenanigans, it's a Sunday afternoon, and I've got places to be and boys to see."

"I promise you'll be glad you came in a minute." I check the time on the microwave. One forty-five. Thank goodness I told him an hour later than the party really started, so he didn't have to witness a room full of twelve-year-olds pigging out on hot dogs.

She raises an eyebrow. "Just tell me, and I'll be the judge of that. It's going to have to beat Alex from that phone case stand in the mall with his shaggy, floppy puppy hair you just want to brush out of his face. He's already waiting at the coffee shop for me. Not that he won't keep waiting." She grins.

I'm not even sure if she's mentioned Alex before, but I'm certain he's no Xander. I lower my voice. "I've got one of the magicians from the other night coming to do a surprise performance."

She tenses like she's surprised, and then rolls her eyes. "Nope. Sorry. Alex wins." She gives me an air-kiss and heads for the door with a wave of her fingers over her shoulder. She pauses just before she shuts it. "Do not forget to text me."

I have to question our friendship if she thinks a boy with nice hair trumps magic tricks.

The door clicks shut behind her.

I don't have time to worry about it, though. Spilled orange soda is calling my name.

"Present time!" Parker shouts while I'm searching for more paper towels.

Deb nods, catching my eye as the kids sprint into the other room. I told her about my surprise. She loved the idea. She squealed and clapped her hands, and I felt a little guilty about trying to show her up. I wanted to win, while she just wanted the best party for Parker.

The doorbell rings, and I dart down the hall and pull open the door. Xander's not dressed as flashily as he does for the stage. He wears dark jeans and a black shirt and carries a deck of black cards in his hand, shuffling them back and forth like he never really stops.

Already my blood thrums with anticipation—no, from proximity to him. I can feel his magic.

I wave a hand, beckoning. "What are you waiting for? An invitation?"

Xander cracks a grin and deliberately takes a step across the threshold. I'm not one for a vampire joke, but he is, and I feel like I owe him one after holding a stake to his chest last night.

I shut the door behind him. "This way."

I start to turn away when someone knocks at the door. I frown. All the kids are here. Everyone showed. Turns out, Parker's really popular.

Maybe Stacie changed her mind.

I pull open the door, ready to make a comment about Alex's floppy hair not holding magical birds in it, but it dies on my lips.

He almost looks out of place in the daylight. His skin's so pale it's like blinking into the sun, and his dark auburn hair shimmers with copper threads in the light. He still wears black slacks and a wrinkle-free white button-up shirt and suspenders.

I don't even get a chance to say anything before Xander pushes in front of me. "You shouldn't be here." Xander's voice is tight and angry. "What are you doing still following us? You already got what you wanted."

"Did I?" Roman cocks his head slightly, like he's trying to see me.

I try to step around Xander, but he shifts, blocking me.

"Worried?" The boy's voice is deep and calm—not the kind of calm used to soothe a crying child, but the kind that sends shivers up my arms.

"No," Xander says just a little too fast for it to be true. "What do you want?"

"Same thing as always, to check up on you."

"I'm fine, thanks."

"Well, you're not the one I care about." The ring of sincerity in his voice startles me.

That's why I don't shut the door in his face.

I duck under Xander's arm because he's gripping the door now like he'll close it.

"What are you doing here?" I ask him. "Tell the truth."

Roman hesitates. "We were following him. I was hoping for a word with you. But we saw the balloons on the porch, and apparently, Willow loves birthdays."

Willow pokes her head out from behind Roman with a wide grin on her face. "Hello!" Her eyes subtly shift to Xander, carefully assessing him. If she thinks he's a threat, she doesn't show it.

"I'm very sorry to intrude. I just miss birthday parties so much."

"Because you have a big family you haven't seen since you started training?"

She looks surprised. "You remembered that. Yeah." She hesitates. "We had at least one a month."

Xander stares down at me. "You know them?"

I glare at Roman, whose expression doesn't change. "He told me to stay away from you."

Xander barks a laugh. "Well, I'm guessing that encouraged her, so thank you."

He's right, of course, but I don't know how he'd know that about me yet.

Roman says nothing, but he's staring at me like he's trying to figure out a puzzle, and I don't like it.

Xander jerks his head toward Willow. "You have one too this time."

"Yes, she's very good." Roman looks me over again. "Yours seems rather delicate, which is why I warned her off in the first place, like you should have."

I bristle.

"She has quite the bite," Xander replies with a smirk.

Roman stares at my lips for a moment too long, like he might be picturing the fangs I keep hidden underneath, and I have to stop myself from announcing that I'm not, in fact, a bloodsucker.

"Ava?" Deb hollers from somewhere in the house.

Whatever's really going on here, I don't have time for it.

"I've got to go. I've got a house full of twelve-year-olds waiting for a performance."

Willow holds up a slender case in her hand. "Can I perform too?"

"Umm . . ." Three magicians are better than one, but I also don't want to piss off the person who offered to train me.

Xander's scowling, but he shrugs at me.

I pull the door open wider. "Come on in, then."

Willow squeals. "You won't regret it." Spinning around, she sets the case she's carrying on the entryway bench, pops the latches, and pulls out a shining silver flute. I don't know what I was expecting, but it wasn't that.

"Is it all right if I go first? I get stage fright, and I'll be even more nervous if I have to wait."

Xander looks at me, and I shrug.

"Be my guest," he says with a dramatic little bow. He turns to

Roman, who's slipped in the door behind us. "She doesn't seem like your type."

Roman gives him a dark glare. "I don't play like that."

They look one second away from ending up in a brawl, and Xander certainly has more muscles, but there's a hardness in Roman's face that tells me not to underestimate him.

I clear my throat. "Follow me, then."

I show them to the living room, where Deb has the partygoers all sitting in a semicircle. Willow doesn't even give me a chance to introduce her. She puts the flute to her lips and lets out a few low, haunting notes before she gives us all a wink and the tune picks up into the lilting dance of Irish maidens. Some of the kids clap along, even though they look a little confused.

I'm starting to wonder if she's just a performer and not a magician at all when she holds one note a little longer and a large bubble forms on the end of the flute and then releases into the air. The pace picks up, and now an array of bubbles spurts out with each note, floating around the room in a lazy way that contrasts with her tune. Some of the kids get on their feet and reach for them, popping one and laughing as soap rains down on them.

It's really kind of brilliant.

"I told you she was good," Roman says to Xander over my head. They're standing on either side of me.

Xander says nothing.

Willow ends on a high note and a burst of tiny bubbles that leaves the kids laughing. She gives a little bow as she heads back to us.

She pushes her way between Xander and me. "What'd you think?"

"Brilliant," I say. I mean it too, but I can't wait to see what Xander does.

He's already heading to center stage, his cards flowing with unnatural ease through his hands as he asks the crowd who the birth-day boy is.

Parker's grin is so big it pulls my own lips into a smile. A real one.

Xander performs a few sleight-of-hand tricks that put Shin Lim to shame before fanning his cards out for Parker to pick one. He tells Parker to put it in his back pocket and then asks him immediately to pull it back out. Parker reaches for it but comes up empty.

Some of the other kids holler at him to check again, and he does. He turns out his front pockets too just for show. I guess we both enjoy being onstage. Maybe his blood is singing the same way mine does.

Finally, Xander points to a package on the table. It's from me. A red bag with Rey on it.

"Open it," Xander commands.

Parker reads the tag first because he's a polite kid like that. He smiles at me and then tears into it, revealing *The Last Jedi*.

"Thanks, Ava!" He forgets all about the magic trick, but I don't. I'm waiting.

Xander rocks back on his heels, casual. "Keep opening it."

Parker's brow furrows. He uses his teeth to tear into the cellophane wrapping on the DVD. Glancing at Xander for confirmation, he opens the case. A single black card falls out.

"Is that your card?"

Parker nods, mouth gaping. His friends go wild, and Xander takes elaborate bows before the kids start to crowd around him, fighting for a chance to examine his cards. He lets Parker shuffle his deck.

"Ava? Weren't you going to perform?" Deb asks. I don't know how long she's been next to me. "I can get the room calmed down for you."

I was. But how can I follow that? Parker's looking up at Xander with an awe he's never had for my cheap coin tricks.

"No." I turn and meet Deb's eyes. "Thanks, though." And I hope she knows I'm thanking her for more than just the offer—it's the best I can do.

She nods.

"Wait," Xander says. "We have one more . . . don't we?" Xander jerks his head toward Roman. "You came all this way."

Roman turns a look on him that would probably wilt flowers. But all the kids are staring up at him with wide, waiting eyes, and when he notices, his cold face melts a fraction. The corners of his eyes crinkle like he's smiling, even though his lips don't move. He takes a few long strides to the center of the room and stands there until the chattering kids settle back down, and then he waits a little bit longer until the silence starts to feel uneasy.

Just when I'm about to give up and announce it's time for cake, he brushes a hand through his hair. A knife appears in his fingers when he pulls his hand back, and he spins it so fast the pearl handle becomes a blur of white. He stops just as suddenly and balances it on a single finger.

"Would anyone care to test if this is a real blade?" he asks softly.

Several hands shoot up.

Deb gives me a look. We probably shouldn't let twelve-year-old kids handle knives.

"I'll do it." I make my way to the front of the room before he can pick someone else.

Roman hands me the knife. It's beautiful and heavier than I thought. I run my finger along the blade and let out a tiny gasp as I draw a drop of blood.

"I can't believe you were going to let a kid test this," I hiss.

He's staring at the drop of blood on my finger like he's just as surprised as I am.

He clears his throat. "Well, I wasn't going to suggest they actually try to cut themselves."

He pulls the knife back from me.

"Don't do this at home," he says to his audience. "Unless I'm in your home, of course."

The kids laugh, but he doesn't.

He holds out his empty hand, palm down, and then slowly places the knife, which still has my blood on it, directly above it. He looks straight at the audience as he pushes the knife slowly through his hand and then pulls it back out again.

No one claps. He takes a black handkerchief out of the pocket of his slacks and dabs away the tiny amount of blood, or what looks like blood, on each side of his hand.

I don't know where the knife went, and I'm not sure if he tucked it away without my notice or if he made it disappear.

"More?" he asks calmly.

Most of the kids are chattering and pressing in closer to get a better look. But there are two girls with their fingers over their eyes and a boy in the back who looks like he might cry.

Deb's pulling at the collar of her shirt. She gives me a wide-eyed, pleading look.

Grabbing Roman's hand, I tug him away. The kids are standing up like they're going to follow him and ask to see him stab his knife somewhere else, so I pull him past Xander's glare and Willow's clapping and past the entryway and into the downstairs hallway that's always a little too dark.

"Time for cake," Deb hollers. If anything can steal the attention of twelve-year-olds, it's cake.

Good. I stare at Roman. He's leaning against the wall, arms folded across his chest, looking down at me.

"That was a little much," I say.

"They seemed to like it." He pauses. "So did you."

I bite my lip. It's true. It reminded me of David Blaine pushing an ice pick through his hand with people standing right next to him. He didn't have blood as part of his trick, though. Roman's was more dramatic.

"Can I see your hand?" I ask.

He seems surprised, but he unfolds his arms and pushes off the wall to stand closer to me. He holds out his hand, palm up. I stare at it without touching at first, but I can't resist. I grab his fingers and pull it closer to my face before flipping it over to look at the other side. There's blood on it.

I look up like I've caught him at something.

"I think that belongs to you," he murmurs.

It takes me a second to realize what he means. My finger's still bleeding, and I've dragged it all over his hand. "Shit. Sorry." I drop his hand and then grab it again, because I should probably clean it off. I'm not sure with what, though.

But he already has his handkerchief out again and is wiping up my blood while I keep holding his hand, and I don't know if I should let go or not, but the hallway suddenly feels too narrow and too dark.

"It's fine," he says, looking down at me. "A little blood never hurt anyone."

I drop his hand and step back.

"Can I see the knife?" I ask.

"You're very curious," he says.

"I want to learn."

"Because you don't know anything." He steps back and leans against the wall. "I remember what that feels like. I used to love this. But you won't keep that love if you stay on this path. Having real magic takes the wonder out of illusions."

He's turning to Mr. Doom and Gloom and Vague Warnings again.

Part of me understands what he means—how it's more impressive to create the feel of magic than use actual magic—but he's also wrong. Even knowing it's magic, there's the mystery of how it works. I like figuring out what parts are magic and what are illusion, because according to Xander, they're all a little of both. "You're not going to show me the knife, are you?"

The blade is out and against my throat before I have time to blink. He steps toward me, but the blade doesn't move at all. Instinct screams at me to step back, but I don't. He's so close that I have to tilt my chin up to meet his stare, feeling the faintest kiss of metal against my skin as I do. His eyes widen.

"I wanted to see the knife, not feel it."

"It's not a trick blade."

"Yeah, I know."

Impossibly, he takes one step closer, so we're flush against each other, with his steady hand still holding a weapon against me.

He sighs. "You're very foolish."

"You called me brave last night."

"They're the same." His low voice vibrates against me, and it feels almost like the hum of magic.

"You're just trying to scare me."

"Because you should be scared. There are no trick blades or rubber bullets in this competition." He steps back and flips the knife into the air, catching it carefully by the blade before holding the handle out for me to take.

I grab it and press it to *his* throat.

He folds his arms across his chest.

"Aren't *you* going to step away?"

"I've been known to be a fool."

"Tell me why you hate them."

"Or you'll stab me?"

"Find out."

His hand is on my wrist in an instant, and the blade is gone from my hand. I don't even see where he tucks it away. He steps back and leans against the other side of the hallway.

"Tell me why you hate my troupe."

I swear an entire storm rages in his eyes. His jaw tightens like he's clamping it shut for good, but he seems to change his mind. "*Your* troupe," he repeats. He pauses like he's giving me a chance to take it back.

I don't.

"The year I was an apprentice, my twin sister was an apprentice for *your* troupe. There was one cuff that year. I'm standing here, so obviously she lost. Xander was in charge of her training. He didn't do a good enough job."

"So you're immortal, and she's not." I can see how that could hurt, but Xander's been a magician for only four years, so Roman can't be that old himself. I shrug. It doesn't seem worth his bitterness.

"I haven't talked to her since," he grits out, like the words are a struggle.

So it caused a falling-out between them. It still doesn't seem like enough to justify trying to scare off all of Xander's apprentices.

"There's only hurt in this, even if you win."

I shrug. Hurt's all over the place. It's just about choosing how you want to suffer.

He shakes his head, like he's giving up on me, and starts down the hall, then pauses and glances over his shoulder. "I wish I'd met you sooner."

He continues down the hallway without another word, and I want to chase after him to ask what he meant.

Instead, I lean back against the wall for a minute. My pulse still races from all that magic.

I'm sure it's the magic.

When I come back out, Xander's standing by the front door.

"Where's Willow?" I ask.

"They just left," Xander says. "Roman said something about over-staying their welcome."

"They weren't exactly welcome in the first place," I say, even though I feel a tiny pinch of loss.

Xander grins. "The true talent remains."

"You can stay for cake if you want," I offer.

"I'd love to," Xander says with a wink.

I feel my cheeks flush and want to kick myself. He probably just wants cake.

When we reach the kitchen, the cake is almost gone, and I grab one of the last pieces. Xander leans against the counter. He watches me even as he says something to one of the kids, and I move closer to Parker.

Frosting sticks to the corners of Parker's mouth. His eyes are bright. "This is the best party ever."

I give him the biggest grin I'm capable of forming. My eyes sting, and I force myself to get a grip. He's getting the party I always dreamed of giving him—it doesn't matter if I wasn't able to do it all by myself. At least, it shouldn't matter.

I grip my plate and slip away to the bottom of the stairs. Sitting down, I let the cool wood bring me to my senses. I take a bite, and the sweetness drowns out everything else. White cake with chocolate custard filling—his favorite. Deb knows him well.

I'm digging into my third bite when Xander walks into the hallway carrying his half-eaten slice of cake.

"I thought I saw you come this way," he says. "May I?"

I nod.

His shoulder bumps mine as he sits beside me, and I get the same charge I felt onstage with him the first time. Maybe it's not the stage and applause I crave. Maybe it's just him. I'd rather it be the rush of the stage. That seems more attainable.

"Hiding from the kids?" I ask.

He chuckles. "I may not have long."

I snort, spewing some icing on my knees in a most unattractive manner. I brush it away like I don't care. "How'd you get away?"

"Magic." He winks, and I tell myself he's not flirting. He nudges my elbow with his. "Are you okay?"

My throat tightens around my answer. "This was the perfect party." My words don't warrant the emotion behind them, but Xander nods anyway, like it's valid to be upset about a kid's birthday party going perfectly.

"You have a great family," he says.

I know the words are meant to be kind and generic, like most words are, but these ones hurt.

"Parker's my family. Deb's our foster . . . whatever."

"Oh," he says. He doesn't say he's sorry or any bullshit people usually say when they find out.

I draw a jagged breath, and he places an arm around my shoulder.

The touch makes my eyes sting again, and I'm seconds away from giving in and maybe crying for the first time in years.

Instead I clear my throat a little too aggressively. "I should probably get back to Parker."

He stares at his half-eaten cake. "I need to go too, actually. See you in the morning?"

"I'll be there."

The rest of the party is a blur of Parker's happy laughter and the tears I'm barely keeping in. I need to keep it together. I don't want to ruin my last day with him before however long I'll need to be gone. I should have asked that. I feel like there are a million things I should ask, but I'm not sure any answers will stop me from wanting to go. I plaster a smile on my face anytime Parker looks at me. I don't get to spend as much time as I wish with him, but watching him smile is enough.

I'm cleaning the kitchen after the kids have gone when Deb calls to me from the living room. "Ava? Can you come in here for a minute? We need to have a family meeting."

My heart plummets. *No. Not yet. Not* today.

I force myself to walk over, pausing just inside the doorframe.

Deb sits in the recliner. Parker and Jacob both sit on the couch. Jacob smiles at me. Parker doesn't look at me. He knows what this is. You don't call a family meeting with foster kids unless it's to tell them they have to go. The reason will be vague: it's just not working out. We've been here before. I can't believe she'd do this on his birthday though.

I failed. Deb felt safer than most, and I dropped my guard. I didn't pretend to like her the same way I did for some of the others. I could have smiled more, done the dishes, dusted the old banisters that haven't been cleaned in ages, said thank you for the clothes.

Now I will pay for it.

No, *Parker* will.

Deb's eyes crease as she watches me. "Ava?"

How long have I been standing here?

I move toward the couch. I want to sit by Parker, but he's on the side already, hands clenched in his lap. Jacob sits on the center cushion with his legs crossed underneath him. I have no choice but to sit on the other side of the couch. Leaning back against the cushions, I trace the roses on the couch's print. It reminds me of the twins and the exploding flowers at the end of their trick—the way it filled me with awe and fear and curiosity.

This will mean I can't go with Xander's troupe. I'll have to get a job and get custody. With Deb, I had planned to stay in the system until I turned twenty-one. She wanted me to live with her while I went to the local college. She helped me fill out all the paperwork. I can't believe she went through all that trouble when she wasn't sure about us. But we don't need Deb. It just means forgetting that I almost had everything: revenge and a glimpse of the life Mom had before me. I hope it doesn't make me bitter.

Deb rests her elbows on her knees, her hands coming together in a tent.

"There's something Jacob and I want to talk to you both about."

She smiles. Jacob's grin stretches across his face.

The ball of dread in my stomach morphs into something else altogether.

"We both already consider you part of our family, but we want to make it official."

"What?" Parker's eyes water as Jacob bounces up and down on the couch, making the rest of us wiggle with him.

"Brothers, man. We'll be brothers. I always wanted a brother."

He doesn't say anything about a sister.

Parker and Jacob chatter about all the things they'll do as brothers, which is pretty much the same things they do now.

I try not to cry. I'd like to pretend the threatening tears are made of joy. I can still go. I can still train with Xander, but this means Parker won't come with me once I'm an established magician. He'll be fully attached to another life by then.

Still, part of me always wanted this for Parker—a real family. I wanted it for myself once upon a time when fairy tales were something I could hold on to. I'm past that point. This isn't for me, anyway. Deb and Jacob want Parker, and they're willing to let me come along too.

"Ava?" Deb asks.

For once, I want her to say my name and have it not be a question. If she can't do that, how can she really want me?

I just stare at her.

"We want you, too. I know you're eighteen, but it's never too late to be a part of a family. It's not too late."

I want to believe her, to stay and pretend like I'm just as much a part of this family as Parker.

Parker and Jacob's excitement spills around the room. It seems to touch Deb, and she glances toward them and smiles before looking back at me. It doesn't touch me. It builds around me like a suffocating cocoon, but not one that will give me a shield to grow so I can finally break out and join. It's one I will wither and die in.

I nod. My eyes water.

I won't stay. Whatever part of me that wanted to linger is gone. Maybe not gone, but shoved down where I won't be able to find it again without removing my own organs. Now I can leave with Xander without packing guilt in my backpack along with my few belongings. Parker is secure. He has a family. He's always had a family with me, but now he has a *home*. If I stayed, I would only be in his way, the constant shadow in a family photo that doesn't really belong to anyone. Deb and Jacob don't really want me, they're just not cruel enough to leave me out. I'm doing them all a favor, and it's not like I won't ever come back.

I slide off the couch without Jacob or Parker noticing. Deb tracks my movement like I'm a wild deer she wants to tame.

I ignore her. When I reach the stairs, I take them two at a time as they creak in protest.

My chic pastel room never felt like mine, but in this moment, it feels so wrong that I can't bring myself to sit on the bed. I sit in the corner of the room. The cool wood floor soothes me and cradles me with its silence. Parker's excitement still floats around me. I turn it into a borrowed blanket. I let it comfort me even though it isn't mine. My own excitement about Santa Cruz is a distant, shapeless thing, but tomorrow I will make it real. Tomorrow I'll try to fit into a family and leave Parker to his.

The stairs call out a warning, and then someone knocks.

"Yeah."

Parker pokes his head in, his eyes going to the bed first and then finding me on the floor. He steps in and shuts the door behind him, then comes and sits cross-legged in front of me.

"It's what we've always wanted," he says.

"Yeah." It's only a half lie, like our magic tricks tonight. I always wanted it for him. I stopped wanting it for myself a long time ago. I can't go back in time and make myself want it again, even for Parker.

"Don't pretend."

Damn, kid. Why does he have to choose now to notice how I'm feeling?

"I'm not." I give the most convincing smile in my bag of tricks and ruffle his hair like I did when he was younger. He hates it now, but he lets me do it anyway.

He sees through it.

"You won't be less of a sister if Jacob's my brother. We're already like brothers anyway. Nothing will change."

But it already has. Of course they're brothers. I saw it the other night when he forgot movie night—our family tradition. I'm still every bit his sister, but that doesn't mean he needs me in the same way.

Perhaps he's always been the strong one, not me. I thought he was too soft, too innocent to handle the life we had, but maybe he's always been better at it than me. He was just holding out for this moment. He protected his dreams while I let mine shatter. That's strong.

And now he doesn't need me.

His sharp eyes bore into me. "Are you okay?"

An impossible question. I don't know how anyone ever answers it. Isn't everyone always okay and not okay at the same time? Okay in the sense that they're breathing, making it through another day. And not okay in any number of major or insignificant ways.

It's not a yes-or-no question. Either answer makes you a liar.

Yes: because he will have something I didn't at his age—Deb loves him, Jacob loves him. And I know more than one person can love someone at a time, and that makes their life better, not worse.

No: because I don't love Deb and Jacob the way Parker does. I could stay and try, but I don't believe that kind of magic exists for me, and when I leave, Parker might love me a little less.

But he'll have a family. A home.

"Yes," I say. "I'm always fine."

"I know." He turns innocent and naive again right before my eyes—the way I want him to stay. He pushes himself off the floor, heading for the door. "Deb wants to take us to Giovanni's for pizza to celebrate."

He grins. I love pizza. But the thought of it turns my stomach right now.

"You guys go without me. I have a stomachache."

His smile disappears.

"Too much excitement," I say.

"Okay." He pauses at the door again. "Hey, let's watch a movie when I get back. Just the two of us."

And just like that I'm back in a magician's box, and I've forgotten to pull my legs up and the saw is tearing me in half, and part of me will stay here and part of me will go.

"Yeah, sure," I say, and he's gone.

I stand for a long time outside Parker and Jacob's door in the night before I go, listening to their laughter sprinkled with gunfire and groans when one or the other gets hit. Parker's laughter is just a little more high-pitched than Jacob's, and I let it needle into me like guilt. I wonder if it will be deeper when I get back. Part of me hopes he misses me. Part of me hopes he doesn't. I write him a note and tape it to his door.

CHAPTER 8

The drive down takes several hours in the early morning traffic, and for most of it, everyone's asleep except me and Aristelle, who's driving. And neither of us are talkers, so I mostly stare out the dark window and wonder if I made the right choice.

Eventually Xander wakes up. We're in the middle row of seats, and he fell asleep on Diantha's shoulder on the other side of him, but the seat dips as he slides closer to me. He nudges me with his elbow and then doesn't move away again.

His hand rests on the seat between us, just barely grazing the back of my thigh. His fingers tap up and down, gently hitting my leg as he stares out the window, and I wonder if he knows just what it's doing to me—how my heart seems to stutter with each little touch.

But then he turns from the window slightly and glances down at me until I look up and meet his eyes.

The corner of his mouth curves ever so slightly.

He knows.

I look away first. His fingers continue their tap, tap, tap.

I can hardly breathe. I might have to jump from the car just to get some air. It's not just the revenge and the magic and the mystery of who Mom really was that's propelling me. I want his easy flirting, too.

He stops when we turn off the main road and head into the woods down a one-lane road hugged by the giant trunks of redwood trees. He's still leaning against me, so I can feel his body tense. Maybe he's claustrophobic. The forest feels like it's trying to box us in, like the road might narrow to a stop at any moment.

Pale morning light peeks through some of the trees, but as soon as it does, fog creeps in as well, drifting among the fern fronds that cover the ground. It surges higher the farther in we go, wrapping the trunks until the trees rise from a sea of gray.

"Is it always this foggy here?" I whisper. Reina and Diantha are stirring, but the twins are still asleep.

"It's not normal fog," Xander says softly, close to my ear.

I shiver like I'm already standing in its icy grip.

I didn't think it could get denser, but it closes in on the windows so tightly, I can see only the barest shadow of the forest. I don't know how Aristelle can even drive through it. Her pace hasn't slowed. I lean into Xander to look out the front window. Nothing but a wall of gray.

"How can you even see?"

"I've driven this enough times to do it with my eyes closed." Aristelle turns around and stares at me for a long moment while her hand still twists the steering wheel.

I really didn't need a demonstration.

Just when I think the fog will swallow us whole, it clears a fraction. The trees end too, revealing a clearing of ferns.

And then I feel it: the change is like leaving a burning summer day and stepping into icy air-conditioning. But it's not a matter of hot then cold. It's the magic. It's like it has gone from nothing but a hum in my veins that I could barely feel to a song on the radio that's just a little too loud.

I gasp.

Xander laughs. "You get used to it."

The way the magic buzzes in me isn't the only thing I'm reacting to. A huge metal arbor looms in front of us. Wild roses grow up the sides of it, and they don't look like they've been trimmed in years, but on either side, perfectly cut towering hedges run, stretching into the fog so I can't see where they stop.

I jump from the SUV, and Xander follows, lightly grabbing my fingers in his as he tugs me toward the archway.

He pauses as a sleek black car pulls up beside us.

Willow hops out first. She gives me a bright smile and a wave.

Roman unfolds from the driver's seat and takes us in. His eyes dart to Xander's fingers in my hand and then up to my face. I can feel the heat on my cheeks, and I have to fight the urge to pull my hand away from Xander. I don't even know why I consider doing it. Xander's hand is warm and welcoming. Roman is anything but.

Aristelle marches forward. "No time to waste."

Xander drops my hand and beckons me to follow, but my phone rings, and I stop, pulling it out of my pocket. Stacie always texts. There's only one person I know who calls me. My chest squeezes as I look down at Deb's name. I left her a note too, telling her that I was leaving with the magicians. I had hoped she'd just let me go—that we wouldn't have to do this. I wish I could just hit ignore, but she has Parker. I owe her an answer.

I pick up. "Hello."

"Ava, are you okay?" Her voice is tight.

"Yeah, didn't you get the note?"

"Yes. That's the problem. You ran away with the *circus* and left a *note?*" I've never heard her snap like that before.

"They're magicians, and I didn't run away. I'm eighteen."

There's a pause on the other end of the line, and then she sighs. "I know, but this wasn't your plan."

"Plans change."

We sit in silence for a moment, and I'm wondering if I should hang up when she starts talking again. "You didn't . . . you didn't have to run. I would have understood if you didn't want to be adopted. It wouldn't have hurt my feelings. I know that must have been a complicated ask. I'm sorry I sprung it on you like that." Her voice isn't angry anymore. It's sad.

It's the sadness that kills me a little bit. "It wasn't that." Part of it was, but I try to make my voice as earnest as possible. "This is my dream. I wanted to follow it, and I knew you would take care of Parker for me. Right?"

"Always." Her voice is strong. "But Ava, you can come home anytime."

"Thanks," I choke out. But Deb's house isn't my home, and I can't go back to my real one. I hang up before she can say anything else. I don't want her to say she loves me or something.

Everyone's watching me. Even Roman and Willow. I glare at Roman, and he has the decency to move away and tug Willow after him. They both pause in the archway, framed by the tangle of roses— Roman in a black suit, looking like some sort of gothic prince, and Willow trailing right behind him with her long, tangled hair and a flowing white dress that makes her look like a wraith. Roman casts one look over his shoulder at me before they step through and disappear into the fog that seems to be trapped inside.

I follow. The vines grab at me, and I have to twist around them to stop them from snagging on my clothes as I step through the arch. Rosebushes surround me on both sides. The fog is so dense it's hard to see in any direction, but we continue down a path made of stepping-stones with pebbles between them. As the fog twirls and shifts around us, I catch glimpses of red beneath my feet, and for a moment I think they're petals from the rosebushes lining the walkway, but they're tiny red stones as small as drops of blood.

The farther we go, the more the roses hug the pathway. Stray branches reach out, and hungry thorns bite at my skin. I'm pretty sure they draw blood more than once. I'm wondering if Roman's going to have to hack through the branches with his knife when the wall of fog in front of us rolls away, revealing a huge mansion of gray stone that peeks through the moss covering most of it. Dark turrets rise up, and the fog hugs them like it's trying to keep them from climbing into the sky. An array of crimson flowers grows haphazardly around the base of the walls and reaches over the sides of the wide stone steps leading to a massive front door. I can't decide if it looks like a castle for monsters or princes.

Xander opens the door and waves a hand at me, and I step into a grand entryway with wood floors so dark they border on black.

Willow steps in beside me. "Yikes," she mutters.

She's not wrong. There's no warm welcome rug here. No pictures hang from the dark burgundy walls. No tables filled with warm flowers, nothing to give a hint of welcome. Ahead of us, a grand staircase winds upward before splitting in two different directions. Iron spikes studded with red gems that match the ones in the magicians' cuffs decorate the railing. Balconies wrap above us, framing the entire entryway like watching the arrival of guests is some type of sport. Nobody is up there, though. This feels like stepping into a haunted house that's been vacant for years. The hollow silence in the room almost suffocates, like I could die right here and the room would just absorb me.

Or the magic. The magic here is thick and probing. Before, I could feel it in my blood and sense it in others, but now it rolls over my skin and tugs at my flesh. My tongue is heavy from it.

I swallow. "I wouldn't want to fall from the balcony."

Willow jumps as my voice breaks the silence. She shakes her head, unwilling to break it with me. Her eyes are rounder than usual. She looks like she's going to faint.

"This is actually kind of what I expected." I try to laugh. The walls swallow the sound and spit it back out at me in a cackling echo.

Willow winces.

Xander steps into place beside me, followed by the others.

"What took you so long?" I ask.

"This is the worst decor yet." Reina squeezes in between Xander and me and crinkles her nose. "You would think it would try a little harder to impress the new guests."

"Just a few vases of fresh flowers would've done the trick," says Diantha, stepping around us and smoothing a hand over her bright blue, fifties-style skirt that's stitched with daisies. It seems like a casual gesture with casual words, but her hand trembles slightly.

"I like it," Roman says.

I stiffen at the sound of his voice.

Xander snorts. "You would. It matches your soul, I would think."

I finally look at Roman. Xander's not wrong. Roman's face holds no expression even as his eyes meet mine for the briefest moment before looking away again.

Aristelle brushes past me. "See you at the opening ceremony." She pauses a couple of steps up the stairs and looks back at Xander. "Make sure she's dressed appropriately."

I bristle at the implication I can't dress myself.

"I already have it covered," Xander says. Apparently he's thought of it too.

The others start to break away, leaving just Xander and me, and Roman and Willow.

Roman gives me a polite nod. "See you later." He beckons Willow, and she follows him tentatively up the stairs.

"What opening ceremony?"

"The start of the competition."

I freeze. "You said I had time to train first."

Xander gives me a breezy smile. "Don't worry. The real battle doesn't start yet. This is just a chance for everyone's apprentice to show-case their skill," Xander explains. "Earn a spot to keep training."

I swallow. "I don't *have* a skill."

"Your coin trick will do. It just has to be something to prove you belong here." He gives me a reassuring nudge that does nothing to fill me with confidence. "Don't worry. This is the easy part."

"I wasn't worried." But I am now.

I step forward and run a hand over one of the points on the railing, pulling back with a wince. A line of blood appears.

Xander snaps his fingers, and suddenly he's pressing a white hand-kerchief to my palm, dabbing away the blood. My blood is the bright-est thing in the room.

"Don't feed the magic any more than needed," he jokes. At least I think it's a joke. There's a humming vibration in the room now, like the house's stomach is grumbling. But maybe I'm imagining it.

"The magic here is—" "Dangerous" comes to mind, but I pull the word back to me. "Strong," I give instead.

"Magicians have been contributing to the spells in this place for so many years that the magic is overflowing now."

"I can see why you like it here," I lie.

He frowns a little. "'Like' is a strong word."

He doesn't explain, but I understand. My skin doesn't feel like my own, as if my body doesn't quite belong to me, and if I don't own that, what do I have left? I try to swallow down my uneasiness. It must be like living at a higher altitude. My body will adjust. Xander takes my hand and bounds up the steps, half pulling me behind him. He pauses at the landing.

"Which way?" I ask. A hallway opens up on either side.

"Doesn't matter. We'll end up where we need to be no matter what. Everything is always shifting here. You're always lost and never lost at the same time. You just walk and the magic takes you where you need to be. Which way do you want to go?" he asks.

Back out the front door, I think, but I head left instead into a wide hallway with wallpaper made from dried yellow rose petals. White doors with rose-shaped knockers appear every ten feet or so. I stop in front of one, turn the handle, and step inside, bent on testing Xander's claim.

Another hallway opens up. This one is darker with purple-and-black diamond-patterned wallpaper and dark wood paneling rising halfway up the wall. Old black-and-white photos of magicians break up the pattern. I gawk at them as I walk across the gleaming onyx floor. I pause at a black door with a brass handle fashioned like a full, blooming rose. I twist it and push the door open.

A huge room sprawls before me. I step inside, and my boots sink into lush, green carpet. A cherrywood bed with a simple black bedspread helps fill the enormous space. Matching end tables frame it. The only decoration in the room is a massive painting of the ocean in the moonlight hanging above the bed. It almost blends with the dark blue walls.

"Do you like it?"

I move to the bay windows, past the two chairs and table set up there, to stare out at nothing but fog that doesn't just sit and hug the ground; it swirls and dances like it's performing for me.

"I need to go get settled," he calls over his shoulder. "Your outfit is in the armoire."

I pull it open and find green pants. Green.

"No way." I turn, but he's already gone.

CHAPTER 9

I've stepped into one of Gatsby's parties.

No—Gatsby would faint with jealousy of what lies before me. This room teems with life and magic and possibility. It's jarring compared to the emptiness I stepped into this morning, like I'm in a different world instead of just a different room. As if everyone here snapped their fingers and appeared, and I should clap for a trick well done.

An impossibly long gold table stretches fifty yards down the center of the cavernous room. But that's not what takes my breath away. Miniature stages line the walls, each one no more than three feet in diameter, painted gold and covered with elaborate designs—swirling vines, roiling clouds, and twisting branches. A single magician performs on each one.

Xander stands at my shoulder. "What do you think?" He doesn't wait for my answer. "I see someone I need to talk to. Aristelle and the others should be at the table." He starts to turn before twisting back. "And Ava, be careful. The games start early."

Even that vaguely ominous warning can't pull me out of what's in front of me.

To my right, a woman painted gold from head to toe swallows a golden spear longer than her own leg. She doesn't pull it back out. She turns to me and bows. I force myself to keep walking. She tracks my movements—at least I think she does.

I duck as an arrow flies just feet above my head. The man on the next stage laughs. I glare at him as he nocks another gold arrow with black feathers. He jerks his chin at me, and I follow his line of sight to the opposite stage, where a blindfolded woman dressed all in black stands waiting. The arrow sings above my head again, and before I can register it, the same arrow quivers between the woman's bronzed lips. She smiles, revealing the sharp tip caught between her teeth.

I turn back to the man, and he bows and then winks, his eyelids flashing gold against his dark brown skin.

I smooth my hand over the billowing white shirt I'm wearing with my green pants. "She did the hard part," I say.

He laughs, pulls out one of his arrows, and swallows it before I can blink, raising a brow at me.

"Not bad, but I just watched someone else swallow a spear." I smile, and he does too.

The next stage is only an ice sculpture. A woman in a flowing gown with one upraised hand, finger pointed out at the audience. I can't resist. I lift my finger to hers.

She cracks, splintering from her finger to her arm and up across her smooth cheek until all of her is veined. Then she shatters, leaving behind a real fair-skinned woman in a white dress. She turns silver eyes on me and smiles. As she pulls herself into another position, the chips of ice around her feet shift, climbing up her gown, molding into solid, unblemished ice as they go.

MARGIE FUSTON

I take a teetering step back and shiver, turning to the banquet table instead. It looks like pure gold, but I'm not somebody who can tell the difference between fake and real. Vines of ivy seem to be trapped underneath the gold, and it's not just a carving. Real leaves sprout from the design. I can't help myself. I step forward and bend in front of one twisting table leg and run my finger along the smooth metal and then the fine, papery texture of a leaf. I wonder how it stays alive in there. A silly question, but I can't seem to stop myself from looking for the strings behind all this.

At least one string exists—the magic itself—but from everything I've gathered, it isn't something you can find and observe to learn how it works. *Dangerous.* The word springs to my mind unbidden. I try to push it away, but it lingers, taunting me, reminding me why I'm really here: I want the magic to make *me* dangerous.

The leaf, still under my finger, turns a winter brown and then black, cracking beneath my fingernail and falling off. A solid gold leaf grows in its place.

I jerk my hand back and step away from the table to take it all in. Black drapes cascade from blacker walls. The shining black marble floor reflects my pale face when I stare down. The only color comes from the table and the array of strange and colorful people surrounding it. All the black around them gives them an extra-glorious light—gods floating in an otherwise dark and empty abyss.

Beautiful. I take the word and wrap it around the danger. Beauty is an excellent mask for danger. Nature uses it all the time. People use it too. I can't afford to think of the danger, not if I want to stay, not if I want them to choose me in the end. I need to trust in this magic.

"You must be Ava."

I turn to face a white guy in bright red. Every piece of his attire, from his shoes to his slacks to his tie, is the exact same startling color.

He's almost painful to look at, like an open, glaring wound.

"Who are you?" He stands so close that all I can see is the perfect knot of his tie. I take a quick step back, and his mouth widens like he's scored some type of victory over me. I glance around, but nobody watches us.

I'm unremarkable on a good day. Among these people, I'm invisible. Everyone mingles around the tables in outlandish dresses and suits in every color. The styles range from modern sleek gowns to corsets and skirts straight out of Henry VIII's court. A woman passes in a dress that appears to be made of live roses.

I wonder about the thorns.

I pull my attention back to the boy in front of me. He's staring at me with calculating amusement.

"What?" I close my expression off to him, letting my face slide into a perfect blank mask. The mask I wore at many awkward foster-whatever dinners where I didn't quite belong. It's comfortable. I can pull off my own illusions.

"That's better," he says. "I could see everything you were feeling a second ago." He smirks. "Not that it wasn't entertaining."

I resist the urge to grind my teeth. Blank. I am blank. "Who are you?" I ask again.

"You don't know who I am?" He adjusts his already perfect tie. "I know about you."

"I wouldn't ask if I knew, would I?" I raise one calm brow—a neutral, almost indifferent expression.

He thinks about this, like I've asked him something profound. "Lots of people ask questions they already know the answer to. It's much easier than asking something you don't know and having to guess if you'll like the answer or not." His smile is smug.

I snort, dropping my mask for the briefest moment to knock him off his pedestal. "I bet you stayed up late thinking of that." I slide my face back to impassive just as his twists in brief fury before matching my own.

He shrugs like I simply can't understand his wisdom.

"So, what do you know about me?" I ask. I'm not entirely sure I want to know, but it may help me in the long run.

"You're Ava. You belong to Aristelle's troupe. They picked you up like a stray dog on the way here." I tense at this. He sees it, and his lost smirk comes back. "You don't stand a chance against me once the competition starts." I just barely manage to keep my face blank.

"You're an apprentice?"

"Bingo." He shakes his head. "You really don't know anything. I thought everyone was exaggerating."

"What do you mean, everyone?" A twinge of panic shoots through me. I'm already behind. I know it, but I didn't realize everyone else did too.

He catches my mask slipping again, and his smirk widens into a full-on grin.

Bastard.

"You really are going to make this easy on me." He looks me up and down. "Nice pants."

I cringe as I glance down at myself. I do feel underdressed. Everyone else seems to be in elaborate ball gowns or stunning suits, but I didn't exactly pack any of that stuff, and this is what Xander thought I'd look good in, apparently.

I step around him. "Excuse me. I need to find my friends."

As I draw even with him, he reaches out and clasps my elbow. "I'm Ethan, by the way. I wouldn't want to be rude and not answer your original question." I pull my arm from his grip and keep moving.

"And Ava," he calls over his shoulder, "you don't have any friends here."

I don't look back at him, so he can't see his words sinking into my gut like stones.

The immense desire to prove him wrong makes me smile at the next guy I see. My smile's fake, of course, but that doesn't mean it's not friendly. He appears to be an apprentice as, like me, he seems underdressed, in light jeans and a button-up black shirt. Square black glasses are pushed up into the too-long bangs of his shaggy black hair, and his pale white skin glows as if it's never met the sun. He looks like he belongs bent over books in a musty library.

He doesn't smile back.

"I'm Ava." I try not to cringe as I give my name out like I'm a friendly person. Where's Willow when I need her?

"Barry," he says before brushing by me.

At least there are people in this world who are less friendly than me.

I turn away, and my gaze settles on a regal girl in a green velvet cape draped over a dress the color of wet red dirt. Her bloodred hair makes her look like a goddess that's stepped out of an enchanted forest. She looks like she belongs here too much to be an apprentice. She nods at me as she catches my stare, and I take that as all the win I need right now.

I press onward until I see Reina and Diantha both smiling warmly as I approach. Aristelle is sipping from her wineglass, but even she looks up and gives me a quick nod.

Ethan wasn't wrong. Reina, Diantha, and Aristelle look like friends sitting together, but I'm not one of them. I barely know them.

Reina stands and pulls out a gold-plated chair for me to sit next to Aristelle. When I sit, the chair is warm, heated with magic, no doubt.

Diantha leans across Reina and Aristelle. "You look lovely."

"I'd say the same to you, but it seems grossly inadequate." She's wearing green with an ivy pattern weaving down the planes of her skirt. The tips of the leaves are threaded with gold. She's the mirror image of the table itself.

She nods at my sloppy compliment.

Xander walks up and perches in the seat beside me. His eyes are sharp as he twists to look around. "Any sign of Lucius yet?" His eyes rest on me when he asks the question, as if I should know who that is.

Aristelle shakes her head and takes a long drink from her glass.

Diantha fidgets with one of the leaves on her skirt until Reina wraps her hand around hers.

They all look like they want to talk about something, but nobody says anything, and I get the sinking feeling it's because I'm here. I knew they were holding something back.

"Who's Lucius?"

"He's the head of the Society," Reina says.

"Why do you all look like he's going to come out here and murder everyone?"

"He's just a little . . . intense," Xander says.

"Understandably," Diantha says softly, looking around like she expects the guy to be listening in.

Maybe he could be. Maybe that's something magicians can do.

"He *really* hates vampires." Aristelle nods like this is the best compliment she can give someone. "He's the one who created these." She holds up the cuff on her wrist.

She lets that sink in. This man is old. Ancient Rome old. The whole idea makes my skin crawl. It's one thing to be sitting next to a girl who's been frozen at seventeen since 1969. It's another to think about someone who's been alive for centuries. I'm imagining him with paper-thin skin and frail limbs and dim eyes. I'm imagining him like a classic creepy vampire. A threat.

"What do I need to know about him?"

Aristelle gives me a look like she's deciding whether or not to take me off a need-to-know basis. "When magic was first discovered, there were a couple of friends who just sort of took charge, Lucius and Numerius."

"I thought a woman discovered it."

"She was smart enough not to keep pressing for more," Reina says.

"Men aren't as smart," Diantha mutters.

"True," Xander says.

Aristelle snorts, but she also gives Diantha a hard look.

They *are* worried about him overhearing. My uneasiness spreads, and I glance around the room, even though I don't know what he looks like.

"Lucius and Numerius were the ones who got into blood magic. Numerius is the one who went too far and became the first vampire. But once he realized his powers were gone, he went on a rampage. He killed his first magician and realized that by drinking magician blood, he could have everything: immortality and his old powers back."

"So Lucius stopped him." I respect that. Whoever he is, it had to take courage to do that.

"Not at first," Aristelle adds. "Not until Numerius killed Lucius's sister."

Revenge formed this group. It feels right that I'm here, then.

"Numerius's own sister turned against him at that point and teamed up with Lucius. She's the one who gave her life to make these stones while Lucius cast the spell. She thought it was right. A sister's life for a sister's life."

I nod. I understand. I feel like I know Lucius now, because I know what it's like to be hardened by death. I know what it's like to give up things to get revenge.

"Did he kill him?" I ask.

"No," Xander says. "Numerius is still out there. He's still making vampires—he's not the only one, of course. Any magician playing with blood magic can become a vampire and trigger a new line of the curse. But Numerius is the most dangerous. Lucius almost never leaves this place anymore because they're both still hunting for each other. It's why he takes this competition so seriously. We're at war."

I'm not just signing on to hunt a few vampires. I'm signing on to a centuries-long quest for revenge, but it feels good to take my personal loss and fit it into the larger story. I'm not alone anymore. I'm with a group of people who all understand that vampires are real and that they hurt the people they kill *and* the people who get left behind.

An eerie sort of calm comes over me. I'm almost certain Mom was a part of this, and that a vampire killed her because of her magic, but I still don't know why she left. Wouldn't it have been safer to stay with her troupe?

I'm about to finally tell them about Mom's journal entries when all the talking stops. The sudden shift is enough to send my heart racing, as if something terrible happened and nobody's entirely sure yet what it was. I meet Willow's wide, startled eyes. She gives me the faintest shrug, and we both turn with everyone else to the head of the table as a man appears.

He looks to be in his midthirties. His beauty is cruel and cold, like a winter landscape you might try to cross even though you know you'll freeze before you can make it. His skin is white enough to show his blue veins underneath. His mouth twists into something resembling a smile, but it looks out of place between his sharp chin and long nose. On top of his long, white-blond hair, he wears a glowing ruby crown that seems to suck all the radiance off its surroundings and into itself. Everything else in the room now seems somehow duller. It's no wonder everyone decided to wear such finery. They would all become absolutely lifeless next to the glow.

A small, delicate white woman who appears to be a few years younger than him holds his left hand. I wonder if anyone even notices her next to him. She, too, seems faded. Her hair looks blond at first glance, but as she tilts her head to survey the room, it shines silver against her white dress. The only white dress in attendance. She stands out like a tear in the canvas.

They're flanked by two hulking magicians who give off Secret Service vibes, except for their flashy gold suits.

"Who's the woman?" I ask Xander.

"His consort."

As she sits, I finally notice who sits beside her. The twins. She looks at them, and a glimmer of happiness lights her wide eyes. She reaches out a hand toward them, and they each clasp it.

"Are the twins . . . are they . . ."

"They're her sisters," Xander says. "Her name's Annalise. She was an apprentice almost nineteen years ago—maybe the most powerful one there's ever been. Lucius fell in love with her and canceled the whole tournament just because he wanted to make sure she joined us. She only agreed to be with him if he'd make her sisters immortal too."

"Then why are the twins in your troupe?"

"Because I trained Annalise," Aristelle says softly. "And I trained her well. Lucius didn't want the kids to be here all the time, so Annalise asked them to be placed with me, and I've kept them safe ever since."

Something else is nagging at me. If she got to keep her sisters, then that meant there were three cuffs given out at the same time. "I thought there weren't usually that many cuffs?"

Xander's face is dark. "A lot had died that year."

"How many people died this year?"

"We don't know yet."

I must look as queasy as I feel because Xander reaches out and squeezes my arm. "We'll find out soon enough. Lucius will announce whether there will be a competition or not."

I look at Lucius just as he turns his head, and I see his profile for the first time. My blood freezes. Gripping the table, I lean forward and stare. I know his profile well. I've stared at it for hours—his face tilted just like that, gazing hungrily at my mom. Which means . . .

Mom wasn't just a magician.

She knew their leader.

From the photo, it looked like they performed together. Maybe they were in the same troupe. Although she talked about her former troupe all the time. Why did she never mention Lucius's name?

"Ava?" Xander says.

I'm breathing a little too heavily.

"I know him," I whisper.

"What?" Xander puts a hand on my arm, trying to pull me back in my seat.

Aristelle's head whips toward me.

"I have a picture of him with my mom. I need to talk to him. He knew her."

I'm staring at Lucius, not at them, but I know Xander and Aristelle are sharing a look behind me.

"You didn't mention you had pictures," Xander says softly. "You didn't mention your mom did real magic."

"She didn't," I snap. "I wasn't sure she was one of you until just now." I push my chair back and start to stand. "I need to talk to him."

Xander and Aristelle both say no at the same time they each grab a side of my chair and tug it toward the table.

"Do *not* make a scene," Xander says.

"I just want to talk to him."

"Ava," Reina says softly. "If your mom was one of us, then she left." She pauses and shakes her head. "Lucius doesn't take kindly to deserters of his cause. He may hold it against you in the competition."

I'm not sure I care. I might trade everything for one good story about my mom and the life she had before—the stories she would have shared with me when I was older. Those lost stories are gaping holes in me, and now there's someone who can fill some of them just a short walk away.

"Please." It's the pleading in Xander's voice that stops me. He sounds scared. "Win first. Don't risk this." I look at him as he waves his hand between himself and the rest of the troupe.

This. He means a future with them. If I go searching right now for my mom's stories, I risk losing the potential stories I'd have on my own. Do I want to give up my future for a tiny glimpse of the past?

I lean back, and everyone around me relaxes.

The meal is nothing short of amazing. Platters of food instantly materialize in front of me, waiting long enough for me to decide whether to take what's offered or not before winking out of existence, another plate appearing in its place. I end up with a steak sprinkled in rosemary, buttered asparagus, and roasted beets. I've never actually had beets before, so I take a bite of them first, savoring the sweet, unusual flavor before letting my knife sink into the steak. A basket of rolls appears in front of me, and I grab one before they disappear again. Butter leaks out of the center. I tear into the roll, and it drips down my chin so fast I have to snatch the black napkin from my lap and wipe it off.

I glance around to see if anyone noticed. Xander's slicing into a chicken breast, and Reina's taking dainty bites of mashed potatoes. Roman's watching me, though, with a faint smile on his face. At least it *looks* like a smile from this distance. It's hard to say, and he doesn't seem like one for smiling. I'm not sure why he's still bothering to watch me anyway. He didn't get his way. I'm here. It's too late to scare me off.

I turn to the head of the table. Annalise sits in front of a full plate, staring down the table at nothing, while Lucius skewers a piece of meat and surveys everything. His eyes land on me, and the asparagus chunk I'm lifting to my mouth freezes in midair. I don't look away, even though I'm screaming at myself to do so. Common sense says that if you're in a staring contest with the oldest immortal at the table, you should probably let him win. But I don't do it. I keep staring. His eyes narrow, and he finally turns from me, placing a hand on Annalise's arm. She flinches like he's woken her from a trance and lifts her fork, spearing a carrot and placing it in her mouth without ever looking at her plate.

"What are you doing?" Aristelle follows my gaze to Lucius, and the fire in her eyes turns cold. "Don't."

"Don't what?"

She goes back to her food without answering.

I drop my fork and stare at my untouched wineglass.

My glass blinks out of focus, and then it's filled with a golden liquid.

"Who did that?"

Reina giggles. "I think you did. The magic read what you wanted." She turns to Diantha. "Did you see that? She is a natural."

I reach out and take a sip of apple juice. It is what I was thinking of. The familiar sweetness calms me in this sea of chaos. It also makes me think of Parker, how I used to pack the lunches in the mornings for him and some of the other foster kids, and I would put two apple juices in his. I would've given him two of everything if I could've gotten away with it. I saw him once sharing his lunch with another kid and going hungry himself. He was always too softhearted. I tried to tell him not to share. He told me it was the kind thing to do—not the right thing, the kind thing. He saw a difference.

Something tells me he wouldn't survive here. These people are sharp. There's a greediness in the way they dig into their plates of food, eyes barely connecting with those around them. Even though the plates of food flicking in and out in front of me are constantly full, I can't quite shake the sense of urgency in the meal. It makes me put my own fork down just as everyone's plates disappear and the table is suddenly naked and gold. Without anything on top of it, it seems almost obscene.

I run a finger over the smooth top until Xander intertwines his fingers with mine and drops our combined hands between us.

Lucius stands at the end of the table. All eyes turn to him as he scans us. This time his eyes shift over me without stopping. "My troupes," he says, "as the keepers of magic, we have an obligation to feed it, protect it, and most important, use it against those who would abuse it. It is time to replenish our ranks once again." He holds up a closed fist and lets a single, gleaming red cuff drop from his pinched fingers. "Samuel was murdered, and now we must find someone to take his place and continue the fight."

One immortality spell. I search out Willow and find her looking at me too. She looks radiant, with pastel pink flowers woven into a crown on her head to contrast her bright pink gown. Two would have been nice. I shift my gaze to Roman, but for once, I don't catch him looking at me. He's staring down at Willow, his lips pulled into a tight frown, eyes worried. He looks like she just got a death sentence.

I'm still watching Roman when Lucius says, "But first, let's see what you've brought me."

The table splits down the middle, and the floor rumbles and shakes as we all move backward, leaving a gaping black hole in the center of the room. Narrow golden pillars carved with elaborate designs that look like they belong in front of a temple rise from the dark.

I have to fight to keep my cool. It's one thing to realize people can move objects with their minds; it's another to see whole rooms split open.

"Take your places," Lucius says. "We begin now."

People rise from their seats and crawl across the table to jump onto the pedestals. Ethan leaps up a few chairs down from me and launches himself onto the pedestal like he's a gymnast sticking a landing.

"Time to show us what you've got." Xander stands and holds out his hand, waiting.

Now or never. I take his hand and crawl up onto the table, suddenly glad I'm in pants and not an elaborate gown. I step forward and stare down into the gap in the table from where the pillars have risen, expecting the same black tile floor as everywhere else in the room, but the blackness beneath me is endless and thick as smoke. The bottoms of the golden pillars aren't even visible. The anticipation in my blood fizzles out as I glance to the tiny spot I'm supposed to land on.

But the muscles in my legs are already tense and ready. I make the jump as easily as Ethan, then keep my chin up so I can't look down.

"Afraid already?" Ethan asks.

"Only fools don't have any fear."

"That sounds like a line *you* stayed up all night thinking of."

I give him a fierce grin and a matching one spreads across his face. Usually I'd want to lie low in a new group. I never had any desire to be the favorite kid in the house, but this is different. This potential rivalry feels good because there's something I want to win—and someone I'd be happy to step over to do it.

Lucius stands and makes his way behind the magicians still seated at the table until he stops in front of one of the apprentices on the pedestals—a pale girl with two strawberry blond French braids that reach her waist. She springs a bouquet of pink carnations from her sleeve and floats it in the air in front of her. The next person wears a sky-blue leotard stitched with swirls of gold thread, and it looks so stunning against their warm brown skin that I feel self-conscious again in my simple green pants. I forget about my discomfort when they do a series of flips and spins on that tiny platform. They're only centimeters from one wrong step sending them plummeting. The moves wouldn't be that impressive on solid ground, but on a one-foot square? They must be using magic. Unfriendly Barry goes next, making a pair of cards flap above his head like one of Reina's birds. I'd be pleased that his was the worst so far if my stomach weren't sinking with the surety that my coin trick's going to be even less impressive.

The next one stares forward and does nothing until a sharp slap rings out and a cool smile spreads across the boy's face.

A few people gasp.

"What happened?" I ask Ethan. I'd rather talk to Willow, but there's another girl between us.

Ethan shoots me such a nasty glare that I'm surprised when he actually answers. "He's a mentalist. He made Lucius smack himself in the face." There's a trace of awe in his voice. "Mentalists are rare. It takes an incredible amount of power." He gives me a look. "We should both be worried."

But Lucius is waving his hand and the two men who flanked him before lumber over and grab an older man from the chair in front of where the mentalist just performed. They pull the man up by his shoulders, and one of them twists his hands around his back.

"Edgar," Lucius says. "What a shame you brought a dud after so many years."

The old man says nothing. He just looks tired.

But the woman sitting beside him leaps to her feet. She's older too, with long, tangled, graying blond hair that falls to her waist. "Everyone in this room felt that magic," she hisses.

Lucius is silent for a long moment.

Nobody says a thing. Nobody backs her up.

The woman stares Lucius down, face furious. She leans back the slightest bit, like she wants to hit him but also knows she should run. She holds her ground, though.

"I felt nothing but a fly on my face . . . one easily smashed," Lucius says slowly. "Sit down, Julia."

The names together make me stand up straighter. Mom talked about an Edgar and a Julia in the troupe she was with before she joined my dad. She talked about a Samuel too—could it be the same magician who died? Am I fighting to fill the spot of a man who Mom told me stories about? I hope not. I try to search my memory of the pictures in her box that I didn't steal. Do Julia and Edgar look familiar? It's been too long to recognize them, but they have to be the people Mom knew. I can feel it in the way my heart speeds like I'm close to something I want.

Julia opens her mouth again, but Edgar catches her eye and shakes his head. Her mouth closes, and she steps back, chest heaving. Lucius waves a hand, and the man gets escorted out of the room. I turn to the mentalist apprentice. A smug smile sits on his face, like they knew this might happen and were willing to pay the price. It wavers as Lucius gestures with a finger for him to step down. It seems like the whole room holds their breath until Lucius points behind his shoulder at Annalise. "You're done. Please wait with her. Memories will be wiped at the end."

To his credit, the boy holds his head high as he walks away.

I glance down the line at the rest of the apprentices. Some, like Ethan, stand calmly, but most of us fidget, sharing glances with each other.

Ethan's next. He pulls out an old-fashioned revolver and points it in my direction. I try to step back and teeter, my foot almost slipping off the edge, but he's already raised it above my head. He fires. The blast leaves me trembling. My ears ring. I put my hands over them in a delayed reaction and glance around. What the hell did he shoot?

My eyes land on Willow. Her hand is pressed to her head, face frozen with her mouth slightly open. Roman's standing up at his spot at the table, saying something I can't hear, probably her name. Willow finally drops her hand. One side of her flower crown is in tatters. Ethan fired a bullet right next to her head and right over mine—an impossible shot that didn't line up right but somehow was perfect anyway.

I glance back to Ethan, and he's got that same smirk on his face I saw earlier. I want to rip it off. He dips his chin and mouths, *Your turn.* Or maybe he says it. My ears are still ringing.

I turn around to meet Lucius's bored stare. He waves at me in a *carry on* motion.

I'm already holding my coins, clenched so tightly in my fist that when I open it, George Washington's face is indented on my palm. I don't even remember reaching for them, but all I have to do is show a little bit of potential, and I can do coin tricks in my sleep.

I start with a classic four-coin flourish, transferring them to my other hand and then back into my pocket, pulling out just the two I need for my favorite trick—passing the coin through the hand. As I slam one quarter into the back of my hand, I let my hidden quarter drop from the other side. I even step it up a notch and catch it, so I don't lose it into the abyss.

Nobody claps or cheers.

Disappointment flashes across Lucius's face. He waves at his henchmen, and they stride in our direction.

Xander's on his feet in an instant, holding his palms out in a stop motion. "Wait. Wait." He turns to Lucius as he shifts to stand behind Aristelle's chair. "You *know* she can do more than that."

I'm confused. How would he know that? People have been talking about me, but why would they know what I'm capable of?

"Not from what we just saw," Lucius says. He looks downright bored until he smiles at Xander, and his face turns instantly cruel. "Looks like you bet wrong."

My heart pounds too hard, and I feel dizzy. This all seems too intense. Wrong.

Xander climbs on the table and grabs my arm. "Try again. You have to use your magic. You must still have some from performing with me. It's in you."

I shake my head. "I don't know how. Why didn't you tell me I'd need to do that?"

"I saw you," Xander practically shouts. "I saw you use magic to move your coin to your pocket."

Outside the club that first night. I played it off like I knew what I had done. My stomach sinks. "I did that on accident."

Fear so intense crosses his face that I jerk back from it, and only his hand on my arm keeps me from slipping.

"You have to try. We can't be split up."

His fear seemed like too much for the situation, but when he says those words, I get it. They're a family, and one of them is going to be ripped away from the others. She might still be alive, but it's going to hurt almost as much as a death.

"Performing magic on accident is even more impressive. You can do this. Dig deep. Believe you can move those coins with nothing but your mind, and then do it. Keep it simple. Float one." He lets go of me and jumps back down from the table, eyes shifting from me to the men approaching.

I hold my hand out with my coins. The same ones Mom gave me. They may not be magic, but they do hold power. I focus in on them and only them.

"Enough of this," Lucius says, and my stare jerks away just long enough to see the same men who dragged Edgar away reach Aristelle's chair. Her eyes go wide. I force my focus back on the coins, trying to feel that buzzing in my blood that Mom talked about. This is for my new troupe, but it's for her, too. I am her daughter.

Believing in myself is like believing in her.

The coins explode from my hand, multiplying in a swirl of silver that rises from my palm, growing bigger and bigger until there's a five-foot tornado of clinking coins spinning around my head.

"Amateur," Ethan mutters beside me, but worry leaks into his voice.

I turn toward him, and my coins do too. They dart away from me and swirl around his legs, rising higher and higher until he's completely surrounded.

I gasp. I didn't tell them to do that. I didn't tell them to do anything, but something inside of me pushes them on. My blood's singing an angry revenge song with my heartbeat as the base.

"Enough," Lucius says.

I turn to look at him. His expression is confusing, like he's angry *and* impressed.

"I said enough," he snaps.

Stop. I don't say it out loud. Just to myself. I created this, and I believe I can control it.

The coins crash down in an instant, clattering against Ethan's pillar until he stands with a pile at his feet. His cheeks are flushed, and there are tiny red lines across his whole face where my coins got too close. He looks like he wants to murder me.

I open my mouth to tell him I didn't really mean to do that, and then I snap it closed again. I can't admit that.

I've just turned a rival into an enemy.

I glance back to my troupe. Their faces are white. Lucius has already moved on to the next girl.

I check the pocket of my pants and find my four coins safe and sound.

Julia is giving me a hard look, with her bushy brows pinched together. I want to jump down and talk to her. The rest of the apprentices continue to perform, but I can hardly focus on them except to watch Willow release bubbles from shaky fingers. All I can think about is the power under my skin. It feels like a dam has broken where before there was only a trickle, but it also feels like there's more to come. It's almost as if there's too much magic inside me, like it might wash me away if it all escaped at once. I swallow.

Nothing pulls me out of myself until Ethan says, "You need to see this."

Whatever he wants me to see is definitely going to hurt, not help.

I glance at him, and he nods down the line at the gorgeous girl in the velvet cloak. I was really hoping she wasn't an apprentice because she looks like she undoubtedly belongs here.

"Her name's Nadine. With the mentalist gone, she's the second best here."

"Let me guess, you're the first?"

"Naturally."

Nadine clutches the edge of her cloak in her hand and pulls it as she spins until she's lost in a green cocoon. After a few seconds, the cape drops to the ground in a heap. A small rabbit the color of her dress hops out and sits for a second before burrowing back under the cloak. The forest-green velvet spins and rises until the edges peel apart and Nadine stands there, brushing back one stray lock of hair.

"*She's* number one," I say to Ethan.

He doesn't answer. He knows it as well as I do. Neither of us are the best.

I zone out again. I'm worried that what little confidence I have will vanish if I watch anyone else.

My limbs shake when we're finally allowed to hop down. Xander practically has to lift me from the table.

"I need more training," I say.

"Tomorrow," he says.

I nod and search for Julia, catching a glimpse of the back of her head as she slips from the room. I'll find her tomorrow too. Lucius knew my mom, but if Julia is who I think she is, then she did too. I know which one I'd rather talk to.

I search out the two apprentices who failed: the mentalist and another boy who just stood there for a long time until Lucius moved on. Annalise leads both of them away.

"What's she going to do with them?"

"Annalise is a mentalist too. She'll wipe their memories and have them taken home," Xander says.

"Annalise is a mentalist *too*? So that boy did have the power?"

Nobody says anything.

"What happened to Edgar?"

Xander frowns like I shouldn't know his name or something. "He was separated from his troupe."

"It all seemed so . . . dramatic."

"We're all performers," Reina says way too lightly. "Let's get you back to your room. We have to start harnessing all that power tomorrow."

I nod. I can't let that power out if it's going to hurt people—even if that person's Ethan.

CHAPTER 10

Stepping out the front door of the mansion, I expect the dense fog of yesterday to greet me, but blue sky is actually visible today even though wisps of clouds linger low and gather around the high hedges that surround the compound. A breeze brushes the tips of the sequoias outside the enclosed area, but inside, the clouds don't move. It's eerie. So is the massive courtyard in front of me—it looks like something out of *Alice in Wonderland*, and I'd be tempted to believe in magic if I didn't already.

Low three-foot hedges that match the larger ones on the perimeter split the courtyard into squares. Gray or red paving stones make up the ground in each box, and pathways like the one I walked in on divide them further. It looks like a giant checkerboard with deep-green moss sprouting between the cracks. A tree rises from the center of each section.

"Welcome to your training grounds," Xander says. "There's a section for each apprentice to work in. You all train out in the open, so you'll know what you're up against."

Xander leads the way down the path. The sun's barely up, but a lot of apprentices practice already. We pass Barry circling playing cards in the air around him, but it's still nothing compared to Xander's butterfly. In another yard, the girl who pulled flowers from her sleeves last night frees peacock-blue lace from the cuff of her blazer, and it twists into the air above her like a whirlpool. When it reaches the end, she grips the material as it continues to rise, pulling her feet off the ground until she's doing a graceful twirl in the air.

Shit.

This isn't someone who got scouted on the street a few days ago.

Xander's hand settles on my back and pushes me forward. "Don't focus on what everyone else is doing. We have about three weeks to get you into shape."

I don't mention that that seems short—that I know how long Willow's been training.

I shiver. A chill seeps from the stones beneath my feet. You'd think they could warm it up with a little bit of magic. Almost makes me wish Aristelle the human bonfire was here.

We enter the first open training square. A cherry tree grows in the center, branches heavy with red. Aristelle leans against the tree, her lips a perfect match for the cherries.

Well, be careful what you wish for, I guess.

Aristelle's Victorian-style lace-up boots click against the pavers as she circles me, slowly looking me up and down. "I guess we can fix your attire after we fix your lack of skill."

I sigh. "I thought Xander was in charge of my training."

"This is my troupe and my . . ." She stops. "It's my reputation on the line."

Xander shifts on his feet like he's uneasy with her intrusion. He can get in line. But I shrug. I'll learn from anyone I can.

"Let's see what you've got," Aristelle says.

I feel for my magic. It feels faint—muffled even. "I think I used the magic all up."

"Impossible," Xander says. "You would have gotten more from your performance last night."

I pull my quarters from my pocket, fanning them between my fingers. I can do a few tricks to get it flowing.

Aristelle slaps my hands and sends my coins rolling across the ground.

"Hey!" I spin on her.

"Coin tricks aren't good enough."

"People love them."

"*Children* love them."

Xander bends to pick up the quarters. I ignore the brush of his fingers as he places them back in my hand. "She's right," he says. "You need another skill. One that will impress a crowd full of badass magician vampire hunters. Last night was . . . interesting, but you need something more versatile."

"No pressure," Aristelle says. "But I'm here to help you."

"Aristelle . . ." Xander's giving her a look that says he doesn't like what's coming but is totally resigned to it.

"I want to have first crack," she says.

I don't like the sound of that.

"Fine." Xander crosses his arms over his chest and takes five steps back.

I'm not sure why he needs that much distance between us or why Aristelle's smile is brighter than I've ever seen it, but it can't be good for me.

Aristelle claps her hands to get my attention. "I'm going to ask you to do things, and I want you to try it. Don't question. Just believe you can do it and try."

I nod.

She doesn't answer. Instead, she holds out a hand and unfurls a crimson piece of lace long enough to touch the ground. She thrusts the lace toward me, and I grip the coarse material without thinking.

"Put it up your sleeve," she commands.

I hesitate. Xander waits ten feet away from us, watching blankly. I try to shake away the foolishness I feel as I pull out the cuff of my jacket and begin stuffing the lace inside. *Believe.* The piece is long. Too long to comfortably fit. I open my jacket, reaching in and shoving my other arm down my sleeve until I touch the end of the lace and pull it up toward my armpit, finally making the last of it disappear inside my cuff.

I zip my jacket back up, trying to relax my loaded sleeve like nothing is there—like I'm a real magician and it's disappeared into my skin. But it itches like hell. I want to crinkle my nose, but I don't.

Aristelle wouldn't give me any sympathy.

"Now pull it back out and make more."

My mouth gapes. It's not like I haven't seen this trick before—magicians pulling endless streams of knotted silk scarves from their sleeves, mouths, and other orifices, looking like they've just gotten done shoplifting every silk nightgown from a lingerie shop. It's not a hard trick to figure out. But this isn't a trick. I don't have a second stash of lace. Even my damn underwear is cotton. I need to make more lace from nothing. They're expecting me to do what that other girl was doing. How in the world am I supposed to believe I can do that?

They both wait expectantly.

"Just do it," Aristelle says.

"How?"

Aristelle huffs and waves an impatient hand at my sleeve. I glance at Xander, and he gives me a single nod.

I pinch the tip of the fabric and yank it, trying to believe I have the whole Victoria's Secret catalogue stashed in my hoodie. The other end flops out and hits the muted-red cement pavers.

Silence.

I laugh, the noise loud and angry. "That was fun."

"Shut up." Aristelle cuts me short. "Next test. Believe you can catch fire."

"Wait . . . what?"

I see the wicked curve of Aristelle's lips a moment too late.

An orange glow bursts to life in her palms and then hits me, sliding up and over the arm of my jacket, turning it to flame.

I scream and stumble back.

"Control it," she yells.

Another glowing ball forms in her hands. My arm grows hotter, even though it only seems to be dancing on the surface of my clothing. My other arm ignites, the flames never touching skin. Sweat beads on my face. My skin will blister. It's like leaning too close to the bonfire as a kid, staying there even when it feels like you're moments away from combusting and joining the flames—all for the perfect marshmallow.

But I'm not burning. My magic buzzes in me like a fire alarm. I'm choking on the heat, but I'm not burning.

I hold my arms out from my sides. "Put it out!" I yell.

"*Control* it," Aristelle says again. Another ball rolls in her palm.

"I can't." I sputter on the smoke.

She throws the other ball of flame at my head. I duck, and it erupts above me, floating into pieces of ash that turn to water as they fall. The drops lick away the fire from my sleeves.

I expect my jacket to be ruined, but it looks the same as when I left this morning, a little worn but in one piece.

　　　　　　　　　　　　　MARGIE FUSTON

Xander claps. Claps.

I glare at him.

"What? That was better."

"She couldn't control it," Aristelle hisses, dusting her palms across her jeans.

"But she didn't burn." Xander sounds hopeful.

I run my palms across my arms. They're not even hot. "You thought I would burn?"

Aristelle smiles sweetly. "I believed in you."

"I didn't," an annoying voice says behind me. "I knew last night was a fluke."

I spin around. Ethan stands beside the hedges of the practice square. Of course he'd get placed right next to me.

"That's what I've been telling everyone," he continues. "I'm not sure they believed me, but they certainly do now." He gives a single breathy laugh and then waves a hand, gesturing for me to look.

I make the mistake of doing it. He's not the only one who's stopped their own training to watch mine. I did put on quite the show last night, but each time I meet someone's eyes they glance away. They're embarrassed for me.

Ethan smirks as he pulls the gun from his holster. It takes everything in me not to step away from him, but he aims it over his shoulder and pops off three quick shots. Three lemons explode on the tree in the center of his courtyard, and a burst of citrus floods the air.

"And that's how it's done." He gives me an obnoxious wink that belongs in a bad western movie.

"Has anyone told you that you're a tad bit annoying?" Xander says. He stands close enough for our arms to touch, and it feels good to have someone beside me when staring down a bully.

Ethan shrugs.

"I'm guessing your parents," Xander adds.

Ethan's face darkens. I don't want to feel sympathy for a guy who almost shot Willow in the head, but I hate the way he looks down for a moment before he meets Xander's stare.

They hold each other's glares like they're about to duel until Xander yells, "Natasha!"

I didn't even notice the two magicians sitting on the benches on the far side of Ethan's training ground, but now they share a look before rising and walking toward us. The girl is petite, with a pink pixie cut. Her face is all sharp angles except for her rosebud lips. They cut up into a smile as she reaches us. The guy with her has a matching pink haircut, but he's four times her size. They have the same lips though, and I wonder if they're siblings.

"Problem?" Natasha asks.

"Please collect your dog," Xander says. "All his barking is getting on my nerves."

"A little smack-talking is part of the game, isn't it?" Natasha's smile holds so firmly that it's obviously fake. I'm pretty sure she's not even trying to pass it off as real.

"It's for the weak," Xander says, folding his arms across his chest.

"Then maybe your apprentice should try it."

I bristle. I wish I could do another display to put them in their place, but they just watched me fail miserably, and I'm not exactly sure I believe in myself right now.

Aristelle sighs behind us. "Walk away, Xander."

Natasha's smile finally seems real. "Seems like someone's being summoned."

Xander doesn't budge. I decide to walk away though. Aristelle's the one in charge of the troupe. She's the one I need to impress more than Xander.

"Don't tell me not to listen to them," I say. I don't need a pep talk. I need power.

"You *should* listen to them," she says. "If you can't use your power consistently, you *are* weak."

I hate that she's right. I hate how vulnerable I feel. I've spent years training to hunt vampires so I wouldn't feel like this, and now that I'm with real hunters, I'm that little girl wandering the dark streets with nothing but a sharpened pencil. Out of my league.

At least then I was alone. I can't help but glance around again at the people watching me. One in particular catches my eye, but she's not in one of the training courtyards; she's standing on one of the paths that surround them. Her hair is long and straggly, and she wears a flowing skirt and patchwork vest that make her look like a witch who's stumbled out of a different story.

Julia.

"Who's that?" I ask, nodding in her direction.

Aristelle follows my stare. "Julia? She lost her apprentice last night. She's nobody to worry about."

"Why is she older? And why are all the apprentices so young?" I don't know how I didn't see it before, but most of the magicians seem around my age. Midtwenties at the oldest.

"Lucius realized that the younger you are, the more likely you are to be able to believe in yourself enough to learn the magic, so now we focus on the young, but not too young. If you give immortality to someone who hasn't discovered who they are yet, then how can you expect them to hang on to their humanity?" Her eyes drift up to where the twins have come out to sit on the steps of the mansion. They sit with perfect stillness, one on each side like stone lions. "The older magicians have been here the longest."

I turn back to Julia. "I need to take a walk." I spin around before

Aristelle can protest. I can sense people watching me as I make my way down the paths, so I keep my head down and focus on my feet crunching across the gray stones mixed with the blood-drop jewels. I look up only when I know I must be getting closer to Julia.

She's gone.

I stop walking. The people in the courtyards next to me are staring. With no destination, it looked like I was running away, but a peppy tune catches my attention, and I keep striding forward. I know only one person who would play something that bright and happy after last night. I end up outside a courtyard with a sleek black piano underneath an orange tree so full of ripening fruit it reminds me of pancake breakfasts at Deb's. She was always getting fresh-squeezed orange juice at the farmers market anytime she could. The smell suits Willow's pretty little song. She has a light smile on her face as she plays. I can see her fitting in perfectly with Deb's constant cheerfulness—much better than me. If I had been that lighthearted, maybe I never would have needed to leave. For a second, I can't tell what magic she's doing, but then I notice the orange peels opening like blooming flowers and closing again. No wonder it smells so strongly.

Willow notices me and stops playing.

Roman follows her stare and scowls but says nothing as she gets up and runs to the hedge.

"Hi!" She waves brightly.

"Hi." I nod at her piano. "Your music is stunning. I've always loved music."

"Do you play anything?"

"No. I grew up in the system, so I didn't really get a chance." I don't know why I tell her that. It's not something I usually share with someone I barely know. It took me weeks to tell Stacie, and she's the type of person to ask a million questions. I only told her because she told me about her experience first.

She nods. "I grew up in a house full of siblings, and after-school music programs were the only thing my parents ever said yes to. They thought sports were a waste of time when they needed my help at home, but music was culture." She laughs. "I learned a lot of instruments."

"Willow," Roman says. He doesn't shout it or make any move toward us, but his voice is so commanding, I almost step away.

"Wait," Willow says. "Thank you for getting him back. Yesterday," she adds when I don't immediately answer.

It takes me a minute to realize she's talking about Ethan. She thinks I tormented him to pay him back for shooting the flowers right off her head.

I open my mouth to admit that I didn't do it on purpose, but why not let her think that I did? I already made an enemy—an ally might be useful. At least for now.

"You're welcome. I didn't really mean to scratch him up." I'll admit just that much. I didn't intend to go so far.

"He deserved it," Willow whispers.

Roman appears at her shoulder. "You need to be training." His eyes land on me. "*Both* of you."

I can't argue. Willow gives me another little wave and then heads to her piano as I step back onto the path. I consider scoping out what everyone else is working on, but I don't want the stares.

Xander and Aristelle are arguing in whispers that stop the second I walk up.

Neither one looks happy with me.

"Go ahead," I say to Aristelle. "Hit me with your best shot."

Neither cracks a smile.

Xander rubs his hands together. "It's my turn."

I groan. "What'd you have in mind?"

He scowls as if he doesn't like what he's about to say. "The magic is all about believing. The audience believes, and that feeds it, but you have to believe and feed it too. Technically, with unlimited power, what you could do with it would be limitless, but even if you had that, you'd still have to believe you could do whatever you were trying. It's harder than it looks, which is why most of us have specialties. Things we were good at *without* power that the power can amplify."

I glance at Aristelle. "Were you an arsonist in a past life? How do you have an affinity for fire?"

"I'll tell you one day when you're one of us."

When you're one of us. Maybe she believes in me after all.

I turn back to Xander. He still hasn't told me exactly what he's thinking. He twists his mouth up like he doesn't want to spit it out. "Given your skill with a stake, there's an obvious leap to make."

"Knives?" I try to stop the smile that's spreading across my face, because the wider it gets, the deeper Xander scowls. Of course he doesn't want me to do knives. Roman does knives.

"You don't have to be so excited about it," Xander grumbles.

Aristelle taps her chin. "I actually think Roman'll hate this."

The corners of Xander's mouth tip up. "You might be right." With a flick of his wrist, he holds up two matte-black throwing knives as long as his hand. He strides toward me, flipping one and catching the blade in his palm so he can offer me the handle. "Give it a feel."

I wrap my hand around the cold metal and take it. I do like the weight of it, the security in holding something sharp enough to wound. It's the same feeling as carrying a stake.

He points at the trunk of the cherry tree just ten feet away. "Try to hit it."

Xander slides up behind me in a way that makes my breath hitch, even though I try to hide it. His right arm curves around mine as he adjusts my grip on the knife. His fingers are warm. "You can do this," he whispers. My blood whispers in answer.

"Okay, just throw it already," Aristelle says.

I can't see the look Xander must give her, but she rolls her eyes.

Xander shifts to stand beside me, and they wait.

I throw one and then the other.

They both limp out of my hand half-heartedly, falling short and skidding across the cement until they hit the base of the tree with weak thuds.

I shrug like none of this matters, but I spare a quick glance for Xander, who's hanging his head and examining a crack at his feet.

Aristelle sighs, shaking her head so that her dark ringlets bob around her face. "You need to believe in yourself first or the magic will never obey you."

Easier said than done. The only person who's ever believed in me is Parker, and I believed in my ability to protect him because there was no other option. But I never believed my life would amount to anything beyond survival.

She looks to Xander. "Help her."

He comes up behind me again, just a hair away from touching me as he leans close to my ear. "I believe in you, Ava."

I shiver. The whisper under my skin picks up until it's a rushing song of power.

They're metal. I've been manipulating metal all my life. These are just bigger and sharper chunks, but I've got strong and careful fingers.

Xander rests a hand on my shoulder, so light I can barely feel it, but it's there.

I jump as two knives reappear in my palms, and I don't know if

Xander or Aristelle summoned them, but it wasn't me. Regardless, my fingers close against the cool metal on instinct. Only this time they don't feel cold and foreign. My palms seem to melt into them, giving blood and life to the metal until they feel hotter than my own skin. I give a little yelp of surprise, and Xander squeezes my shoulder.

Aristelle remains stoic. "Try again," she commands.

I jolt as my knives pull in my palm, angling toward her, reading my darkest thoughts and longing to obey.

I grip them harder, taming the heat in them.

Aristelle draws her brows together in a frown. She notices everything. Then her lips curve like burning paper. "I don't think you can do it," she says.

My magic blazes.

"Aristelle, that's not helping," Xander snaps.

She ignores him and smirks at me, but it's not a cruel expression, only satisfied. She takes in my fingers clenched around my knives and nods to herself. Her doubt makes my own belief double, and she can tell. I don't know whether to be grateful or angry. I go with anger because it's what I need right now. Plus, it's easier.

I force myself to turn from her, focusing instead on the tree.

My palms burn. I need to release the knives. They grow hotter in my hands by the second. I don't have any choice.

I know where they will fly.

The knives loosen in my grip as they slip down until I'm holding just the ends of the handles firmly in my fingers. In an instant, I shift my stance and let the knife in my right hand fly. Taking the slightest step forward, I snap the left knife after it.

The first knife glances off the side of the tree and clatters onto the stone.

But the second thuds into the bark.

Xander chuckles, letting go of me and clapping his hands in slow appreciation.

Aristelle even looks pleased.

My chest heaves, and my palms itch to have the knives back.

Aristelle brushes invisible dust from her black skinny jeans. "My work is done here. Train her." She strides away and leaves me with my mouth hanging open.

I turn to Xander. His smile is wide and open—whatever hesitation he had about me is hidden or gone.

"Welcome to the troupe," he says.

He lifts my hand, bending to press a light kiss to my knuckles, and I'm pretty sure the thrum in my stomach when he does has nothing to do with the magic.

I expect him to drop my hand and end our little moment of flirting, but he doesn't. He laces his fingers through mine and tugs me forward, past the cherry tree and out of the courtyard to the dauntingly high hedges at the very edges of the compound. We stand there, facing the wall of green.

"What are you doing?" I ask.

"Showing you around, giving you a taste of what you're fighting for."

I stare at the dense green leaves in front of me. "Uh, yeah, nice plant. Matches your hair."

But then the leaves start shifting, pulling back as the branches wind into each other, slowly revealing a glossy black door with a copper handle. "Think of somewhere you were happy," he instructs.

The command makes my chest ache, and for a second my mind is painfully blank, but then he opens the door and steps through, and I hear the steady roar just before my boots sink into sand. Ocean waves foam against a beach littered with shells and sand dollars.

"Damn," Xander says. "It did mine. Not yours."

"How is . . . how is this possible? We're deep in the woods."

"It's an illusion," Xander says. "We've been building the magic of this place for so long that it can make almost anything feel real—think of what you want, and it can be behind any door. I meant for it to be your happy place, though, not mine."

I swallow the lump in my throat. "No. This was mine, too. My mom loved the beach."

A wave breaks on a rock to my right, and droplets of salt water coat my face.

"Why is it yours?" I ask, but I can already guess the answer. He looks like a piece of him gets tugged out from shore with each wave.

"My brother loved it. We both loved it. He wanted to surf, though, and my parents only ever let us use boogie boards. They said he could paddle out with the sharks when he turned eighteen if he wanted." He chuckles. "Our mom *wasn't* a fan of the ocean."

"Your parents . . . do they know what you are?"

He swallows. "They blamed me for taking him to that party. They never said it outright, but I saw it on their faces every time I visited. I don't visit anymore."

It looks like a surfer rides a wave out in the distance.

"Is that . . . ?" My heart beats a little harder as I glance around the beach, like I might see Mom kneeling down in the waves, washing the sand from a shell she'll string onto a necklace later.

"No. No illusion is strong enough to make the dead seem real," Xander whispers.

"But this is something," I say.

I sit down in the sand and tuck my knees up to my chest. Xander sits beside me—close enough for my shoulder to press into his upper arm. We may not have who we lost, but there's some wholeness in pressing two broken things together, even if they don't quite fit.

We sit there for a long time and watch the sun get swallowed in the flaming horizon.

At some point, Xander takes off his shoes and splashes into the waves, but I don't.

Mom never did teach me to swim. We were always at the beach, but she said it wasn't the place to swim. The waves were too aggressive for learning such a delicate thing.

I can picture it so easily: me trying to dive into the water just to see where it would take me, and her hand gripping mine, keeping me onshore, her voice saying, *Power like that will swallow you up, Ava.*

CHAPTER 11

Just over a week later, Xander smiles at me from a stone bench, legs stretched out before him. I've just sunk my knife into the cherry tree for the hundredth time.

But today I have an audience, and not just Ethan glaring daggers into my back or the sideways glances of the other apprentices. I've gotten good enough in just a week that the glances I get are worried, not snide. Diantha and Reina sit on either side of Xander while Aristelle paces to the right of me. If I squint, I can pretend she's not there, but her eyes still burn into me even when I can't see her. I don't know if it's part of her power or just my reaction to being judged.

You would think I'd be used to it. When you're a foster kid, everyone's always judging if you're a good fit for them or not. But I've let myself forget this is a competition.

I've already fallen into a routine. I train with Xander during the day and then visit our pretend beach with him before he leaves with Aristelle to hunt vampires. They still won't take me, not even after a full week of training. Apparently Santa Cruz is a vampire hot spot. They're drawn here—even the ones that don't know what hunting magicians can give them. They sense the power of this place radiating through the whole city, even if the spells keep them from finding it.

I get stuck hanging out in Reina and Diantha's room with them and the twins. None of them like hunting vampires, so Xander and Aristelle are happy to pick up the slack while we sit on an overstuffed green velvet couch and watch the *Tomb Raider* movies on repeat. Or *Indiana Jones* if I get to pick. Sometimes I play Yahtzee with the twins. It all feels oddly normal, even though when I leave their room to go back to mine, I step into a magical hallway that may or may not look the same as it did when I walked in.

I've started to become part of the troupe, even if I feel like the kid who's not old enough to go out with the grown-ups.

I walk forward and rip my knives from the trunk. It heals itself immediately.

At least the twins, eyes always shifting in unison, aren't here. They still creep me out. And I *know* they cheat at Yahtzee.

The metal hilts heat in my hands until I struggle to keep my grip on them. My anger at everyone watching, at letting myself forget that I'm on trial, seems to make me believe in myself more and calls the magic rapidly against my will, or maybe because I can't control my own will. My magic presses against my skin, more like a scream that wants to be free than a hum. I don't know that I could control *that*. That doubt stops me from totally letting go.

I bite the inside of my lip and taste blood.

A slender hand closes around my wrist, pressing fingers against my throbbing pulse. Reina's curtain of black hair brushes against my bare arm as she stands next to me.

"Breathe," she whispers. Everything about her is soft—a cloud to smother my anger.

My pulse backs down, letting go of some of the hurt pushing it.

I turn and meet her round eyes. They crinkle at the corners as her face breaks into a proud smile. She turns from a cloud to the sun in seconds. While Aristelle clearly makes the decisions, Reina is the true center of the group, giving us all just what we need. For me, it's open smiles with nothing hiding behind them.

Everyone goes to her from time to time to soak in her warmth.

"Diantha," she calls. She lets go of my wrist and turns from me.

My time in the sun is up as Diantha rises from her bench. She hesitates, running her hands down her green capri pants, looking only at Reina. I can't see whatever look Reina gives her, but it's enough. Her arms relax by her sides as she comes to stand by the pillar.

Diantha closes her eyes. Sparkling white shadow and green liner flash against the fog. It's thicker today. I can practically taste the magic in it.

Diantha starts to hum a low, sweet lullaby, swaying back and forth so slightly I almost don't notice the movement. She always looks ready for the stage, but she's the only one I've never seen perform.

Nothing seems to happen at first, but then a slender green vine sprouts from the base of the tree, twining slowing around the trunk, thickening as it grows, stretching upward as if it longs to wind together with her song. When it reaches eye level, the humming intensifies and then breaks off as a drooping red lily erupts from the tip.

I clap for her. Reina beams and laces her fingers into Diantha's, squeezing softly. Diantha brushes her black hair behind her shoulders, shifting her feet.

"Why don't you do that for the show?" Surely the crowd would love this.

Reina stills beside me as Diantha's smile fades. Her eyes dim despite the bursts of color around them.

"She's too good," Aristelle says. "Without the possibility of a rational explanation, belief turns to fear. It ruins the magic."

Reina nods. Diantha just dips her head and moves back to her seat. I try not to stare at her as she does.

Reina waves my attention back to the flower. "Sever it from the stem," she commands, stepping back to her seat, leaving me the sole performer.

I gulp the stale, cold air. All I've been doing is tossing knives into a six-inch-wide chunk of wood. What she's asking is the next level. My fingers warm. I let my first knife fly. It slices through the flower, destroying the delicate petals. A cool shot, if I hadn't been aiming for the vine that held it. Frustrated, I focus on my second knife, staring at it in my hand for a moment. Xander said focusing on the shape of it can help me visualize exactly what I want it to do.

Ethan fires off an annoying loud shot, and I grimace. I wish my assigned training courtyard were next to Willow. I can barely make out the notes of her haunting flute today. Her music would make it a lot easier to focus.

I glance up at my mark. But the vine has crumbled to the ground, leaving only the flower pinned like a sad party game.

"You're welcome," Ethan says. His gun still points in the direction of the tree.

I twist toward him, power rushing to the tips of my fingers.

"Well, now I need somewhere else to throw my knife." I let my gaze wander over his chest. I grip my knife tighter, not because I'm going to throw it, but because I'm worried about my magic listening to my desire without waiting for me to give it the green light.

Ethan steps back, and I'm shocked I've intimidated him until he opens his arms wide, inviting me to take a shot.

"You two have good chemistry," Natasha says. I didn't even see her stroll up to the hedge. I was too busy fantasizing about where to hit Ethan without causing serious damage—just a little flesh wound.

"What?" Ethan and I both say at the same time, and then share a look of disgust that we're in sync with each other.

Natasha ignores us. She turns to Aristelle. "Maybe they should perform together . . . say, tomorrow night?"

Ethan starts to open his mouth, but Natasha gives him a shove in the other direction. He glares at me over his shoulder, like I'm the one who suggested it.

I'm desperate to get onstage, but not with him.

Aristelle glances at me and pulls me to the side. "It's time to start performing more for an audience. We need to build up your magic as much as possible before the competition continues, and performing with other troupes can increase the takeaway from a show."

"Where?" I don't really want to perform again for the other magicians until I'm absolutely ready.

"In town. Different clubs. Sometimes the street."

"Can I stake him afterward?"

Her curling smile says she's not entirely opposed to the idea. "I'm beginning to think you're more vicious than I am." She turns back to Natasha. "We're going to pass."

Natasha scowls. Ethan looks even more annoyed that we turned them down.

"Thanks," I whisper to Aristelle. I consider it a victory that she consulted my feelings.

"Back to work," she snaps.

I stride forward and yank out my knife. The tattered flower falls and slumps off my boot.

"Up the stakes," Aristelle calls out as I stride backward.

Xander grins, jumping from his seat. "I've been waiting for this."

He practically skips to the tree, pausing to pull a cherry from a branch. For a second, I'm worried he'll ask me to aim for something that small, but he only winks, popping it into his mouth as he holds an ace of spades out against the wood, pinching the tip with two fingers that could easily be removed by my blades.

I shake my head. "I could cut you."

"You won't."

His confidence in me does nothing to stop the tremors in my fingers. Because I don't trust myself. My magic falters.

"I want to kill vamps, not you." My grip tightens on my knives.

His card blinks out of sight, and he moves forward, stopping just in front of me. His hand closes around one of my fists, and I resist fighting him as he pulls my fingers apart and frees the knife from my grip.

He places his other hand, palm up, between us. We stand so close his fingertips brush the front of my Rolling Stones T-shirt.

He draws my knife across his palm before I can react, leaving a thin trail of blood. I cringe like I inflicted the wound myself, but he doesn't even flinch, just passes the knife back to me. My fingers close naturally around the hilt, even though part of me doesn't want it back.

He holds his hand up as the skin pulls itself back together again. The blood lining his wound bubbles like it's evaporating.

I'm caught in the glimmer of the jewel at his wrist and the blood still on his hand. My breathing speeds as the red of the cherries in the tree blurs together. Xander asks me if I'm okay, but I barely hear him.

I remember something. I spend so much time thinking about Mom that it's rare for me to remember something new, but looking at the blood and jewel together just triggered memories that got overshadowed by what happened the next day.

I was playing a game with Parker next to the little glass outdoor table that Mom had picked up at a yard sale. It had roses painted on the top, and wherever we pulled our trailer, Mom would set it up outside between two folding chairs. I was jumping over it and running around the other chair. I think I was yelling "now you see me, now you don't" while Parker laughed. Until I tripped and fell into the table. The glass shattered. Something bit into my stomach, and I was wailing, and there was blood. A *lot* of it. And then Mom's white face as she looked at me and ran. I cried for her. I couldn't understand why she left. But when she came back, her red-stone choker glinted around her neck. My stomach hurt worse for a second, but then she told me to sit up and that it was only a scratch, but there was so much blood in the dirt.

We moved right after that—to the campground where Mom was murdered the very next day.

I must have been so lost in what happened after that I forgot about what came before. And why would I have remembered that? I was always getting little scratches and breaking things I shouldn't.

But now I see that memory in a different light.

Mom *did* use magic—at least once—the day before she died. And she put on the choker she never wore. The choker with the stones that match theirs. If there was any doubt left that she was immortal once upon a time, it's gone.

I feel like I've been stabbed in the stomach all over again. Mom used a massive amount of magic—enough to make her a beacon to any vampires around.

And she did it to save me. She *knew* not to use her magic. She wrote about how much she missed it, but none of that compelled her to use it. I did. My hand presses against my stomach. I don't even have a scar—not there, at least. It's what happened the next day that left me gutted.

Her death was probably my fault.

I try to tell myself that I don't know for sure, but part of me always wanted to blame myself anyway. What if I had woken up earlier? Maybe I could have scared them off or called for help before it was too late, but those were always just the thoughts of a kid who needed someone tangible to blame, even if that person was themself. I let go of those thoughts as I got older, but *this* information brings them back full force. It makes my guilt a living thing that grows like thorned vines inside me.

Part of me wants to tell them about it, but I don't want to say the words out loud. Instead, I focus on what I need to know. Facts.

I take a step back as Xander holds up his perfectly smooth hand. "It's okay, Ava. I'm fine."

"How did you do that? Did you just use blood magic?"

It seems like it. The way the blood disappeared from his palm was the same way it disappeared from my skin but not the ground that day with my mom.

"Healing is incredibly hard," he says. "Vampires can do it instantaneously because their curse uses the blood magic automatically. For us, we need to think about using blood magic, and for more serious wounds, we usually need more power too." He holds up his cuff. "But the only time we use it is when it's already spilled, and only to heal."

I don't like it. I don't like the way it blurs the lines between them and vampires.

But Mom did it . . .

And then she died. There were consequences.

"Let's get on with this," Aristelle says.

Xander's nodding, heading back to the tree.

But there's a tremor in my fingers that I can't stop.

Before I can even consider throwing, Diantha and Reina step in front of me. Diantha searches my eyes for a moment as Reina says, "I think we should stop for now and have a girls' night."

I groan. "I can't take one more viewing of *Tomb Raider*."

"No," Reina says. "We're going out."

We don't get many tourists in downtown Sacramento. It's more for the people who live and work there. You can count on seeing the same faces on the same nights—tired people looking for the same escape. On some nights, it feels less like an escape and more like a different side of the same cage.

Downtown Santa Cruz is different. Energy and excitement buzz along the tree-lined streets. Tourists gawk in windows at beach-themed novelties while locals stroll by on the way to a market everyone else passes without a glance. People perform on the street. I fish a dollar out of my pocket and toss it in the guitar case of a man strumming his own tune with his eyes closed. He's not any good, but he looks like he's playing for nobody but himself, swaying slightly to his own lack of melody.

We stroll under a canopy of leafy trees that line the street every twenty feet or so. Even though night has already closed in, it's bright. Streetlights punctuate the sidewalk, and strings of round bulbs connect every lamppost.

Reina and Diantha both wear sequined dresses that fit them like gloves. Diantha's is the dark green of ivy and Reina's is the pale blue of morning sky. I'm pretty sure they turn every head as they walk by. No, *we* do. Aristelle came in and tossed a little silk black dress at me while we were getting ready. Plus, she lent me some high black boots that were loose enough to strap my knives into. I think she's starting to like me.

Still, it's hard *not* to feel like a third wheel when you're hanging out with the hottest couple alive.

Diantha and Reina slow, like they noticed me falling behind them. They unlink their arms and drop back to either side of me, then slide their arms through both of mine instead. My first instinct is to pull away, to keep walking separately, but they seem to sense that in me and both give me an extra little squeeze.

And I stay. Because it feels right. It feels like this could be our Friday nights for years to come. I'm not a third wheel. I'm the one who moderates their debates on who's the hottest Lara Croft: Angelina Jolie or Alicia Vikander—I always side with Reina and pick Angelina because I can play neutral for only so long. I feel like I'm a part of something with them. Something special.

It scares me. I'm letting myself build a whole life, and futures can be ripped away so easily. This one's even more precarious—I still have to win. But in some ways, that makes it feel more secure. They want me. Whether or not I get to stay is in *my* hands. Nobody can take away something that I win.

Except Lucius. I think of Edgar's tired face as he got dragged off, but that's avoidable as long as we play by the rules.

We come to a stop outside of a place called Blueroom, with a large, ominous black door and windows trimmed in turquoise. It's an odd combo, but it fits my mood. Reina drops my arm and pulls the door open with a little bow. "Ladies," she says, waving us forward.

We step inside and the hostess greets us. "At the bar or at a table?" But her eyes narrow on me a little bit, like she knows the bar isn't an option.

"Table, please," Diantha says.

The hostess leads us to a red faux-leather booth tucked into a corner that's away from the glare of the windows. Soon, we're stuffing our faces with the best crab-spinach-artichoke dip I've ever had. Okay, it's the only crab dip I've ever had, but I'd bet money on it being unbeatable. It takes us only ten minutes to polish off the whole thing.

When the waitress comes to take our dinner orders, I eye the empty dip tray.

"Actually," Reina says, "I think we'll take another dip and some mozzarella sticks." She winks at me as the waitress walks away.

Maybe I'm easy to read.

Or maybe Reina's starting to know me.

It's weird to have other people anticipate what you want. The only other person who's done that for me since Mom died was Deb, but it was always so clear she loved Parker that I had to wonder if taking care of me was for his benefit. But with my troupe, I know it's for me and no one else.

I sip at my water. I don't know why, but I feel embarrassed about it, like I've messed up somehow by letting them get close to me—by letting myself get close to them. But at the same time, this feels right. It's just as easy as sitting on the couch with them, watching movies.

Like I used to do with Parker. I push past the pain in my chest. I just talked to him this morning. I thought he'd be hurt, and I'd have to explain that it's not forever—that I'd be back to visit soon—but he sounded excited for me. He said he hoped I upgraded my coin tricks, and I grumbled that he has no appreciation for illusion, and it felt normal. It didn't make sense that the conversation made the hole in my chest from being away from him open up a little bit more. He's starting a summer soccer program next week. He's always wanted to do that. He's happy. I have to repeat that a few times before the pain goes away. He's happy. I can chase . . . whatever I'm chasing. It's gotten more complicated. At first it was the magic, then the chance for revenge, but now . . . it's moments like this, too.

I want too much.

It scares me.

The steaming dip comes, and I dig in so fast that I burn my tongue and have to guzzle my drink and wave at the waitress for a refill.

It doesn't deter me from going for another scoop.

"So what are your stories?" I blurt out around bites. I've been wondering for the past week, but there never seems to be a good opening to ask just how old someone is . . . or isn't . . . on the scale of immortality. I glance around the place before continuing. Most people are at the bar, and no one is paying attention to us. "Was it the magic or the killing vampires?"

"Neither," they say together—just as in sync as the twins, but cute instead of creepy.

They grin at each other.

"I worked at a pet shop," Reina says. "Birds were my favorite, so I trained them."

I choke on my water.

"They're trainable without magic," Reina says, turning to Diantha. "Why does everyone always think that's strange?"

Diantha gives her a patient look, like she's explained before why that's weird. Reina huffs.

"Can I ask what kind of tricks?"

"I taught them to wave at kids and fly on command. Things like that. I can show you a nonmagical trick." She cups her hands together, then stops. "Okay, this first trick is magical. I don't carry birds up my sleeves, but then I'll do a regular one."

Before she can conjure a bird from nowhere, Diantha bumps her shoulder. "I told you no birds in restaurants."

"Fine." Reina gives a dramatic pout before all expression leaves her face. "I was walking home one night when a man grabbed me and shoved me into a building. He tried to rip my purse from my hands, but I was so scared I couldn't let go. He lifted his fist, and I still couldn't move even though everything inside of me was screaming to do something—anything—to fight back. But I guess part of me did. Pigeons came out of nowhere, and it was like a scene from *The Birds*. The guy ended up screaming as he ran away down the street with the flock trailing him. Aristelle found me, and I told her no at first, but I was so afraid to walk alone anymore, and she wasn't just offering me magic, she was offering me power. I wanted it." She pauses. "I didn't want to feel like that ever again."

Diantha twirls her straw around her drink and stares down at the swirl of water in her cup. For a second, I don't think she'll answer at all, and I'm about to tell her never mind. Nobody has to share their story if they don't want to. I haven't even shared all of mine. But then . . .

"I grew flowers in my backyard and sold them at a farmers market on the weekends. I'd wear big poofy sleeves and pull a daisy out for kids who walked by." She's still looking at her drink, but a fleeting smile crosses her face. "It drew people to my booth. I started getting custom requests during the week . . . to the point that I was bringing in more money than my husband. He didn't like that. It was mostly yelling at first, but one day he came home, and I was in the backyard pruning roses, and he started screaming about me not having dinner ready on time. He hit me." She looks up and stares straight into my eyes. "He didn't get a chance to do it again. I fell into my roses, and all I wanted was for them to scratch him to pieces instead of me, so they did. They grew out from their beds and pots until they swallowed him whole. I just sat there and watched and listened to him scream, but I didn't want it to stop. We lived in the country, so nobody heard him. I just sat down on the garden bench for hours, until I heard a car pull up the gravel driveway." She smirks now, like she enjoys this part of the memory. "Aristelle strolled through the back gate, took in the whole scene, then grabbed the shears and cut him loose. Then she held him by the collar and lit her hand on fire and told him to never try to find me. He seemed terrified. He looked like I had been feeling for weeks. I left with Aristelle and never turned back."

I nod. I can understand the need for power. If I'm honest with myself, that's a driving force for me too. I want it all: revenge, magic, power.

But something else nags at me for the first time. Diantha never looked back, and I can understand why she wouldn't, but I don't want that.

"Do you still visit anyone from your previous life? Do they know about you?" If I can't see Parker once I stop aging . . . that would be enough to scare me away.

"I don't," Diantha says.

"Well, my parents love her." Reina squeezes Diantha's hand. "And the Japanese side of my family is close. Most of them live around Los Angeles, so we go visit a couple times a year."

"How?" I don't know how long ago they became immortal, but at a certain point it'd start to be obvious.

Reina glances around before smiling at me. At first, I don't notice, but then I see it—a few wrinkles around her eyes and deepened laugh lines around her lips. It's not a huge difference, but she looks maybe ten years older.

"You can learn this too," she says. "It's not the easiest illusion, so some people don't bother, but if you love your family, you can do it."

Diantha clears her throat and nods her head toward the bar.

Reina's eyes shift in that direction and back to me. "Sorry, Ava. Looks like duty calls."

I sit up straighter. "A vampire?" I whisper.

"Vampires aren't the only ones that prey on the vulnerable," Reina says. "Xander and Aristelle tend to focus their energies there, but our interests lie elsewhere. Look behind you and to the left. The woman and man who are about to leave."

I turn just in time to watch a woman in a silver dress stumble as she slides off her barstool. A man catches her by the arm, and she looks at him like she's surprised to see him, like maybe she doesn't know him that well. He wears jeans and a button-up blue shirt that fits like it's expensive, and he smooths chin-length light brown hair back from his face. He flashes the people around him an apologetic smile. His round baby face makes it look sincere.

I know fake smiles though. This one makes my skin crawl.

The woman steps away from him, brushing her dark brown hair out of her dazed green eyes. She might just be drunk, but she could be drugged. Either way, something doesn't feel right. The man drapes her coat and his over his arm and hurries after her as she weaves her way to the front door. She never once glances back to see if he's following.

My guess would be a first date.

I turn back around as Diantha lays enough twenties on the table to cover our bill three times over, and then we're on the move. I trail behind them as we burst into the night. I may not be hunting vampires, but I'll watch and learn this too. I'll never say no to helping someone who might be preyed upon—no matter who the predator is.

Reina and Diantha glance down each side of the street.

"Damn it." Reina's fists clench as she stalks back and forth. "Did they hop in a car already?"

"Wait," Diantha says. "I see them." She stalks straight into the street, making cars stop for her. Reina strides behind her, and I hurry after, feeling like that awkward sidekick in a movie who's going to end up hiding while the badass heroine takes down every bad guy who ever dared breathe near her—at least, that's definitely the vibes Diantha and Reina are giving off. Alicia Vikander and Angelina Jolie don't have anything on them. Their shoulders are back, their steps are sure. *This* is why they're here.

We follow the couple into a parking lot across the street that's sandwiched between two buildings. There's only one row of parking spaces, and from what I can tell, they're all full of city buses. The other side of the lot is just a stone wall with ivy dripping over the edge. Solar lights line that side, but the dim glow doesn't reach the shadowed buses.

Reina and Diantha do nothing to hide the click of their spiked heels, and the man turns his head to glance at us as he grabs the woman's elbow and leads her around the side of the last bus.

We turn the corner as he pulls open the passenger side door of a flashy car.

"Hello there." Over-the-top sweetness drips from Reina's voice, like she's about to make him choke on a bag of sugar.

The man doesn't respond. "Get in," he tells the woman.

She takes a wobbly step away from him.

"I said get in," he grits out.

"I don't think she wants to go." Reina steps toward the girl.

"I have an obligation to take her home."

"Right." Diantha moves closer to him. Her normally warm voice drops below freezing. "And *are* you taking her home?"

There's one damning moment of hesitation before he says, "Of course."

"We'll be taking her from here," Reina says, like we're friends offering a favor.

"Like hell." He lets go of the woman and takes a threatening step toward us.

I glance between Reina and Diantha. Maybe I should reach for my knives. Diantha's face gives nothing away, but there's a slight curl in

Reina's lips that stops me. I'm not going to need my knives.

Wings flutter. I was so focused on the man that I didn't see them before. Three seagulls sit perched on the stone wall. They take off and fly at the man's head like he's got a sandwich on top of it. He swears and bats at them, stumbling forward where his toe meets a root that's just grown out of a crack in the ground. He falls forward and lands on his hands and knees before darting up again.

"What are you? Fucking witches?" he growls before the birds are diving at him again, pecking at his head as he slaps at them.

Diantha steps calmly around him and slides under the girl's arm, helping her move away from the car as the man stumbles around the front of it, muttering the whole time about witches, until he reaches the driver's side. He gets in and slams the door behind him. The tires squeal as he pulls out. The gulls squeal too as they drift upward and fly away.

Reina waves at them, and it only seems a *little* weird.

The adrenaline I didn't even register fades as my muscles relax.

"I'll run and get the car," Reina says. "She's in no shape to walk that far." She turns around and pauses, eyes narrowing, and for a moment I think she's looking at me, but then I realize she's staring over my shoulder.

"Hello, ladies."

The hair on the back of my neck stands up. His voice is so neutral and flat that it almost sounds inhuman. I fight the urge to spin around. My instincts are screaming that sudden movements would be bad, like he's a rattlesnake coiled to bite. But he's not a snake—he's something so much worse. I can feel it, not with magic but in my bones.

"You all smell lovely this evening."

Everything else he says is monotone, but he rolls "lovely" across his tongue as if he's tasting it. My heart hammers in my throat.

Reina's wide eyes meet mine. Diantha releases the girl she's holding, letting her slowly sink to the ground as she places herself slightly in front of her.

"When I said I was visiting California, everyone told me Santa Cruz had the best drinks, and I have to say, it looks like they're absolutely right . . . maybe even better than New Orleans."

I've been slowly turning this whole time, and now I see him: wispy blond hair reaches his shoulders. He wears tight leather pants and a lavender tank that seem out of place in this beach town.

I meet his eyes, and he cocks his head at me.

I don't even see him move. It's like one second he's casually standing, seemingly relaxed, and the next I'm staring up into an open mouth flashing extending fangs. The only thing that stops them from sinking straight into my neck is Reina's arm darting in front of me.

She hisses in pain as the fangs sink into her wrist.

I stumble back and grab a stake from one boot and a knife from the other.

The root that tripped the creepy dude shoots out of the ground and curls around the vampire's ankle, but he kicks and the wood snaps in an instant. The seagulls are back too, but he doesn't even register them as they bombard his head. He laughs, even with his teeth buried in Reina's arm. Some of her blood leaks down his lips.

Her other hand is free, though, and she lunges with a stake I didn't know she had on her. He swats it away. I need to get a shot in. His back's against a bus, and she's trapped in front of him, so I don't have a clear one.

More roots crawl across his feet.

I can't get his heart, but I can get something. I send my knife flying into the side of his arm. He hums a little at the impact but doesn't release Reina. Instead, he plucks it out. He twists it in his fingers, shifting slightly. Aiming.

I start to duck, but the blade doesn't get a chance to leave his fingers. He's yanked to the side with enough force to rip his mouth from Reina's wrist.

Roman steps out as the vampire stumbles, dropping my blade, but he doesn't go down.

I see my window and take it.

I focus on my stake and will it to fly as I pull back and release. It soars past Roman's shoulder and sticks into the side of the bus. Next to the vampire's head. The vamp turns to look at it and then raises his eyebrows as he shifts to the side so Roman stands between us. Roman's glaring at me.

I guess I did cut it a little close.

I walk up to stand by him, since he's still got a stake in his hand. He turns toward the vampire as the creature takes another step back. The vampire sniffs the air and pauses as his eyes narrow on Roman. "Hmm, interesting."

Roman tenses, his fingers flexing and then loosening against the stake in his hand.

The vamp coolly scans the rest of us. "Three against one was a delight, but five against one is a *little* too much." He twists on his heel and strides into the night.

I take one step after him. "Should we really be letting him go?"

Roman's hand grips my shoulder. "He's too strong. It'd take a whole team of us to take down someone like that."

I glance around. Seems like we have a whole team. Willow's here too. I didn't see her come up, but she's helping the girl back to her feet.

"A whole trained team," he says, reading my mind.

I grit my teeth but don't argue. There's nothing I want more than to stake a bloodsucker, but I also want to be in one piece at the end of it.

I turn to Reina. "Are you okay?"

She lifts a smooth, perfect wrist. "Hazard of the job. I'm all healed up." But there's a tiny quiver in her voice. Her wrist might be fine, but given what she's been through, I can't imagine getting attacked by a man, vampire or not, doesn't bring up stuff. One glance at Diantha's worried face tells me I'm right.

Roman stands there watching us with his hands folded behind his back.

Reina scowls at him. "I guess I should thank you."

"Didn't do it for you." His eyes flick to me.

"We had it covered," Diantha says, wrapping a hand around Reina's wrist as if holding her where her wound was can bandage something else.

"Of course," Roman says. He steps back, but his eyes linger on mine.

"Can I help you?" I ask.

He shakes himself. "Maybe." He plucks my knife from the ground. I reach my hand out for it, but he's not even looking at me. He taps his thumb against the sharp tip.

His eyes move back to mine while he runs a finger down the edge of the blade. I force myself to meet his stare. Two can play this game. One side of his mouth quirks up the tiniest bit. Finally, he speaks. "I'd like you to perform with me."

I feel a tiny zing of excitement at the thought of performing with a guy who stabbed his own hand in front of a group of kids, but I don't answer.

"No, thanks," Reina says.

"I'm in need of a second knife thrower for a new act. Don't you think you owe me a favor?"

"Why me?" Surely there are other magicians who throw knives.

"I need you," he says simply.

Those three words are nice. They distract me from my line of thought. When someone says they need you, it makes you want to toss yourself into that need, expand yourself to fill it, or cut yourself in half like a magician's assistant if that's what they require, because helping them will make you feel whole for a moment. Until they don't want you anymore, and you're left contorted and gangly, and you can't quite remember your original shape.

The words pull at me like they always do, but this time I swat them away. "I don't want you throwing knives at me."

"I'm quite good," Roman says.

"I don't care."

Roman tosses my knife in the air, catches it by the blade, and holds it out to me. "I won't hit you, and what's more, I'll give you a turn to throw at me too." His voice is solid, firm, unquestionable—almost tangible enough to hold on to. It makes me trust him.

I hesitate for a moment, then, "Fine, I'm in."

Reina groans.

CHAPTER 12

Their names were James and June. Cute. Too cute, like Hallmark poetry. It made sense, though, since they were a Hallmark couple. They even had a golden retriever. Our last foster home had been cold. We were two of three foster kids in the home. The oldest was a teenage girl who went in and out and didn't really speak to us. It felt like nobody really spoke to us besides telling us to come to dinner or get ready for school. It felt like we were ghosts that appeared only when someone needed us to do something.

So when we got to June and James, it was like coming alive again. We were the only foster kids. We had our own bedrooms there. Blank rooms—not generically decorated to appeal to a string of kids. We got to go to Target and pick our own bedroom sets. We got to paint the walls, which felt precious and permanent. I didn't get yet that walls are easily painted over again. At the time, I just knew they wanted us. I also knew we were on trial, like when you have so many days to take a sweater back to the store if you don't like the fit.

We were out back playing with the golden retriever, Molly—I

don't know why I still remember her name. I had my hand wrapped around a damp tennis ball while Parker laughed and ran circles around the dog. I was smiling. Then they called us inside and our caseworker was there. They said they loved us but weren't ready for the responsibilities of two children.

I think it was the last time I smiled without some ulterior motivation behind the expression. My smiles became tricks meant to disarm my audience and let me perform my sleight of hand. Convince them that Parker and I were no trouble. Worth whatever they were getting paid. It kept us together.

But when I smile at Xander as I wait to go onstage for the first time as a real magician, it's an aching, real thing. The only other real smiles I've allowed myself in these last years have been for Parker.

I want to be here, performing illusions more real than fake. This was how Mom must have felt before she gave all this up.

The club we're in is bigger and shinier than the one in Sacramento, full of chrome and hard edges, with none of the comforting wood paneling that reminds you of a grandparent's house. I miss the old, musty smell underneath everything. In here, the metal only amplifies the heavy, sweet scent of alcohol.

I stand with Xander on the edge of the stage, waiting for the show to start. He wasn't thrilled to be performing with Roman, but we did owe him one. I didn't mention my excitement at performing with another knife thrower.

Earlier, Roman laid out our plan for tonight's performance, an easy enough trick. Xander and Aristelle will perform before us because Xander insisted on performing too and muttered something about not leaving me alone with a wolf.

The lights black out, and the crowd hushes. In the darkness, the anticipation becomes palpable.

MARGIE FUSTON

Fire flares to life in Aristelle's palm, illuminating her foot tapping to a drum beat I recognize immediately. Foreigner's "Hot Blooded" seems a little too on point, but those in the audience who recognize it cheer and laugh, giving her early applause for being clever. I can't see her face, but I doubt she acknowledges them.

As the guitar picks up, she sashays forward, her skintight black jeans and red crop top, moving with her toned body, drawing a few whistles from the crowd.

The opening chorus starts, and she whips a lit hand behind her as she rolls her body and then drops to a crouching spin, leaving her own flames chasing her. As Lou Gramm cries out about his fever of 103, Aristelle rises, spinning again as her arms burst into flame from wrist to shoulder. She waves them at her sides, letting the audience gasp at what they think is an impressive trick before she calls the flames back to her palms.

"Wish me luck," Xander whispers next to my ear before he strolls onto the stage behind her. He wears a blue vest shimmering with hints of red, the perfect burning contrast to her. He eyes her up and down as he stops beside her, pulling out his deck and fanning it out in front of her. She pulls a card and lights it on fire, letting it burn down to her fingertips while Xander's mouth drops open. He re-fans the deck and holds the cards out again. She gives them a withering glare, and they burst into flames without her even touching them. Xander lets them drop and brushes his hands together as Aristelle dances away, all fire and heat. Smiling his signature grin, Xander moves after her. When she rounds on him, he holds up his empty fingers, snapping a card into existence. It turns to smoke in his hand, and another takes its place.

As the chorus hits again, Xander pours out his cards, and Aristelle turns them into a waterfall of fire. The audience cheers as the cards run out. Aristelle spins until her back presses against Xander's chest.

They roll their bodies in time to the song. Xander's fingers drift down her arms until she lights them up again, and he pulls back, shaking his fingers like he's been burned.

He's fine, of course.

I'm the one burning.

I try to tamp it down. It's just a performance. How easily their bodies move together on the stage makes no difference to me. But I can't help wishing it were me up there with him. We've been flirting, and I like it. I like how easy it is to joke with Xander, and part of me thought he might be just what I needed: a boy who could smile despite all the hurt in his past, a boy who could kill vampires and come home and laugh with his family.

But maybe I've been reading into things. Xander's pretty flirty with everyone. But this is the first time I haven't gone running when a boy looked twice at me.

I let my eyes drift out of focus until Aristelle and Xander are nothing but blurs of heat and green moving around the stage in a fluid dance.

"Ava." Roman's deep voice pulls me from the dark, unseeing place I've drifted to. "We're up."

I didn't even notice him take Xander's place beside me, but he appears to be evaluating my every movement. I wipe my hands on the thighs of my leather pants. It only makes them sweatier.

I shake myself loose just as Aristelle and Xander come off the stage. Sweat gleams on their faces—probably from both the heat and the movement of their bodies.

Xander grins at me like he's just experienced the best performance of his life.

His sticky hand catches my arm as I move by him. "Good luck."

I just nod, sidestepping him to follow Roman out in front of an audience still buzzing from the heat they just witnessed.

Roman clasps my hand in his as we make our way to the center and give a brief, solemn bow to the audience. Their tittering dies down as they anticipate what *we* will give them—our silence leaves them wondering, builds the tension so the reveal will spring them into early applause. Willow and Reina wheel out a large, cloth-covered object. Roman leads me toward it, holding my hand in his raised one as if he were a courtly gentleman escorting a lady to a dance. A small part of me wishes we were doing something sexier with our knives. My face heats at the thought, and I jerk my hand away from his.

Roman gives me an odd look, like he can sense my wayward thoughts, before he pulls back the cloth, revealing a circular board with six golden stars painted around the rim. The crowd cheers, applauding for a classic trick they know and love. Everyone loves a classic as long as a hint of danger lurks on the edge—something could still go wrong even if the trick has been performed a thousand times before.

Roman takes my hand again and helps me step onto a small platform, my shoulders fitting just under the curved, padded bars that they adjusted to my height earlier. My hands grip the handles, and I lock my muscles into place before Roman spins me.

Then movement makes it impossible to focus or anticipate the throw of the knives. Only the vibration and the tearing of metal through wood lets me know a hit's been made. Each time, I'm mildly surprised to still be physically whole.

The twirling stops, and Roman lifts me down, holding me for a moment as I find my legs again. His hands that were so cold a moment ago feel hot against my rib cage.

He pulls his six knives from the board and turns, speaking to the audience for the first time.

"Again?"

Like we practiced, I shake my head. "Your turn."

The crowd laughs. I want to let the sound sink into me, fill some part of me always longing for appreciation. I barely register it.

Roman pulls my shoulder bars out and stands in my place, using the higher bars already installed. I grab a discreet handle and yank the thing into a spin, stepping back with what I hope looks like the stealth and grace of a knife thrower.

I pull my first knife from my ankle, twirling it between my fingers. The crowd claps and then goes silent, letting me concentrate. The magic pools in my fingers, and I send the knife flying. It hits just to the left of his foot. Exactly where I aimed.

I shift my stance as I bend for the next knife. A charred queen of spades pokes out from under the toe of my boot. I pause for a fraction of a second before grabbing the second knife, twirling it as the magic rushes.

Half the queen's face is gone.

Aristelle and Xander twist and burn in my memory.

My magic grows cold a second before my knife leaves my hand.

There's no comforting sound of metal hitting wood. Metal hitting flesh just doesn't have the same ring to it.

A few people in the audience cry out. Roman doesn't.

Willow has already stopped Roman's spin. My knife protrudes from his thigh.

I utter a word I probably shouldn't say onstage and dart forward, but Roman's already jumped down from the board with movements too graceful for someone who just got stabbed. He removes the knife from his leg, ignoring my startled face as he strides by me and grabs my hand, squeezing it like I'm the one who needs support as he wipes the bloody blade on his own pants and pulls me to center stage again.

"Put a mask on," he says gently.

I don't have to ask what he means. I turn my panicked face to stone as we stand before the silent crowd. He holds the knife out for them to see, slaps it against his palm to show that it's solid. Then he uses it to tear away the fabric of his pants, revealing his flawless leg. No wound. No blood.

The crowd claps, half from excitement and half from relief, but the fear they felt moments before drowns their enthusiasm. I feel only half the magic I felt from the other performance. I've cost us some.

Roman gets down off the stage and lets some of the people in the front row inspect the knife, trying, I know, to milk out the applause I lost.

I scurry off the stage.

Willow reaches for me, but I brush her off.

Aristelle's fists are clenched at her sides.

"I know. Don't say it."

"You cost us a lot of applause," she says.

"Are you okay?" Xander asks. He slides a hand up and down my arm until I shake him off.

"Fine." I don't mean to, but my eyes flit between him and Aristelle as she stalks off. He sees it.

"Ava . . ."

I blush at my reaction to all of this, trying to invalidate my own feelings, but they linger, insistent.

Aristelle shakes her head and moves to intercept Roman coming off the stage, probably intent on making sure my error doesn't cost us in some way. I meet Roman's gaze and then look away as Aristelle drags him off.

I spin on my heel and dart down a metal hallway until I find a heavy red door with an exit sign on top of it. I pop out on a deserted side street.

Xander comes out behind me like I knew he would.

"It's just a performance, Ava."

"I know." Didn't look like one though. But he doesn't really owe me an explanation. All we've done is flirt and hold hands, and that shouldn't mean as much to me as it does.

He runs a hand through his hair, takes two steps toward me, then stops. "No, you don't." He sighs. "I'm sorry. I should have told you. I should have known better. I've been performing for so long, I don't even think about it anymore. You're new to this. In the beginning, it's harder to separate yourself from the performer. When you've been doing it for four years . . ." He pauses. "I'm not myself up there. I'm just a machine giving them what they want and collecting the power I need." He closes the distance between us and takes my hand.

We stay like that for a moment, and I try to be content, but the leftover adrenaline from the show won't let me.

Finally, Xander drops my hand and steps away from me. "Want to go back in?"

I shake my head and lean against the side of the wall. "I just need a minute alone."

He hesitates, and I hate the scrutiny in his eyes, so I smile. I wait until the door clicks shut behind him before I leave.

I don't have my backpack or my stake, but for once I don't care, because vampires aren't the things that are haunting me.

CHAPTER 13

I'm feeling more reckless than usual. I need a distraction, and a little bit of danger, to pull me out of my head. I don't have a stake, but I'll make sure to stay in the crowds and away from dark corners. I head to the boardwalk—the glare of the rides scraping the night sky makes it an easy place to find. I don't go in though. Bright lights, colors, and smiling faces will only turn my already sensitive stomach.

I failed. On an easy trick I believed I could do without a second thought. Maybe I'm not the natural Xander keeps telling me I am, but there were other factors. I let myself get distracted. Roman paid the price. And then I ran out like a coward, the one thing I always told myself I wasn't. You don't survive years in the foster system as a coward without it breaking you, and I'm not broken. A little worn, maybe, but not broken.

My steps take me to the wharf and the benches lining the road back to open restaurants where guests wander in and out. Enough people to keep me safe, but few enough for peace. I sit there and watch the neon lights of the boardwalk. This is where I'm most comfortable—on the outskirts of someone else's happiness. Laughter trickles off the beach. The blue and red lights from the rides shimmer in the always moving ocean. The ocean must be lonely too—always barely touching the beach. Always moving. Never really home on any one stretch of sand.

I watch the churning water for a long time, until my mind wanders back to the performance, but I don't think about Aristelle and Xander. I remember Roman's perfectly calm face despite my knife sticking out of his leg. That had to take an incredible amount of strength, and he still found a moment to be there for *me*—the girl who stabbed him because I was thinking about Xander. And then I ran.

I need to forget.

My hand moves toward the quarters I still carry in my pocket even though I haven't done a trick with them since I began training, but I stop myself. They're a security blanket.

Instead, I pull one of my knives from my boot and spin it through my fingers carefully. Despite my earlier disaster, the movement *is* natural. It reminds me of the way Xander maneuvers his cards, which makes sense, since he's the one who taught me. I stop twirling. I need my own tricks.

I spread my left hand on the bench beside me, then begin lightly tapping the tip of my knife between my fingers. The warm tingle in my hand tells the knife just where to hit, and it does, every time. I speed up until my hand moves the knife swiftly and surely, twirling between my fingers like they're nothing more than reluctant dance partners. I close my eyes. When I open them, my fingers remain unscathed.

"Nice trick you've got there."

Two men stand beside my bench, watching. One is short and burly. His hands move in and out of his pockets like he's lost something and doesn't know what. The other is tall and lean, and even in the dark, a mean glint lights his eyes. His teeth flash, caught somewhere between a smile and a sneer.

Dangerous. A warning zings through my blood. The same way it did every time an older foster kid approached me with want coupled with cruelty in their eyes. They usually wanted me to steal something from the foster-whatever for them so that if it went wrong, I would take the fall. I always did it. As an unspoken rule, they came to me and never Parker.

I hope he's okay at his new home with Jacob and Deb. I hope all my protecting did him good, left him innocent enough to live a normal life.

It left me hard, so even when I feel the brush of danger, my muscles tighten and then loosen with the familiarity of it.

I smile one of my many smiles. This one is meant to disarm.

It works. The men share a glance.

"Bad time of night to be out here alone," says the skinny one.

I ignore the threat lurking behind the words.

"Would either of you like to make a wager?" I ask.

The question throws them. The shorter one frowns as he looks toward his friend.

The tall one bounces his eyes back to me, intrigued. "What'd you have in mind?"

I wave my knife hand. "Twenty dollars says I can stab this between my fingers without drawing blood."

"No dice. We just saw you do it."

"Blindfolded."

He raises his eyebrows, and I give him my best predatory smile, like I'm the overconfident one in this situation. He holds out his hand to his friend, who grunts and fishes a wrinkled-up twenty from his pocket. I pull my own twenty out and lay it on the bench before digging out the handkerchief from my pocket that was there for the final part of my trick with Roman. I fold it into a narrow line and fit it around my eyes, fumbling with the tie.

"I can help you with that." The tall one's voice is smooth, charming almost, if you ignore the acid underneath.

"I've got it."

Without my eyes, the knife grows warmer in my hand, like it knows I need something extra from it. I drown out the roller coaster in the distance, the shuffling feet of the men, their heavy breathing, and focus only on the rough wood under one set of fingers and the heat in the other. Knife to wood. Knife to wood. I believe in the movement.

I slam it down.

Then I smile for real because I'm not bleeding. I leave my knife standing upright in the wood while I pull my blindfold up.

Indifference on the short one's face. Anger on the other's.

"I was really hoping you'd bleed," he says. "Double or nothing." He fishes money from his own pocket this time and adds it to the pile while I dig out another twenty and pull my blindfold down again as I rip my knife out of the wood.

I raise my knife again, chanting what I want from it before swinging down.

My shoulder jerks as someone bumps into me. My knife goes off course, digging through the tender skin between two fingers with a sharp stab of pain.

"Oops."

I yank my blindfold up to find the tall one standing right next to me. So close, it's a wonder I didn't hear him move.

"You lose," he whispers.

"Shit." My blood stains the bench, enough that it will be a nasty sight in the daylight for someone enjoying their morning jog.

The short man frowns at my blood. One hand pulls at his beard as his beady eyes shift from my wound to my face to the long knife still clenched in my good hand.

The tall one gives a slow, calculated chuckle. He looks me straight in the eye as the other shifts on his feet. "This is why little girls shouldn't play with knives."

Burning. My hand clenched around my knife almost catches fire, the magic hot and angry enough for me to worry my knife will melt and drip between the cracks in my fingers. I stand up to face them as the magic calls to be used, to meld with my desire to see this man bleed—a magic to grant all my wishes.

"Just take the money and go," I grit out.

"We don't want the money," the tall one says. They both stare at my bleeding hand as I realize I misread the want in their eyes earlier.

The blood in my veins feels like it stands still—like if it doesn't move, they won't pounce—but it's not frozen. It drips from my hand as I take the tiniest step back and glance around for help, but I didn't notice the restaurants closing behind me. I'm alone, but even if I wasn't, I'm the one who's supposed to be a vampire hunter. I'm *not* putting someone else in danger.

My grip tightens on my knife. It might not be a stake, but it's still going to wound them.

Their eyes track the subtle movement, and the tall one grins. He's close enough for me to see the flash of his fangs, and I fight a shudder.

All I can think about is those fangs in my mom's neck.

I bite my lip and taste blood. The magic wants his blood. *I* want his blood. We are one want.

I've never felt so much power. Anger and being backed into a corner turns my belief in myself into a rabid, snapping thing, and the magic loves it, giving me all the power I want.

I stagger toward them. All the fingers on my injured hand drip.

The tall one's lip curls back, caught between a snarl and a smile.

"You're going to taste so good," the short ones says, sniffing the air.

"Good evening." The voice is chillier than the deepest part of the ocean.

Roman's shirt glows bright and startling against the dark as he stops just beside me.

I don't take my eyes off the bloodsuckers. I need to release my knife soon, before it burns through all the nerves in my hand.

"Go away," I grit out, even though his solid presence beside me eases some of the tightness in my chest. All I can think about is the kill I want.

"I'd listen to the lady." The tall vampire spits. It lands close to Roman's gleaming black shoe.

"No," he says simply. He eyes the knife clenched in my hand with a frown before stepping around to stand half in front of me. "I'd rather not."

A glint catches my eye. The short one holds his own knife.

Strike now, the magic sings.

The tall one pulls out a knife too.

"Vampires with knives?" Roman asks the question, but his voice sounds disinterested. "You must be new, and this is not a fair fight."

"Knives get more blood flowing. Otherwise, it's like drinking from a damn straw," the tall one says. "And you smell almost as good as she does."

The short one chuckles. "I've got dibs on her."

"No way," the tall one says.

Roman turns slightly without taking his eyes off them and says to me over his shoulder, "Would you like me to kill them for you?"

"No. I want to do it. Just loan me a stake."

He pulls a stake from somewhere inside his jacket. "My apologies, but I only have one."

The tall vamp strikes so fast I don't see it. One second he's a few feet from us; the next he's pressed up against Roman with his fangs inches from Roman's neck.

I jump back before I can catch myself. The vamp's eyes over Roman's shoulder blink slowly, like they don't even see me.

And then Roman pushes him away. He stumbles back over the corner of the bench and crashes to the ground, gasping and pulling at his shirt.

I take a step forward. I want to see it happen.

Roman grabs my shoulder and spins me to face him. I try to turn my head away, back toward whatever he's just done to that creature, but Roman grabs my chin and forces me to look up at him.

"Ava." He says my name a few more times, but all I can think about is my need to watch that creature die. "Ava."

I finally focus on his face.

"Have you ever seen a vampire die?"

I try to shake my head, but his hand's holding me too tightly.

"Don't watch, then," he says.

"I want to see him suffer," I say. I think I shock him. I shock myself a little.

His brows draw together for a split second, and his hand loosens, and I jerk my head from his grip, but the vampire I thought he killed is gone.

Then I spot the short vamp running in the other direction.

I move to dart after him, but Roman grabs my arm, and it's like trying to run while shackled to a wall. My feet skid against the wooden planks, and I don't make it another inch.

"He's getting away." I yank harder and get absolutely nowhere.

Roman glances after him. Then down at my bleeding hand.

"You need to fix that."

"I can fix it after he's dead. Give me the stake. You let them both get away."

We both stare at the stake still in his hand and watch the blood on it flake away into ash until it's perfectly clean, like nothing happened. Roman tucks it back into his jacket without letting go of my arm. "Not both of them," he says, pointing to where the other vampire fell.

I walk over and stare at the pile of gray ash blending with the worn wood.

"So that's what happens to them." I've pictured the way they might die a thousand times, and turning to dust was definitely one of the ways I imagined.

"It's a little more violent than that."

"I wanted to watch," I say, moving back toward him so I can look him in the eyes, so he can know just how much I mean that. I want to shock him again, but he studies me with the same impassive expression as always.

"You lost someone," he says.

My mouth clamps shut.

Roman squats down in front of me and picks up the knife I dropped earlier, wiping my blood from it with his handkerchief. Still kneeling, he lightly grips the back of my calf. I jump at the softness of his touch. It sends my heart speeding like there's another threat—but no, it's not that type of fear that's making my blood pulse. I'm overly aware of the brush of each of his fingers as he slides my knife back into the sheath in my boot. That's scary in a different way, and I don't know where this feeling comes from, but I need to focus on something else. Like Xander.

Standing, Roman grips my elbow, and I startle at that too. He gives me a worried look, like I'm more fragile than he thought, but at least he doesn't know what I'm actually thinking as he leads me around the bench to sit.

He takes my clean hand in his first. My fingers still curl as if they're holding a knife. He coaxes them open and examines the angry red indentations—the markers of my rage. He lays that hand in my lap and lifts the other, dabbing at the blood with his handkerchief.

"You're still bleeding." He sounds surprised.

"No shit."

"Why aren't you healing it?"

"I . . ." My hand leaks a steady flow.

"Xander didn't teach you?"

"No." I certainly didn't ask. I don't want to use blood magic.

He lets out a low hiss. "He didn't teach you a lot of things."

I'm sure he means earlier when I blew his whole show.

"I'm sorry."

"It's not your fault." He doesn't have to specify who he thinks the fault belongs to. He cups my hand in one of his and loosely grips my wrist with the other. "You have to pull the magic to the spot you need healed. Focus on the blood you've released there—use all that power leaking out of you."

"I won't use blood magic. That's for vampires."

"But you want one of these?" He holds up the bloodred jewel in his cuff. "Do you know how they were made?"

"Blood magic. I know, but that was once a long time ago."

He frowns, reaching out and touching my lip. I wince as he pulls his thumb back wet with blood. "Looks like you already used blood magic yourself. You were putting off a lot of magic for an apprentice. You're telling me you did it on accident?"

My stomach lurches. Of course I bit my lip on accident. I would never . . . but it did feel like more power than I'd ever felt before.

"You're stronger than I thought." He looks at me, then past me, searching the waves.

"Um. Thanks." My hand's bleeding into his now. I need stitches.

He snaps back to me. "It's not a compliment. Raw talent means nothing if you haven't had any training."

I bristle. "Xander trained me."

"Not well enough. It's like you have the potential to be the world's greatest acrobat, yet all you know how to do is walk on a balance beam. You'll never make it through this competition."

I almost jerk my hand out of his grip. "That's not true. You haven't seen half of what I can do."

"Then heal yourself."

I stare at my split skin. I can feel the magic burning around it, hungry for a command I'm never going to give. I try to pull my hand away, but his grip tightens.

"You won't do it." It's not a question. He shakes his head. "You could have healed this in an instant with all the magic I felt rolling off you."

"Not worth it."

He studies me before turning back to my hand and moving to press his fingers against my cut.

"No." I try to tug away from him. "I don't want it used *on* me either."

He doesn't let me go, though. "We're not walking back with you dripping blood like a magician buffet."

"You don't have to walk with me." I try to escape his iron grip again.

He lets out an irritated growl as his hands tighten around mine. "I thought you wanted to win this competition? You can't do that if you're dead. Let me do it for you, just this once."

He must see the hesitation on my face because he looks back down at my hand and runs a finger across my cut before I can say no again. A tingling pours from his touch and my hand itches, and then the pain is gone. He passes me the handkerchief so I can clean away the rest of the blood.

I begrudgingly take it without saying thank you. It's only one time, and only because he didn't give me much of a choice.

He rises from the bench. "I will still take you back."

"I can make it myself."

"Of that, I have no doubt." He smiles faintly. "Regardless." He holds out a palm, gesturing for me to rise.

I don't take his offered hand, but I get up with a sigh and walk beside him.

We move in silence until Roman stops just before we reach the club.

"What are you doing?" I ask.

He pulls something from his pocket and comes toward me, pressing it into my hand. I stare down at a wad of bills. More than one boasts a hundred on it.

"Get on a bus and go home," he says.

"No." I shove the bills back at him. I can't believe this was all a ploy to get me to leave—to eliminate some of Willow's competition. Plus, when I think of home, I think of Parker's smiling face, but I also think of Diantha and Reina linking arms with me, Xander's flirty little comments, the twins playing dice. Hell, I even think about Aristelle constantly looking frustrated with me.

Home feels more complicated than ever.

He doesn't lift a finger as I continue to extend the money.

"You don't know what you've gotten into. You don't understand the risk, and you are not ready for it." His deep brown eyes are cold but sincere. "Go home."

I wince. "Tell me what I've gotten into, then."

He shakes his head, dark curls shifting in the shadows.

He's worried I can't heal myself, but what are the odds I injure myself beyond repair?

My limbs are heavy. It's been a long night. The bills feel light and carefree in my grip. I open my hand and let the wind take them. Roman makes no move to chase them, even though I must have been holding at least three hundred dollars.

He sighs. "Let me train you, then."

"What?" I jerk my head up.

"You need to learn from another knife thrower."

"Xander's doing just fine." I turn and head for the door to the club.

"Wait." His hand grips my right elbow, and I almost pull away, but there's a hint of desperation in his eyes that sparks a little bit of fear in me. But I'm not afraid of him. He seems like a statue that's witnessed years of pain, all while staying strong for the next person to lean against.

So when he steps toward me until my elbow brushes his ribs as he leans down slightly toward my ear, I don't even flinch. I feel safe with him, and it's such an unusual feeling, especially for someone I just met. I can hardly make sense of it. I didn't even feel that with Xander, not at first. But maybe I'm reading into it, and my comfort is built on the fact that he just saved me from a vampire attack—not that I couldn't have handled them myself.

I turn so I can look up at his face, which is tight and nervous and so close to my neck that if a vampire hunter saw us, our position would make them do a double take.

"I can give you what you really want," he says. His voice is so low that I can barely hear him. I glance around the street, but there's nobody out here but us.

My betraying thoughts wander to his firm hand steadying me after the performance, and then the careful way he tucked my knife back into my boot. My cheeks heat with how foolish I'm being, and I take a deep breath before answering. "And what's that?"

"I don't think you care about being a magician at all. You want to kill vampires."

Killing vampires *is* more important to me, and for a while that was all I wanted, but now I can see another future using these new skills to make a life for myself.

"They told me it was too dangerous, that I needed to have one of those cuffs first."

"Not if you know what you're doing."

"And you'll teach me that, too?"

"I'll teach you everything."

"Why?" I don't try to hide the suspicion in my voice.

He sighs. "Because I scared off their last apprentice. I'm the reason you're not trained properly, and I don't want to live with that kind of guilt."

"That's not really on you."

"It is," he bites out.

I shrug. I don't want to try too hard to absolve whatever guilt he's feeling. His offer is too tempting. He's giving me something I want now—no competition, just training. But that means getting closer to him, and that seems to have its own dangers.

"Xander won't like it."

"Xander doesn't need to know."

"What about Willow?"

"Aren't you best friends or something?" he grumbles.

The wound on my hand is gone. All that's left is smooth, unmarred flesh. I don't want to learn that particular skill, but I know he can teach me others. I can practice with Roman and see how it goes.

"Yes," I say before I can stop myself. "Yes."

"Good." He doesn't smile. Whatever he gets out of this arrangement, it certainly won't be joy.

CHAPTER 14

Roman drives down the dark, curving road that hugs the coast. Willow's in the front seat, singing along to "Cardigan" for the third time in a row.

Xander wanted me to perform with him tonight, but I begged for more training first, claiming I was nervous to get onstage again after last time. It's not really a lie. I feel the tiniest bit of guilt, but I'm not foolish enough to put all my trust in one thing when Roman's offering another way to get what I want. A backup. I can't turn that down.

The beach we end up at is dark and secluded, and we're the only car parked along the cliff side. Standing on the edge of what must be a steep path down, I swallow loud enough to hear. It's so dark I can't even see the water.

"Willow," Roman says.

Willow closes her eyes, lifting her hands up in front of her and humming a low song like a prayer to the sliver of moon. Two orbs of steady white light grow in her hands. She lets out a soft rush of air as her song finishes.

"Why do you sing?" I ask.

Her face flushes in her own glowing lights. "It's how I pull the magic out of me. I need music to call it."

"I hope you don't expect me to sing. It won't be anything close to magical."

"The singing is a weakness. You can pull the magic out of you with just your will alone. Willow has to lean on something she's naturally gifted at to believe in herself." Roman's voice is terse. In the dim light his face shows nothing. He doesn't so much as glance at Willow as he says it, focusing on the path below as he takes the first step.

Willow's light flickers, and he looks back.

"Come."

We both obey. Willow goes first, with me following behind them both, my feet skidding every once in a while on a loose patch of dirt and stone. When we hit the sand below, Roman kicks off his loafers and rolls his black slacks up. The sleeves of his white-collared shirt are already pushed up to his elbows, revealing a set of knives strapped to each forearm. Why he didn't change for the beach, I don't know. He probably sleeps in slacks and a white shirt.

I almost ask him, but he doesn't seem in the mood for jokes. He never seems in the mood for jokes. Willow's already in sandals. I bend and unzip my combat boots, revealing my own knives.

We trudge after Roman, Willow's lights creating shadows in the grooves and dips in the sand.

I may not be able to see much of the beach besides the faint white of foamy waves hitting sand in the moonlight, but my other senses don't disappoint. The cold air bites at me. The smell is hard to describe, salty and tangy, alive compared to the city. The sand grabs at my toes with each step, as if it wants me to just be still for a moment. We walk until we reach an outcropping of rock, cutting us off from the beach on the other side of it. The waves are louder here, hitting more stone than sand.

Roman glances around and grabs a stump of driftwood, dragging it backward to the edge of the cliff and propping it against the jagged rock. He nods to Willow, who steps over to him and reaches one glowing hand in the air, leaving her light floating there like she's a goddess hanging stars. She puts the other one ten paces back, next to me. I resist the urge to touch it and see if it's hot like a light bulb that's been on for too long or if it burns like the magic in my palms the night before.

Roman holds a knife in his hand until it glows red-hot before running it in an X across the driftwood, leaving charred wood in his wake.

My hands tingle, ready. As Roman steps away, I lean down and yank a knife from my boot, tossing it almost before I'm even upright again. It hits the center of his X with a dull thud.

Willow claps, making my blood sing.

I try to keep smugness off my face and fail.

"Again." There's no hint of praise in Roman's voice.

I pull another knife from my boot. This time I twirl it around my fingers, the same way Xander twirls his cards—until suddenly metal clangs against metal, and my knife falls to my feet while a slim, white-handled knife buries itself hilt deep in the sand just a yard away.

"What the hell?"

Roman hasn't moved an inch, but one of the knives at his wrist is gone.

"You could have hit me."

"Yes. And it would have been good practice for you too."

Willow gapes between us, shifting in the sand from foot to foot. She throws me an apologetic look as Roman strides toward me and removes his knife from the sand. He doesn't pick up mine while he's at it.

"Stop playing with your knives like they're cards. You're too good for that."

I ignore the subtle dig at Xander. "The audience loves it."

"A vampire's going to love it too when you give it time to rip your throat out. You're dipping your toes in the lake of your power like you're a child playing in a puddle. The lake will swallow you if you don't know how to swim."

My cheeks flush. I doubt he realizes how personal the metaphor is to me given that I really *don't* know how to swim. I certainly won't tell him.

He seems to be waiting for me to argue with him. I don't.

"Back up ten steps."

I back up until wet, crisp sand greets my toes. Any more and I will be in the water.

I hesitate. The throw is farther than I've ever tried.

"Do it."

I pull my second knife and let the magic rush to my fingers the way Xander showed me, and then I let it fly. It travels true until it loses momentum and drops somewhere into the sand.

My blood heats, not from the magic, but from my own human embarrassment.

"When am I ever going to have to make a throw like that?"

"What about a vampire running away from you? You could have wounded the one the other night before it got away."

"Let's not pretend *I'm* the one who let it go," I say.

Willow gasps. "What vampire?"

Neither of us answer her.

"Stop complaining and do it again."

I pull out my third knife and throw again. It eats sand even though I will it to eat wood.

"You're not pulling the power to you. You're letting the power come if it feels like it. *Command* it."

"Maybe I should sing?"

Willow smiles. "You can try it."

"Maybe a little Bon Jovi?"

Willow sings the first few lines from "Shot through the Heart" and then bursts into laughter, and I almost let myself join her, but Roman's glare stops me.

"This isn't a joke."

Willow twists her lips in a grimace at me and looks away.

"Willow needs to sing. You do not. I doubt it would even work for you. Focus on the source of your power, call it out from there, order it if you have to, and then send it where you wish it."

"Okay." I walk to the target and free my knife before scanning the sand for the others. Damn. I'm about to get on my knees and start digging for them.

A hand settles on my shoulder. I almost shiver under his touch, despite the fact that he's definitely not flirting. I shake my head like that will help me focus.

"Make them come to you," he says.

"I can't—" But then I stop myself. Why can't I? I've had enough people in my life tell me I can't do things. Roman's telling me I can. I need to tell myself too.

I focus. Power pulses, hot and white. I believe in it. I ask it to come to me. Tentative at first, but then more demanding—soft, but with the understanding that I will accept only one answer.

"Yes," Roman says. "Pull it to your fingers and call the knives."

I listen, coaxing the magic down to the tips of my fingernails, wishing for the knives.

They shoot from the sand toward me faster than I can throw them.

My hands find their handles through pure instinct. It's a wonder they didn't slice through flesh.

My mouth hangs open.

Roman removes his hand, and I try not to miss it.

Willow rushes over and swings her arms around my neck from behind. "You're brilliant, Ava. I don't stand a chance against you."

"True." I laugh. But then regret it. Willow's smile is so wide and sincere that I have to wonder if it's real or if she's just the best illusionist I know. She can't love that Roman's training me. How would I feel if Xander were training someone else on the side? But Willow and I are competitors, not just friends, which means I have to look out for myself.

I glance at Roman.

"That was good," he says gruffly.

Willow giggles like she's used to his sad attempts at praise and links arms with me as Roman starts to head back the way we came.

We straggle behind him, his crisp white shirt a fading beacon in the moonlight. He never glances back to see if we follow or not. I doubt he would care if we turned around and swam out into the ocean and just disappeared.

"Is he always like this?" I ask.

"No. He's in a good mood tonight."

I snort, and she snickers, brushing her pale hair behind her ear.

"Why do you put up with it?"

"I want out."

"Of what? Didn't you say you had a big family?"

She sighs. "That's what I wanted out of. I'm the oldest of ten kids. I felt like I was an extra set of hands and nothing else. All I wanted was to get a scholarship for music, but I didn't have time to practice, so before I learned to tap into my magic, my talent was average. Roman found me on one of those rare nights I got away from tucking kids into bed. I was playing a guitar out on the street and singing, and he dropped a hundred dollars in my case and walked away, but I ran after him to say thanks. He was kind of cute." She laughs.

"Are you . . ." I don't know what I'm asking, but if she has a crush on him or something, I'll stop feeling whatever it is I'm feeling. I shouldn't be feeling it anyway.

"Oh, gosh no." She laughs louder. "He's like a cranky older brother now, but did you know he plays the piano? That's how I ended up training with him. He could hold his own talking music."

"I didn't know that." I stare at his tense shoulders leading the way ahead of us. I'm sure he can hear us talking about him.

I slip on a rock, and Willow's grip keeps me from falling. My knees would be bruised and bloody without her. We keep walking like it was nothing.

"Thanks," I say, about ten seconds too late.

"Anytime." She says the word casually, like an automatic response, but deep in my gut I know she means it. Even if I'm probably hurting her.

CHAPTER 15

Xander's at my door in the morning, bright and smiling way too much for how early it is.

"Where were you last night?" he asks.

I rub my eyes to give myself time to push an explanation to my lips. Did Roman tell him? Was helping me just part of his game to rile up Xander? "I can only watch *Tomb Raider* so many times," I say. It's not a lie.

"You weren't here."

I stare at him. He never looks for me in the evenings, and it's not the first time I skipped out on movie night with Reina and Diantha. "You weren't hunting?"

"Night off. Self-care and all that." Something sharpens in his expression. "You're not answering the question."

I shrug. "I was with Willow."

"Reina checked. She wasn't here either."

"What's with the interrogation?"

He holds his hands up like I'm the one overreacting.

"We went out to one of the magical doors. Hers goes to an orchestra performance. I like music."

"Sounds fun." I half expect him to ask me to sing a tune I heard as proof, but he steps back. "See you at the training yard in fifteen?"

"Make it twenty," I grumble.

He raises his eyebrows and stares pointedly at my flannel pajama bottoms. "You got it."

It takes me only minutes to toss on a pair of jeans and get to Willow's door.

When she opens to my knock, she's unfairly bright and smiley just like Xander, and it hits me that they're a matching set. And Roman and I are a matching set.

"Ava." She's surprised, but her warm voice is like opening the door to a cozy room with a stoked fire. "Come in."

I step inside her room onto a periwinkle rug. Her walls are a soft beige and her furniture is white and polished and a pink velvet comforter covers her bed. The magic's good. It looks like her.

"Did Xander come by to see you?"

She laughs. "Why would he do that? Is Roman trying to make a trade?"

Her smile is wide like it's just a joke, but this time I'm *sure* it's not real. Her illusion is cracking. There's a tiny bit of hurt in the pinch of her eyes when she says it.

"You don't have to do that."

"What?" Her smile holds steady, like a magical shield of positivity, but it's not magic. She's just the type of person who smiles to hide the pain because she always had an audience: her siblings. She probably joined up with Roman because she couldn't smile anymore, and now she's doing it for me.

"You don't have to keep smiling when you're upset."

Her smile breaks. She stares at me for a second like she resents the fact that I saw through her. Maybe I shouldn't have pushed like that, but I want to be real friends—not illusions of ones.

"Do you not want me to train with Roman?"

She stares out her window at the sun brushing the branches of the sequoias, and I worry she's going to tell me to stop, and then I'll have to decide if I really will or not. What's more important to me?

"No." Her smile bounces back. "He *is* the reason you had so little time to train. He *does* owe you. He's just been acting weird with me lately, like as soon as they announced that there was only one immortality spell up for grabs . . ." She bites her lip, ruining her smile. "He's acting like I can't win."

"That's bullshit. You're amazing."

"Thanks!" Her voice is cheerful again. "I don't think I'm going to come tonight though. I'm glad you're getting extra help, but I just can't be there."

I nod, even though it stings.

I hate asking what I'm going to ask next though. "If you see anybody from my troupe, will you tell them I'm with you? Say you left me in your room or something . . . anything? I don't want to hurt them."

"Right. Yeah," she says. "But I wish we really were hanging out."

"Me too," I say, backing toward the door before she can hug me, because I worry she will, and that will make me feel even guiltier. Because even with her blessing, I now *know* I'm hurting her.

That night, I still can't hit the target, but I can send my knives speeding into the side of the cliff. Another one goes wide, and rocks break loose and crumble.

"If I keep this up, I'm going to chip away at this until the road comes down on top of us."

White flashes in the dark. It could be Roman smiling, but I wouldn't bet my life on it. I wouldn't even bet one of my quarters. Roman's been sitting on his own piece of driftwood, watching me throw again and again. Sometimes I hit the X. Not often enough.

"Even with the magic, it helps to aim."

I grind my teeth. "I *am* aiming."

Roman stands up, dusts the back of his pants, and moves toward me. "Grab a knife."

Holding it in my palm, I immediately draw there the power needed to carry it. I glance at the tip and then at the target ahead of me. I will make it.

"No. You'll never hit it like that."

Roman slides behind me. One hand reaches around my neck and lifts my chin while the other flattens out across my back. I almost jerk away from the surprise of it. Xander is always moving me this way or that while we're training or putting a reassuring hand on my back. But Roman is different.

"Do not tilt your head to look at your knife as you throw," he says "Do not curve your spine as you prepare. Keep your eyes where your knife will go. Know where it's going, and it will go there."

"I know where it's going."

"If you did, you would have dug a hole through that piece of wood by now."

I don't laugh. I know he's not trying to be funny.

"Okay. I got it."

I expect him to let go of me. He doesn't. His hands are like ice against me, and I fight a shiver.

"Throw it now."

I take a deep breath, holding it because I can't remember how to let it back out again. His hand moves slightly on my back, and I wonder if it's to distract me.

"That's your other problem."

"What?" I let the damn breath out in a rush. My spine tries to fold in, but with Roman's hand locking my chin in place and the other one pressed along my spine, I can't do anything but stand up straight, which is of course what he wants.

"Breathing."

"Everyone knows how to breathe."

"Not you, apparently."

Funny. Again, I don't think he means to be.

"Treat your breathing like a second magic. Pull it in as deep as you can and then release it. Don't hold it so long that it's burning you up from the inside out."

He's remembering the other night when I mixed magic and rage to the boiling point, when I called on blood magic without meaning to, but if he won't mention it specifically, neither will I. I breathe, letting it in and out over and over again. I debate telling him the hands on my chin and back are distracting, but instead I focus on breathing past my discomfort, which I'm pretty sure is what he'd tell me to do anyway.

"Now throw the knife. Don't look anywhere but the target," he whispers, as if the very sound of his voice might interrupt my breathing. But it's his breath on my ear that does that. This time I lose the fight and shiver. His hands twitch ever so slightly where they hold me, but he doesn't pull back.

I tell myself I'd tremble like that if anyone blew out a breath so close to my ear, but his hands feel scalding against me.

I pull my arm back and throw as his hands shift slightly with each minor move of my body, keeping my form absolutely perfect as the knife sails from my hand.

It sinks deep into the wood at the center of our X.

I twist toward him, and his hands move with me instead of

dropping, and I'm staring up at him, his face half lit in the moonlight, with his hand still under my chin and his other one pressed into my back. The hand at my back moves, pushing me slightly so I take a step closer, closing the distance between us. His eyes widen like this is a surprise to him, like it's not his hand moving me.

This is a really bad plan. It's one thing to take lessons from a rival troupe; it's another to share a moonlight . . , whatever this is. I clear my throat.

His hands drop, and he steps around me. "That's enough for one night."

By the end of the fifth night, I stand so far from the target that the waves nip the backs of my ankles. I try not to shiver as I breathe in and out. Shivering makes it hard to keep my breaths steady. One wave dares to rise a little higher, soaking my pants up to my knees. Distracting. Probably the exact reason Roman wanted me to back up so far in the first place—to see if my form will hold while I fight the cold seeping through me.

I pull back my arm and breathe, setting the knife free on the exhale. It hits its mark, and only then do I splash out of the water toward the drier sand, searching Roman's face for some kind of excitement at my progress. I've come far in five days, practicing with Xander during the day and Roman at night.

I want him to share some type of emotion with me. If he did, I'd be tempted to call him my friend. Isn't this what friends do? Help each other when they get nothing in return? Maybe he's getting something out of this that I don't know about. Or maybe we are friends. Maybe he's as bad at making friends as I am . . . was. I have more now than ever before.

Roman stares off down the beach. When he turns back to me, his brows pull together.

No excitement, then.

"And the stake."

I grimace. We've been practicing with knives *and* stakes, but I don't have the same affinity for controlling wood as I do for metal. Still, I do as I'm told—only this time I stand much closer to the target. I throw the stake, and it lodges into the wood a few inches from the knife.

Roman nods, like that's good enough, before giving me a hard look. "I need to teach you one more thing." He says it with a trace of reluctance.

I almost joke with him. I almost tell him not to be sad our time is over, that we can still be best friends. The seriousness on his face kills the words on my tongue as he says, "I need to teach you to heal."

"No," I say. "You know how I feel about that."

"I don't, actually. You didn't explain."

I swallow. My throat burns like I'm gulping down sand. "A vampire killed my mom. I don't want anything to do with them or their kind of magic."

He nods like he already expected as much. "Why do you assume the blood magic is evil? What's evil about healing yourself or others?"

"Vampires use it." That feels like evidence enough.

"Why are you assuming vampires are evil?"

"They killed my mom."

"One," he says. "One killed your mom. People kill people all the time. That doesn't mean all of them are evil."

"But they *all* kill people to live. They're monsters."

"They do not."

"But Xander said—"

Roman's voice drops so low I can barely hear him over the rumble of the waves. "I don't give a damn what Xander said. Xander buys into whatever the Society tells him."

"But you killed the vampire," I remind him. "You're teaching me to kill them too."

"I killed the vampire that was trying to kill you. I'm training you to defend yourself because I've already seen that you're reckless enough to walk around at night like bait. I have no qualms about killing an actual killer. But not every vampire is one."

"How do you know?"

"What?"

"You have a lot of vampire friends?"

Roman looks away from me, out into the dark and endless ocean behind us. In the moonlight, I can just make out the tension in his eyes and the way his jaw is so tight that it seems like his teeth could break.

I take a step back from him. "You loved one." It comes out harsh, like an accusation, because I mean it like that. I take another step back.

"Wait." He doesn't try to follow me, but his normally firm voice breaks like a wave against a rock, and for some reason, that's enough to stop me. "Let me tell you."

I'm still tempted to turn around and forget about him and go back to Xander. I don't want my hatred for vampires to be complicated. It's been my fuel for so many years that I'm not sure who I'd be if some of it got stripped away. But for the first time in my life, I feel like I owe someone something, so I nod.

Roman sighs so softly I can barely hear him, and I wonder if part of him wishes I had just turned around and walked away.

"I didn't end up in the competition because I hated vampires," he says. "I know troupes sometimes look for people whose lives have been destroyed by one. Revenge will make people do wild things."

He nods at me. I don't like that he sees that desperation in me. The way he says it makes it sound like it's something to take advantage of, like I'm being used.

"My sister and I came from a wealthy family in New York. We started doing magic tricks as a way to piss off our parents, but then we fell in love with it." His teeth flash in the night, and I realize he's actually grinning at the memory of it. It's short-lived though. "We got good. We were performing, and a troupe found us. They offered me an apprenticeship. I wouldn't do it without Beatrice, but they knew another troupe out in California that needed an apprentice too, so we said yes. We both signed on because we loved the gasps a crowd makes when you pull off the impossible. We loved the applause. And we loved pissing off our parents."

"Why don't you quit?" I ask. "Go home to your sister."

"I can't," he says.

I can sense the hurt there. But it doesn't quite add up. He hates my troupe because Beatrice didn't get to be an immortal magician, but Roman doesn't seem like the kind of person to crave immortality enough to ruin his relationship with his sister. Why would he waste his time taunting Xander? Why not go home and give up the thing that caused the rift?

I think I know. "Your sister's not back home."

He shakes his head.

"She died."

He gives me a short, sharp nod, like he doesn't want to acknowledge those words. Still, he says nothing.

"During the competition?"

Another nod.

That makes more sense, but the revelation causes my stomach to feel like it's being tossed at sea. "Apprentices die during this?" Nobody mentioned that. I was imagining a more intense version of *America's Got Talent*, but not one where I could actually die.

"I told you there weren't trick blades."

"I thought you were trying to scare me."

"I was, but you don't seem to have a sensible bone in your body," he grumbles. He looks at me with an odd mix of annoyance and admiration. "You have to push yourself to extremes to win. The Society figures you need to be a little reckless to hunt vampires."

"Do a lot of apprentices die?"

"You should still consider leaving. You're not too far in yet."

His nonanswer tells me he's still trying to scare me, but even if his sister was the only casualty in all these years, that's not nothing. So I do consider walking away, but he's right. I *am* reckless. Every dark alley I've looked down was me sticking my neck out, knowing I might get bit but doing it anyway because I needed some type of closure, no matter the risk. Am I really going to stop now? I thought I could live without it, but if that were the case, I'd be back in my pastel room at Deb's, waiting for Parker to remember it's movie night, and I'd be content with that.

But I'm here, and I'm not like Roman's sister. "You said Xander didn't train her well, but he's been training me every day since I joined."

"He's different with you," Roman grits out, like it kills him to admit it. "Not that it excuses them bringing you in at the last minute, but with Beatrice, it was three years ago—Xander's first year in the Society. Beatrice would go on and on about how many vampires they killed. They trained her for their obsession, not the competition. They wrapped her up in their bloodlust and made her think she was serving some higher purpose."

"But they don't let me hunt vampires."

"Then maybe they learned their lesson."

"But you're training me for that."

He glares at me for suggesting that he's like them in some way. "I'm training you for everything. I'm not letting you die in this competition either," he bites out.

His expression is so firm, I believe him. It calms my rolling stomach.

He clears his throat. "For me, the vampire killing came after the competition," he says. "I killed them without a second thought. It seemed noble enough, and I needed an outlet for my anger. But one day I found this girl curled up in an alley just waiting to die." He shakes his head. "There are plenty of ways for vampires to get the blood they need to survive without killing: a willing partner, underground vampire bars with voluntary donors, and it's fairly easy to buy blood bags. But the last two cost money, so for some vampires who were turned against their will and don't have someone looking out for them, they have two options: take what they want from victims or die. She was obviously choosing to die. . . . It takes a lot of strength to let yourself die even when the alternative is harming others, and I was trained to let her or maybe even finish the job for her. But when I crept up beside her and she looked at me, I didn't see any evil. I just saw something broken, so I scooped her up, took her home, and . . . I gave her my blood."

I'm glad it's dark so that he can't see the revulsion that must be on my face. But he can surely sense it.

"I know what you're thinking, because I never could've imagined doing it myself, but when there's not violence behind it, it's . . ." He hesitates, and his voice sounds strained. "Nice."

This time a little noise escapes me. I can't help the fact that my stomach turns. But I can hear the pain in his voice and the lingering love for someone who's only a memory. I recognize it, and that's why I keep listening.

"She was a freshman in college who got turned walking across campus late at night. We built a weird little life together, going to museums during the day where I'd just listen to her rattle on about color composition, and at night I'd still go out and hunt because each troupe is supposed to kill a certain number each year, but I got more selective. If they weren't hurting anyone, why should I hurt them?"

"Because they have the potential to hurt someone," I say. I'm trying hard to cling to what I believe, even with his grief standing there, matching mine.

"You can say that about anyone," he says.

He's not wrong.

"So where is she?" I ask, even though I already know the answer. I can tell he needs to say it.

"Dead."

For a second, the waves seem to quiet in deference to that word, but I know it's only because my grief and his grief are somehow the same and yet make no sense together, drowning out everything else around us.

"How?"

"Killed by Society hunters," he says.

"Xander?" My heart seems to pause as I wait for an answer.

"No. I don't know who killed her. It was probably my own troupe. It wasn't just me back then, and we still performed together every week, so we stayed in the same area. But I only know that she didn't come home, and she never would've just left me without a word. Plus, you saw what happens to vampires when they die. And I found a pile of ash two blocks from our place."

"So are you saying the Society is evil?"

"I'm saying there's evil and good in everything, and nothing's a simple binary."

I want to forget about this, to block it out and hang on to my pure, red-hot anger and let it drive me without thought, but that's not who I am. I can still have my revenge. It's just not as simple.

"So you *really* volunteered to train me to teach me *this*. Make sure I do it the right way?" That finally makes sense.

"And to give you a chance to do it without the Society."

"You said they weren't all bad," I remind him.

"They're not, and ultimately, it's your choice," he says. "But if you don't let me teach you how to heal, I'll make sure you're out of the competition."

His voice is hard. I don't know how he'd stop me, but I know this is not an idle threat. I nod.

He strides toward me, steady and unwavering. Kneeling in the sand, he gestures for me to do the same. Even though the warmth of the day has long worn off it, the sand cushions my knees. My bones relax into it, almost begging me to just lie down there and find some sleep. I fight to stay upright.

Roman braces my shoulder for a moment, sensing my impending toppling.

"I'm sorry," he says.

For a moment, I think he's apologizing for working me until I'm near dropping, but then he reaches for one of his knives at his wrist. Of course. To teach me to heal, I need to bleed first. My mouth turns dry like I've been guzzling salt water all day. I can't sit still long enough to let him stab me. I don't need to know how to heal. I need to be careful.

He notices my response and hesitates, then puts the knife he's drawn back in its sheath. He can't do it either. I hold my sigh of relief as he unstraps his entire sheath of knives.

We sit knee to knee in the sand, and I let him pull my limp hand from my lap into his, then place his knives against my forearm and buckle the two leather straps to hold them there before putting my arm back on my own legs. The leather is soft on my skin, the knives the faintest weight.

"These belong to you now."

I gape at them—the worn brown leather, the fine pearl handles that catch and hold the moonlight. Exquisite. Personal. Too personal. They look like a family heirloom. He still wears the matching set on his other arm.

"Why?" It pops out of my mouth instead of thank you. Two hard words for me.

"You need better knives," he says simply, pulling out another from his remaining sheath. He doesn't pause to create the awkward silence sometimes used to manipulate a thank-you, just moves on like he doesn't need or want the words from me.

It must be why they're off my tongue before I can stop them. "Thank you."

He raises his head to look me in the eyes for a moment, then moves back to examining the slim blade he holds between us. "These blades are narrower than the ones you've been using. The wounds heal faster. Give me your hand."

"I don't think so."

I half expect him to reach out and take it anyway. He doesn't. He just waits there in the sand and stares at me with little emotion.

"I'd rather you go first."

He gives me a chuckle, perhaps a bigger gift than the knives. Then more waiting.

Finally, I hold my hand out to him. He takes it and pricks the end of my finger before I can second-guess myself. In the half-light, my blood bubbles up black.

"It's the same as drawing the magic to your knives, but you're also calling it back. You just want something different from it. Tell it what you want."

"I want to stop bleeding."

He sighs. "Don't tell me."

I pull the magic down into my fingertips as they itch for my knives on instinct. *No. No knives*, I tell it. *Fix me.* It doesn't. My finger throbs. I stare at the blood on it, commanding the power to come back to me and do my bidding. At last, it does. The tip of my finger grows hot, and I feel the moment the blood stops escaping. Roman produces a handkerchief from the air or from his pocket and dabs the blood off my finger. My fingers jerk toward my new sheath of knives, practically begging me to throw them.

"Focus," Roman says. "You pulled too much magic for such a small wound. Don't let it control you. That's why blood magic is so dangerous. Once it's outside of your body, it has a will of its own."

He takes my hand in his as if inspecting my work. Before I get a chance to register the movement, his knife slices toward my hand again, plunging through the soft center and out the other side.

I forget how to breathe.

Roman's grip on the hilt tightens.

"No no no—"

He yanks the knife back out in one fluid movement.

I scream and then scream again, hoping it will release some of the white-hot pain radiating from the center of my hand. The ocean takes my screams and swallows them, offering me nothing in return.

I bend at the waist, folding my hand between my stomach and my thighs. Pressure. Wounds like this need pressure. My head hits Roman's chest as I fold in on myself. He doesn't budge.

"Bastard," I hiss.

"Yes," he admits, and moves on. "You need to breathe."

I *am* breathing. My breaths are just ragged and unfulfilling, leaving me gulping at the salty night air.

"Focus, Ava."

Roman's fingers find my chin, pulling upward until I'm forced to unfurl myself and look at him. In the dark, his brown eyes turn into cavernous black pits threatening to swallow me just as surely as the waves at my back. I let some of myself sink into those eyes and draw my focus away from my hand.

"It's the same as before, Ava. You need to draw the magic to the wound and call back the magic spilling out. The longer you wait, the harder it is to heal. Do it now, Ava."

He keeps saying my name like that will ground me somehow. It doesn't. The memories of every time someone has used my name to get me to do something—usually after wounding me in some way—come rushing back to me, blending with the pain in my hand until all the wounds become almost indecipherable.

"Damn it, Ava, come on."

"Shut up," I grind out.

He does, holding me there with his hand and his eyes.

I throw a wild grasp at the power, rushing it to my hand so fast that my skin down my arm tingles to the point of pain.

The flesh on my palm knits together as tears run down my face. Roman doesn't flinch as they hit his hand.

Then, just as fast as I drew the power to me, it's gone. I gasp, empty and shivering in the ocean breeze. Roman and I both look down at my hand, healed on one side and not the other.

"Bring it back."

I try, reaching for the magic. I'm not empty; I feel it there, dancing just out of reach. But I can't access it.

I shake my head, and Roman drags his finger across my hand, through the blood, healing it almost instantly.

The pain lingers like a phantom, even though the visible cause is gone. I roll over onto my side in the sand as Roman stays kneeling.

I want to curse at him—to call him every crude name I ever learned.

"Why are you *really* helping me?" The question I've been asking myself since the night on the wharf. It feels like his reasoning goes beyond what he's admitted to.

Roman's quiet for so long that I wonder if he heard me over the tide battering the rocks.

The sand scratches my face, rubbing it raw as I lie there.

"I don't know," he whispers.

I don't believe him. People are cruel for no reason, but rarely kind.

"We need to go," he says. "Rest up for tomorrow."

"What's tomorrow?"

"Tomorrow I take you hunting," he says. "As promised."

CHAPTER 16

We park down a side street in front of some unassuming houses. My hands are even sweatier than they were performing. I'm such a weird mixture of emotions that I can barely focus: anticipation of finally doing something I've wanted forever and some fear, of course, but there's also a tiny bit of excitement to walk the boardwalk instead of staring at it from a distance. It seems like such an odd location to hunt vampires, but Roman claims the place is teeming with them after dark. Unaccompanied teens make easy targets for a quick sip and run, apparently.

Just because they're not making kills doesn't mean they don't deserve to die.

The streets we take on the way to the boardwalk are tired—accustomed to being used only as a means to get to another spot. I walk a little slower because of it, counting the cracks in the sidewalk just so the street knows I'm paying attention to it.

I don't look up until Roman comes to a stop in front of me at a crosswalk. "What do you think?" he asks.

I told him I'd never been to a boardwalk before.

I steady myself, suddenly afraid to see it. Nothing's ever as good as you think it will be. I'm pretty sure the longer you wait to enjoy something, the less likely it is to meet your expectations. If all you feed yourself is a steady diet of dreams, how can reality actually compete?

But I tell myself to just look. I'm not on vacation. I don't need a big dramatic moment.

It still takes my breath away.

Everything is color. A sea-blue ramp leads up to the entrance. In front of it, kids climb on giant stone beach balls painted bold colors while parents snap their pictures. A turquoise building sits just to the right where three golden seahorses watch the crowds from its domed top of woven metal like they're gloating escaping the net below them. Palm trees rise sky-high in the background.

It sucks the city clean around it, leaching all the color into this one glorious spot.

The light changes, and we cross the street with a family of squealing kids. I remind myself that I'm too old to squeal too. But when we pass through the entryway, a smile almost breaks my face.

I catch myself though. I reach inside the black jacket Roman gave me and feel the outline of the two stakes hidden on one side to remind myself what I'm here for.

Roman leads us farther in, and the cacophony of sound almost swallows me—kids laughing, people screaming from some strange mix of terror and excitement as they free-fall on a ride, a shrill buzzer from a game, the click-click-click of the roller coaster climbing to its drop, a hip-hop song in the background that I can't quite make out, and behind it all the faint, peaceful rush of water.

The ocean. It's been so long since I've seen the real thing—something that's not an illusion—except while practicing with Roman, and then it was so dark I couldn't see it at all, just hear it. Right now, the sun is setting. Darkness is still a few minutes away, and we're not as likely to find a vampire in the daylight, so I stop focusing on following Roman and turn to fully take it all in.

It's funny—it looks the same as my magical pretend ocean, but it *feels* different. The vastness of it guts me in the strangest of ways. As if each time a wave licks the sand, a piece of me goes with it. I end up standing there watching until I turn hollow—hollow in a way that leaves me open for something better, something new. So many possibilities exist on the endless horizon where the ocean never meets the sky.

I feel Roman standing at my shoulder, and I glance to see if the view has the same effect on him, but he's not staring out at the water. He's watching me.

I blush in the dimming light, and I'm not sure why.

"This place it too alive for vampires," I say, ruining the moment because, once again, I need to focus.

He looks around. "I think that's why they like it here. It's as close to life as some of them are going to get."

"Where do we even find one?"

"Our best bet is the far side—there's a section closed down back there, and it makes for a perfect make-out spot for couples. That's where we should go." He pauses and clears his throat. "I mean, because that's where the vampires will be."

We keep walking, Roman half a step ahead of me, looking so out of place in slacks and suspenders that people glance at him. It's a good thing we're not spies.

Roasted corn, garlic fries, deep-fried everything, and the sweetness of cotton candy overpower the undercurrent of salty ocean breeze. I pause again in front of a booth dangling with pink, blue, and purple cotton candy bags, as if someone captured the disappearing sunset and sugared it.

"Do you want one?" Roman comes back to stand beside me.

The question startles me. I'm packing two stakes and four knives on me, and I want to rid the world of a vampire tonight. Now doesn't seem like the time for cotton candy, and Roman's always so hyper-focused on the task at hand that I can't believe he'd offer. Must be a test. I start to say no, but he's already walking away from me, handing the girl at the counter some money, and bringing back a bag of pink fluff.

I hold it in my hands and just stare at it for a second.

He clears his throat and then takes the bag from me. I guess it was a test, then. I try not to be disappointed as I follow him to the fence between the boardwalk and the sand, but he doesn't throw the cotton candy away. Instead, he opens the bag and holds it out to me, and I can't resist. I pull out a piece of fluff, and it's like tasting color—like everything bright and alive about this place was spun and whipped and bagged. I take another bite as I look up at him.

The faintest smile tugs at his lips. It wavers when he catches me watching, like maybe he doesn't want to be seen as anything besides stern and serious, but he doesn't let go of the smile. It expands, and his eyes widen with something like shock.

It surprises me too. The way he's looking at me—it reminds me of the way Dad looked at Mom in that single video of them performing. Before I came out and blew up the trick.

I shove a giant puff of pink in my mouth to hide whatever I'm feeling . . . I'm not even sure what it is.

He clears his throat. "You really like this stuff."

"First time I've ever had the real deal—not just a bag from the dollar store." It's way different. This is sugared air, and the cheap stuff is dense and overpowering.

This time his smile fades. "You have a lot of living to do."

"I've lived plenty."

"Not the good kind."

I want to snap at him, but I'm not sure I can argue. "Why aren't you eating it, then?"

"I'm not a sugar person." He shrugs.

"Sounds like you need to get better at living too."

He stares out at the ocean for a long second before turning back to me. "Probably. It gets harder to do when you're focused on killing. The killing will take the good away until you don't remember who you are anymore."

My stomach tightens. He's not lying to me. There's a hollowness in his voice and a sadness in his eyes, and it takes everything in me not to reach out and grab his hand. I know what hollowness feels like. Sometimes I just need to hug Parker for a minute or see him smile to fill that hole again, and in that moment, I want to be that person for Roman.

The way he's staring at me makes me think I could be.

"Are you sure you want to do this?" he asks. "You can't undo it."

His words stop me from reaching for him just in time, and my stomach suddenly sours. I take the bite of cotton candy still in my hand and toss it in the trash. "I can't undo what they did to my mother."

He nods and folds up the top of the cotton candy bag before throwing it away too.

"I had to try," he says.

I don't answer. Maybe there was no real moment between us—just an illusion to manipulate me.

He starts walking away, and I follow.

The crowd trickles down the farther we head to the edge until we reach a closed-off area with silent, unmoving rides behind flimsy panels of fencing. Roman pulls back one panel, and I slide through. They're really not trying very hard to keep people out. We wind back down a walkway, past giant turquoise columns that seem to be supporting some out-of-service ride. Round globes still light the walkway, but it's darker back here. Empty. We stop at the very edge of the park, next to chain-link fencing. Dense trees grow on the other side, making this little nook feel even more hidden. A turnstile exit sits back here, but it pops out into a deserted side street.

"So we just wait for them?" I ask.

"We can bait them."

I reach for one of my knives, but Roman grabs my wrist to stop me.

"No. I'm the bait. I'll do it, and then they'll be gunning for me instead." He pulls out one of his knives and twirls it between his fingers.

The tiny burst of his power makes my skin tingle. I raise my eyebrows. "I thought you didn't like being showy."

"Never said I didn't have the skill." He tucks the knife back in his sleeve. "We need to seem preoccupied."

"How so?"

He's not quite looking at me, which is odd. I'm used to his direct stares that see right through me.

Then I get it. This is the make-out hunting section.

"Oh," I say. I try to chuckle. "Is this how you and Willow hunt vampires?"

His eyes widen, and he rocks back on his heels. "No. Willow and I aren't . . . I didn't mean we should actually . . ." He sighs and composes himself. "It's just the most practical position."

It gives me a little thrill that I got him flustered for a second.

"Okay, then, where do you want me?"

He doesn't even crack a smile as he points to the fence. "Put your back against it."

I listen. The metal digs into my shoulders, and I can't imagine actually choosing to make out with someone in this position.

Roman closes in on me, using his hands to brace himself against the fence so our bodies are close but not touching, but if someone stumbled on us from behind, well, it'd look like we were two people enjoying a private moment.

He leans down so that his chin brushes the top of my hair. His voice is a low whisper. "Pull out your stake. It'll come up behind me. We don't kill until it bites. I'll spin, and you'll hit it in the back."

I balk. "You're going to let it bite you?"

I feel him tense. "You want to do this right, don't you? What good is your revenge if you're killing an innocent? How would you be any better than the ones you want to hunt? It's the only way to know for sure that we've got a bad one."

His words shame me. I believed him when he said they weren't all evil. I nod. I can let go of a tiny piece of my hatred. I'll save the rest for those who deserve it—those who take without asking. Those who kill.

"How do you do this alone? Isn't it dangerous?"

"Yes. *You* shouldn't do it alone." His tone suggests that his own safety isn't a priority.

"So I do need a troupe."

He sighs. "Get ready."

I pull the stake out from my jacket and clench it in my fist.

"Don't hold it so tight."

I loosen my grip and try to breathe, but my chest feels too tight. My fingers shake. All the times I suffered through a vampire movie in hopes of gleaning some kind of useful information, all the interviews I watched with Gerald, all the hours spent doing push-ups or practicing jabbing a stake through someone's ribs, all are about to pay off. I don't know if I ever really believed I would get a chance to kill one, but now I'm so close, and I wonder who I'll be afterward. I hope it's someone better.

Roman's voice is only a murmur. "Here we go."

"Maybe it's just a security guard or something."

He dips his head so we're nose to nose. "I can feel them, so it's either a magician who just used magic or a vampire who just fed."

"I can't sense a thing." My heart thuds.

"I'm better trained than you." His head shifts the tiniest bit. "Almost time."

I'm shaking. Suddenly I don't want to do this, but there's also nothing else I want to do. It's a confusing feeling.

Roman's hand brushes my cheek, and for a moment I think it's part of the show we're putting on, but then I see that he's waiting for me to look him in the eyes. "Last chance to back out."

"No," I say. My hand tightens around the stake before I force myself to relax.

"It's coming," Roman whispers. And then his eyes widen as a woman buries her fangs in his neck. He twists, but her back is to me for only a split second. She lets go of Roman and shoves him away before spinning to face me.

My arm's already pulled back, the magic called to my fingers, but then I doubt myself for a moment before I let the stake fly toward her chest. She looks like a soccer mom on vacation, wearing pink capris and a tie-dyed top, sloppy makeup, and a white baseball cap over her auburn hair. I think we've made a horrible mistake as my stake plants itself below her left shoulder. Too high to kill.

She lunges, a blur of bright colors. Her teeth snap together inches from my throat, but then Roman's arm is in front of me. His stake in her heart. He pushes her back, pulling his stake free at the same time, and she crumbles. This time I can watch the red bloom on her chest. It spreads as her legs kick. Her arms flail, and her fingers scratch at the pavement as the hole in her chest starts to disintegrate. It's like she's turning to ash from the inside out. But I can't look away. One minute she's there, and the next she's nothing but burned debris.

My stomach turns, but I hold down my cotton candy. I picture her killing my mom. She wanted to kill me.

I step forward and kick at the ash. One less monster. One less person hurt. One less family shattered.

But I don't know if I feel better.

I just feel numb.

Maybe that's better than anger.

Roman's silent, but I feel him close, letting me have my moment.

When I finally turn to him, I scream his name.

Four people creep up behind him. No. Not people. There's something in the way they crouch slightly that gives them away. The man in front can't be more than twenty-five. He wears a blue plaid shirt and black skinny jeans. As soon as I scream, he straightens, hands raised. A disarming smile spreads across his face.

"Whoa, didn't mean to startle you," he says.

A man to his left straightens up too, pushing thick black glasses up his nose. He looks like he's trying to smile, but it's so strained that it makes my skin prickle with unease. A blond woman dressed in the same style as the one we just dusted leans against one of the light posts. And then there's a goth girl who looks younger than me, with black-rimmed eyes to match her black leather skirt and crop top. She looks like the kind of girl who begged to become one of them, and she's not even pretending. Her lip is curled back, and her fangs are showing.

One of my stakes is buried in the pile of soccer mom at my feet. And despite my improvement with wielding them, I can't call wood to me like metal. My hand itches for the other stake tucked in my clothes, but my knives are closer.

"Ava," Roman says softly. "I want you to run."

I don't quite register what he's saying at first. My hand's almost to the knife at my wrist.

"Ava, *run*," he says again.

My head's pounding with my heartbeat. Roman is more powerful than me. I'd probably just get in the way.

The guy in the blue plaid shirt grins. "I'd probably listen to your friend." He sniffs the air.

And then they all move at once. It happens so fast that all I can do is focus on one. I pick the goth girl since she's barreling toward me like a meteor. She hits me at top speed, and I crash backward into the fence so hard my teeth clank. Her hands pin my shoulders, and I catch the briefest smile on her face before her teeth slam into my neck.

My whole body goes cold except for that one burning spot. I try to push off the fence on instinct. *Run. Run. Run*, it says. How is she so strong? I try not to let it, but the memory of my mom crushes me like another weight. How long did she struggle?

And then she pulls back. Her gaping mouth is wet with my blood. Her hold softens. I finally snag a knife from my wrist and plunge it into her side, but she's already turning to dust. Roman's stake clatters with her to the ground.

He's standing right in front of me, and his eyes are panicked as he glances at my neck. He reaches for it, like he's actually going to take the time to heal me right there, but the other vampires aren't dead.

One is on the ground, pushing a broken leg bone back into place, and I'm pretty sure I'd hurl if I weren't in shock. Another stands, plucking a stake from his chest that must have just missed his heart. He lobs it over the fence. The woman pulls two knives from her throat and rubs a hand over the blood like it's nothing.

I push Roman's hand away from me. "There's no time."

"You're right," he says, and then he grabs me and moves me so fast, I don't even know what's happening until he pushes me through the exit turnstile.

"No!" I scream. I try to push back through, but it's designed to be one-way.

"Sorry about this," he says, and I can't help but think he's apologizing for dying while I watch.

I scream and slap the bars as the three vamps close in on him again. How many knives does he have left? Does he even have a stake still?

One appears in his hand, and he calls a knife into the other.

I will not watch someone die like this.

My pulse slows. The rapid change from panic to calm is jarring, but I've trained for this. I take a deep breath as they rush him and draw the two knives from my boots. I'm a knife thrower with magic. It doesn't matter if I'm behind a fence.

They're on him before I can throw, but then I stick a knife into the head of the woman, sending her reeling back. She drops Roman's arm that she was already pinning down. My other knife hits the guy with glasses in the throat and slows him just enough for Roman to plant a stake in his heart. He goes down, screaming and clawing at his chest. I grab my last stake, the best shot I've got, and send it for the guy in plaid. He's the ringleader, so maybe if he dies, it will give the woman pause. But he's too far away. I hit his shoulder, and all he does is snarl in my direction.

It's not enough. Roman's outnumbered. They've got his arms, and he's not as strong as them. He struggles and then stills. Their backs are to me. I've got one knife left, but what would that even do? I could call the other knives back to me, but I need stakes, and I need to be close enough to use them. Roman twists his head like he's trying to see me. Probably to tell me to run again.

Like hell.

"Don't drain him out in a huge rush like the last one," blue plaid vamp says.

The woman grumbles.

They both latch on to his neck, and I have to bite back a scream. Instead, I move as quickly and quietly as I can to the other side of the gate and the ten-foot chain-link fence that's keeping me from the fight.

I'm sure I'm not that quiet, but neither glance my way as I climb over and down the other side. My breath is heaving, and I can't make it stop. I drop to my knees and search the two piles of ash from the soccer mom and the goth girl until I'm covered in bloodsucker waste. I hope I appear terrifying.

Nobody's looking though. Roman's eyes are closed. His head droops forward. The vampires seem to be holding him up now, their faces buried as they suck his life away.

The woman is closest, so I do her first. I don't miss. She screams and falls to her side, turning to dust at my feet. A rush of power hits me, and for a second, I think it's just that I've done it with my own hand—killed a creature with the same murderous heart that killed my mom—but no. It's real power that's flooding me, the same intoxicating sizzle as applause, but it's different, too. There's a wildness to it, pushing harder against my insides than normal.

But I don't have time to think about it. The other vampire's rising. Roman's on his knees between us, and I have to lean over him to aim for the heart. The vamp catches my wrist right before the stake can puncture. Grinning, he squeezes it so hard that I'm sure my bone will turn to dust like one of them.

I gasp. I can't hold on. The stake falls from my grasp right into Roman's waiting hand. He plunges it into the vampire's chest so quickly that the vamp is still smiling when he starts to combust.

I don't watch this time. I kneel down by Roman and examine the streams of blood trickling down both sides of his neck.

"I'm all right," he says. "Give me a minute."

He closes his eyes, and I watch as the wounds stop bleeding and then heal over.

When his eyes open, they seem softer than usual, more vulnerable, but maybe almost dying does that for a person.

"You saved me." He sounds confused.

"Just paying you back. You trained me for this," I add, but in truth there's nothing in the world that could have trained me for this.

His eyes zero in on my neck. "You're still bleeding." He reaches for it, but I stand, glancing around.

"It's over, Ava." He rises to his feet.

But my blood's still pumping too fast, and my magic still feels like it's pushing against my veins.

"What was that?"

He glances around like he's missed something.

"I felt something when I killed that vampire."

Roman grimaces. "I thought you knew."

I'm getting tired of the things I don't know—both the things I'm searching for and the things everyone forgets to tell me. At least Roman doesn't wait for me to ask the question.

"If we kill a vampire, we take their power."

"We take the blood magic," I clarify.

"Yes."

"I don't want it."

"You take a life, you take the magic. That's just how it is."

I can still feel it in me. It's like restlessness under the skin—an urge to hunt more. The potential to be as out of control as the curse itself.

"You all hunt vampires for the power." It seems a lot less noble than looking out for the defenseless.

"It's a reason for some. For others, it's personal. If it matters, for your troupe, I don't think they do it for the power." He shakes his head like he can't believe he's admitting this. "But there's also a tithe every year when we gather, whether we have the competition or not. Every troupe has to give some of their power to the mansion to keep the protection spells in place. Killing vampires makes it easier to meet your quota."

"And that's why *you* kill?"

"I'll take down anyone who harms the innocent. But it's also just me in my troupe. I have to meet the entire quota myself." His face droops with weariness. He wobbles, like he's still feeling the blood loss, as he looks over at the chain-link fence. "Did you climb that?"

"Yep."

He stares at me, but it's too dark to see his expression. "You're different than I thought. I didn't think you'd actually kill one."

I don't answer. I don't know what to say to that. I always hoped I'd kill one someday, but how do you really explain that kind of drive to take a life—even a vile one? I should be more upset, perhaps. Some distant part of me does feel sick, but it feels right, too.

Roman grabs my arm and pulls me to the fence, and I lean on it again. His cool hand feels good against my arm, like it's soothing the burning magic inside me, and some part of me just wants to press up against him and let his touch soothe all of me.

"Let me see your neck," he says.

One of his hands finds the side of my face, and his thumb presses under my chin and tilts it up. His other fingers slide across the blood on my neck. I wince when he finds the wound, but it takes only a moment for the pain to go away. I can feel my skin stitch back together, but he doesn't let go of me. He steps closer so that his arm is pressed between us.

His ragged breath brushes against my face.

My own lips part and release a breath that matches his.

His cheek grazes mine, and our lips almost touch at the corners.

My mind is a scattered mess of revenge and death and pain and lust and some kind of matching brokenness between us. Turning my head toward him would be complicated and hard.

"Fuck." He pulls back.

The word jolts me. It doesn't fit coming out of his mouth. He's always so calm and cool and put together.

"I didn't mean to do that." His eyes are too dark in the shadows to read, but his voice is hoarse. And he sounds shocked, like he surprised even himself. "I'm sorry. Fuck." He turns and takes a couple of steps away from me. Twisting back around, he runs a hand through his curls, so they stand on end like wild vines. He takes a step toward me and halts.

"It's fine," I say. "Nothing even happened."

"I was supposed to give you an out, not draw you in more." He strides all the way back to me, and for a second I think he's going to finish what he started, and I don't really know how I feel about that, but I stay right where I am and wait for him. But he doesn't try to kiss me. He slams his fist and forearm into the chain-link above my head and stands there, inches from me, his body leaning down toward mine. His breathing is heavy.

Part of me wants to lift my fingers and touch his heaving chest, but I'm not sure what it would mean. Roman was supposed to be just another path to get what I wanted, but what if magic and revenge aren't everything I'm longing for? And am I tempted by him just because Xander's taking forever to make a move? I don't know.

I like holding Xander's hand and just smiling and laughing at his jokes and cheesy flirtations.

This. Right now. Doesn't feel the same. This scares me. For the first time, I'm scared of Roman.

Because this feels too real.

Xander's a fairy tale.

Fairy tales weren't made for me.

But I can handle real and messy, and I want *this*.

I put my hand against his chest, pushing him back and around so that he's the one against the fence, so that it's clear I'm not pinned in, I'm right here, waiting.

He stares down at my hand, then back up at me. I let my fingers wind into the open collar of his shirt. His breath catches. "Ava, wait."

I stop. "You don't want this?" I don't mean for my voice to come out so hurt.

He moves in answer. His lips stop barely an inch from mine, and for once, I don't hesitate. I don't think about what's right or best. I do what I want. I kiss him, and desperation blooms there, tangling us together. I push harder, searching for the roots of each bloom. Mine are easy to follow at first, but they become convoluted the deeper I go. His, I can't begin to fathom.

I pull back.

The steady, raspy breath of the distant ocean mixes with our own.

He leans in this time, and his lips move softer, slower, like a balm over the hurt we were releasing before. I want to lose myself in the feeling.

A sharp sting against my neck stops me. My eyes fly open just in time to watch Roman's look of alarm. His face contorts into a snarl as fingers dig into my arms, pulling me back from him. Before I can react, Roman becomes nothing but a blur. And then I'm free, stumbling as I twist around, searching for the stakes we should have already picked up.

In my peripheral, I can see the vampire has his fangs in Roman. I bend and grab a stake before turning to take in the situation. I freeze. Every part of me turns cold.

The vampire doesn't have Roman at all.

Roman's mouth is against the vampire's neck as he struggles and then goes still. For a second, I try to make it something else that I'm seeing. Anything else. Then Roman pushes the vampire away from him. He falls to the ground before scrambling up and running into the night, but for once, I don't care about the vampire that's escaping.

I care about the one standing right in front of me.

Roman turns around slowly. Dark blood coats his lips, and his mouth is still open slightly like he misses the neck that used to be there. The tips of his fangs hang just below his top lip. Lips that I was kissing moments ago.

I bend at the waist and heave. Barely keeping myself from vomiting.

He wipes a hand over his mouth, leaving a nasty smear across his cheek as he steps toward me.

I'm no longer frozen. My nerves are screaming in panic and confusion, so I fall back into what I know. I lunge toward him, closing the distance in a second. The stake and my hand fly through the air. I barely stop the momentum.

My stake presses against his chest.

He doesn't even flinch.

"Do it if it will make you feel better." His voice is low and raw.

The rawness of it reminds me of our kiss—the vulnerability of it, like we were both opening up in some way.

But he wasn't. He kept something back. He kept *everything* back.

My hand starts to tremble, and I drop the stake. I can't do it. He might be a liar, but he doesn't deserve to die. I hate that he taught me that. It'd be so much easier if he hadn't.

"Ava, please." He reaches for me, and I step back so quickly that I stumble and slip, landing hard on my ass. I yelp, and he tries to bend toward me.

"Don't touch me," I snarl.

Tears cloud my eyes as I drag myself to my feet. I'm going to feel the ache of this tomorrow.

I back away. I don't bend down to reach for my stake. If it were in my hand again, I'd feel like I needed to use it—to do the thing I set out to do.

The thought of staking Roman . . . my own heart feels like it's being split in two just thinking about it.

"Please don't tell anyone." There's a desperation in his voice that makes my heart rip further apart. "They'll kill me, and . . ." He cuts off like he's choking on the words. "I can't die. Not yet."

"I'll think about it," is all I can manage to say.

He nods. He opens his mouth to say more, but I shake my head.

"Let me explain," he says anyway.

I almost tell him no, but I need to know. If not for me, then for my troupe. Why would he be masquerading as a magician when they'd kill him if they found out?

"You have two minutes. I guess I owe you that."

"Ava . . . I don't want you to feel like you owe me."

"Don't say my name. You have less than two minutes now."

He swallows. "The vampire I was in love with. Once I knew what life could look like as a vampire, I wanted that instead. I had plenty of money from my trust fund to buy as much blood as we needed. I didn't want to be part of a group of magicians that hunt vampires, but I *did* want to live forever because *she* was going to live forever. So she turned me. And then she died before anyone even knew what I'd done."

"But you're still here. Why?"

He's silent.

"Revenge," I say softly. Everyone's been hurt. Everyone wants to fix it by hurting someone else. I understand it, but more and more, I wonder if I've been wrong my whole life about going after it. "What are you doing?"

He shrugs. "I don't really know. But if I get the chance to show someone that all vampires aren't evil, then that's one more person who might help me change things."

He's talking about me.

"Does Willow know?"

He shakes his head. "Not that I'm a vampire. She knows I loved one though. She knows we're not all bad."

"You might not be a killer, but you're definitely a liar." My fingers brush my lips.

He looks down at his feet. "I didn't mean for that to happen. I've been fighting that since . . . since you stuck your neck into that alley to save Willow without caring about what happened to yourself."

I don't want to think about that—moments when I felt something for him too. "How has nobody found you out? Especially during the annual gathering?"

"Money. I only drink magician blood. As I explained, there's a whole underground blood market. And it doesn't need to be Society blood. There are plenty of other magicians out there using their magic that don't belong to the Society. Some of them make a living building their magic and selling their blood. It's expensive, but vampires drinking magician blood feel like a magician to the senses, can do magic like a magician, can walk in the sun. There's no way to tell." He holds up the cuff on his wrist. "This thing still works. I can still tap that power somehow, and it lets me past the barrier spell. I drive out of town to feed, so nobody feels an odd burst of power from me, but even if they did, I could say it was me practicing magic. There's shockingly little difference between a vampire and a magician."

I don't know how to feel about that last part.

"Will you keep my secret?"

"I don't know." It's the best I can do. "But I want you to go."

He pauses for a second like he's waiting for me to change my mind, but all I want right now is to not look at him. I close my eyes until I hear him walk past me. Then I twist to watch him as he pauses with his back to me. He doesn't turn around again, just waits, like he's giving me another chance to end him if I need to.

I won't. It wouldn't help. Killing him wouldn't make me forget how much I wanted his lips against mine. If it would, I might actually do it.

His shoulders rise and fall with a heavy breath, and then he walks away.

Some part of me wants to run after him, but that's not who I raised myself to be. Instead, I focus on the fading sound of ocean waves and let it pull that thought out to sea.

I tuck my stakes into my jacket—Roman's jacket—and run back to the crowd. Something tells me Roman's still watching me. He wouldn't leave me alone out here. But I can also feel it, like his sadness is a hand on my arm.

Maybe I should have taken one more thing from him: a ride back. I can't exactly Uber to a hidden compound on an unnamed road with no address.

I pull out my phone and light up the screen as I push between groups of teens laughing and jostling each other. I have only one troupe member's number in my phone: Xander.

He's going to hate this.

He picks up on the first ring.

"Ava?"

"I need a ride."

A beat of silence. "Where are you?"

"The boardwalk."

"Alone?"

"I am now."

"Don't leave the crowds. I'm close. I'll call you when we're out front."

He ends the call. Of course he's with Aristelle.

Ten minutes later, and I'm in the back of a van with Aristelle driving and Xander turned around, staring at me with an anger I rarely see on his face. "You were *what?*"

"Hunting with Roman. He trained me," I add.

I can tell that last part didn't make things any better.

"Should have known that asshole wasn't going to give up."

"It's not like that. He didn't try to get me to leave, and I'm better now than I was before."

"He didn't?"

"No. He felt guilty that it was his fault you had to find me so late."

"He does love guilt," Aristelle mutters.

"I'm *not* leaving," I say.

It's dark now that we've left the city's lights, but I feel Xander searching my face.

"I'm with you," I say.

"Then let's make it official," Aristelle says.

Xander's smile flashes in the dark.

CHAPTER 17

I slide my fingers down my borrowed leather pants, surprised for the millionth time at their softness. It doesn't make them any more comfortable, though. Xander wears leather pants too and his signature shirtless vest.

"Are you sure we both need to wear leather?"

Xander only chuckles.

I take a deep, shaky breath. "Seems like overkill."

"You'll do fine. You're ready for this."

I am. Roman made me better. I ignore the sickening twist in my stomach.

I hate that he stood there and offered to let me kill him. It would have been so much easier if he'd been angry or defensive. But all I saw on his face was hurt and sadness and shame, and the bit of hope when he explained—and the way that hope crumbled like dust after I listened and still told him to leave.

Aristelle receives her applause and exits without saying good luck on her way by. I guess I'm in the doghouse in her book.

My hands sweat. I need to focus. Roman doesn't have anything to do with why I started this. It was always about magic and revenge, and the people I'm with right now.

Xander takes one of my hands and leads me out to the center of the stage beneath a harsh light secretly trying to illuminate all my flaws and not my talent. Only the dim lights above the audience's heads illuminate their waiting faces. I pretend I'm performing for a room of skeletons instead of people. Pretty sure you're supposed to imagine them naked, but this seems like a better option.

Xander drops my hand and pulls out a deck of red cards, shuffling them quickly before the audience. "We're going to need a volunteer."

Hands shoot up and Xander gives me a little nod. I step forward and scan the faces in the front before choosing.

A young man darts up onto the stage, pulling his skinny jeans back up after he climbs the stairs. Xander hands him the deck. "Normal deck, right?"

The man shuffles through them so fast he can't possibly see them and hands them back.

"Do you like magic . . . ?"

"Andy."

"Do you like magic, Andy?" Xander repeats. He captures names so easily.

"Sure."

"You don't sound sure."

The audience chuckles.

Xander fans the cards in front of him. "Pick a card, Andy. You know what, pick two cards, Andy, just because I like you."

A few more people laugh. Laughter is good. The applause will be more generous at the end.

"Show them to the crowd, but don't show me. Don't show her

either." He turns and tosses me a wink. "She likes to cheat." Andy follows the directions. "Now put them back anywhere you'd like. That's it, Andy. Perfect."

Xander shuffles the cards, stepping back against a black board we painted and placed earlier. He fans the cards out face-first and holds them against the board. "Now, I'm not sure what cards you picked, Andy, but my lovely assistant knows. Would you pick his card out?" he asks me.

"Gladly." I'm up. I reach down to my ankle and pull out one of three long, beautiful black knives. A gift from Xander. In my hand, the metal pulls the magic from my skin, the knives coming to life. The audience murmurs as I try to look confident.

"Stand behind me," I say to Andy, just for show.

His nervous energy moves to my back, and I take a slow breath to shake it off. The audience believes I'm about to do something fantastic. My skin throbs with it.

I let fly, aiming for the cards spread out against the board.

Xander doesn't flinch as the knife hits inches above his fingers.

I earn applause, and I have to fight the grin trying to spread across my face. *Look cool, Ava. Look like you knew you would hit those cards.*

Xander lets the cards drop to the floor, leaving the knifed card stuck to the board. "Two of diamonds?"

Andy nods, mouth popping open.

People clap.

Xander starts performing bow after bow.

"Forgetting something, aren't you?" This is a line I've practiced.

Xander looks puzzled before he grins. "Right. You had two cards, didn't you, Andy?"

Andy nods as Xander starts fishing through his pockets, coming up empty before he performs his signature move: erupting in a waterfall of cards. Finally he holds up two empty fingers. "Found it." He grins, gesturing for me to go ahead.

I turn to the audience and raise my eyebrows dramatically, then give them a shrug. They give me their laughter, and I try not to laugh with them at how easy it is to control them. I bend down and yank another knife from my ankle, gripping it as the heat rushes into it. This throw is easier. All I have to do is hit the air above Xander's hand. I make the throw swift and neat, and when my knife thunks into the board, an ace of spades sits pinned beneath it.

The audience gasps, and Xander yanks out the two knives and the cards. He strolls back to me and Andy, handing me the knives and Andy the ruined cards.

"Those are your cards, I take it."

Andy nods. He's not quick enough to give a comeback like I was.

"His were in better shape." I say it for him. The audience laughs, and as Andy goes back to his seat, Xander and I bow to their applause. I don't bother looking at their faces.

When we get offstage, only Reina and Diantha are there. They give me my own little round of applause. I flush. They both hug me while Xander steps back and waits.

"The others were starving. They went down the street for Thai. The twins wanted to eat out. We wanted to congratulate you before we went." They move toward the door. "Come join us if you want."

I turn toward Xander with a smile I wish were real.

He smiles back at me like it's the easiest thing in the world to do.

"Do you want to join the others?" I ask.

He shakes his head and steps toward me. His hand reaches up and brushes my hair behind one ear, drifting down to clasp the side of my neck. My mind jumps to Roman, and I don't want it to. I need something else to cover up that moment with him. Something that's not built on a lie.

I thought I didn't want the fairy tale, but maybe that's exactly what I need: the charming prince. I don't need dark and brooding. I'm enough of that all by myself.

So I focus on Xander's touch. These small touches seem to fill all our time together. I've grown used to them, but they still make my palms sweat. Nothing has ever come from it, though, so I swallow down nervousness beating in my throat and try not to pay attention to his bare chest.

"How do you feel?" he asks.

Heat fills my body. Sure, part of it is Xander's close, shirtless proximity, but most of it is from the show, from having a crowd of people want me, applauding for me. It's a rush. Roman was wrong about me just wanting to kill vampires. That's the old me. The new me wants *this*.

"Exquisite." I regret the word almost immediately. It's too much, too vulnerable.

But he doesn't laugh. Dropping his hand and spinning away from me, he sits on the edge of a table with his feet on the bench. His deck of cards is out, shifting between his fingers.

"Want to learn a trick? One without magic?" He focuses on the cards like he actually needs to watch his fingers to do his fancy tricks. He doesn't. He fans the cards in front of him. "Choose your fate."

I pull a two of hearts from the selection. He folds the deck of cards and hands it to me as he plucks the heart from my hand and raises it to his mouth, biting the edge and slowly ripping it from the card with his perfect teeth.

My mouth goes dry. I try to say something, anything, to clear my throat.

"You sure like doing tricks with your mouth." Shit. I want to pull back the words and choke myself with them. In my head, they brought to mind the night we met, when he coughed up my card. Out in the open, with the air already taut between us, they take on a meaning of their own.

The wicked gleam in Xander's eyes tells me he hears only the second meaning.

He pinches the torn card between two fingers and flicks it to the side with enough force to hit the wall and slide to the floor. The other piece he pulls from his mouth and drops between his knees so that it lands face-up on the bench. A red two and a jagged half heart stare up at me.

"Don't we need those for the trick?"

His silence pulls my gaze up to his. "I want to try something else—a new trick, or maybe the oldest trick in the book, depending on how you look at it."

He reaches out and cups my chin, pulling his hand back slightly so I follow until my legs bump the bench, and I stand with his knees on either side of my hips.

We're about to cross the line between flirting and something else.

If I'm honest with myself, I've been wanting to do this with Xander since he whispered in my ear that first night of the show, but I was beginning to think his little flirtations where nothing at all—just his personality. Stacie is like that. She can look like she's flirting with a tree she's just walking by.

I tense. "Why now?" I ask. "Is this because of Roman?"

Xander groans. "Please don't say his name." His eyes sharpen. "Are you saying you had something with Roman?"

I shake my head—a lie to both of us.

"I was afraid he'd scare you away," Xander says. "I didn't want to start something and then . . ."

He didn't want to open himself up to a loss. I understand that. We understand each other better than most.

"Last night you said you weren't leaving, and I believe you," he says, but desperation trickles through his voice, and I'm not sure if it's because he *doesn't* really believe me or he feels safe enough to show how he really feels now. He watches me, waiting to see if I want this too.

I nod.

His eyes drift over me and glaze slightly as he leans forward to place a breeze-light kiss on the corner of my mouth and then hovers there, waiting for something. Permission, maybe.

I give it with a turn of my head, angling my mouth right in front of his, leaving the tiniest breath of air between us.

He closes the gap, soft and tentative at first as the hand holding my chin drifts to my hair, and his other hand presses at my back, trying to pull me closer even though my knees clank against the bench. I break off long enough to brace my hands on his thighs and crawl on top of the bench to get closer to him. His kiss grows hungrier, and he pulls me to him. My hands flutter. I don't know what to do with them. I place them in front of me, on his chest, but he's not wearing a shirt, and the skin-on-skin contact jolts me in a way that makes me hesitate. I move and grip his leather vest instead, the soft material sliding against my fingertips.

I try to memorize it at first—the exact softness and hardness of his mouth, the way my knees begin to hurt from kneeling on the hard bench, the mustiness of the room, and then I give up. He doesn't pull back until I've forgotten who I am, where I am. The feeling terrifies me, and yet I want to sink into it again. It's different than Roman, where our hurt was tangled up with our kisses, which made them too hungry. Xander kisses like he wants to forget the world, not save it. I want that too. At least right now.

He takes a shaky breath. I want to lean in and take it from him.

I lean away from him instead, suddenly overly conscious of my own skin, and it has nothing to do with the magical buzz of my performance. Aristelle's leather pants are unbearably sticky.

"I need to get out of these pants," I mutter.

His eyes widen.

"I mean—" I jump off the bench I've been kneeling on. "They're just really hot." Not as hot as my face, though.

His mouth quivers with barely contained laughter. "I could snap my fingers and change them for you." He winks.

"Nope. Nope. I prefer the old-fashioned way—by myself, I mean." My words slur together in one long, awkward string that I wish could roll back into my mouth. "Don't trouble yourself."

This time he lets his laughter loose. "I assure you it would be no trouble."

Every nerve ending in my body seems to be on high alert. Some of it's the magic, sure, but some of it's the flirting, the way my lips still tingle, and my desire to step back into him despite the awkwardness. It's no wonder I wrote off the magic I felt when I met him as attraction. The two are difficult to distinguish, and combined, I'm so alive I want to puke.

So why am I still thinking about a dead guy?

CHAPTER 18

Xander insisted we finish training early today and have some fun. I'm not sure how I feel about being back at the boardwalk, but the sun's not setting yet, and it feels different, walking this street with him. His bright hair and brighter smile fit this place in a way that Roman never could.

Xander stops abruptly in front of the bright turquoise arcade. A painting of an unfurling orange octopus covers the building above our heads. "I think we should hold hands," he says.

"Oh?" I say, hands firmly buried in my pockets.

"Yeah." He grins. "It's good luck."

I scoff. "I've never heard that one before."

"Of course not, I made it up just now, but it sounds true, doesn't it? Isn't that what counts?"

"Probably not." I pull my hands out anyway, dangling them at my sides, unsure.

"Plus, it's just practical. It's kind of chilly out."

"I'm surprised you're cold—you're wearing more clothes than usual."

He tugs on the strings of his sweatshirt hood and smirks. "You spend a lot of time thinking about what I am or am not wearing."

I snort. I'm a little bit embarrassed, but after so much time together . . . this back-and-forth just feels natural.

"Fine," I say.

He reaches down and locks his fingers into mine. "Try not to be so excited. It could scare the other pedestrians."

"I'll do what I can. No promises." My skin thrums under his touch, either from the magic in our blood connecting or from plain physical connection. I'm not sure it matters anymore which is which.

We walk the rest of the way in comfortable silence. It's so much different from walking alone, where I lose myself in observing my surroundings. Walking with Xander, I lose myself in *him* and how our steps slow or speed up to match each other, the way our fingers tighten and release, the way our forearms brush against each other through our sweatshirts.

We walk past the red, white, and blue ticket booth and step under the arched sign that reads BOARDWALK in huge red letters. I'm glad this isn't the same entrance I came in with Roman. This is different. A fresh start.

Xander leads me toward a pirate ship ride that's flying through the air with the ocean at its back and past the haunted house with creepy gargoyles sitting above the door that remind me of the vamps from *30 Days of Night*. I always particularly hated those ones. We move past a pale yellow gift shop and then a sea-green snack shack until we're standing at a wide expanse of beach.

Whereas the ocean is uniform and endless, the beach is scattered and confined. Every shade of every color pops against the sand like a spilled bag of mixed candies.

Xander lets go of my hand and wraps an arm across my shoulders, pulling me farther down to where stairs lead to the beach. I trudge along in my boots, knowing I'll never get the sand out of them but not really caring. We weave between families under striped umbrellas and sandcastles already falling to pieces. My chest aches a little from all the laughter and smiles. I like being here with Xander's warm arm around me, but the beach feels like a place for families.

But then Xander stops and shields his eyes as he glances around. "There they are."

Amid the color, Reina raises a hand toward us. Her glossy peach one-piece swimsuit glints in the sun like a polished shell. Aristelle and Diantha sit with her on a blue blanket spread across the dips in the sand, giving it the appearance of waves on the shore.

Aristelle's eyes narrow on Xander's arm around my shoulders, and her lips turn down, but the expression is gone just as fast. She opens the cooler and waves at the inside. "We made the mistake of letting the twins go into the store by themselves to get drinks, so we've got orange cream soda or orange cream soda." She smiles, and there's no burning condescension behind it, like the ocean has dampened her usual flames. I can't tell if it's real or fake, but I want to believe it, so I do.

"Good thing I like orange soda, then," I answer.

She hands Xander and me each a bottle before taking a swig of her drink. I pop the lid off my own, and it foams like the ocean.

Xander sits on the other side of me. Diantha and Reina spread out on a towel behind us. Diantha leans forward and points out the twins playing tag in the waves.

We all laugh as one of them slips and the other stands, waiting for her to brush the sand from her bottom, out of sync for once in their lives.

"Which one fell?" I ask.

"Bridgette," Reina says, at the same time Diantha says, "Briar."

We laugh again. It's a beautiful sound when you laugh with people you know. I pick out Xander's deep chuckle, Aristelle's faint and airy, Reina and Diantha both bells, one high and one low, and me. My own laugh comes out raspy and tentative, shy from not being allowed out for so many years. It blends all the same, whispering between theirs to bind everything together.

I pull the zippers down on my boots and yank my socks off, scooting forward on the blanket to bury my toes in the sand. It's so warm that it seems to heat my bones. I thought the sand in my magical ocean playground felt real and warm, but it's never felt like *this*. It warmed only the surface of my skin. It never sank into me. How did I imagine that felt real?

This is real. I'm sitting on the beach with a family. I'm sitting on the beach with people that seem to want me to be *part* of their family. They want me enough to train me to fight for it. This is what I really want—not killing vampires. I thought I had to do that to find peace, but it didn't give me any. This, sitting here with people who always have each other's back no matter what, that's what I really want.

I lean back on my elbows, close my eyes, and let the sun compete with the cool breeze over the temperature of my skin. Xander asks me if I want to get my feet wet, but I shake my head. I don't want anything to steal this warmth from me.

Eventually, the twins run up to us, wet and covered in sand, wilder and more unkept than I've ever seen them.

"We want to ride the rides," they sing in unison.

"We'll take you." Xander looks to me for confirmation. I nod, matching my smile to the twins' like we're triplets.

We take them on spinning swings, a roller coaster with twirling seats that leaves me jelly-legged and stumbling, the famous Giant Dipper, which slams me into Xander with enough force to bruise, and the giant pirate boat that looked innocent at first glance but still lifts my stomach to my throat. Xander lets out whoops and yells while the twins stay silent with the same frozen smile on every ride. I smile too.

When the sun begins to drop, Reina finds us and takes the twins for corn dogs, giving us a wink before turning serious. "Don't be late."

"Late for what?" I ask.

Xander cups my face. My stomach flops, but not from the thrill of a ride. "You'll see."

"I don't really like surprises."

"I had a feeling, but you'll like this one." He pushes his sunglasses up to his head. His green hair flops over the frames in a way that makes me want to fix it.

I grumble, but Xander just takes my hand and tugs me in the direction of those pink fluffy clouds captured in bags.

"I could go for some sweets." He's got money out and a bag of sky-blue cotton candy in his hand before I can protest. He undoes the tie and holds it out to me. I stare into it. At least it's blue and not pink, but of course I still can't help thinking of Roman. The look on his face when he watched me eat it, like he needed me to like it, like me being happy somehow made him happier.

Xander laughs at my hesitation. "It's fine if you don't like it." He pulls it back and takes a big chunk, letting it crust around his mouth before he licks it off, leaving a faint trace of blue. He hums with happiness. He doesn't need me to like it. He doesn't need me to make him happy. He's already found that peace.

He holds the bag out one more time. "You sure?"

I smile and shake my head. "That orange soda was too much sugar already."

"No such thing." He takes another big chunk as he watches the pink in the sky overtake the blue. I watch him. I can feel the smile on my face. I deserve someone who brings out my smiles, not some-one who needs me to bring out their own. I watch him devour the whole bag himself before tossing the empty container in the trash. There's still sugar on his mouth when he looks as me. "Time for that surprise."

Xander yanks off his sweatshirt as we walk, and for a second I think that the surprise is a striptease, and I might be okay with it, but he grabs my hand in the next moment and pulls me so that I'm walk-ing awkwardly in front of him. He wraps the sweatshirt around me.

"I'm really not cold," I say, even though I like the salty ocean-breeze smell of it.

He pulls it back off without answering, and I almost gasp. My own sweatshirt is gone, and I wear a billowing black shirt I've never seen before. Strips of my sleeves are made from nothing but lace.

I laugh, stopping to spin like I'm Cinderella before coming to my senses and crossing my arms over my chest. "Okay, now I'm cold."

But the sweatshirt is gone and Xander's wearing slacks and his vest with nothing under it, and he doesn't look like any fairy godmother I've seen. The excitement in his grin is laced with wickedness as he pulls me under his arm and starts walking. He leans down to my ear. "You'll forget about it soon."

I already have.

We make our way through the thick crowds, and I let myself get lost in the colors and smells, the brightly painted booths filled with stuffed animal prizes and surrounded with people laughing and cheer-ing, the smell of corn dogs making my stomach grumble, the screams of the people on the giant wooden roller coaster.

Normally I'd feel uneasy around so many happy couples and fami-lies, but I blend in just fine.

I'm about to ask Xander where exactly we're going when I spot

Aristelle through the crowd. She's standing above everyone else, and when we get closer, I can see she's on top of one of the stone tables lined up in front of a stretch of food places. She wears a black dress that flares at her knees and wrists. A red glowing pizza sign behind her head casts the perfect lighting for her.

She smirks at my surprised face.

Xander pulls me farther down. Reina stands on top of the next table, contrasting Aristelle in a glowing white feathered skirt stopping inches above her ankles, and the twins stand on the next table with their perfect blond ringlets reaching the puffy shoulders of their old-fashioned blue dresses. They smile at me in unison. Diantha is next in a green gown stitched with cascading roses.

"What is this?" I ask. Some of the crowd has started drifting to a stop around them, waiting to see what they'll do. A few people grumble with hands full of food, looking for a table, but most people just seem curious.

"A welcome," Xander says, "to your new family."

Family. The word starts an ache in my chest, and yes, part of it is the pinch of sorrow, but most of it is the ache of finally finding something you've wanted for years even when you told yourself you didn't. And they do feel like family already. I know Aristelle will talk softly and warmly to the twins one minute and snap at the rest of us in the same breath. I know the twins braid each other's hair in the mornings and take them out right before they get onstage. I know Diantha only truly laughs when she's holding hands with Reina. I know Xander eats sugar like he's in kindergarten.

If that's not family, it's at least the seed of one.

I look at them all and smile.

Aristelle snaps her fingers, and the hem of her skirt and the edges of her sleeves catch fire. She begins to twirl, swift and sure, along the edge of the table, blazing like fireworks personified. People around me gasp. Some step away, but others cheer.

Reina moves with softness and grace—a poised ballerina next to Aristelle's frantic movements. She raises her hands in the air, lifts one foot behind her, then rises onto the tips of her toes and spins like a ballerina in a jewelry box. As she moves, doves burst from beneath her skirts.

The crowd cheers and grows around us as Diantha pulls an endless stream of green lace from her sleeves. Some of Reina's birds flit around her, grabbing the fabric and lifting it over the heads of the audience.

"No way," a girl edging in next to me says, and she positions her phone to capture the lace the birds drop on our heads.

It snags in my hair, and I laugh, brushing it away.

The twins take turns throwing a black cloth over each other, shifting not just their dresses but their hairstyles too. One is in braids and a blue jumpsuit and a second later is in an orange sequined gown, hair perfectly pulled up in a bun of curls.

Impossible.

"Isn't this too much?" I shout above the cheers of the crowd.

Xander just grins, shaking his head.

How anyone could watch them and not suspect the true magic is beyond me, but I guess that's the point. We want them to believe we're special—something just beyond their understanding. Their belief feeds us. My blood already drinks up their fascination.

Xander tugs my hand. "Come on. You belong up there too."

I don't hesitate. My blood hums with pleasure, and I want more. Xander leads me to the last table in the row, where a family sits with a pizza.

"May we borrow your table?" he asks.

The parents look slightly annoyed, but their kids jump up, eager for a front row seat to whatever we're going to do. Xander gets up first and reaches down a hand, pulling me up next to him and steadying me as I glance out at the swelling crowd. Already people point at the new additions to the lineup. I reach down into my boots and pull out the three knives I've taken to carrying there. Some of the crowd steps back from me, and I give them a feral grin.

I don't have a trick planned. I don't have a target set up. Instinct takes over. I fling the first knife into the air, catching the hilt in my palm again with ease. They cheer at my simple trick and magic surges in my fingers, and my knives begin soaring as I juggle them with a grace I never had during my well-practiced coin tricks. I don't even flinch as Xander begins flinging his cards into the path of my knives until each knife holds several victims.

I bathe in the applause, confident enough to scan the faces of the audience now.

A knife slips through my fingers.

I move my foot to keep it from skewering me, and it clanks against the concrete bench before falling and hitting the ground. Xander grabs my arm as I teeter. Once I'm steady, I look up for the face that made me fumble.

Stacie.

I never did tell her exactly where I was, but I did say Santa Cruz, and I wouldn't put it past her to just head down and try to find me, but the thing that really startles me is the face next to her. We first met when she defended me from a bully making fun of my coin tricks, and that's the same boy whose arm she's tucked under now—Adam, I think is his name. He laughs as he sees me recognize him. Stacie gives me a little wave. Why the hell would she bring *him* here?

"Are you all right?" Xander's hand still clenches my arm.

"What are they doing here?"

"Who?"

I try to point, but I don't see them anymore.

I feel sick. "Help me down."

Xander does so without question. I pull the wounded cards off my knives and hand them to him before tucking my knives back into my boots. I look for Stacie and Adam, but the crowd's gotten too dense. People push in around me, trying to talk to me, but all I hear is buzzing.

Until one word rings out louder than the others. "Cops!" someone yells.

The crowd breaks apart around us. Xander grips my hand and pulls me with them before freezing.

"Diantha," he says. "Damn it. We should know better. There's always cops outside on the streets here, and all it takes is one asshole to go running."

He doesn't have to explain himself. Diantha's Black.

We both turn around, and Xander jumps back up on the table, scanning the crowd. After a second, he jumps down. "I spotted her with Reina. Looks like they got ahead of the crowd."

"What about the others?" I glance back, but all the tables are empty.

"They'll be fine," Xander says as he pulls us into the swarm of people moving away from the scene of our show.

CHAPTER 19

One second Xander runs in his performing clothes, and the next, he's just another punk kid in black with unnaturally colored hair. But the cops might be looking for that green hair. I open my mouth to ask if he can magic that away too, but he drapes his coat around my shoulders and pulls it away, leaving me back in my hoodie and tank. It shouldn't surprise me at this point, but my steps falter, and I stumble. Xander grabs my arm to keep me upright, then slides his hand down my arm and links our fingers like we're just a couple on a date and not evading a ticket for a public disturbance.

The initial rush of the crowd fades, and we're able to get back out onto the main street in front of the boardwalk without any trouble. Xander glances around. "Do you see any of the others?"

Someone grabs my other hand, and I jump, pulling away until I realize it's Reina.

"Found one," I say as a thread of relief unwinds in my chest.

Reina sighs as she looks up at Xander. "You should change your hair. You're a flaming guilty sign if anyone gave the cops our descriptions."

"Never." Xander brushes his hair back from his eyes. "It's my best feature."

I disagree, but now is not the time to say so. In the near darkness, the shadows only accent his beautiful face, but his hair glows, refusing to be dimmed.

"Where's Diantha? I thought she was with you?" Xander asks.

"She's safe, and so are the twins. I put them in a cab." A note of fear I didn't think she was capable of enters her voice. "I can't find Aristelle. I felt a vampire feeding during the commotion—probably someone taking advantage of a distraction. If she felt it too . . ." She trails off. I know Aristelle well enough to know that she'd go after it.

Xander's face in the shadows barely changes, but I feel tension in his grip where he still holds my hand. "Let's go," he says, but none of us move. There are too many places she might be.

"I can feel magic," Reina whispers.

Xander nods.

I check my own senses. My magic buzzes from the performance, so much so that it's hard to feel anything else, but then I do. It's like hearing a song blaring from far away, but I hear it under my skin instead, like a thread I grip in my hand and follow.

Xander drops my hand and takes off running as we follow behind him, no longer caring if we look suspicious or draw attention to ourselves. We end up on a dark, rusted metal bridge with a train track running through it. Xander doesn't wait, just walks out onto it, glancing around in confusion.

"She's here somewhere," he says.

"Xander," Reina whispers. She points down to the water beneath the bridge.

We hear a splash and the sound of someone thrashing in the water.

Laughter reaches us—and not the kind between friends. It has the cruel bite of joy at someone else's expense.

"I'm going to burn you to ash." Aristelle's voice is a raspy growl.

"Not if you're half drowned," says a chipper voice.

Xander's already gone, hopping over the railings of the walkway beside the tracks so he's standing on one of the wooden beams that juts out over the water. Then he jumps. There's a splash below. Yelling. Reina's trying to climb over the fence as well, but her feathered skirt snags, and I have to yank her free before jumping over after her. She steps out onto a beam and then slides down so she's sitting with her feet dangling.

"It's not that far," she says as she grips the beam in front of her with her hands and then slides off, hanging for a moment before dropping. I copy her, wishing I had stairs instead, but it can't be more than a twelve-foot drop—six and a half feet since I'm dangling by my arms. I suddenly realize why this feels so familiar. I'm basically reenacting a scene from *The Lost Boys*. But the fool in that movie was joining a group of vampires. I'm joining a family. My stomach twists, and I let go. Water splashes up my legs. The impact shakes me, and I go down to one knee, but I hope it looks intentional. At least it gives me a chance to slide a knife from my boot.

I stand just in time to see Xander shove Adam into one of the giant blocks of cement that support the bridge above us. Adam's skull cracks against the stone so hard my stomach lurches, and I scream Xander's name. I may not like Adam, but I don't want his head split open. What's he doing here anyway? My mind scrambles to catch up with what's happening around me.

But Adam doesn't crumple to the ground like I expect. He lands crouched on his feet. He snarls, lips pulled back in a way that doesn't seem human at all. It's so jarring that I take a step back.

Stacie stands next to him, her body tense like she's in a cage fight and ready to spring at Xander. Reina strides over to where two people I don't recognize hold a flailing, sopping-wet Aristelle.

They got her in the water to stop her flames.

She must have come here to save Adam and Stacie. They were the ones who got taken by vampires, but they were just bait to land a magician.

I'm about to explain to Xander what's happening before he snaps Adam in two, but before I can open my mouth, Aristelle lets out a vicious scream. Her skin steams under the hands that hold her.

"Dunk her again," Stacie screeches.

No. I turn to Stacie, my mouth opening in shock. Nothing quite makes sense. My former high school world and my magic world don't belong together at all.

The vamps aren't fast enough. Aristelle's arms ignite, and they drop her and move out of the water in a blur. Pausing, they share a look with each other.

I've never seen Aristelle so on fire. It gives the scene an eerie light, as if we're all standing on the brink of some kind of portal to hell.

"Get back here and help us," Adam yells.

"Sorry, man," says a vamp that looks like he spent the morning surfing. "You said easy magician blood. I like surfing in the sun, but not enough to take on four." He sprints off into the night with the girl following close behind.

"Four against two now," Xander says. "You're going to regret this."

"Stacie?" I ask, because it just seems like a reasonable question.

Xander straightens from his stance for a fraction of a second and glances back at me. "You know this leech?"

Everything explodes like a scene from an action movie. Adam

springs like a cat toward Xander's turned shoulder, but I don't see whether he lands the hit or not.

Stacie lunges forward with superhuman speed. She's nothing but a flash of blond, glowing red in Aristelle's burning light.

The word "vampire" screams in my head, but it refuses to connect with the bubbly, boy-obsessed girl who paints her nails a different shade of pink every day. Boy-obsessed or blood-obsessed? Maybe all those dates weren't what they seemed. But it makes no sense—we've been friends for a few years. How could she pretend for that long? How much magician blood did she have to drink? I'm trying to make it fit when cold hands with what I'm sure are hot-pink nails grip my upper arms from behind. The very tip of something sharp brushes against my neck along with sticky lip gloss.

I'd freeze if I weren't already standing like a statue.

My knife plinks into the water, and I realize my hands drip with cold sweat.

Vampire. *Vampire.* It's not Stacie at all anymore—it's this one word drumming in my head.

Xander and Reina have Adam pinned against the brick wall. His head snaps back and forth between them, but it's clear he's no match for the two of them together. Aristelle stands in front of him with a stake in one hand and a ball of fire in the other. Her damp hair clings to her cheeks. She lines the stake up with his chest.

The teeth leave my neck, and I feel like I can breathe again even though her hands on my arms are steel traps.

"I wouldn't," she says. Her voice jars me even more. It's still Stacie's voice—every bit as bright and bubbly as usual.

Everyone's head snaps in our direction.

"Aristelle," Xander says softly.

Aristelle passes her stake to Reina before lighting both her hands again and taking a few slow steps in my direction. The fire in her expression makes me want to take my chances with Stacie. I'm not confident that Aristelle cares if she burns me to the ground too.

Stacie drops my arms, but before I can even think about running, her hand squeezes the back of my neck so hard I cringe.

"You know I can snap her neck before you even let go of one of your little fireballs."

Aristelle shrugs.

I'm going to die. *Stacie's* going to kill me.

"Aristelle," Xander snaps.

She sighs, but she's still stepping slowly in our direction. "Fine. Give me her, and we'll let him go."

"We do it at the same time, or not at all. And something tells me Ava doesn't heal as well as Adam," Stacie says.

My name in her mouth pisses me off, and I finally snap out of it and swing an elbow back into her ribs.

She laughs. Her grip on my neck doesn't falter at all. "It's about time," she says, close enough to my ear to make my skin crawl. "I always thought you'd put up a fight." The smallest trace of sadness enters her voice. "Sometimes I even hoped you'd win." Her hands shift to grip my arms again. "On three," she shouts.

Xander nods as Stacie counts, and then I'm being shoved forward, and it looks like Aristelle will catch me, but she only gives me another shove behind her before launching herself at a running Adam. She hits his middle, and they roll together across the pavement and splash into the water. Xander and Reina are there in an instant, pulling him back against the cement block.

Stacie stops running and spins, hissing as she steps toward us. "We had a deal."

"I don't make deals with vampires." Aristelle stands up as Xander and Reina drag Adam to his feet again. "Besides, we did let him go. Not my fault if he's slow."

Stacie takes a step back, even though it looks like she wants to rip everyone's throat out. I'm surprised her face can even hold that vicious of an expression. I couldn't have even imagined it on her before now.

"Don't leave me," Adam growls.

"Sorry," she says. She shoots me one quick look I can't read before sprinting into the night.

Aristelle shakes her head. "Rule number one about vampires is that their own filthy lives matter to them more than anything else. They're not like us." She turns to Adam. "Sucks for you, bloodsucker."

Xander laughs, and the sound is so cold that it stops me from taking another step toward him.

"Reina, care to do the honors?" Aristelle asks.

"I'd rather not, actually. I just painted my nails." Reina glances down at her dove-gray nails.

Aristelle sighs. "You know you can magic them clean."

"They still won't feel the same. You know I hate all that ash on me."

Adam coughs—or chokes, it's hard to tell—and I suddenly feel bad for him. Roman's lesson throbs in the back of my mind. Then Roman's face. The sorrow on it.

"Let's not rush this," Xander says. "Tell us why you were following Ava."

"And you'll let me go?" Adam asks.

The three of them share a look.

"Of course," Aristelle says with a smile that would wilt flowers.

We all know that's a lie, but Adam swallows. A lie's all he has separating him from the stake in Reina's hand.

"We've been watching her for years. We want to find your compound. We're tired of you hunting us. Plus, having a whole blood bank of you would make life easier. This was just one plan of many: become friends with someone who might get tapped as an apprentice and then trick them into showing us where it is once they're in. We thought me showing up with Stacie would send Ava off-kilter—make her want to meet Stacie. Make her careless."

"Why not just follow one of the troupes?" I ask.

"They're too careful."

"Well, joke's on you. I couldn't remember how to get there if I tried."

Adam sighs. "I bet Stacie's disappointed. She devoted so much to this. . . . I mean, being your friend for the past few years? At least I didn't have to pretend to like you." He sneers.

He's trying to hurt me. It works.

"Why me?" I ask. "I wasn't using magic. How did you find me?"

He laughs. "Oh, you *were* using magic. All those silly coin tricks? You were using little amounts, making your grip stronger and your fingers faster. You were just too dense to realize it. I bet you're pretty talentless without it."

He's wrong. Mom taught me those tricks. Maybe I used magic sometimes, but I know I had skill too.

Xander looks Adam up and down. "Full offense intended, but you don't look like someone who could afford years of magician blood to pretend to be human, and evidence suggests you're not that great at hunting. How'd you two pull it off?"

"When I said "we," I didn't mean just me and Stacie."

"Who, then?" Aristelle says slowly.

"Numerius." Adam's lips curl when we all fall silent. "He's closer than you think."

"You're lying," Aristelle says. "If you're working with someone with those kinds of resources, why would you try and take a bite out of me? Fun?"

"He cut us off once Ava left. We didn't have to pretend anymore, and he thought it'd make us hungrier to find her again." He licks his lips. "It's hard to lose the sun after having it for so long. I suggested a little snatch and snack." He shakes his head. "Stacie said it was a bad plan."

"She was right," Aristelle says before turning to me. "I believe the honors of killing this beast should go to you." She plucks the stake from Reina's hand and holds it out.

I take it. I look up at Adam. He looks like a guy I don't like from high school. A regular old bully. This is different from my kills with Roman. *They* had *him* pinned down. *They* were in the process of killing *him*. My actions were all adrenaline and instinct. This is . . . calculated.

This is for Mom, I try to tell myself. But it doesn't raise the same pure fury in me as before. Damn, Roman. Part of me wants it back.

I look into Adam's face. "Did you kill my mom?" He probably knows the story. I think of him and Stacie, sharing a drink while laughing about my mom. It helps harden me.

He shakes his head so hard I think it might pop off. "No. I've only been a vampire for three years. I didn't want to be one at all. Someone attacked me behind a diner after I got off work. I still can't believe I died behind a diner. I don't know anything about your mom. They just told us to keep you close. I don't belong here."

"Shut up," Xander says, shaking him. "We don't care. You were about to kill Aristelle."

"We weren't going to drain her. We just needed some magician blood. We were going to lose the sun again."

"You belong in the dark," Xander snarls. "How many people have you killed?"

He doesn't answer.

Maybe that's answer enough. But the stake's limp in my hand, and I can't get my grip on it to tighten.

"Do it," Aristelle says. "Consider this your last test before you can really be part of our troupe. Show me what you're willing to do to protect a fellow magician. They would have drained me dry so they could keep masquerading in the sun with you. How far will you go for us, Ava?"

I search Xander's face for a way out. He gives me nothing.

What am I willing to do for family? The answer has always been anything. I need to show them they're my family now. Earn it, and then win the competition. If I do all that, then it can't be taken away from me.

I take slow steps until I'm staring at Adam's chest.

"Please," he begs. "I have a little sister."

I shake my head, and then the stake is gone from my hand and in his chest, but I didn't put it there. Xander's hand is tight around the hilt.

Adam gasps, his mouth opening and closing like he's desperate for air.

Red blooms briefly on his shirt before the wound starts disintegrating to a gray dust. Xander and Reina let go of him, and he drops to my feet as he continues to turn to ash from the wound outward. He flails, and one of his hands finds my ankle for a moment, and I stare at that and nothing else until it turns to ash too.

I step out of the water and then I bend at the waist and wrestle down the urge to heave up everything inside me, but even when I'm in control, I don't look up. I can't. I can't look at them at all.

I thought killing vampires would heal my open wounds, but I feel like I've opened a new one instead. Another memory I won't be able to shake.

I hear the others whispering behind me, and when I look up, only Xander's still here.

He's made of nothing but shadows, standing across from me. He prowls toward me like a monster from a nightmare, and I take a step back into the water. Cold dampness greets me, but my bones are colder.

"Hey." His voice is soft. He's not stalking closer—he's moving slowly because he knows I'm spooked.

I just watched *someone I knew* poof away like a piece of newspaper in a bonfire.

I can't make the fantasy of hunting monstrous creatures fit with stabbing a high school bully in the chest with a stake. He sat behind me in math class. I'm pretty sure he threw more than one gum wrapper at my head. He'd walk through the door at the same time as me so he could shove me in the shoulder.

But that was a ruse—his bullying gave Stacie an in to befriend me.

My first real friend was a freaking vampire.

And so was my first kiss.

I'm spiraling, and I need to catch myself. I always knew what my goals were and how to reach them. But things have changed. I don't ever want to do *this* again. I can have a code like Roman. That thought alone keeps me spiraling—I want to model myself after a *vampire* instead of my troupe because his moral code aligns more with mine.

Shit.

Xander's hand is on my elbow, leading me from the water and out from under the bridge. The cool night breeze opens up my airways and helps me breathe again.

"The first time's the hardest." Xander lets go of my elbow and presses a hand into my back, leading us down a walkway into more darkness where more vampires might be lurking, but I've had my fill of vampires for the night.

I don't tell him it's not my first time. I may have left out the part of hunting with Roman where we actually got attacked.

"You have to remember they're not human," he says. "Not any-more."

"He looked human." That's the part I can't shake. He wasn't trying to kill us in that moment. He was someone's big brother.

"You heard his silence when I asked him if he'd killed anyone. You don't know who it was or who they left behind." He turns to me and stops walking. His hand on my back presses me closer as his other hand pulls my chin up to look at him. "You should look at every vampire you see and assume they're the reason a couple more kids are parentless."

I cringe and almost yank away from him for using my past like that, but he's not wrong. That's why I'm out here in the first place, isn't it? That fury of wanting to change something unchangeable? He's also right that Adam didn't answer—or rather, that silence is its own answer.

I need something to help me erase the memory, though.

I latch on to Xander's jacket and push him backward until he's pressed against the chain-link fence lining this side of the park. We're not that far from where I kissed Roman—just on the other side of the fence. The thought propels me. I rise up on my toes and press my lips into his so we can share our darkness—the things we're willing to do for our family. I was always willing to wound others for Parker, and now I have another family to protect too.

Our lips part at the same time. We're nothing but hungry shadows. His hand on my back presses me closer, as if we could meld into one shadow instead of two. His other hand still holds my chin, and his fingers dig into my jaw in a way that should be painful but only makes me tighten my grip on him.

But then the image of his fingers wrapped around the stake in Adam's chest comes back to me, and I break our kiss. His hands drop to his sides immediately, but he doesn't move away.

The heaviness of our breathing fills the night until it's almost suf-focating.

If he knows what's going through my head, if he knows why I broke the kiss, he says nothing. Instead, he just grabs my hand in the dark and squeezes it lightly. "Let's go home."

I nod, but that word doesn't feel right, even though I desperately want it to.

CHAPTER 20

I wear a dramatic black gown with a skirt made of tattered layers of tulle and a black bodice with a single gold thread crisscrossing from my waist to my chest, where the stitching curves around the high neckline in a tangle of wild vines. My hand brushes along the banister of a curving set of stairs. I look like I'm ready to take an album cover photo. I've never worn anything like this, and I'm surprised by how much I like it.

I reach the bottom first.

"I hope we get there soon." We're on the way to the tithe. I pretended like I didn't already know about it when my troupe told me. We've been winding down staircases and hallways for at least ten minutes. If the magic can take us anywhere we want, why is it insisting on the long way?

Xander huffs. "The house is playing with us today."

It feels more like trickery than play, but I don't want to say it out loud.

Turquoise paint peels off the next door, revealing streaks of bare wood beneath. Rust coats the doorknob and scrapes at my palm as I turn it. We step into a hallway re-created from a gothic horror movie. Faded blue wallpaper hangs in strips on the walls; the floor's rough wooden planks are cracked and missing chunks; climbing roses reach up the walls and curl across the scuffed baseboards as if they long to drag this hallway into the gardens outside.

For a second, I think the magic's missing from this particular part of the mansion, but then I feel it, a vibration against my skin like a throbbing bass. The sensation smothers my own magic. I glance around again. The magic isn't gone—there's too much. It's grown wild.

"It's fine," Xander says. "We only have to come to this room once a year."

His words do nothing to help the unease that continues to roll down my spine.

We reach another door at the end of the hall. Roses grow up it and weave through cracks in the aged wood. The handle hides among the leaves, and this time I wait for Xander to open it. He jiggles it until it clicks. As he pushes it, some of the vines tear, as if nobody else arrived this way.

I step inside and barely hold back a gasp. Gold coats the floor as if it were poured from hundreds of paint cans, drying in ripples that make it feel like stepping onto golden lava. The same gold drips from the walls in frozen rivers. The room's an octagon, and each corner holds an ornate column made from soft beige stones and carved to look like vines of flowers climbing. At the top, the vines break to reveal a person carved into the stone. Each one lifts their hands upward, and from their fingers more etched vines flow across the arched stones of the ceiling. It reminds me of an ancient cathedral, but instead of an altar, the largest rosebush I've ever seen rises from the center. The twisting branches reach out like they're trying to snag anyone who gets close enough. The closed red rosebuds make me think of drops of blood.

Just like at the opening party, everyone here is dressed in bright colors. They look like jewels against the gold of a dragon's lair. The effect is almost overwhelming. Except me. I stick out like a lump of coal among the treasure. My stare snags on one other person dressed in all black. Roman. I haven't seen him since our kiss. I don't know why that's the first thing that comes to mind. I also haven't seen him since I watched his fangs sink into another vampire's neck.

That's better.

"Why'd you pick black for the dress?" I ask Xander. It appeared in my armoire just like all my other outfits.

"I didn't." Xander's eyebrows draw together. "I thought you magicked it to black. Diantha picked your dress. I know it was green."

My eyes dart to Roman again. I'm a gothic princess, and he looks like a vampire prince.

Xander sees where I'm staring and grumbles, "Of course he would."

Roman lifts his wineglass, acknowledging our stares or his role in my black dress, I'm not sure which. My stomach clenches at the red in his cup. Willow looks my way and smiles happily in her pale pink gown. The breast of her dress is an overturned heart—the point rests in the hollow of her throat, secured by a choker of soft pink jewels. The waist puffs out in white material made of spun clouds. She's sweet dreams personified, and she pops against the gold.

"Bastard," Xander spits, looking back to me.

"Why would he change my dress?" It seems like a childish prank someone might pull at summer camp.

Unless it's a threat. I know his secret. This could be a reminder of how easily he can get to me.

I'm a walking funeral compared to everyone else.

The room fills with even more color. Aristelle, Reina, and Diantha appear at my shoulder in their signature colors. Diantha stares a second too long at my dress.

"Roman changed it," I say. "Green would have been so much better."

"Figures," Aristelle mutters. If everyone else is a jewel in a dragon's lair, Aristelle is the dragon's fire. Her strapless gown starts out red at the top and then fades in color until it becomes a startling yellow that swirls around her feet.

"We could change it back," I say.

Diantha smiles. "It'd draw too much attention. Besides, black suits you."

"Thanks." I try not to notice Xander cringing beside me.

The room begins to fill even more around us, and we get pressed close to the rosebush in the center of the room until the crowd parts and Lucius strides through. He wears a golden suit embroidered with chaotic black vines. As his eyes scan the crowd, they settle on me for a moment. Our outfits are inverted matches, and now I look like I somehow knew. He gives me the briefest frown before turning away to address the crowd. "We all make sacrifices to keep ourselves safe, but more important, to keep the world safe from the curse Numerius triggered so long before. Today, we sacrifice even more to keep our stronghold safe. Because without this place, without me, we are nothing. Vampires will drain every last drop of magician blood, or worse: imprison us so we're nothing more than blood bags, heightening their power until nobody can stand against them." His voice is almost a snarl. The fierceness in his face and the bitterness in his eyes make me lean forward. Other magicians murmur their agreement. Some clap. There's an energy in the crowd that's its own kind of power. People believe him.

I can't help but look at Roman. He's already looking at me,

wondering, I think, if this little speech will draw me in just as certainly as it's drawing in everyone else. Well, almost everyone. Some people look decidedly grim. I catch sight of Julia with her arms folded across her chest. She doesn't buy it.

I meet Roman's stare again and shake my head the tiniest bit. I don't buy into the fact that all vampires are evil—not when I know one, and not when he risked a lot to make sure I didn't end up dead from a trick I couldn't handle or a vampire I couldn't fight off. If the rest of them knew about Roman, maybe they would change. I glance over at my troupe. Despite the rivalry they have with him, I can't imagine them staking him. If he came forward, he could change this. We could be doing good, working with the vampires who don't kill to rid the world of the ones that do. And then I could still be a part of this, because I don't want to leave the people surrounding me right now.

But if I told them what I know, it wouldn't be my life on the line.

My eyes narrow in on Lucius. He lost a sister to a vampire, but all I see and hear is rage. I wonder if he even feels grief anymore or if it's been burned away by hate.

I look at him and see what I almost became.

Roman stopped me.

But he still lied. I can't trust him.

Lucius has stopped talking, and Natasha and her brother approach the rosebush. Each one holds out their hand, and a vine reaches out, winding up their arms. I don't understand what's happening until I see blood start to drip, running down their arms and fingertips.

"Blood magic." I turn to Xander. "You're using even more blood magic."

The blood gathers in a pool near their feet, and when the vines finally release their arms, the red puddle dwindles as if it's being sucked down a drain.

Roman goes up next. It's only him, and he has to stand there forever until his skin's so pale, I'm not sure how anyone could imagine he's anything but a vampire. He wobbles slightly as he heads back toward Willow. She tries to prop him up, but he shrugs her off.

My troupe goes next. Diantha and Reina both cringe and look away from the thorns that dig into their arms. The twins smile like they enjoy the pain. Aristelle and Xander remain stoic. Their blood continues to flow long after the vines release the others. They hold the most magic because they've killed the most vampires. All their late nights hunting, they were protecting the rest of the troupe from this moment. They were making the kills so the others wouldn't have to. I hope they killed only the ones who deserved it, but . . . something tells me there's no distinction with them.

I don't want to watch anymore, so I glance down at my feet and blink. The floor's not just gold any longer. Thin red lines vibrate beneath the surface, branching like twigs. Or veins. My pulse throbs in my throat. Everything feels heavy. The blood magic is thick in the air.

I don't even see Xander and Aristelle finish. I just sense them around me.

"I don't like it," I whisper.

Someone grabs my hand. I look up into Reina's eyes. "It's only once a year."

I'm not sure that helps.

Another lone magician steps up. He turns as pale as Roman as the bush sucks him dry. He wobbles, and still the vine holds him. He sags, eyes rolling into his head, and then he slumps to the ground. Still the blood flows, but now instead of running down his fingers, it travels down his shoulder, streaming over his chest and chin before dripping to the ravenous floor.

Nobody stops it.

I meet Willow's wide eyes.

When the thorns finally give him up, Lucius waves a hand, and the man is carried away.

"He's going to be okay," I say.

But nobody agrees or disagrees.

As the bloodletting goes on, the roses open, and blood trickles from their petals like scarlet rain. The people giving blood last end up with red streaks down their faces and clothes, and there's so much blood that I avert my stare upward instead. It's worse. The blood climbs the columns as well, turning the carved leaves red. The lips on the statues turn the garish color of rubies.

I don't like it, but nobody's dying—at least I don't think so. Maybe this is just another thing to get used to.

Blood magic's not all bad.

Lucius is speaking again, and I have to force myself to listen.

He's smiling, and cold violence lurks around the edges of it. "The competition continues now," he says.

Everything goes dark, even though I'm almost certain my eyes are still open. I close them against a rush of air so strong I can't breathe. When I open them again, I blink up at blue sky framed by towering hedges.

CHAPTER 21

Twisting green branches loom on every side of me. I twist, feet crunching on the familiar gray stones laced with rubies. But I'm not in the courtyard. Every direction looks exactly the same—I'm in the center of an X with hedges lining each path. A maze. I take a single step and get snagged by a scraggly branch from the climbing roses that weave into the shrubs.

Still dressed in my ridiculous black gown, I must look like a gothic princess, escaped from the haunted castle.

If this is our first test, we must have to find our way out.

I close my eyes to see if I can feel the magic of the mansion.

Nothing.

It seems more like blind luck than skill unless I'm missing some clue, but I can't stand in one spot forever. I pick a path and run. At the end it breaks into three other paths that curve off. I check each one, but they only break into more directions. It just looks like trial and error.

A wave of panic gets my feet moving, and I curve around turn after turn, heading in meaningless directions until I stop, panting. Maybe

I'm missing something. *Breathe*, I tell myself. *Think*. A pinch at my ankle distracts me, and I glance down at a rose branch that has wound its way around my ankle.

"What the hell?"

It tightens, and I yelp. My fingers fumble for my knives, and I don't bother with magic. I bend down and hack through the branch. It reaches back out for me, and I run, hissing in pain at the thorny anklet that's still digging into me. I stop just long enough to bend down and unwind it, pricking my fingers too. I should heal myself, but I can't focus. The hedges seem to be closing in, or maybe the roses are growing thicker, reaching out farther.

I run, turning and winding, until a puff of pink darts behind a hedge up ahead.

I recognize the shade. I was jealous of it earlier.

"Willow!" I yell.

She pops back around the corner and squeals.

I've never been so relieved to see another person.

She flings herself into me. I hug her and don't hate it, which is another rare occurrence.

"Thank God!" She pulls back and holds me at arm's length. Her frothy pink dress snags on my scratchy black lace, and the material stays connected even after she lets me go.

My magic tingles with her standing next to me. Maybe that's what this test is about—finding someone to work with.

"Do you know where you're going?" I ask.

"Not a clue. I was just trying to get there fast."

"Maybe we can sense it now with our magic together."

"Worth a shot."

I try again. My magic barely bubbles like an almost flat soda. I don't feel any type of pull. I look to Willow, but she shakes her head.

"I guess we just start moving again." I glance at the darkening violet sky above us. "And fast."

We take off—probably looking like some weird prom photo shoot for a teen magazine.

We arrive at a dead end. A little stone bench with legs that curve like unwinding scrolls sits boxed in by the hedges. Red lilies grow around it, and it's nice to see a flower that doesn't bite. Willow plops down. "We must be missing something. Could you cut through the brush?"

I don't get a chance to answer.

A vine lunges out of the hedge and curls around Willow's throat. Others snag into her dress, yanking her backward off the bench. She screams as I lunge, pulling two knives out and slashing into the vines over and over again until she can crawl away.

"Run!" I yell.

Willow's up and moving, but a branch trips me, and I sprawl on my hands and knees.

Willow crouches beside me. "Are you okay?" Dots of blood ring her neck like a gruesome choker.

I don't answer. I'm bleeding. A lot. My hand landed on a vine full of thick thorns that's still trying to wrap around my wrist. Wet heat seeps from my palm into the stones. I hack the plant away from me.

"Can you heal it?"

I shake my head.

"I can try," she offers.

"Be quiet."

She tenses beside me, but we don't have time for hurt feelings.

I didn't notice it before, but I can feel the blood from my wounds tugging me in a certain direction, an arrow in a compass.

The feeling makes my skin crawl. Like a monster is calling, and my blood answers.

I don't like it.

It's blood magic again. Why is blood magic so prevalent in a group who fights against blood magicians? But maybe blood magic wasn't how we were supposed to get back at all. Maybe I'm accidently cheating.

I swallow. I'm already cut. I can use it just this once.

We need to get out. The sun's gone, and Willow's a faded pink shadow beside me. This isn't just about me.

I rise to my feet. "Follow me." I stride instead of running. My franticness is gone. The magic is calling me to its waiting, hungry mouth, and I only need to listen.

I pause a couple more times to spin in circles and feel for that extra tug of blood seeping from my palm. The pull grows stronger and stronger until we turn a corner and stand in front of a cheerful yellow door.

Willow cheers. "You did it!"

It's too dark to read her face, but I hear a bit of jealousy in the way she says *you* did it and not *we*.

I could have found it without her and had one less competitor.

I flinch at my own thoughts.

"Let's go," she says.

"One second." I bend down and rip off part of my dress, squeezing the material against my palm to stop the bleeding. Now that we're so close to the house, the magic feels like it wants to pull every last drop of blood from my body. The sensation makes my head swim.

"Are you okay?" Willow asks.

I nod and head for the door, opening it and stepping through.

We stand in a circular room with burgundy walls that rise and rise until darkness swallows them. Twelve black doors are spaced evenly in the walls.

We aren't the first ones back.

Barry barely spares us a glance as he pulls open one of the black doors to reveal a wall of bricks. He slams it so hard my teeth knock together, and then he's on to the next, pulling it open on another brick wall.

"He's already checked them all," says a girl sitting cross-legged on the floor. She tugs her two strawberry blond braids. She's the girl who pulled carnations from her sleeve for the opening test. She looks even younger up close, maybe only fourteen. Too young to be here. Where are her parents? It's a ridiculous question I should know better than to ask.

"Shut up, Lucy," the boy growls, slamming another door.

Lucy shrugs at us, nibbling on one of her fingernails. "That's Barry. He's been here the longest."

"Try magic," Lucy says.

"Fine." Barry steps back.

I'm surprised they haven't already. Magic pulses thick and heavy in the room.

I step toward him, then stop. Gold letters are inscribed on the black marble floor. DON'T CHOOSE, JUST DESIRE repeats again and again in a circle around the room's center.

Of course. The magic controls everything here, shifting the rooms and passageways to take the magicians where they want to go.

Barry clenches his fists.

"Wait." I gesture to the writing on the floor. "Did you read this?"

He turns to me with a scowl. "Of course. I know how to read."

"I don't think we should use magic to force ourselves through. All we have to do is want it badly enough, and the door will let us pass. Let me try."

Barry's face contorts with rage. "Nobody wants this more than I do."

He swings the door open again, faces the bricks, and hurtles a blast of power so strong the floor buckles. The bricks turn to dust, revealing darkness beyond.

Barry tosses me a smug look.

I recognize the faint hiss, but I don't have time to register what it belongs to.

I don't have time to save him.

Not before a black arrow sails from the dark and pierces his throat.

CHAPTER 22

My instincts have been honed on survival for as long as I can remember—Parker's and then my own. Nobody else's really mattered to me until now. Parker's not here, and so my first instinct is to save myself and Willow. My arm flings out in front of her.

Barry goes down on his knees and then falls backward.

I spring forward and grab his legs, yanking him away from the darkness, painting an awful streak of blood across the floor, but I need to shut the door. Once he's out of the way, I leap forward and slam it, accidentally stepping in a little puddle of blood covering the word "desire."

Willow kneels next to him, blood soaking through her dress at the knees. She presses her fingers to his neck. He gurgles.

Lucy sobs, rocking in the center of the floor. "I want to go home," she says, quietly at first and then loudly as she jumps to her feet and spins wildly, but the front door we all came through is gone. Only the twelve identical doors remain.

I stare at the blood coating his neck. My stomach lurches, and I can't help but think of Roman's sister, but he hadn't made it sound like dying in the competition was *normal*—just a horrible possibility. The magic's so thick it chokes me. It's thick because this is an illusion. *This is fake. This is fake. This is fake.* I *need* to believe it.

I try not to look at his neck. I try not to think of my mom, but even that wasn't like this. She had two small, almost bloodless wounds. They wanted her blood, after all.

I need to focus on what *I* want. Performing. Killing vampires. This is only a test to see if I can handle the gore of it all. Everything is a test. *This is fake.*

Willow holds one of Barry's hands. Tears stream down her face, but she bites her lip like she's holding back full sobs. Barry's other hand grasps at air. This is a test. And whether the magic knows it or not, it's the worst test it could give me.

I lean down and grab his reaching hand. His eyes are wide, and the determination that was in them before is dulled. Everything is dull.

I brace myself. Illusion or not, I don't want another memory of someone's life leaving them. Will it feel just like Mom? That little twitch? Like a thread breaking after being pulled too tight? My cheeks are hot with tears.

But the moment doesn't come. Barry starts to sink, like the floor's turned to quicksand beneath him and he's Artax, and I already know there's nothing we can do to save him.

Willow's tugging at his hand, but his face is already sinking, the black tiles re-forming over him like hardening sludge.

I step back as he disappears. Even if it weren't an illusion, he's probably getting healed up now. They weren't going to let him just die in front of us.

Blood covers my foot. I gag.

Against the black marble floor, the blood could be mistaken for spilled oil. Why didn't the mansion swallow that too? To make it *feel* real? If so, it's working. I let my vision blur so I can pretend it's not there.

"This isn't right." Willow stands next to me now, whispering.

Lucy pounds on the empty wall where the front door used to be.

"It can't be real," I say. "This is all just an illusion. Part of the game." I wave a hand toward the blood like it will disappear. It doesn't.

Willow swallows. She stares at her red, shaking hands. "It *feels* real."

We eye each other. I'm surprised she's keeping it together. She's stronger than I thought.

We share a nod. Real or not, there is no backward path for us to take.

"Lucy, please be quiet," I snap.

Her panic dies down to a low whimper.

I draw a breath, unlock my knees, and move to a random door. It doesn't matter which one if I'm right.

And I have to be right. There's no other option.

"Don't," Lucy whimpers. I hear the rustle of her scooting away from me and the door.

Willow says my name, but she doesn't tell me to stop. Somebody has to do it, and she's not volunteering.

My hand grips the cool brass handle. It does not heat to my touch like my knives. No magic pulses in it. My fingers feel cold and human. Perhaps it's a sign.

No. It's trying to shake me. I want this. I will not turn around and go back to the life I had before, where I have to rely on someone else to throw my brother a birthday party that puts light in his eyes. I want that power. I will fight for it.

The magic answers me, crawling up my skin like ants until I shiver from it. I twist the handle and pull.

Heat blasts my face, and I step back from a hallway covered in coals flickering red.

A door waits across the path.

I grin in the heat as my feet grow cold. I lift the hem of my dress. My shoes are gone.

Shit.

I step away and try another door, willing the magic to be kinder.

It doesn't listen. More coals.

I open all the doors until I'm sweating from the heat coming off the paths of coal. I turn to Willow. Her face is blotchy from the warmth. She shakes her head.

"I don't think we have a choice," I answer.

Lucy sobs, and I wish she would stop.

Looks like I'm first.

I step back to my original door—the coals somehow seem hotter, red and vicious. A punishment for trying the other doors? Probably. I can barely breathe from the magic rolling around the room with us. It's in control here—not us.

I grasp at it, calling it to me. It bucks away from me like a wild horse, but I fight and coax it all at once, wrapping it around my feet, asking for a shield until my feet burn with their own fire, and I almost cry out from it. Instead, I bite my tongue and run.

The coals roll under my feet like riverbed stones.

What if the other door doesn't open?

I push the thought away when a flicker of heat breaks through my magic. Doubt will kill me.

I reach the door and pull, stepping out onto cool wood flooring.

Turning, I smile back at Lucy and Willow gaping at me.

My smile drops when I glance at all the blood behind them on the floor. Too much.

I decide not to think about it.

"Let's go." I wave my hand at them, coaxing.

Willow keeps shaking her head while Lucy cries.

"You have to."

Resolve finally settles on Willow's face, and she picks up her skirt and runs. I have to jump away as she barrels past and skids to a stop, then hops back and forth on her red feet.

"Are you okay?"

She bites her lip and nods. Her feet look sunburned. "Are you?"

"Little hot." I don't know why I lie. My feet are cool against the wood. I'm almost giddy from the rush of commanding so much magic. I fight down a smile that doesn't feel like mine, like the magic's pulling those strings now.

Lucy's scream jerks our attention back to the door as she stumbles through, going down on her knees just as she passes the doorframe so that we both have to grab her arms and drag her feet out of the coals.

So many blisters bubble on her skin, I have to look away and suck in a breath to drag down the bile working its way up my throat. She didn't use the magic at all.

Whoever brought her here to this competition had to know that she doesn't stand a chance.

Maybe that's why Roman tried to get me not to come. He thought I'd be the girl burning from lack of control.

He was wrong.

I wiggle my perfectly cold toes.

And then I hate myself again when I look back at Lucy, tears running down her face, no longer whimpering.

I turn away and clear my throat. "Let's go."

The hallway is long and curving, and I lead the way as Willow shoulders some of Lucy's weight behind me.

We turn one of the many corners and stop.

A magician's box stretches the full length of the hallway. Inside it, a blue-haired girl turns her head toward us, grinning so fiercely her red lips are a gash across her pale face. Her feet stick out the other end. Her arms are free and dangling from two small holes in each side of the box. The middle of the box doesn't exist. Her bare torso, floating in empty space, connects both sides. A giant black blade floats above her middle like a guillotine.

"Hello." She giggles. "You need one more."

"One more for what?" I don't trust her smile. She reminds me of Harley Quinn, but less stable.

"To cut me in half, silly." She gestures to her stomach. "Three won't do at all."

"No way," Willow says before I can even consider it. "We're not doing it." She looks at me. Whatever she sees there makes her repeat herself. "We're not doing it. We can just duck under the damn box." She lets go of Lucy, who sags against the wall, and steps toward the girl.

Iron bars blink into existence all around the box, floor to ceiling, and we are left standing in front of massive gates locked in the middle by a single torso. Willow scrambles back.

"Silly, silly, silly," the girl sings, shaking her head back and forth so her hair shimmers like water. She stops and stares at me. "You know *you* can."

"What?" I snap, but I know what she means. I *can* do it. I can cut her in half if I need to. She won't be hurt—not for real. Magicians heal. Can they recover from being cut in half, though? I don't know. Although I'd have to hope this girl wouldn't be so overly cheerful if she couldn't.

I move to the blade and tug.

Willow screams something at me, but I am all white noise and action. I can't think or I won't do what needs to be done.

The blade doesn't budge.

I eye the smooth black metal.

Eight grooves for eight hands indent the handle. Four people. We need one more, just like she said.

She nods at me. "He's coming."

"Who?" The word barely leaves my mouth when I hear footsteps. I turn and face Ethan, in another horrible red suit, perfectly pressed. I glance down at my own ragged dress.

He takes in each of us quickly, eyes narrowing on the girl's torso and the blade above it.

He knows what needs to be done. He looks at me again. "What are you waiting for?"

I'm almost glad to see him. "We need a fourth person."

"Let's do it." He reaches for the blade, and I do too. I don't know what it says about me that I'm with him in this. We can't go back. There is no back. When left with no other choice, wouldn't anyone do whatever was necessary to keep going?

Lucy answers for me. "I'm not doing this." She backs down the hall past Willow, who doesn't try to stop her.

Anger flashes across Ethan's face, and he moves forward like he'll drag her back by her hair if he has to, and I don't know whether to grab his arm and stop him or help him do it, but I don't have to make the choice.

Another girl rounds the corner and bumps into Lucy. Grabbing Lucy's arm and righting her before she can tumble, the girl takes us all in quickly with hazel eyes. She wears a stunning purple gown that bleeds to black at the bottom, and I can't tell if it's blood or if the dress came like that. I could take a guess. Her loose, wavy red hair is darkened at the tips with what looks like blood.

"I'm Nadine," she says.

"Don't care," Ethan says, even though I know he knows who she is. He jerks a thumb toward the blade. "Will you help us slice through this girl or not?"

Nadine takes in the scene. Her mouth tightens, but she nods.

"You all are bonkers," Lucy says. She backs into the velvet damask wallpaper—and suddenly the wallpaper starts curling around her and dragging her inside a wall now soft as pudding.

"Lucy!" Willow lunges, but it's too late. Just Lucy sinks through the wall; Willow slams into it, bouncing backward.

Screams echo—faint enough for us to convince ourselves we didn't hear them.

"You only needed four," the blue-haired girl says.

"Let's get this over with." I put my hands on the blade, and the others follow until we all wait for Willow. She looks like she'll be sick. She takes a step back.

I grab her hands and yank her forward, placing them on the blade and then following with mine.

The blue-haired girl laughs as the blade slices air and then her torso as if it were only air too.

The gate swings open, and the boxes the blue-haired girl is in move apart on their own, clearing a path. The girl, in two dripping, bloody pieces, is still laughing as we walk through. The gate clanks shut behind us, and by the time we turn, she is whole and standing in front of the now solid bars. She's naked, but none of us bat an eye. Her blue hair drapes over her chest.

My heart pounds with relief.

"I knew it was a trick," I say.

She meets my eyes and winks. "If you say so, Ava."

I squirm. "How'd you know my name?"

She laughs. "My name's Cecily, and I know things." She opens her closed fist to reveal a key.

"Follow me," she says as she pads softly past us.

Shouts echo down the hallway, and I glance back at the gate that's not a gate anymore. "Others are coming," I say.

Cecily doesn't turn around. "No, they're not. There's only four."

"I can hear them." But when I look back again, all I can hear are echoes.

"Only four," she says again, and this time I don't argue.

We trail her down the hall to a double door, and she pulls another key from behind Ethan's ear with a wink. She pushes the key into the lock and turns it. "Congratulations," she says as she pushes the door open.

CHAPTER 23

We step into the tithing room to a crowd of cheering magicians. Xander beams at me. I try to smile back, but the rush of using so much magic disappears. I wish I could've known it was coming, but I'd asked when the next part of the competition would be, and he'd said they couldn't tell us. The Society wanted it to startle us.

It succeeded.

My knees shake. The nerves I kept frozen before unthaw under their applause. Normally I'd bask in the praise and the magic roaring inside me, but right now I only want to puke.

Lucius waves us to the center of the room so that we have to stand right next to the ravenous rosebush. Blood still drips from the petals and then disappears into the floor below like a vampiric fountain. Lucius's eyes glitter with frost as he looks us up and down, assessing. He smiles at Ethan. Truth be told, he looks better than the rest of us in our torn, bloodied dresses.

I silently thank Roman for messing with my dress. At least no one can tell there's blood on me.

"Welcome back," Lucius says. "You are the final four."

If Ethan lifts his chin any higher, he'll be staring at the ceiling.

"And each of you showed a command of blood magic to get here."

So it wasn't an accident that my cut palm led me out. Blood was the only way free.

"We only use blood magic when absolutely necessary: to heal, to defend, to live. You showed the instinct to do what you had to do to win. Remember this. It may save your life one day." He holds out a hand under the bloody roses and catches a single drop, which he lets run down his finger. "The next stage will begin tomorrow. You may go," Lucius says.

Just like that, it's over. The others drift away. I follow, trying not to stare at my feet and the red veins that run under the golden floor. Are there more of them now? Is this why Mom ran? Did she leave this place and take her chances with the vampires out in the world because this very mansion was a leech?

I'm through the next round. I've proven myself, and now I need answers. I whip back around before I can stop myself. "What happened to the others?"

Lucius turns to me, regarding me with eyes that would make me shiver if I hadn't just cut a girl in half. "They did not have what it takes." His words are slow and pointed.

"Obviously. But what happened to them? Where did they go?"

A smile creeps across his face with the deceptive patience of an adult who's tired of questions from a kid who's not even theirs. I've seen the look before. I've pushed that look to its breaking point one too many times and paid for it. My hands shake, but I clench my fingers into my palms.

He leans toward me. "They go home, little girl. You will go home with the barest sliver of the power you've developed a taste for and no memory of what it's like to have more. Maybe one day you'll feel the buzz of magic under your skin, but you won't understand it. You'll brush it away and go on with your inconsequential life."

I flinch. I love the power, but I could live without it if I got to keep my troupe—my new family. But I won't remember them either.

I shake myself. He wants to push me over the edge. He wants me to drop this conversation and move on. But I'm not good at doing what those in a position of power want—never have been.

It's my turn to lean forward. "I saw the house eat a dying boy today. What about him?"

Lucius backs away from me and laughs. "Illusions, my child. Hasn't your troupe taught you that everything is an illusion?" His eyes slide behind me. I realize for the first time that the entire hall is silent. "Perhaps I should speak to them about their choices." A threat sits coldly in his words, just waiting to be released.

I don't dare turn around to see my troupe's faces, but their fear presses at my back, so I step away from him. I shake my head, dropping my eyes slightly.

For them, I will obey. I will not ask any more questions. At least not to him.

He turns from me without a second look, satisfied he broke me into submission.

I am good at pretending. I hunch over and scurry back to my troupe like a scared mouse.

The fury on Aristelle's face makes me a little less scared of Lucius. "What's the matter with you?" she hisses as she grabs my arm.

I open my mouth to snarl back, but then I see Diantha behind her, trembling so hard it seems only Reina's arms hold her together. They're scared of him—more scared than they were of vampires in a dark alley. I swallow down my defense.

"I'm sorry," I say instead. The words aren't easy for me.

Aristelle lets go of me and stalks away, and it's Xander's turn to grab me, squeezing my upper arms and spinning me toward him. "What were you thinking?"

"Tell me what happened to the other apprentices," I shoot back.

He freezes for a second, like he doesn't know the answer.

"Exactly what he said, Ava. Exactly what we already told you. You go home without any memory of this. Everything else is part of an elaborate show to test you." His words are hard with impatience. As he speaks, he looks over my head in the direction of Lucius. "Just keep doing what you need to do to win." He finally stares back down at me. "Will you?" He gives me a hard shake, and my head bobs from it, looking like a nod.

He lets go of me, satisfied.

Past his shoulder, Roman watches me.

"I'll be right back," I say to Xander.

I push through the crowd, dodging over-the-top magicians that somehow seem garish now in this room that reeks of blood.

I walk up to where Roman's standing, watching Willow dab her newly red gown with napkins.

"Did you change my dress?" It's not the question I mean to ask, but somehow, despite everything, this answer still matters.

I stand close enough that my shoulder grazes his upper arm. And my mind screams *vampire*, but if he's trying to intimidate me, I want him to know it won't work.

"That's what you want to ask me?"

"Yes."

His body rises and falls with a shrug. Answer enough.

"You don't scare me."

His eyes widen. "Ava . . . that's not—"

I'm looking at his face, his lips, remembering them pressed against mine and then pressed against a vampire's throat, and whatever I might understand about vampires, however my feelings might have changed, my gut reaction still makes my stomach heave and my fingers tremble.

I back away, searching.

My eyes settle on Annalise drifting around the edges of the room like a ghost haunting this place. At some point she stood under that cursed rosebush, because red streaks have dyed her hair and tiny specks sprinkle her dress. I move to the outside edges, trying not to look like I'm tracking her. I can feel stares on me, though. Maybe Roman's, maybe my troupe's. I lean against the wall despite the red veins spreading upward like cracks in the foundation, trying to look natural, but the wall's warm. My stomach lurches. I want out of this room, but I take deep breaths, looking out at the sea of faces without really seeing. All I care about is one. I'm directly in her looping path now, and for a second I think she's going to pass right through me as if she's an actual ghost, but at the last minute she steps slightly to the side, walking by me so closely that her hair, spiderweb thin and wet, brushes my arm. I barely hold back a gag. She smells of copper and rotting roses.

"Hello," I say.

She keeps walking.

"Hello?" This time I touch her arm. I don't want to. My hand comes back sticky.

She pauses, tilting her head like *I'm* the ghost whispering in her ear. She turns toward me with big gray eyes the color of pale morning sky. "Can I help you?" Her voice is a light rasp. She seems surprised by it.

"Sorry to bother you . . ." I trail off. I didn't exactly plan what to say. "Shouldn't you be wiping the memories of the apprentices who just lost?"

She blinks. "What memories?" Her eyes share the same dense fog that blankets this place, but they sharpen a little as she seems to register the blood on her. "I'm sorry. I really need to change."

She drifts away, and I start to take a step after her, but a warm, paper-soft hand closes around my arm.

"Best not to draw attention to yourself."

I turn to meet Julia's tired face. Up close, she's older than I thought, with the deep lines on her face of someone who used to experience every emotion without hiding any of them. There's a slight droop to her cheeks, though, like some emotions were too much.

"Julia."

She doesn't seem surprised that I know her name. "You look like your mother," she says.

"You're the first person to ever tell me that." I look like my dad. He had yellow-blond hair streaked with white-blond in the sun. One of the few photos my mom kept out of him was the three of us at the beach. Dad held me in his arms, and it was clear that I was made of all the highlights in Dad's hair and Mom's bottomless brown eyes. I used to hold that picture all the time and smile and point out how I looked like Daddy, and Mom would nod and look away. I think it hurt her sometimes to see him in me.

"Yes. I suppose your hair used to look like your father's." She tenses, and her eyes flit away from me for a moment, scanning the room like she's looking for a lion that might pounce.

"So you saw me when I was a kid. You kept in touch with my mom."

"You could say that."

I don't really know what to say next, so I blurt, "I want to know everything."

"Do you?" Julia raises her brows and then furrows her forehead. "What did Cassia tell you about the Society?"

It takes me a second to realize she means Mom. Mom went by Cass. I never heard her called anything else.

"Nothing." The bitterness in my voice surprises me. I wish Mom had let me in, and maybe she would have, or maybe she would have kept this world hidden from me forever. Maybe she would have seen my troupe's show with me and made up some explanation for how the magic was only illusions. The lump in my stomach tells me I'm right.

Julia actually looks surprised. "But you found your way here anyway." Her voice goes quiet and pensive, like she's talking more to herself than me. "And you have quite a lot of power."

"You were in my mom's troupe."

"Yes," Julia says. "With Edgar and Samuel . . . and Lucius. We were inseparable for a long time."

So Lucius *was* part of Mom's troupe. "She used to tell me about you all, how much she loved performing with you." Not Lucius, for some reason, but I don't mention that. "So why did she leave?"

"Because she fell in love."

"With my father? Was he like you?"

"Joseph?" Julia laughs, although her eyes are tight around the edges. "Not even a little bit. He was a true artist. Each illusion was a piece of brilliant craft to him. He wanted nothing to do with our tricks, but your mom was enamored with his talent and wanted him to join us. He ended up winning *her* over instead, not the other way around."

"She gave up magic for him."

"She gave up a *lot* for him." Julia chews on her lip for a moment, as if she wants to say something else. She doesn't.

"I bet you have stories."

She nods.

"And Lucius and Edgar?"

"Some stories can only hurt you. You're in too deep here to dig into the past."

Mom left, and they don't like deserters. She doesn't need to say it. I'm the wrong kind of legacy.

"I just want to know." A childish begging enters my voice, but Julia's face has already hardened against me.

She looks me up and down. "You have more fire in your belly than your mother ever did."

I don't know whether to take the compliment or be annoyed at the diss to my mom.

"Just don't run like her." She turns and disappears, and I'm not sure if she just fades into the crowd or if she actually disappears. I push after her and plow into a tall man in a gold vest with red sequins sewn into a pattern that matches the blood veined throughout the room. He smiles at me, and the six hoops piercing his bottom lip link and slide, switching places in his flesh while I watch. My fingers go numb, and my brain feels fuzzy until a hand grabs me and rips me away.

I turn my head to Xander.

"Please don't stare at hypnotists too long." His voice is overly bright. "You must be exhausted. Shall we go?" He links his arm into the crook of my elbow and gently tugs me to a cherry-stained door carved with ivy.

"I don't think this is the door we came in."

He chuckles. "You know it doesn't matter."

He opens it, and we're thankfully in my hallway—apparently the magic is too full to play with us tonight. I shudder at the thought. My room is just two steps in front of us, with its rose-covered knob. He cracks it open for me and stands back so I can slip past him. I widen it for him, expecting him to come too. He shakes his head. A coy smile plays across his lips.

"Don't tempt me."

"Why not?" I try to smile seductively. I need a distraction, but it feels so wrong in my torn dress stained with blood.

He leans in and cups my cheeks in his hands, placing a chaste kiss in the center of my forehead. "You have a big day tomorrow."

I don't want to think about tomorrow. I don't even know what I'm doing here anymore. I don't want to see other illusions of people dying—or people *actually* dying. I got what I came for. I can kill a vampire, and when I forget about Roman and think about where I've been happiest lately, it's got nothing to do with hunting vampires. It's walking arm in arm down a street with Diantha and Reina, basking in Xander's easy smiles, and sitting on the beach laughing. It felt like family. It felt like a family that chose me right from the start and wants me to fight to make sure I stay. Now I know what my mom was a part of and what she had to give up to go live with my dad. There's really only one thing stopping me from leaving, and a part of that is standing in front of me, while the rest of it is probably losing at Yahtzee to the twins.

"We could just go." I blurt the words without thinking—even though they've been lurking in the back of my mind from the moment we stepped into the unwelcoming entry room of this place, from the moment the magic started to feel so sticky and heavy on my skin. From the moment I sliced a girl in half.

She's fine. I knew she would be.

Barry's fine too. Everyone's fine. Xander wouldn't lie to me. If I say it enough, I'll believe it.

Xander's already stepping back from me when he freezes at my words. His knuckles turn white as he grips the doorjamb, and then he pushes in past me. The door clicks shut even though I'm pretty sure he didn't touch it.

"What did you say?"

I open my mouth to repeat it.

He holds a hand out. "No. Don't repeat it." He runs his hand through his green hair, sending strands running in different directions. "Don't ever say that again."

I start to shrink in on myself, like a child, again like a child. I stop, pulling myself upright. "Why? What's so bad about saying I want—"

"Ava." He turns my name into a warning.

"Stop that," I say.

"What?" He looks honestly confused, but how can I even explain to him what's wrong? How can I explain to him what it's like when a foster-whatever uses your name only because there's a warning behind it, or anger, or some other negative bent? Or how once your name gets used up like that, once it gets polluted, you can't scrub it clean again? It gets hard to hear it and feel anything at all. And how when you hear it sometimes, on those rare occasions when there's love behind it, you wonder what kind of manipulation lurks there, tainting what should be a clean thing.

I never give people my name if I can help it. Ordering chai tea at a coffee shop, I've been Amber, Brittany, and Jessica. I used to try and give different names at school, but there were always those pesky attendance sheets revealing my name to a room full of strangers who I didn't want to have it. It's risky. It gives them a certain power over you even if they don't know it. Some of them do know it and abuse it.

He doesn't press me when I don't answer.

"Ava," he says, softening my name this time, coaxing.

A trap. A softly whispered name is always a trap.

I battle with my own muscles not to flinch away.

"Ava." He tries a third time, reaching out and running a finger from my ear to my chin. This time my name is just my name. I sense nothing behind it.

I step forward.

"You can't leave now. We can't leave now. What about the others? This is our home."

The home part gets me. Despite the fact that this place gives me the creeps, this is home for them. Home for Xander. They want to be home just as badly as I do, and they're offering to make it my home too. Home is a thing you can learn to love, I hope. It doesn't have to be the perfect place if you have the perfect people around you.

With a deep sigh, I nod my head.

He still has his fingers against my jaw, and they slide around to the back of my neck.

"Thank you," he breathes, leaning down and pressing his lips against mine just long enough to clear my head for one blissful moment.

He steps back from me, but his hand lingers on my neck, as if removing it is too much effort.

I take another step toward him just as he pries himself away.

"Good night, my warrior." His coyness trickles back as he turns and slides out the door.

Even after stripping off the blood-soaked dress, I'm too rattled to sleep. I can't strip off the memories. Everything felt too real to be an illusion. I can't deny that magic can do impossible things, but I'm trapped in Barry's distant stare—a stare that reminds me too much of another one. *The* one. My chest tightens as I try not to think about it. I press my eyes closed, but all I can see are Mom's unblinking eyes or Barry's or both at once. How are eyes so similar when they're dying? It doesn't matter what color they are because you don't see the color—all you see is the dimming light inside them.

I open my eyes and begin to pace back and forth.

I wish I could be out on the street with the familiar sound of people and cars, focusing on that or the feel of my stake in my backpack.

I don't want to think of stakes. They remind me of Roman.

I can't pull myself out of my own head.

Mom left for love. And maybe for me? I asked Diantha, and she told me that immortal magicians can't have children. Their bodies are frozen in every way. Did she leave because she wanted kids? Did she regret it? I go to my nightstand and pull out the journal entries and photos there. I reread the one about her craving real magic. She did regret it—even if she didn't regret me.

But my makeshift family is *here*. I can have the magic *and* them.

She'd want me to win so I could keep what she missed.

I only have four pages, but I pick up another and read it.

> Joseph is a joy to work with. His skill with illusions
> is remarkable. He doesn't need the real thing. Still, I
> suggested him as a recruit, but everyone thinks I like
> him too much, and it's best not to be too attached.

If I'm going to stay, I should at least get more stories. Julia wasn't very talkative, but maybe Edgar would be. I haven't spotted him since they dragged him out of the testing ceremony.

Someone knocks on my door.

My chest actually lightens at the tapping. I hope it's Xander, but I'd settle for the twins asking me to play dice. I'd even rather watch *Tomb Raider* one more time than visualize the tithing ceremony any longer.

But when I open it, Willow stands there . . . with Nadine hovering behind her. Both of them have changed out of their bloody ball gowns, but there's a haunted look in their eyes that makes me think they're still imagining the blood-soaked fabric on their skin. I know the look. I probably have it right now too, but I've had it my whole life, so it's easier to ignore.

I open the door wider, and Willow marches in, tossing herself backward on my bed.

Nadine hesitates before stepping in as well. She appraises me as she does, her eyes sharp and observant, like she's not one to miss any detail. I wonder what she sees—if she notices the ghosts in my eyes or if I'm better at hiding them than she is.

Willow flops her head to the side and looks at me. "I found a new friend." She smiles, but it doesn't reach her eyes.

Nadine grimaces just a little at the word "friend," and it makes me like her immediately.

I shut the door behind them and walk back over to my bed, where I gently gather my papers and photos and set them to the side. I'm not sure I want to share that with them. "So how did you two meet? I mean . . . after what we did."

Willow sits up and shrugs. "I just wanted to walk, you know, and focus on something else." She shudders. "I thought the magic was supposed to take you where you wanted to go. I wanted a nice garden or something. I wanted to feel a little sunshine, even if it was just an illusion, but it just took me to hallway after hallway, then up and down a million creepy sets of stairs, and that didn't help. I kept thinking I heard . . ." She turns away and stares up at the ceiling. "I kept thinking I heard little screams from behind the walls. I mean, I know I imagined it, but I couldn't stop." She swallows and looks back at me. "You know?"

"I get it," I say.

She gives me a searching look. She knows my history. She knows I'm not fine either, and I realize she's partly here to check on me.

"Anyway, I ended up at the front door, and I thought maybe a walk through those dreary roses would suffice, but Nadine was already there, yanking on the handle so hard that I thought she might rip the door right off."

"Wait. We're locked inside?"

"Yes," Nadine bites out.

"It would seem that way," Willow says way too brightly. Her over-the-top cheerfulness about it makes my skin prickle. She's scared.

"I think the ones who didn't make it back from the maze were the lucky ones," Nadine says.

"They lost," I say.

"At least two of us in this room have already lost," Nadine says.

We all stare at each other.

"We knew that coming in," I remind her.

"But we didn't know that two of us or all of us in this room might already be dead," she says. "Willow told me what happened to the guy in your group. The same thing happened to me . . . to my group. Two other girls were with me. They blew a door open together while I tried to read the riddle on the floor." She swallows. "They're dead. There's no way they're not dead. I mean, the magic swallowed them up, but there was so much blood. I was holding their hands—"

"Wait." I cut her off, because I can't hear it. I can't listen to her describe what it's like to hold someone's hand in those final moments. I'm already way too close to falling headfirst into the past. "It was an illusion. They're probably fine. Maybe they got knocked out, and the magic showed us what it wanted us to see."

"But there's still blood on my dress. Illusions disappear."

"Not in here." I wave a hand around my room. "This place is one giant illusion. This place is magic. There are no rules for what's possible or not. And even if it was real, we know that the magic can heal, too. Maybe it healed Barry and the others after they got sucked into the floor."

The three of us contemplate that possibility for a silent moment. Then . . .

"Tell her," Willow says to Nadine. "We can trust her."

"I'm not sure I can trust *you*," Nadine says. "We just met."

"Well, you already told me everything anyway," Willow says.

Nadine scowls like she really, really regrets that.

"She has that effect on people," I mutter.

Willow smiles. "I'm good at getting secrets, but I'm also good at keeping them."

Nadine sighs and looks at me for a long moment. Then she glances at my door and steps farther away from it, like she's worried about someone overhearing. She drops her voice low. "I'm not here for the competition. I'm here to find my missing friend."

"Missing?" I ask.

"Last year we went to a magic show together. It wasn't really my thing, but she was super into it. The people were amazing, I have to admit, but I still shrugged it off as nothing out of the ordinary. Why would I think it was real? She didn't think it was real either, but she was desperate to learn from them. It was all she talked about. Then one day she said she was taking off with them. They wanted her to be an apprentice. I was so happy for her, and she sent me texts for the next couple of weeks, but then they just stopped. She wasn't that close to her parents, but they haven't heard from her either. And then a few months ago, I saw that troupe in my town again. I went to the show, and part of me was hoping I'd just see her onstage, doing the quick-change tricks that were her favorite, but I didn't. I thought maybe she fell in love or something and ran off with someone and just left everything behind, but we were like sisters. I had this sick feeling in my gut that I couldn't get rid of. So I did exactly what she did—I kept going back and pretended I was interested in the show. I used to listen to her talk for hours about her tricks and techniques, so they bought it. They just thought I was a newbie, and it turned out I *did* have the magic in me, and I was a really quick learner. But the deeper they let me in, the more I had to wonder what happened to Samantha."

"Did you ask them?"

"You don't ask a killer where the body is if you don't want to end up beside it."

She's not wrong. I didn't ask my troupe about my mom.

"I thought she might be here at the mansion," Nadine continues. "But she's not. It doesn't make any sense. If failed apprentices go home, then where is she? And after what we just saw . . ." She bites her lip. Her eyes well, but the tears don't fall. "What if nobody leaves here alive?"

Willow gets up from the bed and grabs Nadine's hand in hers. Nadine looks shocked, like she's going to pull away, but I doubt Willow would let go.

I know some people don't leave alive, but I can't bring myself to say it and strip away whatever sliver of hope Nadine has. So instead I say, "I don't know about apprentices, but I know a magician who left."

They both turn to me, and I'm not sure I should have blurted that out, but I can't take it back now. And I really don't want to. I want to tell somebody. I wave at them to follow me over to the bed and start spreading out Mom's journal pages and pictures again. "This is my mom. She used to be part of this. So I know full-fledged magicians can leave. She did. But you're right. The Society doesn't like when people leave. I'm not supposed to let anyone know I'm her daughter. At least not yet."

"Why'd she leave?" Nadine asks. "How'd she do it? Did she send you here?"

Each question hurts a little too much.

"Her mom's dead," Willow says.

Nadine's eyes darken like none of this makes her feel any better.

"A vampire killed her," I say. "She didn't die here."

"But she left," Nadine says, picking up the photo of Lucius and my mom. Her eyes narrow. "Do you know him? You talked to him like you did." Suspicion drips from her voice.

"I was pissed. I don't actually know him from anywhere except this photo. I never knew any of this existed. My mom . . . she always told me magic wasn't real."

Nadine's brows draw together. "Why would she do that if there was anything good about this place?"

I want to tell them about my dad, and how she left for love, but it feels like a sweet lie I've been holding on to since I spoke to Julia. Because there's something else that's not adding up. Julia told me not to dig. You tell someone that only if there's something buried. So instead I say, "We moved around a lot when I was a kid . . . I think she was running from something. Someone. I thought it was vampires, but I don't know that for sure."

I look at the picture of Lucius and my mom again—how he's staring at her and not at the camera. It's strange. There's a possessiveness in the way he leans toward her.

"Have you asked anyone about her?" Willow asks.

"Xander didn't know. I asked him as soon as I recognized Lucius. But I'm not walking around polling people either." I decide not to mention Julia quite yet.

"Because you don't trust them," Nadine says.

"I rarely trust anyone."

"But now we trust each other." Willow stands between us, looking back and forth. "I say we do some snooping."

"Tonight?" I ask. My bones feel tired, but my mind buzzes.

"Are any of us really going to sleep?" Nadine asks.

We all know the answer to that, so we come up with a plan. We'll go together, each of us focusing on the same want to see if the magic will give in and take us somewhere with answers, because there has to be hidden pockets full of secrets within these endless corridors. We just need to find them.

We focus our intentions on finding Nadine's friend first, but all we do is walk and walk until we're at the massive front door again. Each time we check the handle, and each time we're still locked in.

"Maybe this means she did leave," I tell Nadine. "We keep ending up here—at the front door. That has to mean something, right?"

Nadine nods, but her eyes look lost.

Next we turn our focus to finding out more about my mom, but that takes us nowhere at all. Endless hallways and winding stairs that open to more hallways or empty rooms.

Eventually we give up.

"We're just too tired to control the magic," Willow says as we're parting ways. "We'd be better off trying again tomorrow."

Nadine and I nod, but we share a look that clearly says we don't have Willow's optimism.

Nadine heads down the hallway and disappears, but Willow calls me back.

"I'm sorry about your dress," she says.

I groan. "Roman told you he changed it?"

"Roman? No . . ." Her cheeks turn a bright pink. "I did it. I was jealous about Roman training you, and I was just walking, blowing off steam, but I ended up at your door, and I did it without thinking."

My mouth opens and closes. I can't quite believe she'd do that.

"I'm so sorry." Tears line her eyes.

I saw the crack in her earlier. I knew it was bothering her, even if she lied about it. A better friend would have stopped training with Roman. But I am not a better friend.

"Don't worry about it," I tell her, and mean it.

"No. It's not okay. It's not me."

"I know it's not." I reach out and squeeze her hand. "I prefer black anyway."

She laughs as one tear breaks free. "You did look stunning." She still seems nervous as she meets my eyes. "Friends?"

"Always." Until one of us loses, at least.

She grins at that and waves as she walks away.

When I'm alone outside my door, I try again. Perhaps the other two weren't focused enough. Nobody's going to be able to desire finding out about my mom more than me, so I walk down my hallway until it shifts, and I'm somewhere I've never been before: a hallway with dark wood paneling that ends in front of a plain black door with a pearl-white handle. I try to twist it and get nothing.

Why is everything in this place locked?

I walk back until it turns into my hallway again, then continue past my room until the hallway changes abruptly to the wood-paneled one again.

Impossible. I'm back at the door. I grab the handle and jiggle it again. Nothing.

I'm turning around once more with a frustrated sigh when the door creaks open.

Roman stands there in his slacks and no shirt. His eyes look half asleep, and his dark auburn hair curls wildly around his head, leaving shadows on his face from the dim light given off by the wall sconce beside his door.

"Ava?" The question reaches his eyes. There's a hope in them that makes my heart speed up and ache at the same time.

"I . . ." I step back. I don't like how badly I want to step inside. I want to show him everything I just shared with Willow and Nadine.

"I ended up at the wrong place." The magic's supposed to take you to where you want to go, so the fact that it kept taking me to Roman's door doesn't make sense. I'm with Xander. I like what I have with him. It's not complicated.

Roman's expression droops like a wilted flower before he straightens and nods. "Of course."

"Sorry to bother you."

"You're never a bother," he says softly.

I start to turn away but then spin back to face him. "Why'd you take the blame for the dress? Willow confessed."

"I guessed it was her. She kept looking at you like she'd done something." He shrugs. "I thought it'd hurt you more if it were her. I didn't want you to lose another person."

"Thanks," I whisper.

I do walk away then, telling the magic to take me to my room, wondering if it will take me back to Roman again. It doesn't. I don't like the twinge of disappointment I feel when I find my own door again.

CHAPTER 24

The ballroom has transformed, if it's even the same room at all. I can't be certain of anything here. The banquet table is gone, replaced on one side with a large stage—black except for the twisting golden roses around the edge. Gold drips off them and streaks down the side of the stage as if they were painted just moments ago.

Today the competition continues. Today we'll each perform in our chosen specialty and show these people what we can do. I drew last. I won't go until the end.

Everyone clusters around the stage except Lucius and Annalise, sitting on a raised platform in the center of us. Lucius, his face unreadable, taps his long fingers against the deep mahogany wood of his throne. Annalise stares straight ahead with her vacant, pale eyes. It's hard to imagine her as the most powerful apprentice in her day.

I turn away and yawn for the hundredth time this morning, trying to catch it in my hand so Xander doesn't notice.

"Didn't sleep well?" Xander asks.

Nadine stands on the other side of me. I cut my eyes toward her, and she gives me a soft, tentative smile as she runs a hand over her hair and fidgets with the messy bun at the nape of her neck.

Willow and Nadine came back last night and invited me to a girls' sleepover in Willow's room. They called it that, like we were at summer camp or something and hadn't just finished clawing our way through blood and horror for a chance at power. I was surprised to see them at my door again after we'd parted for the night, but I understood why they were there—and I can't say I wasn't grateful for it. They needed to forget for a while. I recognized it on their faces because I felt the same desire. Still, I almost said no. It made sense that Willow had made a new friend. I would just be the spectator again, watching on the out-side like I was with Parker and Jacob. It would be everything I was trying to escape. But Willow linked her arm in mine and practically dragged me to her room.

I sensed the same reluctance in Nadine, but anytime one of us tried to pull in on ourselves, Willow was there bringing us back into the moment.

Xander takes us both in, jaw tightening. "Making friends, I see."

"I'm a friendly girl."

"You're not," he mutters, eyeing Nadine like she's a potential threat. She is, of course. She's my competitor. I haven't forgotten.

Xander leans in and drops his voice so only I can hear. "Don't trust anyone."

I shrug him off. I'm not a fool.

I shoot Nadine an apologetic smile as the crowd hushes.

Willow drew the first performance slot. I remember her saying that she has stage fright and am glad she doesn't have to sit and stew in her anxiety while the rest of us go. She takes the stage, regal and calm in a flowing dress made of all the greens of spring and speckled with soft pink rosebuds. She nods her head toward the audience before sitting on the piano bench and arching her fingers over the keys. She holds the pose, giving no explanation, just allowing us a moment to look and anticipate.

Her first notes are tentative, soft, almost asking a whispered permission before reaching our ears. A tiny breeze twirls her dress as the notes pick up, as if she's no longer worried about whether we want them or not. With each one, a tiny blade of grass grows around the stage. Her fingers begin to fly and the notes skip and giggle together like girls in a field. Poppies and daisies spring to life beneath her, swaying gently in the breeze that brushes my hair against my cheeks.

I can smell them. The sweetness sinks into me, making my eyelids droop like it's a warm spring day and I'm in a hammock and the tune plays only in my head. The ultimate illusion. Magic for all the senses. As she plays, vines crawl up the legs of the piano, covering the lid and the music rack. One ambitious vine punches through her sheet music, lifting it above her head as it spirals upward. She doesn't notice. Her eyes are closed, her head rocking faintly back and forth as her fingers crawl across the keys.

As the music crescendos, the vines hit a high point five feet above the piano lid. The crescendo is brief, just like spring itself, and as it leaves, deep purple flowers erupt on the vines.

The piece ends with soft notes again, a whispered apology for the frenzy they caused.

Stunning.

It makes me giddy and sick at the same time, and I bring my hands up in one solid clap before a hand circles my right wrist and drags it down to my side so I cannot clap again.

I jerk, startled, and find Roman beside me. I twist, looking for Xander, but he's gone.

Roman leans toward my ear, as subtle as he can be when he's at least a foot taller than me. His hand still clasps my wrist. "Do not clap."

I flinch, and he lets go of me immediately. His mouth so close to my neck only makes me think of what he's hiding.

He brings his hands together, eyes focused on the stage, where Willow graciously performs bow after bow.

I open my mouth to protest his hypocrisy. Only he's not really clapping. His hands come together again and again in a slow and lazy tease where they never actually touch.

Everyone else around us claps. Nadine yells Willow's name beside me.

Puzzled, I twist back to Roman's fake clapping with a frown.

"Look up," he says.

A glass orb glows above our heads. The light floating within its center pulses a little stronger as it consumes the applause.

Measuring the applause.

And Roman's giving Willow nothing.

It makes no sense—not if he wants his apprentice to win.

Roman slips away from me and out of the room as the applause dwindles.

I trail behind him, almost running to catch him with the long strides he's making down the hallway.

"Roman." His steps falter when I say his name.

I grab his arm. His bicep tenses under my palm for a second before relaxing, and I almost drop my hand. His face is cool as he turns toward me. His eyes drift to my hand wrinkling the white material of his shirt.

"Why didn't you clap?"

A passing woman with blue lips glances toward us with her purple eyebrows arched.

Roman grabs my upper arms, whirling me into a nook with a statue of a nymph sprouting real flowers around her feet and in her hair. One of her elbows pokes me in the back.

"Keep your voice down."

"Why? Why wouldn't you want Willow to win?"

His mouth opens and shuts in a way that makes me believe he doesn't know the answer. His hands tighten on my arms, but not hard enough to hurt.

My own hand still grips his sleeve. To anyone passing by, it might look like lovers sneaking a moment.

Our little nook suddenly feels too hot.

His eyes dart all over my face like he can find his answer there.

And then he lets me go, spinning fast enough to snap his arm out of my grip.

He stalks down the hallway and out of sight without looking back.

I lean against the wall of the nook for a moment. The nymph's seductive smile looks outward at the passing magicians. Reaching down, I pluck a white, pink-veined flower from her feet. It grows back the second I snap the stem.

I sigh and step back out into the hall.

Xander leans against the wall on the other side, only ten feet away from where Roman and I just stood.

I flinch like I've done something wrong.

His eyes narrow on the flower in my hand and then shoot to my face.

"It's not—" I start.

He turns and walks away in the opposite direction of Roman, leaving me alone with a flower that's already wilting from being cut off from its magic.

I find Xander back in the performance hall. Nadine's on the stage, shaking a black curtain up over her head. When the curtain drops, a peacock stands in her place. It fans its glorious plumage as I spot Xander's green hair and push my way to the front to slide up beside him.

"It's not what it looked like."

His eyes never leave the stage. The peacock disappears in an explosion of blue-green feathers. Nadine reappears from behind one of several colored curtains decorating the stage. The silver jumpsuit she wore a minute ago is now a deep blue dress accented with peacock feathers dropping from the waist.

"Xander."

His eyes slide toward me and away.

"Talk to me."

"I don't have anything to say, but it seems you do." He crosses his arms over his chest. On the stage, Nadine shimmies her black cloth over her head again.

"Roman and I are just . . . friends." I hesitate to say the word "friends," but not for the reason Xander must be thinking.

Xander just nods toward the stage. "You should be watching this."

Nadine pulls the curtain over her head and drops it, disappearing and leaving behind a swarm of monarch butterflies. They drift out over the audience, staying just out of reach of wandering hands.

Beautiful. In a different moment, I would be enthralled.

"I've seen disappearing acts before." Not with butterflies, but they don't matter.

"No. She *is* the butterflies. She's transforming her body into something else entirely." His voice is soft, awestruck. "Not many magicians can change themselves into even one animal, let alone a mass of them. And *never* apprentices."

A bit of bitterness turns my mouth sour. Nadine doesn't really want this, but she's still better than me. I have ulterior motives too, but I also *want* this life. I try to shove my jealousy aside as the butterflies trail back to the stage. It won't help me win.

He finally looks at me, one side of his mouth twisted downward. "So you and Roman are 'friends,' are you? I thought you were just learning from him, taking advantage of him. Are you with this family or not? Because he can never be a part of it."

The butterflies swarm together, slowly shifting from a blob to a human outline. Then, just as they finish taking shape, they disintegrate, raining down like ash. In their wake, Nadine stands in a glorious orange gown, the skirts printed with a kaleidoscope of butterflies.

I burst into applause without thinking, and then stop. Nadine doesn't want this. I don't need to feel guilty about not clapping.

Xander doesn't clap as Nadine bows and leaves the stage.

"She outdid me," Willow says.

I don't know how long she's been standing on the other side of me. Her usually sparkling eyes are muted.

"You were beautiful."

"Of course I was, but she was marvelous." She gives me a faint smile. "Let's hope Ethan sucks." She winks.

"That's a given."

A few stagehands clear the stage, and Ethan lopes up the steps. We get no time between performances, and I'm next.

"I'm going to need a volunteer," Ethan announces, strutting back and forth on the stage in an entirely white suit. The white has a sense of flashiness to it—the wicked dressed in snow. He doesn't pull it off.

I jolt when I realize he's stopped in front of me. His eyes narrow. "Ava."

I wish, not for the first time, that he didn't know my name.

Xander's fingers wrap around my own. "Say no," he murmurs softly.

"She can't." Aristelle appears on my other side, sliding between me and Willow. "She'll look like a coward."

Xander and Aristelle glare at each other around me.

She's right, though. The crowd already murmurs with excitement at Ethan's new twist. They watch *me* now, not him. He's managed to turn me into the one being judged, probably hoping I'll say no and weaken my own position before I can ever get on the stage myself. Clever bastard.

He knows it too. It's all over his face. His raised, mocking eyebrows. His smug smirk. Every second I stand and think about it, I lose the crowd around me.

My only option is to steal his show.

I break away from Xander and head toward the center of the stage, not the stairs on either side. I need to gain back some of what I lost to hesitation.

Ethan moves to meet me there, squatting down to offer his hand.

Ignoring it, I brace my arms on the side of the stage and swing my legs up and over, springing to my feet with a grace I have all my running and training to thank for. Ethan doesn't have time to spring from his own squat before I offer him my hand.

He scowls as the crowd erupts in laughter. They are mine. I allow myself the smallest smirk.

And then he pulls out the gun at his side, spinning it between his fingers until the pearl handle flashes like a star dancing in his hands.

The crowd claps for his party trick. He gets them back. For now.

My fingers itch for the knives I always wear on my wrists and ankles now. I keep my hands calmly at my sides. It won't do for me to start acting twitchy. I will play assistant to him and be done with this. If I can steal the crowd for a moment again, all the better.

"Fellow magicians," he crows, keeping his gun spinning from hand to hand as he speaks, "tonight you'll be in for a real treat. Tonight I will catch a bullet with my bare hands."

I almost snort. It's a used-up trick. Penn and Teller mastered it already. They pull it off beautifully, too. It's enough to make your heart stop for that one glorious moment as you try to figure out how it's done. I've watched the video online nearly thirty times, picking apart the smallest details and moves of their hands before finally searching out how they do it: a sleight-of-hand trick and wax bullets to shatter the glass panes they shoot through. The glass is a nice touch. Ethan can't possibly add anything new to it.

Still, a human crowd might clap for this. Even if they know how it's done, there's still a sense of awe in a trick pulled off. Especially one that requires so many thoughtful, controlled moves. This crowd stays silent, waiting.

Ethan turns and steps toward me. I keep my eyes on the gun twirling around his index finger as he reaches into a pocket and then extends his closed fist to me. I'm forced to leave him hanging or hold out my cupped hands to take whatever he gives me.

Six bullets drop coldly into my palm. They feel real.

He grips his gun and whips open the cylinder, turning it and holding it by the barrel.

"Please," he says.

I fit the bullets into their home without asking for clarification like I'm sure he's hoping I will. I may not know guns, but I've seen some westerns.

When I'm done, he snaps the cylinder back into place, continuing to hold the gun out to me.

He smiles slowly when I do nothing. "Tonight you'll be firing the gun."

Of course. Of course he needs someone to fire it at him to do this trick. I thought I would only be testing the bullets, maybe signing my name to one before lowering myself back into the crowd.

My hands sweat. This isn't the same as being onstage with a

practiced routine. It's not even the same as that first time with Xander. He was playing with cards. Ethan's holding out a gun toward me.

He lowers his voice. "I need someone who can aim. You do knives."

He says it as if that's the only reason he picked me, like he wouldn't have asked me otherwise. He actually needs a favor. I'm not really in the business of doing favors.

But I extend my hand. The gun, heavy and cold, turns the sweat on my palm to ice.

Ethan leans close to my ear. "Don't miss. Aim for my right hand and then my left, alternate between them until the bullets are gone."

Six bullets. Six real bullets. I think. I can't be entirely sure. His trick doesn't seem as silly as it did a moment ago.

As Ethan saunters across the stage, the audience stays silent—from boredom or anticipation, I can't tell. I find Xander leaning forward slightly. Even Aristelle next to him looks tense.

Ethan turns to face me when he reaches the other side.

He mouths something to me as he spreads his hands out, directly in front of his chest. *Don't miss.*

I'd feel a lot better if his hands were out at his sides. If they were, and I missed, then the bullet would just dig into the side of the stage, and the only thing lost would be my pride. But he's raising the stakes. He also better hope the bullets don't sail through his palm and into his chest. I want to ask him if he's even done this before. He must have. He'd be a fool to try something new right now.

I cradle the gun in both hands. One loosely gripped around the handle, the other a resting point for the barrel. I'm pretty sure it's not how you're supposed to carry a gun.

"Now, Ava," Ethan orders.

I let the gun drop to my side, weighing it there before I lift it.

It wobbles, foreign and unwieldy. Not at all like my knives, which fit the curves of my hands and warm almost immediately to the temperature of my body.

I almost toss the gun and walk away from this. Instead, I rest my finger on the trigger, take aim, and pull, realizing a moment too late that I should have tried to use magic to guide the bullet. He probably expected me to.

I miss.

CHAPTER 25

I swear his hands dropped two inches lower the moment before I pulled the trigger—too late for me to adjust my aim.

I hit him straight in the chest, and blood blooms across his white shirt.

Our audience gasps, and a few people cackle with glee.

His knees hit the stage with a thud the same time the gun thwacks from me dropping it. I dart forward, skidding to my own knees beside him.

Even though he's still upright, his head slumps against his chest.

I grab his arm. "Ethan." I shake him. "Ethan."

I can't hear the audience. Either they aren't making a sound or the buzzing in my head is drowning everything out except for my own gasping breath.

"Wake up!" I yell. I scan the crowd of onlookers. Some gape. Some wear slight smiles, like this is part of some marvelous trick. Only three people move. Xander pushes through the crowd to my left with Aristelle trailing behind him. Roman's making his way along the side. Willow stands with Nadine two rows back, both frozen.

My hand is wet. Blood seeps through the lapel I'm holding on to.

He's not healing. Some wounds are too difficult to heal. You can't control your magic when you're losing consciousness. It's why most magicians choose less deadly illusions to play with, Roman had told me.

Suddenly, Ethan's head snaps up, and he grins with blood in the cracks of his white teeth—a mirror of his jacket.

His fingers grope at his bloody shirt, and then he rips it open. Buttons clink around me as he exposes his chest. Removing a clean handkerchief from his pocket, he wipes the blood away from where his wound should be.

There's nothing but smooth skin.

I still grip his lapel like I'm a part of this, like I'm his good assistant pulling open the curtain at just the right moment to complete the trick.

He turns his grin on me before I can drop my hand and get away. I freeze, staring at the blood in his teeth—the perfect touch, just like the breaking glass. It adds the bit of flair that makes your stomach plummet and leaves you cold for the briefest moment before you appreciate the brilliance of it all.

Something flickers in his eyes. I realize a second too late it's resolve. He's not done.

He lifts a hand to my still outstretched arm and yanks free one of my daggers.

"Don't." I barely get the word out, leaning closer to him to stop him from plunging it inside himself. The body can only take so much healing.

Instead, he shoves the knife hilt-deep in my stomach.

It rips into me and lodges itself there as I fall back on my heels. Vaguely I'm aware of him getting to his feet, trading places with me, leaving me to bleed for his show.

"Pull the knife out," someone yells. It's a man's voice. Through the fog building in my head, I can't be sure if it's Roman or Xander. Maybe neither.

Not Ethan, though. He takes his bow in a blur of white above me. The magicians erupt in vicious applause.

I watch my own hand fasten around the white hilt of the knife. It's funny almost. My black clothes hide the blood. It could almost be a trick knife if you didn't know any better. But I can feel the blood, warm and sticky. Maybe the crowd thinks it's a trick knife. I slump backward, twisting my legs underneath me as I go. My movement jars the knife, and I cry out, but the hungry cheers swallow it. I turn my head toward the crowd and realize that they know it's not a trick. They just don't care. This is what they've been yearning for—something they haven't seen before. Death played out for entertainment.

Except I can heal. I don't have to die. I don't even care if it's blood magic—I just want the pain to stop.

I tighten my grip and slide the knife out of me just as Xander's face looms in front of mine.

My hand crashes to the side, and the knife clatters.

"Okay, good," Xander says. His face wars with itself to stay calm. "Now heal. Do it yourself or you'll look weak."

I search for the magic, the ever-present hum under my skin. Silence answers me. Cold silence. I think I'm whimpering. Not really whimpering. It's more of a sharp, animal keening.

Xander touches my stomach—at least I think it's him—still nothing.

"Heal her." Roman's here too, his voice tight but calm.

"I can't!" Xander yells. At least I think he yells. Everything sounds fuzzy. "Lucius is blocking me."

Voices wave in and out.

"I care because I want a fair fight. This isn't one," Roman is saying.

I can't hear the replies of whoever he's talking to.

"You won't have a show without her," he says.

Xander turns his head toward the conversation.

I take in Xander's profile like it's the last time I'll see it. Then he pushes away from me.

Lucius takes his place. I try to focus on his cruel blue eyes, but my own just want to close. I fight it.

"I won't do this a second time. For anyone." I'm not sure if the words are for me or not, but then the magic scorches, and I do not care.

I scream until I'm nothing.

I wake up in my bed, flat on my back. I roll to my side and moan.

Reina and Diantha stand up from the two window chairs and come to my side.

"What happened?" Why is there so much pain? If I healed properly, there shouldn't be any at all.

"You blacked out. Even Lucius couldn't make the magic fully heal you." Reina's face darkens. "At least that's what he said."

"You'll live, though," Diantha adds softly.

But he wanted to leave me bleeding out on the stage. Why? To give everyone a better show? Or because I couldn't find the magic to heal myself? Did I doubt it would heal me? Maybe, for just a moment, before I pulled out the dagger. One second of doubt, but that second must have been enough.

The hum of it is back now. I feel it there beneath the surface, but now fear creeps under my skin, tainting it, poisoning it so I won't know again whether to trust it or not. I shake myself. Trust is necessary to survive.

"How long was I out?"

"It's only been about fifteen minutes."

Wincing, I throw my feet off the bed. "Where's Xander?" I'm

surprised he's not here. I won't soon forget the panic on his face as he crouched over me.

Reina and Diantha exchange a look.

Diantha answers, "He went after Ethan after we brought you here."

"What?" I push to my feet, biting the inside of my cheek to keep from cringing.

"Don't worry," Reina offers. "Roman went with him."

"What?" My voice goes up an octave. I take an unsteady step toward the door, struggling to find my balance.

"Let them handle this," Reina says.

I don't answer. Instead, I straighten as best as I can and leave them behind.

Stumbling down the hallways, I grip the iron railings that weren't there earlier, almost as if the magic is apologizing to me for before, giving me a peace offering, or maybe I'm reading into it and seeing what I want. Either way, I accept them and use them as I wander the halls.

I don't know where I'm going, but eventually I overhear heated voices, and I pause outside an open black door. Inside the cavernous black room, Lucius sits upon his throne with Xander and Roman on one side and Ethan on the other.

"It seems fair to me," Xander says.

Ethan glares at him, his mouth a grim line.

I wonder if blood still coats his teeth—if he found time to wash his mouth out before Xander and Roman got to him. He clearly didn't have time to change.

"What about you?" Lucius's eyes snake toward me standing in the doorway. "Would you see him punished for his stunt?"

I swallow. My throat catches with the movement, and I regret not taking the water Diantha offered. Ethan watches me. I wish he had enough shame to not meet my eyes, but he does. The fierceness in them might make anyone else cringe. I don't. Irrational fierceness is often the result of extreme vulnerability and a willingness to lash out at others so that they never bother to notice the vulnerable parts. I see them. I recognize them because I have them too—or at least similar ones. But I had Parker. I had Parker to make me acknowledge those vulnerable places. He was an anchor that kept me from tearing apart everything and everyone around me. He still is.

Maybe Ethan never had a person to keep him contained. I can't pretend to know his story.

I suspect he didn't. Nothing is holding him back. The scar on my abdomen proves it.

Xander gives me an encouraging nod. I can use this moment to my advantage. This is a game, after all. Ethan played dirty first. I would be justified in letting him reap his reward.

I look to Roman. The two of them dragged him here together. He must want the same thing. His face gives me nothing, leaving it up to me.

Lucius waits, looking like he's teetering on the edge of boredom.

"No," I answer.

"Ava," Xander starts, but Lucius cuts him off with a cold glare.

"She's decided." He stands from his throne. Now it's made of stone blocks, giving it hard edges like someone tried to combine medieval and modern styles. He moves toward the door, looking back for a moment on his way. "It would have made you weak to decide other-wise." His eyes flick to Xander, and then he is gone.

Xander looks as if he's chewing his own tongue in frustration.

Ethan has somehow managed to slip to a side door.

Xander catches his movement. "Not so fast." His muscles tense. He clenches his hands hard enough for me to see veins popping out. This won't end well. Especially for Ethan.

Ethan disappears out the door, and Xander starts after him.

"No." I dart forward. Pain pinches my middle. "I've got this."

Xander slows just enough to turn toward me. "Ava, you need to lie down."

I won't beat him to the door.

Roman steps forward and grabs Xander's arm, forcing him to stop short.

"I need to handle this myself." And I can. It's not the first time I've dealt with a bully in my life. I've handled it just fine on my own in the past. In fact, I took care of Parker's bullies, too. One might say I'm an expert on them.

I shoot Roman a look of thanks, ignoring the hurt on Xander's face.

A small part of me flushes with happiness that Xander wants to take care of this for me. But I can't let him. I've already dropped my guard enough with him. To let him become my knight in shining armor would be a mistake—one not easy to recover from. You can't go back to fighting your own battles after growing used to having someone else fight them for you. Your muscles would have turned to Jell-O and your instincts would be foggy. You'd be dead the first time a beast looked your way and licked its chops.

"I've got this. Thanks, though," I add, hoping that softens the blow.

I take a deep breath and push into the hallway. Ethan's the only one out here. Good. I don't want anyone else to see this if it doesn't go my way.

"Ethan."

To his credit, he stops and turns. He could easily outrun me in this moment.

I wince as I move toward him, refusing to clasp a hand over my stomach.

"What the hell?" It seems like a good enough question to sum up what I'm thinking. The blood on his suit is already drying—if it was even his blood. I'm not even sure if it was magic or a classic illusion.

My curiosity flares, but I shove it aside. I don't really need to know. It's better if I assume it was magic. It means he has a better grasp on it than I do. It means I won't underestimate him again.

He shrugs, tugging down a sleeve stained with blood I *know* is real. After all, it's mine. "It wasn't personal. I just need to win."

"It felt personal." I lift my shirt so he can see the angry red mark that's clearly going to scar.

He doesn't look.

"Look," I growl.

He glances down and away. "You're not as strong as I thought."

His words carry a ring of truth. I should have healed. I *could* have healed from a wound like that if I'd been able to call on the magic just a little bit faster.

Doubt swirls around me. I will lose. If I can't heal a knife wound to the stomach, how will I ever be able to pull off a show worthy of applause? It's not like street performing or doing small illusions on the stage. These people are immortal. They have seen it all.

Ethan watches with cool satisfaction.

This. This is what he wanted more than the shock and applause he earned from the performance. He wanted me to doubt myself, to doubt the magic—to make the magic abandon me in my hour of need.

"You're a bastard," I hiss.

He tucks his hand into his pockets, shoulders drooping. "In more than one way," he admits, winking to cover the vulnerable part of him. "I did you a favor, Ava."

"How do you figure?"

"Now you know. You can't win this. You may be able to die trying, but you will never win. Leave and live," he says casually, like there isn't an implicit threat to his words.

I drag a knife from the sheath on my wrist. I raise the tip to the knot in his tie and let it trail lazily down to his stomach, to the exact spot where he hit me.

Something flickers in his expression, but he does not flinch.

"Go ahead." He leans forward slightly, pushing the knife just to the point of ripping the fabric on his shirt. "*I* know how to heal."

"So do I."

I jerk the knife back, then swing it in an arc toward his face, but I don't hit him. Instead, I lift my other hand and slide my knife in and out of my own palm in one swift movement, praying I don't hit a bone. Bone is harder to heal. I have to grit my teeth against the pain, but I don't hesitate.

Ethan jolts, surprise taking control of him for one moment before he can slide back behind indifference.

I call the magic to me instantly, and it answers, humming a tune in my hand as it sews my flesh back together again. It's not the magic it would take to heal a gut wound, but at least I can prove I have some skill.

"Nice party trick."

"Don't test me again."

We stare at each other in silence before he turns on his heel and struts away.

I walk back to the throne room.

"She needed to do it herself," Roman says. I turn the corner. Roman's hand is still wrapped around Xander's arm. Xander's face is red, and I can't tell if Roman's actually physically holding him there or not.

He drops Xander's arm when he sees me, and Xander spins, jogging toward me like I'm in some kind of immediate danger. Maybe I am. This seems to be a dangerous game.

"Are you all right?"

"I'm fine."

Xander's eyes scan me, landing on the leftover blood on my hand. He reaches for it, but I pull away.

His mouth tightens to a thin line. "I will kill him."

"He didn't do it. I did."

Xander's eyes widen.

"I needed to prove a point." I wipe the blood away on my black jeans. There are definitely benefits to wearing black.

Roman chuckles just behind Xander's shoulder. Chuckles. He rarely cracks a smile, and this is what gets him.

I can't help it. I giggle myself.

Xander's gaping at us, shaking his head. "Show me the wound," he says, refusing to join our funny little party.

I hold up my pristine hand.

"Not that one."

Damn it. One of the girls must have told him. This I don't want to do. Suddenly, that moment of lighthearted giggling seems years ago.

I hesitate, fingering the hem of my black T-shirt. It's new. Somebody changed me while I was out.

"It's not that bad."

"Show me."

Roman looks like he's considering whether he should stay for this or not. I wish he wouldn't.

He decides to wait.

I pull the hem up slowly, revealing a one-inch red line bristling across my pale stomach. I'm almost more embarrassed of how white my stomach is. I could have used some time in the Santa Cruz sun. The thought makes me want to giggle again.

"Shit," Xander breathes, running a hand through his hair and looking at the ceiling.

Roman stares at the wound, checks my expression, and then politely looks away.

"It's not that bad." It doesn't look pretty, though.

I want Xander to lighten the mood—to make some inappropriate remark about the skin he can see. But he just tugs his jaw with his hand.

"Don't you dare," I say.

"What?"

"Do not touch him."

He sighs, glancing back at Roman for whatever support he found earlier. Roman shakes his head. He's with me now. "She's right," he says. "It would only make her look weaker."

I wince, and Xander steps forward, draping one arm around my back and cradling my elbow in his palm. I lean into him even though I wasn't wincing from the pain. It was Roman's words that got me. Going after Ethan *would* make me look weaker, because after today I already look weak. I may have addressed that problem with Ethan, but I can't go around stabbing my own hand in the face of everyone who witnessed the debacle, and they probably wouldn't even find it that impressive—it's not the same as healing from a stomach wound. My own show will need to be above and beyond.

Roman captures my gaze. "You will recover."

I nod. He doesn't mean the wound.

"I'll be fine." I hope it's not a lie, but it sure feels like one.

CHAPTER 26

I wake up shaking, with my hair damp and stuck to the side of my face, but it's not from the stomach wound. My stomach feels surprisingly fine. I was dreaming about their faces while I lay there with a knife in my gut and the life pouring out of me. They reminded me of bored, hungry lions excited by a bit of carnage.

The thought makes me uncomfortable. These are the people I want to join. I'm giving up blood in more than one way just to be here. But Xander's not like that. There was fear in his eyes. Neither is Reina, Diantha, or even Aristelle. I don't know about the twins. Something tells me they might like the sight of blood, with little concern if it's mine or not.

I don't really want to open my eyes and step outside this room and see those faces that seemed to be rooting for me to die.

Something shifts at my feet, like someone's sitting at the end of my bed.

I scramble back so quickly that I bang my head against the headboard.

Roman jumps up from the bed and takes a step back, like he's the one who's scared. He holds a hand up. "Ava, please."

Only then do I realize I've already grabbed the stake from under my pillow. My breathing is heavy.

Roman doesn't seem to be breathing at all. He takes another step backward. "I just wanted to make sure you were okay."

"Well, I'm not bleeding anymore, so there's nothing here for you."

"I wouldn't . . ." He glances at my stake, but it's not fear in his expression. It's sadness. "You sleep with that. . . . You think I would . . ." He grimaces. Hurt darts across his face before he clears his throat. I can tell he's trying to get his emotions in check, but they're still all over his face—a rare occurrence. "I can see that you're fine," he says as he starts to head for the door.

"Wait," I say.

He spins back around—way too quickly, eerily, like he's forgotten to pretend he's not a vampire with me.

The hope on his face feels like a whole different kind of wound.

I don't know if I can trust him, but I do know he won't hurt me.

And I'm starting to think he might kill *for* me.

That's scarier.

I set the stake down on the bedside table. "Sometimes I sleep with it under my pillow. It makes me feels safe. . . ." I trail off. I don't want him to know how much yesterday affected me. I want him to know I'm strong. I don't need his help anymore. Except maybe I do.

Maybe he's the one person who can help me get answers.

I wave at the table by the window. "Are you hungry?" I cringe as soon as the words leave my mouth. "Do you even eat? Regular food, I mean, not . . ."

"Yes, I eat. No, I'm not hungry."

I clear my throat, and then feel self-conscious about the movement. "Well, I am."

A breakfast tray already sits on the table, covered with fruit and croissants and a thick raspberry jam. It was there yesterday morning too, and I don't know if someone brings it in or it just appears. My money's on the latter.

I walk over and grab the ornate copper teakettle and pour us each a cup. Roman tracks my movements as if he's looking for the slightest tremble in me. But I'm fine.

Roman pulls out an overstuffed blue velvet chair and sits, crossing his ankle over his knee.

I sink into the other chair.

The floral tea is so strong I half expect to see blooming clovers in my cup with lazy bees buzzing around them. Instead, it's only a pale liquid. I drop in a sugar cube shaped like a lily and watch it dissolve. Then I sip my cup of spring and sugar. I probably didn't need extra sweetener at all.

I push the second cup toward Roman. He stares at it like it's more than a cup of tea before lifting it to his lips.

"How soon do I have to perform?" I ask. I wouldn't be surprised if it were now.

"Tomorrow. We got you the day off to recover."

I frown. It sounds like they talked to Lucius again, but Roman doesn't explain, so I decide to let it go. I need an extra day.

"I need your help with something." If I can't get the mansion to take me anywhere but to Roman, then I need him to come with me. "Lucius knew my mom," I state.

Roman's eyebrows rise.

"I thought coming here would help me find out more about her. I've been trying to get the mansion to take me anywhere I can find more information, but I keep ending up at your door. It's broken or something."

He sets his teacup down with a clank. "It takes you to my door?"

"Yeah, that's how I ended up there the other night. I wasn't trying to see you or anything." I glance at him and away again.

"Unless you did want to see me." His voice is low and deep, and the sound draws my eyes to his lips. My stomach drops.

"Please," he says.

I don't quite know what he means. But there's a yearning in his voice that makes my heart stutter.

"I can't keep losing people," he says.

"You never had me." I push my chair back from the table and try not to think of our kiss. He had me in that moment.

Doesn't mean he still does.

I stand up. "Never mind. I can do it myself."

He stands too. "No. Let me help . . . as a friend."

I stare at him. He's been on my side this whole time, even though he was lying. I know why he did it, because I would have channeled all the hate in my heart to help me plant a stake in his. He needed time to show me who he was, tell me his story. Help me see.

I do see. I don't want to kill the same way I did before. I definitely don't want to kill him, but he also lied to me. I can't help but wonder if there's something else he's hiding. Sometimes I think I can see it in his eyes—hear it in the pauses around what he says.

But I need him right now. "Okay," I say slowly. "My theory is that if you're with me while I'm looking, then the magic won't take me to your door. Not that it was taking me to what I want," I add, "just to be clear."

"Of course not," he says coolly, but I don't like the lingering hope in his eyes.

"I think it will help if you try to want what I want."

"I already do," he whispers, almost more to himself than to me.

"Okay, then." I clear my throat and rub my hands across my pants. "Let's do this."

We step out of my room and walk side by side until we come to a white door with a gleaming gold handle in the shape of a roaring lion's head. Its open teeth nip at my hand as I grasp it and turn, leading us into a hallway of white marble and golden walls etched with redwood trees. It might be the prettiest hallway yet. If I weren't on a mission, I'd sit and stare at the pictures carved into the walls in such delicate detail, but a matching white door sits at the end, and we step into another hallway. This one's painted plain cream, with a wood floor and a runner made entirely of soft pink rose petals stitched together with golden thread. Each step crushes the petals, and I turn back just long enough to watch them heal as soon as I lift my foot. But I'm not here to marvel at the magic, and another door sits at the end of our flowered path.

"Are you thinking about what I want?" I ask Roman.

I'm starting to think the magic here is lonely, that it's desperate to take a walk with you before it will let you go. Or maybe only one of us is doing the work.

Roman glances at his feet. "I was thinking of you."

I don't like the way his words make my skin tingle the way the magic does.

"Focus," I say.

"Sorry."

I reach out and grab his hand, linking his cold fingers between mine. Cold, like a vampire who hasn't had blood recently and not like the magician he's pretending to be. He *is* hungry, then.

He stares down at our clasped hands in shock. "What are you doing?"

"There. Now you have what you want. You can stop thinking about it."

He clears his throat. "Now I want other things."

My hand feels impossibly hot in his cold one. I look up at him. The longing in his eyes makes my breath catch, and I can't find the words to order him to stop. I shake my head and have to force *myself* to focus.

He nods like he doesn't need me to say it, and we walk to a simple wooden door that could be in any old house. It opens into a hallway of all-black marble from ceiling to floor. It's twice as wide as the other one. This one feels different. The magic in me zings like my GPS telling me I've found my destination.

Photos of different sizes hang on the walls—each one in an elaborate gold frame with a different Victorian design. I walk over to one, and my heart speeds up. Mom stands onstage in a black ball gown with a crown of roses in her hair. Her red-painted lips are pulled back into a wide smile. One of her hands waves to the man behind her on the stage. I squint at him. David Copperfield.

I keep drifting down to photo after photo. Each one feels like an extra puzzle piece for a full picture I've never been able to see. Lucius is in many of them, always looking at her instead of the camera. He's starting to give me creepy stalker vibes until I get to one in a circular gold frame where he's staring straight into the camera while my mom presses into his side and kisses his cheek. It'd be a cute pose if not for the smirk on his face—he doesn't look happy. He looks like he won. Mom looks like she's in love.

This new, bigger revelation locks into place. They were *together*— before Mom left and had me and Parker, she was an immortal magician, and she apparently dated Lucius. If he knows who I am, then it makes sense why he seems to dislike me in particular. She left him and hooked up with my dad, and I'm a walking memory of that.

Shit.

If he knows who I am, he can't possibly want me to win, but maybe he doesn't know. Maybe that's the reason Julia told me not to go digging.

But I bet he has a lot of stories. Maybe I could fill up the years I missed with her with stories of her past. It seems like she had a long one. The realization sends my world spinning. I've always thought of Mom's life as cut short, but that was only her life with me. Does every picture have her in it? I twist and drag Roman toward the end of the hallway, because for some reason I'm still gripping his hand, and I stop in front of huge double doors. Above them are two painted portraits in frames that look like gold-plated roses melded together. Lucius stares down his nose at me with his ice-blue eyes. A golden plaque at the bottom of the frame has his name in curling letters. The other painting is of Mom. She's got her signature rose in her hair with a faint smile on her face. The painter somehow captured excitement in her wide brown eyes, or maybe it's in the slight raise of one of her eyebrows, like she's joking with whoever she's looking at. The plaque at the bottom reads CASSIA.

She looks like the version of Mom I loved most—the one laughing with her toes in the sand.

"Do you recognize her?" Roman's eyebrows draw together as he stares at me.

"That's my mom."

His fingers clench around mine way too tightly.

"Ouch."

"Sorry." He drops my hand so he can turn around to face me, but I can't take my eyes off the painting.

"So I found out something at least. Lucius was in love with my mom." I spin as I take in all the pictures I haven't even looked at yet. "Maybe a little too in love," I mutter.

"Ava."

The hesitation in Roman's voice makes me whip back around.

He points at the portrait of my mom. "*That's* your mom?"

I nod.

His eyes tighten. "Ava . . . the woman in that painting . . . she was the first magician. She's the one who discovered she could move the balls with her mind."

I blink at him. I'm still trying to wrap my mind around her being immortal, but now he's telling me she was *ancient*. Aristelle said it's hard to hang on to your humanity when you live forever, and this information makes me see that weariness in her eyes in a new light. She didn't just give up magic—she gave up *everything* she'd been for so long. It's a wonder she survived it *and* kept her humanity. Because despite the sadness, she was a mom who spent her days making me smile. And she did it all for me and Parker and Dad. The realization makes me love her even more, so much that my lungs squeeze, and I want to cry. The feeling is pure and untainted by her death. I can't remember the last time I felt that.

I move to look at more pictures, longing to explore this revelation. I want to take in as much as I can. But Roman reaches out and turns me to look at him.

I try to ignore his hungry expression.

"That could be why you have so much natural power," he says. "She had a lot of raw magic, and she left and became mortal again, but after building her power for so many years . . . it probably never faded completely. She must have passed some to you." Roman looks me up and down like he's seeing me for the first time. "You might have more than you're letting out."

I keep my mouth shut. I *know* I do. It pushes against my skin like it'll burst from my pores sometimes, but Roman's the person who taught me it doesn't matter without control, and I don't know how much I can control it.

"Do you know what this means?" Roman asks.

I nod. Somehow I've always known. "It means I can win."

If I can let it out without hurting everyone around me.

CHAPTER 27

I stand on the stage in front of the same group of people who cheered for my blood the day before yesterday, but I'm not worried about them. They're almost a pleasant distraction from Lucius, who sits in the middle of the crowd on a raised gold platform. I focus on his chair instead of him, but that's a mistake. The chair's legs are made of thick icicles, the kind you might see on the ceilings of frozen-over caves. The thin points of them dig into the ground. The back of the chair is a fan of icicles with the sharp ends pointing outward. The part that bothers me is what's trapped inside each one: a rose that hasn't blossomed.

Of course I think of Mom. She loved roses.

My hands shake as I pretend to adjust my knives, but I can't stop fixating on those roses. Is it some kind of message? Does he know I'm the daughter of the woman who left him? Xander doesn't. My troupe doesn't. All they know is that I had a magician mother who knew Lucius. But Lucius was going to let me bleed out. Xander said that Lucius was blocking him from healing me. Maybe he blocked *me*, too.

I couldn't feel my magic, but that could also just have been my own weakness. I don't know.

I force myself to look at his face. His eyes are cool and distant, but when he notices my stare, they become sharp and critical, like he's inspecting me for cracks. I turn my expression to ice and glare back.

He smiles. He knows. I can feel it, but I won't be certain until I confront him.

My palms sweat at the thought, but I need to focus. There's a family watching from the audience that wants me to do well so I can stay with them. They *want* me.

I turn my attention back to where I am. Willow and Nadine, dressed in matching black skintight outfits, flank me. I wear dove-gray pants and a short-sleeve black T-shirt. The pants make the black knives attached to my ankles stand out. Everything is about standing out, making the small details unforgettable. I even let Diantha and Reina rim my eyes in darkness and paint my lips in plum.

I dip into a slight bow to Lucius, then rise to address the audience. "Don't get too excited. I'm not going to stab them." A few of them have the gall to look disappointed. Most laugh, though, giving me what I want.

I turn my attention to slightly above their heads, so it seems like I see them but don't. Xander's trick.

My breathing flows in and out of me as consistent as the ocean waves. I can do this. Both Roman and Xander trained with me yesterday after Roman and I got back, or rather, they argued about what would have the most impact on the audience. I ended up making the final call, a balance between their two styles. I will start with flash and end with power.

The orb hangs above the audience. I almost wish I didn't know it was there, collecting the votes as I perform. Swallowing, I raise my hands from my sides, palms up. On cue, Willow and Nadine each pick up a knife from the tables beside them and toss the blades toward me. The magic burning in my palms calls the knives like magnets. Easy. I keep my face grim though as I send them into the air.

Willow and Nadine toss a second set, a third.

My hands fly as I toss and catch, toss and catch. My breaths come short and shallow, and I have to focus on dragging each one down to my stomach and back. Breathing right is the first step to accuracy. I need to be accurate, more than anything else in this.

The only thing I'm missing now is fire. Aristelle coated the tips of all my knives in a clear gel. The fumes from it burn my nose. I don't need to be able to sustain fire the way she can. I only need to light it. The magic's the same magic for all of us. It's only a matter of practice and natural talent. And if you want something badly enough, it will work. I explained it the same way when they all balked at my plan. But they couldn't deny that it *is* what they taught me.

My fingers already throb from it. I push them to the point of aching. Sweat beads on my temples. *Light.* I let the word slip from my mouth, soft and unnoticeable.

Nothing.

The knives move faster, higher, responding to the magic in my fingers.

The magic sings to the metal. I need to change the tune the same way Willow changes the magic with hers. The song I sing now is hard, sleek, and deadly. I need to weave it with fluid heat. I draw images of burning trees and campfires into my mind, but I still struggle to create the song of them. I don't know it.

I'm supposed to give up if I can't do it, move on to my next trick.

I promised.

I make the mistake of looking into the audience. Some watch the high arc of my knives, but some look away already.

Desperate, I find Xander in the front. He shakes his head slightly. He wants me to give it up. I set my jaw and stare at his lips, the angle of his jaw, the way his muscles flex in a casual way when he crosses his arms. But it doesn't work. He's beautiful, but what I really want is to just laugh with him, to be with him and all the rest of the troupe together, to sit on the beach again while we watch the twins play in the waves. I automatically look for Roman. He's on the edges of the audience, a smudge of monotone clothes against a crowd that prefers over-the-top vibrancy. He catches me watching him, but for once, I don't pretend that I'm not. I let myself take in all his sharp edges. His expression stays impassive, but when I meet his eyes again, there's a fire in them. *That's* what I'm looking for. My face heats. I latch on to it and let it spread instead of trying to shut it down. I remember the hunger in our kiss, and not just his hunger—mine too. I sink into the feeling until my fingers sing a new song of liquid, burning metal.

The knives light.

My song turns cold and hard again the moment they do, but it's enough.

My trick keeps them flaming. I give them power mixed with illusion, but they see only power. I deceive them—the only true illusionist in the room. I'm the best of my mom *and* dad. I let myself smirk as I steal their applause, and then I change my throws so the knives fall and stab the ground at my feet in a perfect semicircle.

I receive applause. I try not to judge whether it is more or less than the others. I'm not done yet.

The box my troupe spent hours making sits behind me, its door open and beckoning. I walk back to it and wave at its emptiness before I step inside.

Willow moves forward and shuts the door. Only my head remains visible at the top.

Around the box are more than fifty well-placed slits, waiting to accept the swords and knives piled on the tables.

This will be my true performance. I kick down two wooden flaps built into the inside of the box and pull my legs up on them, putting myself in a crouching position. My knees should just hit the front of the box. I lean my hands back and feel for the tiny nicks in the wood, telling me where to brace them—the exact location to keep my body away from fatal wounds. Only the fatal ones. After Ethan's performance, I need to bleed for these people, but I'm going to do it on my own terms.

Most of the blades should skim by me if I'm in the right position. We spent hours mapping the routes. The ones that hit me, I will need to heal. Again, I will combine power with illusion. It would help if I were an actual contortionist, but at least I'm small.

I nod, and Willow and Nadine move in sync, pulling blades off the table one after another and shoving them through the box. Willow balked at doing this part, but I promised her she wasn't going to wound me *that* badly.

They start at the bottom, and I pretend to wince even though they're nowhere near my legs yet. Some of the audience laughs and hoots at my pretend pain, but at least I'm giving them their desire.

Then the first one slices through my pants and skims the skin of my thigh. I clench my teeth and pull back slightly so I can call the magic to my wound. Another hits the fleshy part of my upper arm. Many slide through without actually touching me, but enough hit me to make my eyes burn. I heal the ones that just scratch me as they go by; the ones that stay embedded I will need to hit with a rush of magic as the blades release. Otherwise I will bleed out and gain nothing from my pain.

Pain's worthwhile only if you gain something.

I made Roman stab me at least fifty times yesterday with varying degrees of severity. He had to heal me sometimes. By the end, I could heal myself 90 percent of the time. Xander refused to stab me at all. He didn't want me to perform this trick. When I said I had no choice, he stopped arguing. He knew it too.

A blade sinks too deep into my thigh, and I actually gasp. It shouldn't have gone so deep. I'm out of position.

Nadine pauses, concern freezing her features.

I nod. Keep going.

Blood trickles down in more places than I can count as I struggle to adjust myself. The last four swords will box in my neck.

Nadine and Willow pick up the remaining swords, placing them so they look like they will pierce through my throat. They push. The skin on the back of my neck opens in a thin line and I almost jerk my head forward into the other blade sliding through. Instead, I hold steady and let myself bleed.

Nadine and Willow stand back and bow. The crowd cheers, and then I call on everything inside of me until my blood screams for me to let go of some of the power. I order the blades away from me and they obey, sliding out of the box as one and crashing to the floor in a beautiful chorus of clanging metal.

The magic, already nearly smothering every inch of me, burns and heals the wounds.

And then I can't hold on to it anymore. It crashes from me like a wave falling away from a rock, leaving me utterly empty, even though I know it will come back. I almost stagger. Instead, I knock the steps back into hiding as Willow opens the box, and I step forward.

My gray pants are streaked with blood. My arms run with it.

Nadine hands me a white, wet cloth, and I wipe the blood away, revealing smooth, unmarked skin. I toss the cloth out into the audience. It lands at Ethan's feet.

I smile at him.

He actually nods with respect.

The audience batters their hands for me.

But I don't have time for the rush of winning. Jumping off the stage, I push my way through the crowd until I'm standing right beside Lucius as he talks to a magician wearing an all-golden suit with golden eyelashes to match. I know he should be able to see me in his peripheral, but he doesn't even glance over in my direction.

It's a power move. He wants me to feel small. Maybe he wants me to feel awkward enough to go away. I don't. I set my feet and cross my arms and wait until the other magician leaves.

"Yes?" he says as he surveys the milling crowd without looking at me.

"We need to talk."

"Agreed." He turns his head and grabs my shoulder, pulling me a step closer to him as a wall of ice rises on all sides of us.

I jump in surprise. His expression is smug, as if he *liked* startling me. I want to step away from his touch, but the walls of ice are too close. I shake as the temperature drops around me.

My fingers go numb.

He watches me as if he's waiting to see if I'll crack from the cold.

I bite my lip to keep my teeth from chattering.

He nods and lets go of my shoulder and rests his palm against the wall of ice. It shatters at his touch, cascading around us in sharp, cold flecks that nip my bare arms. We're alone now—in a small white room with his rose-icicle throne on a platform in the center.

He crunches through the ice on his way to the throne, and I follow behind him until he's placed himself on it, staring down at me.

Another display of power.

"You know who I am, don't you?" I don't see a point in leading gently. He doesn't seem like the type to appreciate it.

His eyes are calculating as he assesses me. "Yes. The question is, my dear child, do you know who *I* am?"

"I know you had a thing with my mother."

"A *thing*." His lips curl in disgust.

"I know she left you for my dad, and I probably remind you of him, but I don't think you should hold that against me. I'm my own person."

His laugh matches the shards of ice around us. "I'm not holding who your father is against you."

"Then why did you hesitate?"

He raises his brows.

"When I got stabbed. I heard it. You stopped them from healing me."

"That wasn't from petty jealousy."

"Then what?"

"Nepotism," he says slowly.

"Because you loved my mom?" My brows draw together as I stare at him. He doesn't seem like the kind of man to favor the child of his ex.

"No. Because I love my *daughter*." His words are slow, like he's waiting for me to catch them.

I step back.

"I can feel the magic in you," he says. "So much of it. Did you think that only came from your mother?" He sneers. "It certainly didn't come from that pretender of a man you apparently thought was your father. Not an ounce of power in him. Weak."

I'd bristle at what he's saying about Dad if my mind weren't tumbling away from me, trying to put it together and resist putting it together at the same time.

"You are *mine*," he says.

I'm so cold, I think he's building a wall of ice around me again, but it's just his chilly expression as he stares, waiting.

"That's not possible. I know your bodies are frozen when you become immortal. You can't have kids." He's playing with me.

He waves a hand, like my confusion is trivial. "Your mother was pregnant before we became immortal. We didn't know anything about what would happen to our bodies because of it. She didn't know that you could never be born. It ate at her. She wanted you. *I* wanted you too, but it killed her to think about the possibility of you. Joseph"—he spits the name—"took advantage of that."

"Don't talk about my father like that."

"*I'm* your father." He says the words like if they're hard enough, I'll believe them.

But he's lying. I have Dad's hair. Mom always agreed when I held that picture of us at the beach and tried to remember whatever piece of him I could.

You have your father's hair, she'd agree. Not, *you have your daddy's hair*, which is how she usually referred to him.

My heart skips a beat. Lucius's hair is an almost white blond . . . just like mine when it's not dyed.

My world shatters, and I try to breathe around the broken pieces stabbing me from every direction. I try to look at him with his cruel, harsh face and pair it with the word "father," but I can't make it fit. I don't want to. All I want to think about when I think of a father is Dad—his smiling face in the ocean picture, the way I always thought I looked like him and Parker looked like Mom.

And *Parker*. It means everyone was right when they said we didn't look like siblings, because we aren't—we're only half-siblings. . . .

I force myself away from that train of thought. It doesn't matter how much blood Parker and I share. Either way, he's not any less my brother. Dad's not any less my father. But I still don't want to believe this man in front of me is *anything* to me.

"But you were going to let me bleed out," I say, as if this is all the proof I need. "You blocked their magic."

He sighs. "I interfered with a competition years ago. For Annalise. She was so powerful, but she lacked the mental strength for competition. I should've realized it meant she lacked the mental strength for this life. There's a reason we began testing people first." He almost sounds regretful. "It angered people. Xander and Roman were breaking the rules by trying to heal you. Blocking them was what I'd do for anyone else. *You* need to prove yourself without everyone knowing who you are. *You* needed to heal *yourself*. But *I* stepped in. *I* had to put my neck out for you." He does nothing to hide the disappointment in his voice.

"So you've known who I was since I walked in."

"Of course, Ava." He says my name as if he doesn't really like it. "I've been waiting many years to call you my daughter."

His voice is still chilly, but did I imagine the thaw in it when he said "daughter"?

"Really," I say flatly. "Then what took you so long?"

He gives a sharp laugh. "Your mother."

He looked for me. She said it in that journal entry.

I want him to explain, but if he says one bad word about her, I'll stick him with a knife. My fingers already itch for them. "She was running from you."

He doesn't deny it.

"Why?"

He shrugs. "I didn't want you to be born. I didn't want Cassia to give up immortality for you. I didn't know if she'd be able to get it back. Nobody's ever tried, but once what was done was done, I wanted to talk to her. I wanted her back. I wanted to see you. I believe she thought I'd be angry with her. I'm a hard man, and any softness I had was for her. But I never gave up that softness for her, even when she kept the thing I loved the most from me."

His eyes are distant. He doesn't mean me. He means *her*.

I think of his hall of pictures. *I'm* the one who took that from him. It wasn't my dad at all.

"Do you still wish I hadn't been born?"

He doesn't answer right away. My stomach pinches. I don't know why I'm bothered by what his answer might be. He's blood, not family. Dad and Parker and Mom are *still* my family. He can't make me doubt that. I shouldn't be upset, but I can't stop myself from needing to hear his answer.

"All I want now is to know you. The daughter of two powerful magicians? A daughter who might be holding more power than anyone else in the world? Of course I want you."

He doesn't really answer the original question. He didn't want me, but he's seen what I can do, and he wants me now.

"Did you know where I was? After she died? Do you know who killed her? Why? Was it . . . she used magic right before she died . . . was it that? Did that bring the vampire to her?" I'm all questions, but I don't really care. I've had old ones burning holes in me, and now I have new ones, and I need to let them all out. I need answers to bandage the pain.

His face shifts into a snarl. "If I could find the vampire who killed her, I'd already have their dust sitting on my mantel."

His fury soothes me in some way. It's good to know I wasn't the only one feeling that way all these years. I wasn't the only one carrying around that pain and hate. He had it too. His eyes still burn with it. Perhaps it was better that he didn't bring me here sooner. With our pain combined, we might have burned the whole world to the ground for a single vampire. I don't want to do that anymore, but his anger pulls at those parts of mine that aren't completely buried.

I think of Roman's cold hand in mine, and the things he's taught me. The anger's still there, but it's where it belongs—directed at *one* vampire. One killer I'll probably never find.

"As for the why," he continues, "it might have been the magic. They're always out sniffing for magician blood, but I suspect they started hunting for her the moment she left—the moment she made herself vulnerable. It was part of the reason I searched so hard. I wanted to offer protection."

"Why would they hunt her?"

"To hurt me."

"For killing them." My voice comes out harsher than I mean it to.

His stare zeros in on me. "Your tone suggests there's something wrong with that."

I don't answer. I'm walking a dangerous line with a killer.

"Who have you been speaking to?" he asks slowly.

I shake my head. "Nobody. I've just seen movies and stuff."

"Ah." He leans back. "Naive, then."

I bristle but don't answer. Better for him to think I'm a silly little girl than to suspect the truth.

"We can fix that. You've killed one, yes?" He raises a brow in question.

I nod.

"Then you know what they're like."

"I do," I say, but I'm not just thinking about the vampires that tried to tear me to pieces. I'm thinking about the one that saved me as well.

"And you want this life?" he asks, but he doesn't seem particularly interested in my answer. He snaps his fingers, and a glass of wine appears in his hands. He swirls it around, sending the liquid in the glass spinning.

"Does it matter? I was born for it."

"Your mother wouldn't like it." He sips the wine and waits for my reaction.

His words shrink me for a second before I puff my chest out. "She isn't here. You are. What do you want for me?"

A slow smile spreads on his face. "Everything." He flicks his hand, and a throne of ice rises from the ground next to him, but he waves a hand toward the door. "As long as you can win."

CHAPTER 28

Lucius's—my father's—words echo in my head: *As long as you can win.* He wants me only if I can be exactly what he needs me to be. He's made that perfectly clear. That's not family. That's what I've dealt with my entire life since Mom died—people wanting me to be something else, whatever fits their lives. Except Deb. She never really asked me to be anything other than myself, but even with her, it was clear that Parker was the one she truly wanted. Still, I'm surprised how much I miss her sometimes.

My father wants me for my power.

But I was never here for him anyway. I'm here to learn about Mom. I'm here because I love the magic. I'm here because my troupe feels like family. My father being here doesn't change any of that.

"Earth to Ava," Willow says. She waves a handful of nail polish bottles in my face. "Do you prefer matte or gloss or clear with sparkles?"

"I don't know. I've never done it before."

"You've never painted your nails?"

"No."

"Not even as a kid?" Nadine scrunches up her face like this is the ultimate cruelty.

There was a time when a question like that would have sent me spiraling into a well of painful memories, but now I let myself laugh. Because we're pretending right now. We're pretending we're not three girls walking around with hidden hurts. We're creating an illusion just to give ourselves a little moment of peace. That's what magicians do in the real world. We should be able to do it for ourselves.

I shake my head and leave it at that.

Willow and Nadine exchange looks of pure evil. We all sit on Willow's pink comforter with a pile of makeup and nail polish in front of us—most of which belongs to Willow. None of which belongs to me. They invited me over to get ready for the elimination ball tonight, because why not have a giant party to celebrate one of us not getting everything we've been fighting for?

I'm much too nervous to worry about my nails.

Still, Nadine holds up a bottle of black polish. Obviously she knows me better than I thought.

I shrug. I'm not saying no.

Willow shakes her head, leaning across the bed as she tucks her hair behind her ear. She holds up an electric-green bottle, smiling slyly. "This color suits you."

Nadine chuckles.

I blush, and I don't try to fight it. In this one moment I have everything I told myself I never wanted. I'm just a girl painting her nails with friends, giggling over a boy, and in a few moments we'll put on beautiful gowns, not to go to some elimination hosted by a questionable group of immortals, but to go to a homecoming dance where the only thing we will worry about is if the punch is spiked and whether or not we'll be queen for the night, not an eternity.

That's the illusion. But one of us may be gone after tonight, and the boy I'm really thinking about doesn't match the green nail polish.

My stomach somersaults. Will I lose my troupe if I choose Roman over Xander? They hate Roman, but what if I can be a bridge between them? Maybe it could work out, and I can have it all. Or maybe I'll lose everything before the competition even ends.

I don't know what to do.

"You're frowning again," Willow says, and I paste a smile on my face. She turns to Nadine. "You're frowning too. You're both ruining the moment."

Nadine's smile looks just as fake as mine. She still hasn't found her friend. We share a look that promises we'll keep our smiles in place for Willow.

So I let them paint my nails green. I protest only a little when they pull out the rack of gowns Lucius has sent for us. I kind of like gowns. I love feeling beautiful when I wear them. When I see Deb again, maybe I'll let her take me shopping. My gown tonight is sapphire blue, the ocean at its purest, with a strapless top, cinched at the waist with a jeweled belt. I look like a pirate's treasure with my flashing nails. Nadine's blue dress is so dark it's almost black. It hugs her legs and fans at the knees, shimmering with the faintest hint of light whenever she moves. Her silver nails turn her into a twilight goddess. Whereas she is the night, Willow is the day in sky-blue taffeta rolling from an empire waist. Her pink nails are the faintest hint of sunset against the sky. We are the night and the day and the sea—all different, yet all beautiful.

We part ways in the hallway as they head down, and I head to my room to wait for Xander to escort me.

My phone buzzes. It's an unknown number, and I move to ignore the call, but it could always be Parker's school or something, so I accept.

"Hello?"

"Ava?" Parker's voice makes my heart leap with nervousness and love, and I suddenly miss him so much that tears threaten to fill my eyes, but I fight them off even with no one watching.

"Hey, kid. Where are you calling me from? This isn't Deb's number."

"Deb got me my own cell, so I could text you, but I wanted to hear your voice," he says.

Next time I see Deb, I'll smile at her for real. My throat aches with happiness.

"Are you still traveling with the magicians?"

"Yeah." I try and pick up on any resentment in his voice. Any sadness. I might go back right now if I hear it.

"I can't wait to tell everyone at school next year. They already think I'm the coolest because I had them at my party. Will you be traveling back here soon?"

"I think so." I don't really know, but I vow to make it happen.

"Jacob's texting me. He got a phone too." He pauses and then laughs. "He wants to know if I want a cookie from downstairs. Gotta go. Love you."

"Love you too."

I tuck my phone away. Parker loves me and has a family. I have friends. I have the chance to belong to something. I just need to earn it.

And I need to sort things out with Xander. I need to be honest with him. If I'm lying to create a place for myself in his troupe, I'm doing the exact thing I refused to do for Deb.

But Xander doesn't show. I push through the doors myself thirty minutes later. My irritation fades as I take in my surroundings.

Tiles cover the floor—each one a different shade of blue, without repetition. I didn't think there were so many different shades of a single color. A band sits on a raised, circular platform in the center.

White columns rise into a swirling ceiling of clouds—real ones.

Multiple tiers of fans drop down from the clouds, each one a different jewel tone, each blade shaped like a bird's wing with stunningly rendered feathers. I bet Reina loves this. I look around for her, already picturing the pure joy on her face, and my eyes lock on Julia. Hers flit away, but I ignore the signal to leave her alone.

She's still looking to the side when I reach her. The tiny strings of beads stitched all over her bohemian-style dress tinkle as she brushes a hand over them and finally looks at me. I expect her to be annoyed, but she just seems tired.

"I'm guessing you knew," I say.

"Knew what?"

"Who my father is."

She's silent. "I was hoping *he* didn't know. That you being here was just an unfortunate accident. I should've known he'd have had people watching you—that he would have found you eventually without your mom keeping you on the run. I used to be one of the ones he had looking for you."

"I thought you were my mom's friend."

Julia gives me an assessing look. "Well, I never found her, did I?"

"He said he wanted to keep us safe."

Julia raises an eyebrow. "He wanted her gone."

Her expression is dark. Furious—with the kind of rage I'm all too familiar with. She thinks *he* murdered her.

But chasing's not killing.

I force myself to say it—the thing I know now. Even though I shouldn't care what she thinks of Lucius. He's not my real father. He made it clear he wants me for my power and nothing else, but I still want to defend him. He's still a piece of me. "He didn't kill her," I say. "My mom used magic the day before she died. A lot of magic, to heal me." It had to be a lot. The memory is clearer now, the dark dirt beneath me that was soaked through with blood. "She died saving me. *I* killed her."

Julia's silent for a long moment, and I expect her to turn that rage on me, but her eyes are soft when she finally looks at me, and her warm hand grasps mine. "Then she died doing the only thing that mattered to her." Her fingers tighten around mine. "That still doesn't mean you should trust your father."

I almost snort at the unnecessary warning. "I don't."

"Good girl."

She lets go of me and twists away, fading into the whirls of blue like ocean foam.

I push into the crowd myself, looking for my troupe. It's hard to find them when everyone's wearing the same color, but I doubt Xander changed his hair.

A woman's gown blows in the breeze from the fans, and its sea blue mixes with the sapphire of my own dress, twirling together like ocean waves until we practically share a gown. She laughs as we struggle to disconnect ourselves.

I stumble away from her, catching the back of my taffeta gown on heels I forgot I was wearing.

Ice grabs the back of my arm and freezes me in place one second before righting me.

Not ice. A hand, unnaturally cold and firm; he's coated his fingertips in miniature icicles. Only vampires should be so cold. Odd that a man who hates vampires would go out of his way to make his skin cold. My pulse thrums too slowly. Long, thin white fingers flick out in the corner of my eye, and the dresses untangle. The woman dips into a low bow, her dress now safely billowing behind her, before rising and darting away.

"Be careful, daughter," Lucius says, leaving his words open and easily attached to any situation—current or future. The sharpness of his eyes tells me he means it for more than just tripping on a dress.

"Thank you," I say, because what else do you say to a vague warning from a vampire-pale immortal ruler who's also your father?

"No need." His stare catches on my stomach where my scar must be under my flowing fabric.

"You thought about letting me die." We both know what I'm talking about because the more I replay that moment, the more I question it. He knew who I was, and for a moment, he chose to let me die. He changed his mind, but that moment still exists.

He stares at me like he doesn't know what I'm hoping he'll say.

He shrugs. "I wasn't sure if I should let you live or not. I wasn't sure if your little troupe brought you here just to hurt me in some way, gain power over me, or maybe just make me watch you die in the competition, so, yes, I considered letting things take their course so you'd never be a weapon against me. But I'm glad I didn't, daughter, because you'll be much more use as *my* weapon. As long as you can harness that power of yours."

My mouth is dry, and not because my father considered letting me bleed out.

"My troupe doesn't know I'm your daughter."

"Of course they do. I've had them watching you since your mother died."

"You're lying." I try to break free of his grip again, but his fingers don't budge.

"I do not lie."

"You said you didn't know where I was, but you've known for ten years. You *left me* for ten years."

A violent storm flashes on his face before he reins it back in. "I needed to see if you were built for this life." He stares down at my arm as I tug against his grip. "I'm still not sure."

Roman appears beside us. Probably out of thin air. He wears slacks and a blue vest so light it's almost white. It makes his hair and pale skin glow with a vibrancy his monotone clothes usually hide. He is breathtaking. "Lucius." Roman bows low, his curls draping forward to obscure his face. He stays there until Lucius gives the faintest nod, and then he straightens. How he could even see him nod with his eyes on the floor and that mess of hair remains a mystery—one I might obsess over if not for my father's hand still clenched on my arm.

My own fingers have grown cold enough to burn. The beds of my nails turn blue, highlighting my green paint. The veins in my arms seem to stand up against the edges of my skin, throbbing, almost begging to come out into the open, to find some kind of warmth. I swallow and wince at the dryness in my throat.

Roman takes in my face quickly before his eyes dart to the hand on my arm and then back to Lucius's face.

Lucius smiles, noticing everything.

I grit my teeth against the shattering, burning cold.

Some unknown instinct tells me not to cry out. I know I am the mouse and he is the cat, with his quiet claws ready to puncture my flesh at any moment.

Roman clears his throat. "Thank you for watching my date, sir." His hand twitches by his side, but he doesn't reach for me.

Lucius looks like he wants to drag me around at his side all evening, but other magicians are beginning to notice. Magicians who don't know who I am. At least I don't think they do. I don't know anymore.

After a long moment, Lucius drops my arm and strides away without another word. The sudden absence of cold burns even more.

Roman places a hand at my elbow, pulling me through the crowd a little too fast. My feet slide in my heels.

"Slow down," I hiss.

"Sorry. I don't like the way people are staring." He scans the crowd. "Where the hell is Xander?"

"That's what I want to know." I can't believe it. There's no way they've been watching me. He's wrong. He's got a bunch of troupes at his disposal. Maybe he forgot who he assigned me to.

A soft, caressing music blossoms from the band. People begin swaying together, and I understand why Lucius made us all wear shades of blue. Everything becomes swirls of wind pushing against water, the ebb and the flow of the tide captured on a ballroom floor. I pass Willow, twirling with a handsome Black guy in a sapphire suit. She raises her brows in question. I shake my head to tell her I'm fine.

Roman reaches the door and opens it.

"It won't be much longer." Aristelle's voice reaches me before Roman pulls me through the doorway.

Roman stops guiding me forward, and I careen into him. He stares at my face with such intensity it takes me a moment to look away from him. To see what he's seen.

Xander presses Aristelle against the wall, his face buried in her neck, one hand in her hair, the other clutching the folds of midnight-blue silk at her waist.

My mouth opens and closes like a fish onshore—one second away from being gutted.

She sees me first, freezing with her hands on his chest. Regret fills her face—whether for me or for being caught, I can't really tell. I don't care.

She gives Xander a light shove away from her.

"What?" He grins down at her like it's a game.

She shakes her head and looks away.

Finally, he glances up.

"Ava." His eyes widen. His hands tighten on Aristelle's dress and then drop away as if he's been burned. I hope he really was.

I stagger back a step, jerking my arm from Roman's tight grip just as Xander moves toward me. His gaze trails over me from head to toe and back again, like he's assessing each twitch of my muscles—a hunter wondering if his prey will run or stand still long enough to receive an arrow in the throat.

I bolt.

CHAPTER 29

There are small and easy ways to break a child. I know most of them—making promises you never keep; saying everything will be fine when it never is; giving a Popsicle to one kid and not the other; saying you love them and then pinching their arm hard enough to bruise; never bothering to look at them at all; kissing their forehead at night and telling them you'll never leave and then dying.

I'm sure other ways exist.

People like to say children are resilient. And they are. Their blood's like glue. Wound them, and their body puts itself back together again. But it's not like a scab that breaks off eventually and leaves the skin unmarred. It's more like a china doll. Even if it looks whole again, there's still that layer of glue there—evidence you can point to—even when no one else looks close enough to see it.

At this point in my life, I'm more glue than flesh.

But this is a new breaking. My skin burns so hot that all the glue holding together every single wound melts, and all my broken parts slowly slip out of place, falling on the hard ground and cracking into more fragments than can ever be put back together.

I stumble, because my feet feel like nothing but dust, and catch myself on the white marble walls veined in blue to match the festivities.

They lied to me. They *all* lied to me.

It's not even about Xander and Aristelle being together, because my ridiculous vampire-forgiving heart was pulling me somewhere else anyway. It was about him pretending to want me. Tricking me. How much of it was a trick? Diantha and Reina laughing with me over dinner? That day at the beach? How much of it was an illusion?

It was like getting to paint a room a different color and then realizing that paint isn't permanent and neither are you.

Suddenly, it is all very clear to me. I may not be able to trust Lucius, but what he said about my troupe was true.

They knew who I was.

I reach the crevice with the stone nymph and slide into it, letting myself pool onto the floor. Today the base of the statue blooms with unnatural twilight-blue roses. Fake. Like everything else. I force the pieces of myself upright and dig my fingers into the stems, yanking the imposters. Real magic doesn't exist. Just because the strings are invisible, it doesn't mean they're not there.

The flowers die and turn the color of dried blood as I pull them free.

And then they grow back.

Once you see through one illusion, another always pops up.

I give a strangled cry and keep pulling, scratching away at the magic. Each time, the statue looks magic-free for five seconds before the illusion comes back like a flesh-eating rash that'll leave nothing but bones.

My fingers bleed.

All that manipulative magic, and they still left the thorns on.

I wipe my hands across the bodice of my dress. The blood turns it a deep, morbid purple.

"It's ruined."

"What?" I jerk my head up toward Roman's voice, letting my eyes stop on his slender throat. His Adam's apple bobs as he clears it.

"Your dress."

"Oh." I look down at myself. More than just my dress is ruined, but he's too polite to say so.

The damn flowers are back.

Ignoring Roman, I twist my fist around a particularly thorny bundle and pull.

Fresh blood drips down my thumb.

Roman takes a soft step toward me and drops to his knees in my pile of dead roses. Vaguely, I'm aware that the thorns must be ruining his pants. He always wears such nice pants.

I hold out my fist of now dead flowers. "At least they're real now." I still only look at his throat. I don't want to see pity on his face.

His chin bobs just in my line of vision. One slender hand reaches past me, latching onto a handful of flowers and yanking. For a while he works with me in this simple and mindless task.

Finally I stop and hold out my mangled hands on my lap.

Roman reaches for them. His are already healed, but traces of blood still linger.

He wants to heal me too, but I pull my hands away. "I don't want to heal."

He nods. "Some wounds take time."

A sob catches in my throat, and I keep it there.

"We need to go," Roman says.

I meet his eyes for the first time, and it's not pity there but anger.

I cringe away from it, and he turns his head from me. When he looks back it's softened, lingering behind concern.

The anger's not for me.

"You knew. Did they do it to Beatrice too?"

"No. But still, I suspected. Last year I noticed that their apprentice seemed a bit enamored with Xander, but I'd also noticed his closeness to Aristelle. I couldn't be sure, though. I think they keep their relationship quiet for this reason. With me chasing away their apprentices, I might have made them desperate." He sighs, rocking forward and bringing his hands together. "Some troupes find their apprentices honestly, and others use . . . manipulation."

Manipulation. It may as well be synonymous with "illusion." Everything has been one big magic trick, and I was fool enough to believe I was one of the magicians when I was nothing more than a bird in a rigged cage, sitting passively as a bloodred silk cloth is draped over the cage, oblivious up until the moment the magician's hand slaps down on it, collapsing it and flattening the bird between the bars. *Oh look*, the magician seems to say. *The cage has disappeared.* The audience claps, of course. Ignorant of the broken bones, the wasted life, all for the sake of them slamming their hands together. The cage, made for the illusion, will be fine. The bird is trash. There's always another bird.

I am a bird. I always have been. Foster kids are a dime a dozen. If you don't like one, toss it out in favor of another. Damaged people are too.

But I'm not crushed yet.

And tricks go wrong all the time.

I fold my hands into fists and wince from the wounds but keep them clenched anyway.

"Did you know that Lucius is my father?"

The pure shock on Roman's face unwinds at least one knot inside me. I don't know if I could take it if he had kept that horrible truth from me too.

"Lucius . . . *how?*" He can't seem to form words around the thought.

"Before they were immortal."

"And Lucius knows?"

I nod.

Roman's voice drops to a hopeful whisper. "And will he make sure you win?"

"He knew when he blocked you and Xander from healing me, so . . . no."

Roman's face darkens. "Does he want you dead, then?"

"He said blocking you from healing me was what he would have done to anyone. I *think* he wants me to win, but I don't think he'll help. But he doesn't want me to win for *me*. He just wants to use me if I prove that I can control my power." I didn't expect it to hurt so much to say it out loud.

"That's all we can ask for with him." Roman scans the hallway and looks back at me. "We should really go before someone sees us."

He doesn't say what I know he must be thinking. I will look weak if someone sees me. Vulnerable. It's something I cannot afford. Especially not now.

Roman offers me a bloody hand, and I take it in mine. Our hands are slick against each other. It seems too intimate. Too symbolic. Even if Roman is something more than a friend now.

But he's still a magician outside of the cage. My cage. It should make no difference whether or not he's the one doing the trick.

"I can make my own way back." I let go of his hand and ball my fists into my ruined dress.

He says nothing, just continues by my side, and when we pass a gilded mirror, I glance at my refection—and then do a double take. My hair's in perfect, glowing ringlets, even though when I lift my hand, I touch a broken thorn tangled just above my ear. My dress has fewer wrinkles than when I put it on, but the strangest of all is my smile, painted across my face like it's always there. Like it's easy.

I immediately know that this is Roman's doing. Anyone who knows me would see through Roman's illusion. But nobody here does.

My mind drifts to Reina and Diantha. They knew, of course, about Xander and Aristelle. And they knew who I was from the start. How could they not? The realization stabs me like a well-thrown knife.

"Stop," I choke out.

"What?" Alarm darts across his features as I glare at him.

At least he sees my actual expression and not the fake smile he's concocted. It's certainly not my first fake smile, but it's the only one that hasn't been my own doing.

I lurch toward the mirror. In the glass, I lift a perfectly manicured hand, and the bloodied, real thing meets its fingertips.

The glass is streaked with my blood.

He steps forward and pulls a black handkerchief from his pocket to wipe away the blood.

I'm grateful he didn't just wave a hand and magic the blood away. He could. It's an odd thing to be grateful for.

"Take it away," I tell him. I want my troupe to see how they hurt me.

"You need to look strong," Roman says gently.

He's right. That's more important than anything. I swallow and nod.

Roman takes my elbow and gently pulls me onward. He doesn't let go until we reach the door of the ballroom.

"They're waiting for you," he says.

The handle slips in my bloodied hand as I pull the door open.

Four golden platforms rise from the center of the room. Ethan, Nadine, and Willow already stand on three of them. Willow flashes me a nervous smile that slips to an outright frown. *She* can see through the illusion. *She* knows me. That fact lifts just a little of the sting. She starts forward like she'll come for me, but I shake my head. She doesn't need marks against her on my account.

A hand grabs my wrist. "Where have you been?"

I shake off Xander's grip and stare straight at him without actually looking up at his face.

He reaches toward me, and I back step into Roman's chest.

"Ava," Xander whispers.

Silence. Whispers around us sneak in to fill it.

"Move." Roman's voice rumbles against my back.

Xander stands his ground for only a fraction of a second before stepping to the side.

I climb onto my pedestal without accepting Roman's offered hand. I only need myself now. He gives me a long, assessing look and then moves to stand next to Willow. All the troupes gather around their apprentices. Except Xander is gone. Aristélle's not, though. She stands in her fire-blue gown holding a giant glass orb of throbbing light. Her face, though paler than usual, is hard and unyielding, mouth set. She did what she thought she had to do, I guess. I try to find a trace of regret in her eyes. She looks down before I know for sure, but I think it's still there. Reina and Diantha both try to make eye contact. I stare above their heads at the turning fans pushing the clouds in one direction, then the other, creating an unnatural swirl of white. Everything in this place is unnatural.

Lucius walks up among us. He begins a slow spin as he addresses the circled crowd. With all their shifting shades of blue, vying for the best position, they create a whirlpool around us, waiting for one of us to drown.

"Tonight we eliminate an apprentice. To be one of us, they must be able to call the magic to them, bend it to their will, and create illusions for humans to devour, which in turn creates the moment of belief for our magic to devour. Without nourishment, everything dies. The orbs represent the applause each apprentice collected from their performance. They will now break the orb and release their applause at the same moment. The weakest will be eliminated."

His stare lingers on me for a second too long. "Hand over the orbs."

Aristelle passes me mine and steps back. A glass dome blinks into existence around me.

"Drop them," he commands.

Without hesitating, I do it. It shatters at my feet and the light swells around me. A barrage of clapping rattles my bones as the glow continues to rise to my ankles, staying just inside the perimeter of my tiny stage. I swirl around. The others glow in contained glass domes as well. Nadine's light bubbles up to her neck. Ethan's hits his chest and he raises his arms above it. Mine dances around my waist, growing into a loud roar. Willow's bubbles at her knees.

Roman, face grim, stands just beside her.

Willow is losing. Nadine has her hands over her ears, grimacing from the noise she's close to drowning in. I catch her eye as she looks out at the three of us. She finds no joy in winning.

Willow finally turns toward me. She eyes my light, just higher than hers, and shakes her head, her expression warring between jealousy and love. She places a palm against the glass as her light turns a garish red-brown, swirling now in a rapid, growing cloud and climbing to her neck in an instant. Her mouth opens to shout something or to scream, and the smoke consumes whatever it was. The last thing I see is her brown eyes wide with fear. I slam my hand against the glass again and again. My own scream rattles in my cage, drowning the dull roar of the entertained bastards I performed for.

And then everything is gone—the liquid lights, the red, Willow.

I sink to my knees and choke back a sob.

My bloody handprints float eerily above me, almost as if they're reaching down to smother me instead of trying to escape.

They wink away just before I panic. The barrier disappears, and I spill over the edge.

I get to my feet in an instant. "Where is she?" I snarl to no one at first, but as I spin around like a cornered cat, I stop in front of *him*. The father who thought about letting me die.

"Relax, my dear. She's only gone from our world, not yours. You won't remember her, of course, but maybe fate will bring you together again when you get back."

When you get back. The words are a slap. He'll call me *daughter*, but only in private, because he doesn't believe in me. Nobody's placing bets on me. My hands clench, and then I relax them. Why would I want to stay here anyway? What good is all the power I'm fighting for if I don't give a shit about the people around me? I care about Roman, but I can't imagine an eternity here, looking at the people who betrayed me.

I want out.

I give Lucius a slow, accepting bow of my head and stumble away. People—or rather, *magicians*—clear a path for me. Most of them don't have enough humanity to be called people. Roman starts toward me, but I shake my head. He's the one thing that might stop me.

Nadine catches me in the hallway. Her eyes are damp, but there's a hardness behind her unshed tears. "I don't think she went home."

"There's only one way to know for sure. I have to get out before they wipe my memory."

Her eyebrows go up.

"There's nothing for me here. I found out . . . my troupe's been lying to me. Everyone here is a liar."

"You got your answers, then." She waits to see if I'll explain.

"Lucius . . ." I pause. I don't really want to say the words out loud again. They feel like a lie. Worse than a lie, even—a truth that you wish were a lie. "Lucius is my father."

Nadine takes a step back. I don't like the suspicion that crosses her face, but I get it. I'm not quite on the outside anymore. I'm part of the thing she hates, even if I don't feel that way myself. She seems to shake herself, though, and reaches out to grip my hand.

"Then you can get answers *here*. About Willow. About . . ."

"I want to, but you saw how he just treated me. I'm nothing to him." I don't mean for my voice to crack on the last few words.

It makes Nadine squeeze my hand even harder. But it's one part sympathy and one part pressure. "Try again. For *Willow*."

She lets go of me and walks away like she has faith I'll do whatever I can.

I believe in myself, but I don't believe in him, and there's someone else who might help me.

I'm not sure what place I'm looking for, so I focus on the who: Annalise, with her hollow cheeks and faded eyes. Eventually, I come to a dead end in a plain hallway with faded yellow wallpaper and a built-in bookcase that's stacked with classic children's stories. I glance behind me, half expecting to see the ghost of some Victorian child, and I almost leave, but there's a pull, like the magic is clearing its throat, exasperated that I'm not understanding. I step up to the bookcase and start tugging the books. When I yank on *The Secret Garden*, one side of the bookcase springs forward. I'd be impressed if I had time for it.

I'm expecting another hallway or maybe a hidden library, but my feet sink into wild clovers, and my eyes squint against the sun in a sky without clouds. I hear trickling giggles before my eyes adjust to the light.

Flowers of every kind grow haphazardly from the field of clovers, so that it looks like a green canvas with splattered paint. It's so bright and vibrant that it's hard to stare at, like it shouldn't exist, and I guess it doesn't, really. A whimsical swing set rises from the center of it all. It's nothing like the cheap metal ones in neighborhood parks. The bars are wood carved into perfect spirals. Vines curve around it and down the ropes of the swings, where the twins sit, pumping their legs back and forth. Annalise stands in front of them, bending down and plucking a handful of tulips at her feet. She tosses them into the air, and the twins laugh.

This is her happy place—just her sisters, away from Lucius and the rest of the magicians.

She doesn't look at me as I run up to her.

"Where's Willow?"

"Who?" Her voice is so faint that she sounds like a distant owl in the night.

"The apprentice who just went home. Did you already wipe her memory? Did they bring her to you?"

Her face pinches like she's thinking it through.

"Swing with us, Ava!" the twins yell.

When I look back, there's a third swing now. The vines around the whole set seem to be growing. I glance from it to Annalise's vacant stare. One of the twins gives a little yelp as a new vine grows over her hand. A trickle of blood drips down her wrist.

"Annalise." The vines keep growing until I touch her arm, and she looks back at me. "Why don't you get rid of the thorns?"

She seems confused for a second.

I point at Briar's or Bridgette's arm, but it's already healed.

"Maybe there are too many thorns in my mind," she says, but her eyes are sharp and clear when she looks at me. "I can't give you what you're looking for. I haven't seen her."

She bites her lip, and blood runs down it before it heals, and then she turns, laughing and clapping her hands as she watches the twins soar higher and higher. There's clearly no answer for me here.

I only have one more option.

I am his daughter—I may not feel it, but it's still true on a basic level. Maybe I can use that. Maybe I'd be allowed to leave and go see Willow, just so I can know she's okay. He could have some sort of magical crystal ball to show me. He might agree to bring her back—not as a competitor again, but as a friend.

It doesn't seem like too much to ask. I need a reason to stay. A father who shows a glimmer of care for me would be a good place to start. I can give it one more try, and then I'll carve my way through the front door with my knives if I have to.

My intent is clear as I push into the hallway. The magic snaps and bends around me. One second the hallway is a brick corridor, the next it's cherrywood paneling with glowing sconces, the next it's lined in a forest-green damask wallpaper. But it gives in to me eventually, and I'm standing in the black marble hallway. I stride down it, trying not to linger on the pictures of my mom. I reach the giant black doors and glance up at her portrait. Her eyes look wary, like a warning. Did they look that way before?

Reaching out, I pound on the door. Something tells me Lucius appreciates boldness.

He doesn't answer, though.

I try the doorknob. Locked.

I knock again, and the door opens. For a second, I think he opened it, and I wait for him to step out, but there's nobody on the other side. Then I realize . . . *I* opened it. My magic. I hesitate for only a moment—I don't know him well as my father, but from what I've heard and seen of him as a ruler, I'm afraid to get caught.

But if I have a chance to look around for answers, then I'll take it.

I step inside. The room's so warm it startles me. A fire blazes in a gaping fireplace. The mantel looks like it's been made from roses woven together and dipped in tar. I step toward it. It's so realistic that there are tiny thorns that appear sharp enough to draw blood. I don't test it.

The rose theme continues in the rest of the room. A rug of deep burgundy with black roses in vines around the edges takes up the center of the room. The long tufted couch and two matching chairs are the color of wilted red petals. Even their dark wooden legs boast a faint carving of the blooming flowers. Mahogany bookcases line the room, their arched tops carved to look like vines of roses dangling down and reaching for the books. An open door leads to the next room, and I can make out a four-poster bed that's almost certainly carved with the same design.

Either he loves roses as much as Mom did, or he *really* loved her, and this is as much a shrine as the hallway.

My skin crawls. It feels more like obsession than love.

The most stunning thing in the room is the solid-glass square coffee table. Inside, a captive rosebush repeatedly blooms and then wilts. It's eerie to watch the birth and death of the petals again and again. Perhaps it's soothing for an immortal. Magic radiates out from it, and I step forward to inspect the most beautiful thing I've ever seen—not the table, but the small box on top of it.

I bend down and examine it. It's gold-plated or maybe pure gold. Careful swirls of wind or fog are carved into every inch of it, weaving together like an uncontrollable storm, and every so often a flower emerges in the swirls. I press a finger to the lid and jerk my hand back. The smell of rotting flowers coats the back of my throat. This table isn't magical at all compared to the power coming off this.

I take a deep breath and lift the box again. There's no lid. I can't even find a seam. My magic pulses in me, testing it, trying to give me what I want, but nothing happens. I flip it over and inspect the bottom, running my fingers along the swirls until something bites at my skin. I stare closer at the tiniest thorn sticking out from the center of a rose. The stain of my blood disappears as I watch, and then the swirls shift as the metal turns molten, sliding away to reveal a perfect seam around the middle of the box.

An uneasy thrill zips through me. I used to sneak peeks into Mom's secret box. It seems fitting that I should do the same to my father's.

I grip the top and lift it, setting it aside as I peer in.

What's inside is so jarring I can't quite register it at first. I was thinking of Mom's box, so I must be imagining what I see. The magic's playing a trick on me. It has to be. Nothing else makes sense.

Her necklace winks up at me: the gold choker with the black velvet tie and five ruby jewels. It's the one she wore to heal me. If it were only that, then I might think it was a replica. But her journals sit beneath it—the old one with the fading brown ink that was missing the back cover, the one with the leather tie that wrapped around it, the one with the bright violets and the coffee stain. It's been so long since I've seen them, but I'd know them anywhere.

All the things the vampire stole.

They're *here*.

Impossible. My brain wants to connect the dots, but I'm not ready. *Impossible. Impossible*, I repeat over and over again until I can't anymore.

There's only one way he could have these things.

He killed her.

I'm numb with the truth of it. I sit back and watch the roses trapped in the glass table wilt. The dead petals drift to the bottom like they're falling through glue.

There could be an explanation. He could have heard of the attack and gotten there just after and taken her mementos with him before I woke up.

No. She was still alive. I held her for her last moment. If he was there, it meant he left her to die.

My fingers tingle as I lean forward and dip my hand into the box. Part of me expects it to close in on me and trap me like a monkey with its hand in a jar. It doesn't, though. My fingers wrap around the journal on top—the worn leather one.

My stomach flips. This is what I've been wanting. The other parts of the story. From Mom. The one person I can truly trust.

I open the journal and begin to read.

> I'm starting to wonder if it was ever about the vampires. He's been telling everyone that they have to kill to survive like wild lions, but I met one the other day. I was going to stake her without asking questions, like we've been taught. Kill or be killed because they want the power they lost. I know they do kill us for it, but it's not all of them. I know that now. I snuck up on this vampire, but she turned around just before I could slip the stake between her ribs and into her back. Her round face and wide brown eyes reminded me of Lucius's sister, who I found killed by Numerius so many years before, and there I was, about to kill a girl who could've been her twin. I couldn't do it. I put my stake down, and she grinned and thanked me for not killing her. It was the type of thing his sister would

have said too. And then I did something else we're not supposed to do: I talked to her. She told me she doesn't kill anyone at all. She works as a nurse, and it's easy for her to steal blood. And she uses her own blood to heal some of her patients. Can you imagine it? A vampire healing humans . . . doing more to help the world than the rest of us. She doesn't even know any other vampires. They're not all in on a plot to kill us—some are, but I have to wonder if they would be if we stopped hunting them. Couldn't there be some type of truce? We could give them our blood willingly to help counteract their curse. Imagine what we could do if we worked together.

The next entry is short and chilling.

I told Lucius my thoughts on vampires. It was a mistake. He stared at me in silence for a long time, and I knew what he was doing: picturing me in his garden. The garden he says is a necessary evil, but what if it's actually the root of all the evil?

I don't know what she means about the garden, but it feels ominous.

I put that journal down and pick up a plain, soft pink one with a gold spine. I flip it open. It bends automatically to a place where a page has been ripped out.

Probably by me, so I scan backward until I find the start of the entry.

Ava did it again today. She got mad because she wanted a different type of cereal, and she threw her spoon across the room like she always does, but it wasn't a harmless drop to the carpet. I felt her surge of power from the other room, and when I got out there, I saw the spoon stuck into the wall six feet away. Lots of children with magic in their blood display accidental power, but nothing like that. I have my theories about why she's like this. I was pregnant before Lucius made me immortal. I knew I was, he knew I was, but neither of us knew our bodies would freeze completely—that the fetus would stay immortal as well for as long as I did. I never would have done it if I'd known. I thought she'd still grow and be born, and if she wanted to choose immortality later, then fine. I didn't know that I'd never ever get to see her—that she'd stay a memory of a different life that was always inside of me. She was with me for every single performance, so what if she was collecting magic all that time as well? It's the only thing that makes sense. She's years and years of unused magic trapped in a tiny body.

We've already packed up and run again. Nobody's going to notice a little magic, but if any true magicians were in the area and felt that, they'll come. Last time, when Ava made her stuffed animal disappear, I spotted Julia in town. We locked eyes at the grocery store, and I knew. She didn't come after me, though. She might be scared enough of him to obey some orders, but she still gave me time to escape.

Julia lied about that. She found us before—she just didn't tell Lucius.

The next page is gone, but I know what it says. I've spent nights staring at it, wondering who the *he* is in it. I have it memorized:

> I don't know if he's coming after her or me. Probably both.

I flip to the next entry.

> We bought a cheap motor home. I have a plan—a spell I can do. I helped Lucius build the compound and make the spell to both trap and cloak the magic within it. I can do the same thing to Ava—trap her magic inside her while hiding it at the same time. It'll take a lot of power, though. I don't dare put my necklace back on, but I can perform with Joseph and collect magic the old-fashioned way. Joseph hates it. I promised to give it all up, but he understands why I have to do it. We'll just have to keep on the road to stay one step ahead of them. If I can get the spell in place and keep it there, eventually it will start using her own magic to feed it. She'll be hidden forever.
>
> Unless they find her or she meets another practicing magician. Then it might shatter.
>
> And there would be nothing I could do to keep her away from the magic after that.

Mom hid who I was. All those times I asked her if magic was real, she'd stare right at me, her own daughter brimming with magic, and lie to me. I know she was doing what she thought she had to, but there's a deep ache in my chest for what might have been if I'd been allowed to be myself. Maybe I'd be stronger now. I'd have more control over this raging river within me.

But none of it was her fault.

Everything that's gone wrong in my life leads back to one person. Lucius.

I want him dead.

Rage burns through me so hot that I worry I'll light my own hands on fire.

Mom spent her whole life protecting me. She died to keep me from the very place I'm sitting now. I already know that revenge leaves you hollow, but then again, I didn't kill the right people. Maybe I should start fresh.

My fingers itch for my knives.

But how could I possible beat him? I don't have the skill. I don't even have a troupe to back me up anymore.

What would Mom do? I run my hand over the journal she worked so hard to keep out of my hands, and I know. She'd want me to go home. She'd want me with Parker. She'd want me to work just as hard at keeping us together as she did.

My legs wobble beneath me as I stand, gripping the journal in my hands. I don't want to put it back and let him hold on to any piece of her, but I'm smarter than that. Leaving it could buy me more time, so I tuck it against the black velvet lining and replace the lid, watching the swirls swallow the seams.

I can't look back.

I have to let go of all of this—the revenge, the magic, everything. For Mom.

When I push my way out of the room, I expect to be in the same hallway as before. I expect to see the photos of Mom one last time, but I'm in a hallway with no doors and generic paisley wallpaper that looks like it came out of a motel that hasn't been updated since the nineties.

I focus on what I want as I walk, but it doesn't shift again. I run, but there are no doors no matter how far I go. I stop as panic bubbles up inside me, and once I stop, I can feel it. The magic in this place tugs at my skin like I'm walking through thorns. It knows what I want, but it doesn't want me to have it, like it's begging me to stay, clawing at me to keep me here. But it can't. I slam my fist into the wall, and it crumbles away. I make my own door.

I step into a hallway of pale lavender and stop. It feels familiar. It takes me a second to realize it's the exact shade of my bedroom at Deb's—that warm, calming color I never really liked. The magic's trying to trick me. I want to be at Deb's, so it's trying to give me Deb's instead of letting me out. At least this hallway has a door in it—that looks exactly like my bedroom door at Deb's house. I push through it, a tiny part of me hoping to find my silly, shabby-chic room on the other side. What I get is a hallway covered in the same floral wallpaper as Deb's stairway.

I put my hand on a fading mauve bloom. It's so real, but this isn't where I want to be. It's not about the paint or wallpaper. I need Parker. I think his name as I push a wave of power from me. I don't even smash the wall. I walk right through it onto the brick pathway lined with fog-drenched roses. I glance behind me at the mansion, all stone and moss and darkness, and wish I could have said goodbye to Roman, but when I start forward, I don't look back.

The path is straight. It doesn't try to wind and trick me. I keep calling my power, pushing it out ahead of me with my desire to leave, and then I'm through the iron gate and at the thick tree line. I look back, expecting to see the whole place having disappeared, hidden again behind the spell, but it's still there, looming and pulsing. Strange, but I don't have time to think about it. I don't have a car, and I need to reach the main road before nightfall.

I follow the narrow road, but I don't walk directly on it. I pick my way through the ferns twenty feet into the forest where I can duck down if anyone starts driving up. I haven't been moving long when I hear the faint crunch of gravel. I crouch down and press myself into the trunk of a thick redwood. All I see is a blur, and then I hear the grinding of feet skidding on gravel.

I peek around the tree. Two people stand in the middle of the road.

"Holy shit," says a petite woman with fire-red hair braided down her back. "There it is."

"I can *feel* it," the man next to her says. He runs a hand across his buzzed black hair and licks his lips. "We've checked this road before. They're getting sloppy."

"Unless it's a trap?" The woman cocks her head.

"Best not to find out with just the two of us," the man answers.

I shift slightly so I can glance back the way I came. The mansion is still there, fog hanging around its peaks.

Shit. Whatever protection spell was on the mansion seems to be gone. I pull a stake from my boot and grip it in my hand, debating what I should do. I want to kill vampires less than ever, but if they're looking for the mansion, maybe I should. Nadine is in there.

And Reina and Diantha. The twins.

The vampires turn and start jogging back down the road. I have to act now, or I'll have no chance of catching them. I move to spin around from my hiding place, but a hand grabs my arm and shoves me back against the bark. I point my stake in that direction on instinct, stopping it just above Roman's heart.

He holds a finger to his lips. He doesn't seem the least bit worried about my stake. He doesn't need to be. I let it fall to my side. We stand in silence until the vampires' chatter fades.

Roman steps away from me and glances back at the mansion. "I believe you shattered the protection spell."

"Not my problem," I tell him. "I'm leaving."

"You can't go," he says.

"I am." I wave a hand around me. "I'm already out."

"Please, Ava. Trust me. You need to see one thing, and then I won't stop you. I swear."

The only reason I nod is because I *do* trust him.

His cold fingers reach out and wrap around my elbow. My skin feels fevered under his touch. I barely pay attention to my surroundings as he leads me back through the arched entryway to the compound, through the twirling paths of fog and roses, to a wooden door tucked in the side of a towering hedge.

We step through, and my feet hit a cobblestone path. Sculpted hedges grow to our knees on each side. The walkway winds and curves in front of us, veering apart in some places and meeting up again farther down. A giant maze with small gardens planted in the middle of each crossing path. Roman holds out his elbow like I'm a lady he's taking for a walk in the garden with our chaperone trailing behind.

"I'm not in the mood for this."

"Take my arm and act natural."

The other side of the maze opens to a field of ferns. Roman glances over his shoulder once before stepping into them and pulling me with him.

"Tell me where we're going."

"Not yet." He looks back again. The hairs on my arms stand in response to whatever threat he senses that I don't.

I keep my mouth shut as we reach the end of the ferns and start down a narrow path through a dense forest. The fog grows so thick that I can't see anything at all, and I don't know we've reached anything until my boots squelch into mud.

I pause, and Roman has to pull me forward as the fog shifts to reveal the edges of a lake.

Roman crouches and then springs out over the water, landing on a billow of fog.

"Are you coming?" He holds out a hand toward me.

I shake my head. I haven't mastered floating on clouds or water or whatever's holding him aloft.

He waves a hand, and the mist rolls back from the water directly in front of us, gathering in a dense cloud on either side of a floating bridge—if you could even call it that. Whole sections dip sideways into the gently lapping water while some boards are missing altogether.

He frowns at my expression, which says he's a fool if he thinks I'm following him, and holds out his hand again. "You *need* to see what I'm going to show you."

"Not this bad."

He doesn't answer, just waits, giving me time to accept what he already knows I'm going to do.

I shrug like it's no big deal. I don't even take his hand. The water's not deep here, and I may not be able to swim, but I can certainly stand on my own. I slosh into the water up to my knees to where the bridge begins and place one soaking boot on a plank. It bobs under my weight.

I sense him waiting to catch me if I lose my footing, and it makes me grit my teeth and drag my other foot up. I brush past him and hop onto the next board.

Which doesn't feel like holding me. My knee hits the wood, hard, and I slip toward the water. Roman grabs the back of my shirt and stops me from taking a bath.

"Thanks," I grumble, pulling myself to my feet as he slides around me.

"Follow me," he says, hopping from board to board with the perfect balance of a squirrel leaping from tree branches. He's a lot more graceful than he looks with his tall, thin frame.

I clunk behind him. A lot clumsier than I look.

After a few close calls on my part, he jumps off, splashing into shallow water and wading onto shore. A lighter fog rolls across the small island, accenting soft grass and clusters of purple flowers. I drift toward a tangle of wild roses growing at the center. Their intoxicating smell glides along with the breeze, filling my head with summer gardens and fog-soaked gullies.

I take another step toward the roses as Roman grips my wrist. I try to jerk away from him, but his fingers tighten.

"You still don't see it."

I barely hear him. The roses beckon, bright and red, singing to my blood like a long-lost sister.

"See what?"

He sighs. "The magic's hiding it from you." His lips are on my ear before I can react. "Open your eyes. You broke the entire barrier spell around the mansion. You can break this too."

His voice shivers down my spine. His fingers on my wrist heat as his magic pulses, shattering the peaceful air around me.

I shut my eyes against the feeling and shudder. My own magic explodes out of me and then stills.

When I open them again, I wish I hadn't.

The smell hits me first. The fog and flowers were only one small thread in the blanket of stench covering this place. The tang of blood and rot is strong enough to taste. My stomach lurches as I take in where it comes from.

People lie tangled in the roses and vines growing out of the hard rocks.

I know immediately where I am. The garden. The one my mom thought Lucius wanted her in.

I take a stuttering step toward them, hitting my toe on jagged stones—the soft, rolling landscape of flowers from moments before is gone.

They seem asleep at first, wrapped in vines like cursed people in a fairy tale just waiting for a knight to save them. I surge forward like I'm the hero in their story. Roman follows, his long strides taking him easily over the rocks I scramble on.

When I reach the edge, I freeze. No one here waits to be saved. The vines don't just hold them in place—they weave under their skin, piercing through chest and limb. Blood dribbles down anywhere the skin breaks. And the vines, some two inches thick, pierce everywhere. Smaller, thread-thin ones weave around the eyelids and lips, giving them the appearance of gruesome, hand-stitched dolls.

I stand in front of a brown-haired girl with a vine weaving in and out of her still-pulsing throat. Her mouth dangles open, and a red rose blooms between her lips. I touch a petal. My finger comes back red with blood.

I turn and heave, fighting my raging stomach.

"What the hell is this?" I brace my hands on my knees in case I hurl again.

Roman's eyes glaze as he looks at me. "Haven't you wondered why there's so much magic here? How it lives outside of us, controlling the very shape of the building?" He turns his head toward the carnage before us. When he looks back, his eyes are sharp again. "We feed it. And these . . ." He lifts his wrist where he wears a simple black band with one of the same red stones every other member of this society wears embedded in the middle of it. "I bet they fed you a story about how one magician's blood sacrifice created these stones with the immortality spell, and now we can feed the spell with our performances instead of blood." I don't even have to nod. He knows. "That's a half-truth at best. Their performances make them strong, but the immortality? It still takes blood to make that spell work." He waves his hand toward the garden, where droplets of blood slowly drip like morning dew, then waves down at his feet. "He linked the stones."

The ground is covered in pebbles coated in blood. There's so much red that at first I don't even notice the sparkle as the mess shifts under my feet, but it's not just pebbles. Red jewels matching the one in Roman's cuff soak in the blood as well. The same jewels I've seen woven into the decor of the house. They're all fed here—everything is linked to this horror.

"Society magicians don't have to consume the blood themselves because they feed the magic blood out of sight. They get all of the benefits and none of the curse. He never found a way around the constant need for blood to feed immortality. He only found a way to make it prettier—at least for the immortals themselves."

"Then they're *all* vampires," I say.

He doesn't refute it. The magicians live off blood just the same as he does.

I shake my head. "No, they're *worse* than vampires. They go out and kill vampires and pretend they're not just as bad."

He looks sick. "I agree."

It makes even more sense now why he chose to become a vampire. He was choosing a better life—a bloody one, but one where the blood was bought or given, not stolen.

"Where did they get all these people?" I can't even tell from here how deep the garden goes. "Never mind, I don't need to know." I straighten and back away, rocks cascading around my feet.

"Wait."

I don't stop.

"You can't go home."

His words slap me. Of course I can't go to a place that doesn't exist for me, but I can get the hell off this island. Roman doesn't follow as I scramble away from the garden of death.

"It needs more than just any old blood," he calls after me. "These are the failed apprentices."

CHAPTER 30

My steps stop at the same time my heart does.

"No." I turn slowly back around, search his face for a lie, and find only truth. I race back toward the thorns, smashing my toes on rocks, slipping on the blood coating them as I race around the edges of this death trap. My knees hit the ground enough times for the blood to soak through my pants and warm my skin. I fight the urge to gag until I finally find what I'm looking for.

She's bent backward at the waist as if frozen in some sadistic game of limbo. Vines enter through her spine and erupt in blooms that run down her chest like buttons, holding her in her constant dip.

When I reach her, I grasp her long blond hair in my hands, pulling it off the ground where it had been soaking up blood, the ends tinted in a morbid dye job. Willow wouldn't want her hair dirty.

I drape it around her neck and shoulders and then yank out a knife. They will not keep her.

I strike through the vine, and it yields easily. I brace myself to pull it though her flesh, trying not to think about the thorns and where they grow.

Roman's hand closes around my fist.

I rip myself free of him and spin, my knife slashing through the front of his shirt as he jumps back. Surprise crosses his face. He holds up his hands, but he doesn't draw his own knife.

"You did this," I snarl.

He shakes his head faintly, confused.

"You told me not to clap for her." My voice cracks. "*You* didn't clap for her."

His face falls as he takes the blame I throw at him and carries it. "I know. I . . . I thought she was stronger. That she could win and be an ally once she saw this. I could tell she'd be the type of person who'd help my fight, but I began to realize that she didn't have the strength to win. I'd hoped that there would be no competition this year, that I would have more time to train her or figure out how to stop this whole thing, but . . ."

"But you chose yourself."

And me. He chose me.

I turn back and grip the vine I cut.

"It won't help," he says.

"You don't know that."

"I do."

I pause. The truth in those two words breaks me.

"Let me show you," he says.

When I don't move, he grips my arms and pulls me away from her.

My hand trails across her warm arm, brushing her perfect, pink nails. "They're not dead, at least."

Roman swallows. "Worse. As far as I can tell, the magic keeps them alive and young while constantly feeding off their blood."

"We need to do something."

"I've tried."

Roman turns and heads deeper into the tangle of thorns and bodies, and I consider not following him at all, but leaving's not even an option anymore. Not with Willow ensnared here. Not without her. I squeeze her hand. I'm not sure if she can feel it, but I hope she knows that it's me, and I've found her, and I will *not* let her rot here.

I step around her and end up face-to-face with a boy stretched out in an X with so many vines holding him in place that they look like a suit of leaves. I almost don't recognize him without his glasses. Barry. A rosebud grows from the exact spot the arrow hit his throat.

I close my eyes for a minute and take a deep breath. I know Lucy must be here too. I can't stop picturing how young she looked. She was probably close to my age, but she seemed like the kind of girl who should be home sitting on the stool of a kitchen island, eating raw cookie dough while she bakes with her mom. I swallow. I don't want to see her.

I keep my eyes on my feet as I move after Roman, but watching bloody rocks and gems slide under each step isn't any better. I look up and try to focus on Roman's back instead.

Finally, Roman stops in front of a girl who must have once been beautiful. Her dark brown hair fans out, tangled around so many vines that it makes her look like she's been caught in a windstorm. Even with the blood caked in it, you can see veins of auburn. Her features are sharp and petite. Dark purple bruises and scabs mar her pale skin. If her eyes were open, I bet they'd be the deepest brown.

"Your sister."

"Yes."

"You tried to cut her out."

I stare at his profile, the tight jaw, the way he keeps swallowing as if something is lodged in his throat.

He pauses and lifts a hand toward Beatrice before dropping it again. "She failed and ended up here, so I can't leave. I can never leave." He shakes his head again. His deep auburn curls blend with our surroundings like blood-slicked vines, like he's spent too much time here. Something tells me he has.

Sympathy washes through me. I know what it's like to be caught in a horrible memory, to have it always with you. Roman can actually visit his. He can smell the blood and see the always fresh wounds. It makes me sick. My memory is vivid and alive, but if I could actually visit the scene every day, I don't know if I'd still be moving.

But rage whispers in with my sympathy too.

"Why the hell didn't you tell me? All those vague warnings? You could have led with this."

"I couldn't. Why do you think I said my sister was dead? We're all spelled so we can't say a thing about it to anyone who doesn't already know. The only reason I can talk now is because *you* broke through the spell. You're not supposed to be seeing this. We don't show you the truth until you win. But when you broke the barrier spell, I thought maybe you could break this one, too."

But that only explains one of the things I'm angry about. "Why bring an apprentice at all if you know they'll end up here if they don't win?"

"Because if we don't bring an apprentice, then the oldest member of the troupe gets placed in here instead." He points out Edgar, bound in so many vines they look like a cocoon. His mentalist apprentice who made Lucius slap himself is next to him, dangling by vines piercing his arms, feet not even touching the ground. "Lucius has thought of everything. It's brilliant, really, because it also gives him the chance to get rid of the oldest and more powerful magicians."

"Why don't people leave?"

Roman points to a man next to Beatrice with golden hair that reaches his waist. He's held up by the roses piercing through both wrists. "He ran two years ago. People don't escape."

"Except my mom."

He's silent.

"He killed her."

Roman takes a step toward me, but I don't want him to hold or comfort me here, in this place he condemned Willow to. I hold up a hand to stop him. "You still put Willow here."

Shame blooms on his face, as garish as any of the roses, and it almost makes me reach for him. Almost.

"Every single one of us here chose ourselves to be here. Or chose a loved one. I think that's why we work in troupes. If we're not willing to condemn some random person to this to save our own neck, then we might do it to save someone we love. I scared away my own troupe's apprentices until it was down to me, and then I had to make that choice. If it was just about me . . . but I couldn't leave her here." This time he does reach out and touch Beatrice, rubbing away a bit of dried blood from her elbow. "It wasn't for me," he says, but his voice is hollow, and it holds no forgiveness for himself.

I'm not ready to forgive him either.

"Why did you train me to beat Willow?" It wasn't fair. He should have given her everything.

He stares at the wet stones beneath his feet. "It was the way you stepped into that dark alley with me and Willow the second time you saw me. Reckless. Fearless. I couldn't imagine you in here. And then . . ." His eyes are pleading as he finally looks up at me. "I felt how powerful you were. I thought you'd be a good ally. You were literally going to risk your neck to help Willow in that alley, and you didn't even know her." He glances back down at his feet. "But then, later . . . I also just wanted to be near you, to be with someone who seemed to feel something close to what I did." He looks around the garden. "Maybe I should've left you alone."

"You wanted to use me." Like my father. Like my troupe.

He takes a step toward me, the jewels and stones sliding under his feet. His hand reaches for me, hovering in the air beside my cheek for a moment. He lets it barely touch me before dropping it to his side again. "At first, but then I wanted more than just an ally. And that seemed so dangerous . . . not just for you. Watching you in this competition and knowing every second that you might end up here?" He closes his eyes. "I wasn't sure I could live through another loss."

This time I reach out. My hand hovers next to his, and I let our fingers brush before I jerk back again.

His eyes pop open, and we stare at each other.

There's been something between us for a long time, but it felt too raw, like it was built on both our wounds. Yet maybe having the same wounds makes it possible to heal together. I thought I wanted easy. Healing is hard.

Still, I take a tiny step back. Now is not the time—not when more hurt is piling around us. We have work to do.

"What do I need to do?"

He spreads his hands. "You have no other choice but to win. You can't lose. You'll end up here. You can't run. They will hunt you. Just like they did your mother."

Silence hangs between us.

"I want to burn it down," I say. "How do we do that?"

Roman hesitates for a moment. "The only way to do that is to kill Lucius. He crafted the spell and built this place. If he's not here to control it, then I think it will wither."

"Then let's do it."

He huffs out a frustrated laugh. "If it were that easy, don't you think I'd have already done it? Lucius isn't just any other magician. Not only has he been gathering power for years, he wears a crown made of these jewels." He holds up his cuff again. "He's funneling more power from this place than anyone." Roman frowns. "I suspect he's funneling magic from Annalise, too. She wears a crown, but I believe it's linked to him and not this place. He's draining her dry."

She looks like it.

"We need more allies," he says.

"How many do you have?"

"You."

My stomach drops.

"And . . . other vampires."

I step back. "No way."

"Wait. Hear me out. There are many here that want Lucius gone. There'd be peace without him, Ava. He's the one fueling an endless war. But no one in the Society is brave enough to go up against him, and I can't do it on my own. I've always known that I would need vampires backing me up on this, but I just couldn't figure out how to get them in. Once, I tried to bring a team into the woods to show them where the mansion was, but there's an alarm built into the barrier that senses anyone without one of these." He holds up his cuff. "The magicians came out and slaughtered everyone. I only got away because they thought I was out there killing them as well. But you just took that barrier down."

I'm shaking my head. Trusting Roman is one thing; letting in an entire group of vampires and trusting them is another.

"When I broke the barrier . . . those vampires I saw . . . they were with you?"

He shakes his head. "No, but most likely with the same group. They were probably in the area and felt the rush of magic when it broke. I bet the barrier's already back up now, but your power is stronger than anyone else's. If you win, we can work on growing it. You can break the barrier again when we need it."

"And how long is that going to take?" I snap. "I can't—" I cut myself off. I can't condemn innocent people while we figure it out. I can't be like him.

He looks away. Even though I don't say the words out loud, they still bite. "We need you to win first, and then we'll figure it out. But we have to go back. We can't get caught here."

I bite my lip, and without another word, I turn and move down the trail, the occasional sliding of stones behind me telling me that Roman follows. As I walk, I take in every face. I draw the images of their suffering on my skin with promises to free them. Promises I can keep only if I stay and fight.

The fear I felt going across the bridge the first time is no longer there. I am empty, weightless enough to float on the surface of the water. I leap across the boards without hesitation.

Once we're through the woods and back into the real garden with flowers not watered in blood, the sweet smell of them is almost too much. I can't shake the scent of blood still lingering on my skin.

Roman turns to me as we go back through the ivy-covered door.

"Will you fight tomorrow?"

Fight. Not compete. This goes beyond competition, and I'm the only one who knows.

I say nothing. The cost of winning may be more than losing.

He nods his head, accepting my nonanswer, and walks away.

I drag myself, wet and tired, through my bedroom door.

Xander raises his head as I do, his face unreadable. Seeing him there, his green hair contrasting with my black bedding, sends fury racing through my blood, heating it almost as swiftly as the magic. It's just as deadly, too. My fingers clench around invisible knives.

"Get out." I try to make my voice cold enough to freeze his blood—so cold that Aristelle won't be able to unthaw him—but I'm too hot. My words hiss out like steam.

"Ava."

"Don't you dare say my name." It has no place on his lying lips.

His mouth forms around the *A* again, and I swear I will pull my knife and cut it from his tongue before I have to hear it.

I never should have talked to him so long ago on the sidewalk outside the club. If I'd kept walking, I'd be back with Parker, Jacob, and Deb, eating chocolate pancakes with fake syrup, pretending to be one of them. Better to be a pretender than to be the one being duped.

Xander must feel the violence rolling off me because he chokes down the start of my name.

I wish he would suffocate on it.

I open my door back up, holding it for him. I already told him the only two words I needed to say. He gets nothing else from me.

He stands and strides for the door, and I think I've won this one piece of dignity when he pulls the door from my hands and shuts it again.

"Please," he says. The word is shallow and meaningless to me.

I shake my head.

"I need to explain."

"What do you need to explain, Xander? The vampiric garden you keep? Because I already know. I've seen it."

His mouth opens and closes. "How?"

"Roman," I snap. I wince as I say it. Roman will be in trouble if Xander says anything, and there is no love between them, but fury loosens my tongue. I take a step closer to him. "*Why?* I was already part of the troupe. You already had your sack of magician blood. Why mess with my feelings, too?"

The shame flickering on his face cools. He pulls a wallet from his back pocket and hands me a creased picture from the folds. Everyone's in the picture: Xander, Aristelle, the twins, Reina, Diantha, and a girl I don't know with short, wild blond hair and a grin that makes everyone else seem sour. "Who is she?" I ask. I can already guess, but I need the story. I need something to make me hate them just a little less. I already carry around too much anger. I can't keep adding to it or I won't be able to lift my head from the weight of it.

He takes the photo back from me. "She was part of our troupe. Two years ago, our apprentice left right before the competition began—thanks to that bastard Roman. We didn't have time to find anyone else to enter, much less train them. It would have been a death sentence, and Sarah was too nice. Better than all of us. She refused to bring someone in without a chance of winning just to save herself. So we were punished. They took Sarah as our sacrifice."

I look up into his face, but he isn't looking at me.

"Aristelle and I decided to never let that happen again. We needed our apprentices to be as invested as possible."

My rib cage feels like it's being pulled from different directions.

"Sarah was Diantha's best friend," he adds.

My chest splits with sorrow for Diantha . . . and also for me.

"We thought you were with us—that you were here for all of us, and I didn't need to take it that step further—but when we found out you were getting close to Roman . . ."

Xander kissed me the next day. He went all in because they thought I was going to walk.

"So you pretended to like me." I nod. He was the bait. "But I liked

Roman," I add. I want him to know that he never had me, not really—that my heart was always pulling me in a different direction.

Xander sighs. "I know."

I slap him. He takes it and says nothing.

My eyes sting, and I fight the tears. I almost never cry, and this makes twice in one hour.

I want to hate him, and I do, but I also understand him. How many people would I lead over the edge of a cliff if it meant keeping Parker safe? It wouldn't even be a choice. I would do it again and again. And that's how my father keeps his control.

"Did you know Lucius was my father?"

He somehow looks more ashamed at this. "Yes. We were tasked with watching you, and when Roman scared off our apprentice so close to the competition, well . . . we knew right where you were. We thought you had to have a lot of power—that it wouldn't be a death sentence for you to not have the same amount of training. And we were right. You can *win* this, Ava."

His confidence means nothing to me. I don't need anything from him.

He takes a deep breath. "I need to know what you plan to do."

I bark out a violent laugh I don't recognize. He didn't come here to check on me or apologize. He came to see if I would still fight for him. Because he knows I'm powerful. He doesn't know I broke the barrier spell, but he probably suspects I have it in me to actually get out—even if I won't get very far.

"I'm not asking just for myself," he adds. "If you leave, it'll be Aristelle in that garden."

Despite everything, the thought of her tangled in those vines twists my gut. The swallow I take is full of knives. They scrape down my throat and leave a gurgling trail of blood in their wake.

In my mind, the vines in the garden of death are already creeping around my ankles, and part of me wants them to just take me and be done with it. A larger part of me wants to ruffle Parker's hair again. I hope he still lets me. I hope I still get that chance.

So I will stay and fight, because there is no other choice.

But I want to make Xander suffer.

"What I do is no longer your concern." I pull open the door for him again.

I force my face to remain blank even as his collapses into a sadness I cannot fathom. He did this. What right does he have to feel pain over it? None.

I turn my attention to my wet boots. Did I leave a trail of bloody footprints? Something tells me the magic swallowed it up.

When I finally look up again, he's gone.

CHAPTER 31

The ballroom has transformed again, forsaking its black walls and floors for pure white. Any spilled blood will glare against it—like Ethan's well-chosen suit from the last round. I shake the thought away. The stage is gone, replaced by stadium seating with maybe fifty square feet of flooring left open in the center. On one side sit Lucius and Annalise, each on a throne of white marble carved with intricate swirls that give it the appearance of frozen clouds.

I stop walking and turn toward them, taking a step in their direction. A beautiful golden choker with five red stones is cinched around Annalise's pale neck. The same necklace I held only yesterday. It doesn't belong to her.

My eyes shift to my father. His lips curl. Does he know I was in his room? Maybe Annalise always wears the necklace for special occasions. I turn away, trying to keep my face neutral.

A woman with purple hair and matching swirls of tattoos along her forearms beckons me forward into the ring. Ethan's already in the center, his orange suit flashing against the white. A few people cheer for him already, remembering the show he gave them last time at my expense. My eyes track those who clap for him. I will remember them later when I win. When I control enough power to make them regret it. I push down the thought uneasily. The pressure is turning me rabid. The pressure or the power. I need to be careful or I will slide into it and let it remake me into something unrecognizable—someone like them. I don't want to be the person who cut a girl in half and hoped for the best. I will *not* be her, even though I feel her creeping just beneath the surface of my skin. Parker needs to be able to recognize me when I get back or I will have lost anyway.

I wear leather pants and a red top, the same outfit I wore the first time I performed with Xander. I hope it brings back memories for him as he watches.

For me, they are just clothes now. I slide my memories of him into a vault. I search out his face in the crowd and scowl when I find him, already tense, the corners of his mouth tight. Worried, even though he must be relieved I didn't run.

Nadine finally arrives and squeezes in between Ethan and me.

"I need to tell you something," I whisper. I tried to find her last night. She deserves to know what the stakes are, where her friend might be, but she wasn't in her room. She was probably wandering the halls looking for answers.

She looks tired. Her eyes focus on me like she didn't really hear what I said.

I open my mouth, but the boisterous crowd turns silent as Lucius stands. He claps. "Let the next trial begin."

Nothing else. No other instructions. Even Ethan turns toward us with a frown, his hand fingering the handle of his gun.

Then the ground spins. I fall to one knee, cracking it hard enough on the marble to jar a curse from my mouth. Nadine calls my name as black fog swirls around us and then fades.

Maybe it's better if I don't tell her right now—processing what might have happened to her friend could distract her.

My own white face stares back at me, my curly brown hair hanging loosely just below my chin. My pulse throbs in my throat. Pulling myself to my feet, I leave my image behind, only to find my eyes reflected in thousands of tilting and angled mirrors making up the walls and ceiling. We can no longer see the audience, but I can feel them just on the other side like I'm a criminal in an episode of *Law & Order*, staring into the glass of an interrogation room, knowing my fate's being decided.

The problem is, I don't even know if I'm innocent or not. I know what waits for Ethan and Nadine should I win. At the very least, the knowledge makes me an accomplice.

Or I lose. Maybe Roman finds the solution he's been looking for and frees me. Or maybe I never see Parker again.

Maybe he's right and my winning will help him. Together we can break this system if I play the game to the end. I need to believe it.

Ethan's cocky grin flashes in the mirrors.

I care less about his fate than Nadine's.

In the center of the room, the glass floor shatters upward, the shards forming a jagged pedestal. A black top hat winks into existence on top of it. Magic curls off it, beckoning, wrapping around us until we move forward as one.

Ethan laughs, somehow excited by all this. "Going classic."

Nadine's brow furrows.

I glance around the room, finding nothing but our confused expressions.

"What are we supposed to do with it?" Nadine crouches,

studying where the top of the hat balances on the glass.

"Pull a rabbit from it, of course," Ethan says.

"I can make myself a rabbit," Nadine suggests, straightening.

"We need to take a rabbit out, not put one in." Ethan rolls his eyes.

"Don't be a dick," I say.

He shrugs. "I'm just trying to help."

"Then stick your hand in there and see what you get." I smile sweetly.

"Fine." Ethan strides to the hat and sticks his hand in up to his shoulder. His brow furrows as he moves his arm, feeling around for who knows what.

He yelps, face draining of color, and yanks his arm out.

Nadine and I both step back as he stumbles from the hat, swinging something around in his hand. No. Swinging something *attached* to his *skin*. A snake hangs on, fangs dug in deep, just below his hand. Ethan stops moving long enough to grip the snake by the back and pull. His skin stretches with the fangs, and he screams as he jerks it, but it will not give. He lets go, panting. The snake twines its body around his wrist like a bracelet.

"Well, that didn't go well." My voice shakes. "Snakes. Why'd it have to be snakes?"

I try to joke and fail. Either nobody here's an *Indiana Jones* fan or they're just not people who joke in crisis. Reina and Diantha would get it. I made them watch *Indiana Jones* almost as many times as we watched *Tomb Raider.* I imagine them laughing in the audience and immediately hate myself for even thinking of them.

Nothing else happens with the hat. It sits there, waiting. But I feel it, the vibration coming off it, asking us to step forward.

"Do you feel that?" asks Nadine.

I nod. "We're not getting out of this."

"Good," Ethan grunts.

We both ignore him as we approach the hat together. I glance inside and find nothing but smooth, black silk. *Touch me*, it says. *Caress me. I don't bite.*

"I'll go," I say.

"No, let me." Nadine bounces on her toes, swinging her arms back and forth in front of her like she's preparing to run a sprint. She dips her hand in, elbow deep, her face tight, waiting for something bad.

She winces but doesn't scream as she pulls her hand back out.

She holds a blooming red rose. The same color drips from her fingers down to her wrist where the long, needle-sharp thorns have broken her skin. She keeps her grip on it despite the pain—or maybe she can't let go. I'm afraid to ask.

"A freaking flower," Ethan grumbles behind me.

"Shut up," I mutter, facing the hat.

I run my fingers over the rim, listening to the hum of magic there, letting it flow into my own blood until the hat and I share the same song beneath our skin. Even though I can't sing to beckon the magic like Willow can, I still hear the melody of it. I let my skin, my blood, my bones all sing the same tune until we are indistinguishable. Then I ask for what I want—a way to win. When I dip my hand into the rim, I let it sink as low as it will go, ignoring any fear lingering around the edges of my mind. It will give me what I need. My fingers brush icy metal so cold it stings. I release a little of my own magic to warm it, and then it's mine. I pull my hand out of the hat.

A brass key reflects a thousand times in the mirrors. The head is an intricate design, depicting a solitary knife in the center. Vines of roses and a single snake twist around the knife, growing out in five loops surrounding the center design. The key's teeth are unnaturally sharp.

I am the only one who didn't bleed into the hat. I hold the key out for the others to see.

Nadine's answering smile is grim. "At least we know who it likes."

Ethan looks away with a scowl.

And then the dark fog takes us again.

When it rolls away, we stand in a field of golden grass long enough to brush our knees. Nothing else exists besides the blue sky, the blistering sun, and three wooden boxes. The one on the left is flat and horizontal, like a coffin, with a curving snake cut out from the sides. The one in the center is upright and narrow, with a key carved out of the top. The last is square, with a hundred little slivers carved out to make a blooming rose.

The door or lid in each opens at once.

The grass rustles in the breeze, a faint, mocking chorus.

"I bet there are snakes out here," Nadine says. She glances at Ethan. "Besides the obvious two."

I snicker.

Ethan glares before heading to the box on the left. "I could use a nap."

The snake still curls around his wrist, fangs secure in his skin, which has turned black around the bite. Perhaps he intends to get in his box and just lie down and die.

That might be nice for the rest of us.

Still, I say, "Stay alert," as he climbs in.

He sneers at my concern for him.

Nadine opens the cubed box and steps inside, giving me an encouraging nod as she sinks in and shuts the lid.

I step into the center box and close the door. The heat inside turns my skin slick within seconds, and the smell of cedar is strong enough to choke on. I struggle to breathe as I run my hand along the door I just shut behind me. If I could get one more breath of fresh air, I'd be fine. But there's no handle. I press my nose up toward the key cutout, the only thing letting light into the box.

I tense, recognizing the threat immediately.

One of the most important aspects of a perfect illusion is the sound—the singing of a blade being pulled free, the music of a synchronized shuffle, the startling crack of a gunshot. The best illusions engage more senses than just sight. It's the kind of detail I used to appreciate. It's also how I recognize the sound of a saw's teeth nipping at the wood of my box.

I'm not the only one. Ethan lets loose a string of curses to my right, muffled through the thick wood between us. Nothing but silence comes from my left.

I hope it's because Nadine has a plan.

I bend, listening for where the saw might break through. Another saw starts, joining its sister's song. As far as I can tell, they come from different directions at the bottom of the box. The first few teeth gleam, sharp and dangerous, through the wood about one foot up from the ground.

It would be low enough to step over, except another set of teeth are biting through the other side. Impossible.

I let out my own stream of curses to join Ethan's.

A gunshot echoes. Then a second and a third.

I jerk at each one, losing precious seconds.

Damn Ethan. The saws move steadily through the box, too thick to just step over, only four inches from hitting either leg.

I move without thinking, grabbing the only thing I have at my disposal. Knives. I pull them from my boots and slam two into each side of the box, making wobbly steps. I brace my hands on the wood and place one foot on the knives. I don't have time to test their strength.

I lift my other foot, cutting it so close the teeth scrape through the leather of my pants.

Ethan screams and screams until I tremble from the pain in it.

His screaming drowns out the third saw so I don't see it coming. It rips through the wood and into my hand, tearing skin. I let go of the sides and duck, barely catching myself from slipping off my steps. Pulling two knives from my wrist, I dig them into the wall so I have the balance to keep myself upright.

Two more saws pass above my head.

Nadine's still silent.

Ethan's stopped screaming.

Only the saws move now, carrying on their vicious task.

I don't move for a long time after they clear through the wood.

Finally, my door opens. The full sun burns my eyes like I've been in there for days. I retrieve my knives and stumble from the box, sucking in the warm, open air.

Ethan lifts the lid of his coffin and sits up like a vampire movie cliché.

"I thought you were dead," I say. "You screamed like it."

"Don't sound so disappointed." His voice is hollow, missing the usual snark he'd lace those words with. He pulls his legs out of the box. The cut-off bottoms of his orange pants bunch around his ankles.

My mouth opens and closes.

"I did what I needed to," he says, looking away, straight into the sun.

Faint red lines ring his calves. He let the blades cut through him and somehow managed to stay conscious and heal.

I swallow back the bile in my throat.

Nadine's box finally opens. A small gray mouse creeps to the front. Genius.

That kind of display of power is sure to impress our judges. All I did was a desperate balancing act. My relief slides into something deep and ugly. I push it away, leaving behind unease—not with the competition, but with myself.

"Now, that just doesn't seem fair," Ethan says.

He points his gun at me.

No. Not at me—just past my shoulder at the little mouse, and I'm close enough to him to jump, to maybe grab his arm and ruin his shot.

I scream at myself to move, but my arms hang dead at my sides, frozen, as Ethan aims his gun at my friend.

CHAPTER 32

I shake myself and lunge.

The gunshot tears by me, shutting down everything in its wake, leaving only a dull ringing in my ears.

I turn to Ethan. For once, no trace of cockiness lingers on his face. His cheek twitches before he turns to stone. He's not even looking at me. His gun, still extended, shakes as if touched by a faint breeze.

I turn, following the veins of broken wood to the black, smoking hole at the center where a mouse sat just moments before.

I bend over and vomit. Then in one fluid movement, I reach a hand to each wrist and release two knives. I lunge, not bothering to call the magic to me. I don't need it. Fury is enough to drive home my blades.

Ethan stumbles back, jerking the gun in my direction now.

I drop as a bullet cracks to life, sailing over my head.

I dive for his legs, my cheeks scraping against the long grass. My shoulder slams into his knees hard enough to knock my teeth together. Hard enough to bring him down. I scramble on top of him in an instant, sinking my knife through his snake and his wrist before he can regain control of the gun. It falls from his grasp. I grab for it as his other fist smashes into the side of my head, sending me sprawling. Pain races from my ear to my jaw as one side of my vision blackens.

I spit dry grass from my mouth as I force myself to roll over onto my back.

The sky sits blank and calm above me. No clouds. A shadow looms across me as Ethan drops to his knees beside me. Blood drips from his wrist to my face as he places the gun just above my nose.

"I win."

Nadine crashes into his side, flinging him onto the ground next to me. She holds a hand on one shoulder where blood leaks through her fingers.

My head twists to Ethan beside me, but he hasn't even lifted his pistol. The expression on his face is relieved for one second before it hardens. "I thought I killed you."

"You're not as good of a shot as you think." Nadine focuses on me. "Are you okay?"

I nod—too stunned to answer.

"Good, 'cause I'm finished. This is *real*, Ava." She holds up her bloody palm. "Sam wouldn't want me to die looking for her." Her face turns bleak. "Not when she's probably dead herself." She spins around and shouts in every direction. "I'm done with this shit."

"Nadine, wait!" I struggle to my feet, but it's too late. A thick swirl of fog surrounds her, and she's gone.

The ground erupts beneath us, cracking and sliding to pieces, and I don't have time to dwell on my guilt. We fall into the same dense smoke that took Nadine moments before.

I hit coldness and scramble to my feet, bracing for an attack. I find Ethan ten feet from me, gun trained in my direction.

I bare my teeth, sinking into the wild part of me I always kept just beneath the surface. But even though his gun is on me, Ethan's turning his head, taking in our surroundings.

"We have other problems," he says. He lowers the gun, keeping his finger on the trigger.

It's enough for me to take my eyes off him.

We're back in the center of the room, although I'm sure we never really left. The audience is there, leaning toward us, eyes greedy for our blood, safely behind a thick pane of glass like we're in a giant fish tank. I glance up at the solid glass ceiling over our heads and know in my bones that I'm not going to like anything that comes next.

"Look." Ethan kicks something on the ground toward me, and I look down for the first time. Four stakes lie at our feet.

I eye him. "Why? We're not vampires."

Ethan nods over my shoulder. "I'm guessing they are."

I turn and watch two people rise up from the floor in a cage on a glass platform. It jerks to a stop, and the cage door drops open with a crash that sounds like it shatters the glass floor.

A giant man with a red beard and a bald head jumps out. He looks like he could snap me in two even if he weren't a vampire. He grins in our direction. His beard is streaked with a darker red that drips through to the ends. The girl hasn't turned around yet, and she looks slight, but that doesn't mean anything for a vamp.

Ethan holsters his gun. "Truce?"

"Never," I say, but I sheath my knives *and* my desire to kill him. I can pull both back out with little effort.

We reach down and grab the stakes.

"I've got dibs on the girl," Ethan says.

"You're kidding me," I say, but then the girl lifts the hair from her face as she jumps out of the cage in sky-high heels and a leather mini-skirt. Stacie. Her eyes zero in on me. She seems surprised, but then she breaks into a ridiculously charming smile, like we've just happened to bump into each other at the mall.

"Ava," she calls.

Ethan looks at me. "Looks like you get her after all."

My body goes cold like *I'm* the vampire. "Never mind. I want the guy." He's still lumbering toward us—each step sounds like a stone falling.

"No way. You'll be dead in five seconds, and I'll have to fight two. Good luck with your friend." He winks and heads for the man, spinning his stakes in his hand like they're flashy guns in a western. I do not like our odds.

Stacie stalks toward me.

"You killed Adam," she says casually. "He was an ass, but we'd been together a long time, like a family member you don't like but can't shake." She hesitates, like she's realized she's being vulnerable and shouldn't. "I honestly didn't think I'd miss him."

"I didn't do it myself. I couldn't," I admit. I want to step away from her, but I drop into a crouch instead. "He told us everything before he died, though. Who you work for. Why you pretended to be my friend."

Her eyes soften. "I didn't pretend. Not at the end."

Her voice is so sincere that I almost believe her.

"Why do it at all, though?"

Her expression hardens. "Because when I first got turned, I found other vampires. We pooled our money and lived in an impossibly small apartment so we'd have money for cheap blood. We didn't kill, but that didn't stop one of these troupes from wiping all of them out one night after we came out of a club. I was the only one left alive. I couldn't afford blood without their help. It became kill or die, and instinct swallowed me. That's when Numerius's people found me." She shrugs. "I agreed with his cause even though I didn't always like the method."

She turns away as Ethan gets tossed ten feet across the tank. He pulls out his gun and fires off a couple shots that hit the vamp in the chest and seem to have the same impact as a fly on a semi.

Stacie chuckles a little as she watches, like she's flipped a switch back to careless vampire, and I know this is my moment. One stake sliding into one heart, but I hesitate, and an inhuman hunger lights her eyes when she turns back to me. I know this is kill or die, and I know which one she's choosing—the one she already chose. I swing one of my stakes at her face and the other at her heart. She whacks the one headed for her face away like it's nothing. The other hits something hard, and my stomach lurches with the feeling, but she's smiling at me. I look down and see my stake piercing through her hand. She yanks it out of my grip and out of her flesh like it's a splinter.

"I guess you do have it in you," she says.

I scramble for one of my knives, but she slams a hand so hard into my chest that I feel my ribs bending. I'm on my back, and she's on top of me before I can even think of the right move or how to use the magic inside me.

Pinning me by the shoulder, she grabs my chin and yanks my head to the side. My cheekbone hits the glass floor. A long stretch of my neck is exposed, and I don't know if I've ever felt so vulnerable. I kick and squirm, but it's like being trapped beneath a fallen tree.

I almost yell out to Ethan, but somehow asking him to save me seems even worse.

I stop squirming. Her hot breath brushes my neck.

I whisper Parker's name like he'll hear it wherever he is and know I love him.

She sits back and lets go of my chin and shoulder but stays straddling my waist. My neck burns like I've pulled a muscle in it when I turn my head to look up at her. She stares down at me like she doesn't even see me.

"I had a younger brother once. He's forty-two now, and I watch him sometimes. He thinks I died a long time ago. Maybe I did." She laughs, and it sounds like my friend cracking jokes while we eat pretzels at the mall.

She reaches behind her, grabs the stake I dropped, and tosses it on my chest. "They're going to kill me one way or another, and it'll be less pretty than this. You should do it."

The stake is heavy on my chest. "I can't."

"You'll never see your brother again if you don't."

"You'll never see yours again if I do." I can't stop picturing a sad girl outside the window of a house full of family—stuck forever as a teenager with nobody at all. The image pulls at me. I don't want to have something in common with her, but I can't stop myself from relating.

"Like I said, I'm already dead."

I shake my head.

"Do it!" she screams. She grabs my hands and forces them around the stake. "Do you know how many people I've killed?"

My fingers clench around the stake.

Her lips twist into a smile. "Do it or you're dead."

And then she lunges. My hands move on instinct, and I can feel the moment I break her skin—the grotesque pressure of it—and I keep pushing and watch something like relief flicker across her face, and then she's turning to dust on top of me. I close my eyes so I don't have to watch.

Her power slips into me like a song I don't want to hear.

When the weight of her disappears, I sit up, and the ash clings to me like regret. I climb to my feet and stare at Ethan, smiling over a body that's slowly crumbling.

He glances at me. "I thought you were a goner." He sounds disappointed.

"What's next?" I ask.

He doesn't answer me, but the arena does. Water flows down the glass, distorting the already gruesome faces of our audience.

The freezing water is at my ankles in seconds, stirring the ashes of the vampires into a sick cloud around my legs. I try not to look down. I can't think about it.

I slosh toward the wall, slapping a hand against the glass. It must be about a foot thick.

I move around the perimeter, ignoring laughing faces, and some worried—those few magicians with enough humanity left to care about this outcome and not just the show. I try not to look for Roman or my own troupe. I need to focus. I reach the other side, finding nothing.

Ethan shakes his head, slamming a bloodied hand against the glass and leaving a print that washes away in the waterfall in an instant. "I thought this was about killing vampires, huh?" he yells. "Pretty sure we passed."

All we get is laughter from the other side.

The water hits his knees and my thighs.

We look at each other and back at the glass.

I pull a knife and slam it with all the force I can muster. My hand aches from the impact, and a sliver of glass breaks away. I try again. This time I heat the knife until it burns my skin, then plunge it into the glass. It breaks through, sinking hilt deep. I try to take it back out again and fail. One knife down.

Ethan draws his gun. "Back up," he says, like he gives a damn about shards hitting me.

I do it anyway.

The blow digs out an inch of glass.

"How many bullets do you have?"

"Not enough."

The water laps at my waist and I grit my teeth to stop them from chattering.

"Look," Ethan says.

I follow Ethan's finger to a bit of flashing gold near the top of one of the walls. We move toward it. The water pushes against me, fighting my every step.

Fear, colder than the water, bites into my bones. I can't swim. Ten minutes. I calculate ten minutes until I'm drowning.

We stand together, looking up at the one and only anomaly in this glass wall—a solid gold keyhole. I pull the key from my pocket. "Looks like the magic loves me best."

"How are you going to get to it?"

There are no footholds to climb, nothing but smooth, unyielding glass. The keyhole itself is buried two inches beneath the glass.

"We can wait until the water rises enough to take us there," he says.

"We can't risk it. We'll only have seconds before the water fills in." Plus, I'll be dead by then.

I plunge into the water and pull two of my thicker knives from my boots. The water steams off them as I pour heat into the metal. I plunge one at chest level and the other above my head. The glass takes the blades and leaves the flat hilts visible. My wet boots and hands slide as I try to pull myself onto them.

"Help me," I grit out without looking at Ethan. I try not to wince as his hands grip my waist, giving me the height and stability to place my boots on the knives. The hilts slide against the heels of my boots, keeping me as stable as possible.

Ethan braces my calves as I pull out one of my smaller wrist knives and plunge it through the wet glass. The water turns the handle slippery in an instant, but I only tighten my grip. Carefully, I lean down and grab another knife, placing it as high as I can reach.

"Let go!" I shout down to Ethan. I grab another wrist knife, digging in and pulling myself up at the same time before I can overthink my movements. My left foot hits a knife and slides off. I jerk my right foot out, searching for grounding as the smaller knife and my right arm take my full weight.

Ethan yells something I don't hear. My left hand grabs a knife from my wrist and connects it with glass. Dangling, my feet claw until they find the knife hilt. My arms shake as I regain my balance.

Three more knives in my boot. Three more at my wrist.

I can make it. I'm smarter this time. I focus on the tingling magic, let it consume every other thought, every desire I ever had until I'm numb—nothing but a vessel for the power. The magic likes me this way. My limbs move, pulling knives, sinking them with barely a thought. My last knife goes in just below my goal. I grip it with both hands as my right foot fights to balance on a hilt. My left foot dangles with nowhere to go.

I let go with one hand and pull the key from my back pocket, slamming it into the glass blocking the keyhole.

The force clatters up my arm. I grasp at the hilt of my knife until I'm holding nothing at all.

I fall.

Cold water envelopes me, pushing up my nose. My limbs flail as I try to escape its grip, but it's everywhere. My boots scramble against glass, and I kick up in an instant. Air greets me, and I choke on it, the water sloshing under my nose. I stand on my tiptoes.

Ethan watches as the water rises above my nose, and I jump to get a breath before going under again. My heart slams, trying to escape my own drowning body. I fight the urge to thrash my limbs. Focus. My knife ladder is only five feet behind me, but it seems like miles as I jump up for another breath, the water pulling me back down like it's made of tiny, vicious hands intent on ending me.

I jump again, barely getting enough traction.

"Help," I gasp out.

I see my mistake written all over Ethan's face before I go under again—the realization I can't swim coupled with the same chilling resolve he had right before he stabbed me and shot Nadine.

My eyes sting under the water. His legs move toward me. I'm seconds away from losing the grip on my last breath when his fingers close on my shirt and yank me upward. All I can do is breathe when I break the surface. He fumbles for the key still clenched in my hand. And I have nothing left to fight him with—all my knives are stuck into the wall behind me, and the water has sapped my energy to the point where I'm about to let it take me.

His fingers pry at mine. I shift the key and sink the teeth into his palm.

He loses his grip on me, and I swallow water as I drop.

This time his hand closes around my neck as I surface, spewing water in his face.

He doesn't flinch as it streams across his set mouth. His other hand yanks the key away.

He screams, his hand tightening around my neck. My vision blackens as I claw at his wrist.

"What did you do?" Rage shatters his features.

I can't answer. There's not enough air in my lungs to make words.

His other hand grasps my arm as he releases my neck. The key winks at the bottom of the tank.

I shake my head as I try to take air down my damaged throat.

"It won't let me hold it," he says. He assesses me. Calm replaces rage so quickly it's like whiplash. He needs me again. "Go get it."

His grip tightens, and I'm shaking my head as he forces me under. I fight it, thrashing, but his other hand finds the back of my head and holds it down. My hands hit the glass bottom and drift until I feel metal. The last of my air bubbles from my mouth as his hands pull me to the surface.

The water's to his chin now. He fights through it, pushing us back toward the wall. He shoves me up it as the water slides into his mouth. "Hurry."

I almost want to give up just so he'll drown in here too. My limbs are ready to. They wobble as I grip the knives. It *should* be easier this time since they're already placed in the wall, but I know it won't be. I move, pushing the magic into my fingers so the water evaporates off the knives the second I touch them. I call so much of it, my own skin seems to melt, becoming one with the metal so it hurts to pull away and latch myself onto the next. I reach the top faster than I thought possible.

The glass isn't so much as dented from my last attempt. Even if I had a knife, it would take too long to chip away.

Ethan treads water below, his gun above his head.

"You need to shoot it!" I scream.

He nods, paddling back, aiming his gun.

I close my eyes and brace myself.

Tiny shards of glass pelt my face and arms like hail.

I open my eyes. An inch of glass remains.

"Again!" I yell.

He bobs with the flow of the water.

I try not to think about what will happen if he misses.

Glass bites me again. So many tiny cuts open my skin, it feels as if

I'm bleeding from my very pores. I'm bleeding magic, and I can feel the hunger of this place—its desire to have me in its garden.

The keyhole is visible. I put the key in and turn.

The glass melts into liquid.

I slam into white marble.

My knives clatter around me. I sit and pull my knees up so I can stick my knives back into the sheaths in my boots. My skin bleeds. I don't bother calling on magic to heal it. I don't want to.

Noise drifts over me—laughter, clapping, exclamations of who won this round. My name and Ethan's get shouted in equal measure. Someone takes bets.

I pull myself to my feet and turn to him.

"We make a good team." He smiles without feeling, his only purpose to get a rise out of me.

"I will kill you," I snarl, stalking toward him. My bones scream in protest. My body will be blooming bruises soon. Nadine is a gaping hole in my stomach. She wouldn't have quit if he hadn't shot her.

Roman is at my side in an instant. Lips near my ear, voice carefully soft. "You know she's not completely gone."

The garden. I know. I can't stop picturing it.

I fight the desire to see Ethan bleed and straighten.

Ethan runs a hand through his wet hair and stands it on end, turning to address Natasha coming up behind him.

Roman lays his hands on my arms and my wounds disappear.

I thank him, even though part of me wanted to keep them. They reminded me of the thorns tearing Willow's—and now Nadine's—skin to pieces. The cuts gave me a little piece of their suffering to hold on to. Otherwise, I might quit. I might leave in the night and see if I could make it out without the magicians catching me. I could hide like my mother tried to, but I'd have to leave Parker for good.

"Thank you." The voice behind me is unusually tentative.

I turn and meet Aristelle's eyes. She doesn't drop her gaze, and neither do I.

"I didn't do it for you." I glance behind her at Reina and Diantha. "Any of you."

I turn and walk away.

CHAPTER 33

I wear chains, both literally and figuratively. My top is nothing but a black corset laced up the front with a thin silver chain. I had to heat the metal and solder it together myself. The irony is not lost on me. All my own choices led me here, even if I made some of them based on half-truths and lies. Sometimes I imagine myself back in the moment Deb offered to adopt us. I would smile this time. It wouldn't be real, of course, but I would try it out anyway. Sometimes if you live in an illusion long enough, it becomes reality. You forget the strings to your own trick.

I sigh, running a hand across my heavy skirt made of black taffeta and chains that clank from my waist, falling in uneven lengths toward my feet. I can't run in this. I can barely move. My heart beats unevenly at the sensation of being trapped in my own clothes. Lucius ordered this dress—maybe to remind me who is in control. He also ordered Reina to help put me in it.

I ignored her as she worked. Some cruel part of me enjoyed watching her squirm in my silence. When I arrived here, these people opened me, helped me become a softer version of myself. Now I'm colder and harder than ever.

Ethan stands ten feet to my right, dressed in a white suit again, although this time his shirt, vest, and tie are orange, green, and pink. His hand brushes Natasha's arm.

He catches me staring and glares.

I turn away. I wonder if she loves him or if she's pulling his strings the way Xander pulled mine.

Doesn't matter. Either way, we're both here, waiting below on platforms that will carry us up when the time comes. We will be lifted onto the stage, and these killers will decide which of us to let into their sick cult.

Heavy footsteps approach behind me, weighted with more than just his tall frame. I recognize the extra weight as sorrow now. Roman comes around to stand in front of me. His eyes drift, briefly, to my overexposed chest before darting to my face.

"I know." I grimace.

"No." He clears his throat. "I don't think you do."

My face flushes, and he turns his attention to my knives, busying himself with pulling them from the sheaths at my wrists and checking the points.

"I sharpened them this morning." It's become my ritual—a way to deaden my mind from anything besides the tip of my blade. Roman keeps checking anyway. Always overprepared.

He hesitates at my long skirt.

"They're there." I know he won't lift the hem to check them, so I add, "They're sharp."

He nods, then finally meets my gaze, holding it so long that I fidget with a chain, clanking it against the others.

"I'll be fine," I say. "Either way."

His face is grim. He doesn't reassure me, but I know that if I end up in the garden, he'll fight for me the same way he's been fighting for Beatrice these last years. I wish it gave me comfort. I wish I knew I was worth fighting for. I think of the soft O that Stacie's lips made when I killed her.

"What will the last task be?"

He hesitates, glancing around at Ethan and Natasha just out of earshot. Whatever it is, he's not supposed to tell me.

He leans in like he will brush a kiss on my cheek. My skin tingles, even though he doesn't actually touch me.

"You have to kill him."

"Who?" Realization slaps me the second I ask. Of course. Only one of us can win.

My head jerks automatically toward Ethan, but Roman's hand is suddenly on my cheek, keeping my head pinned forward between his palm and his cheek.

"He'll go to the garden, though, right?" I can sentence him to that fate. It's his fault Nadine is there.

Roman's head shakes beside me. His curls brush my forehead. "Not this time. They'll use every last drop of one of you to create a new immortality spell. The stones on the cuff are still linked to the garden, but the immortality spell breaks when the magician wearing it dies—it needs a new sacrifice to be cast again. We've all been here. We've all done it." His voice is hard, straight to the point.

"What if one of us had died, though? In the last challenge?" It sure didn't seem like anyone was going to stop Stacie from ripping into my neck if she'd wanted to.

Roman grimaces. "Then they would have plucked someone from the garden just to kill them permanently."

My legs shake under the weight of my skirt. Of course it's not as simple as slapping a bracelet on.

"I don't want that. I don't want to be a—" Murderer. I don't say the word. All of them have blood on their hands or they wouldn't be here.

Roman's fingers twitch against my cheek. He knows what I was about to say and doesn't answer.

"There's no other choice for you, Ava."

He didn't tell me yesterday because he knew I would take my chances and run.

"There's always a choice. Sometimes there just isn't a good one." Too much of my life has been spent without choices. It's why I'm really here, why I craved power. And now they want to strip away choice in exchange for power? That's not power at all.

"I won't do it."

Roman pulls back from me. His jaw clenches.

"He won't hesitate."

"I know."

"He tried to kill you first."

"I know."

"Please, Ava. What about Willow, Nadine?"

I turn my chin away from him. I believe that Roman will find a way to free them eventually. But what will be left of *me* if I do this? Killing those vampires was one thing. That was self-defense. But Ethan? He's horrible, but he's just as trapped as I am, and he's a person with a family—even if that family is the one he found here. I can't go back to Parker as a murderer. Would I even want myself around him like that? He'd be better off without me.

All my choices drop away from me. Perhaps choice was always only an illusion, and I've been destined for this particular fate my entire life. I can find only one way out of it—stop fighting back. Let him kill me and be done with it—the only path that gives me an ounce of power is surrender, refusing to give them one last show.

My limbs are numb. I ignore the magic buzzing in them, ordering me to get ready.

But then Roman says my name, soft and pleading, and I can't stop myself from turning back to him. He looks me up and down like he can't decide where to focus. One finger reaches out and traces the chain lacing the front of my corset. He meets my eyes as he hooks a finger through one, pulling gently. Gently enough that I don't have to follow, but I do. He pulls me against him, and I tilt my chin as he bends over me, hesitating. But we don't really have time for hesitation anymore. I wrap my fingers around his suspenders and pull him down to me.

That familiar desperation is in the way we press together, but it's somehow stronger now. His lips plead with me, beg me, and for a second, I give in. I kiss him back like I'll never leave him.

But I'm a liar. Just like he is. Just like everyone here is.

I break away. His eyes are wild and panicked. He knows what I'm going to do.

I lean forward and whisper, "My father will stop it. He won't let me die." I wish I believed that. I don't, but maybe Roman will.

Roman's saying something to me as my platform jerks and begins to rise. More emotion rages across his face than I've ever seen. I wish I knew if he were more upset about losing me or losing his potential ally in his crusade against the garden.

As for my troupe, this is what they've been training me for ever since the day they tried to get me to stake Adam under the bridge. They wanted to see how far I would go. If I could draw blood and keep going. I did it with the Cecily. I didn't know for sure she would heal, but I was willing to take the chance if it meant getting what I wanted.

My stomach clenches. I've come very far—perhaps too far. They've pushed me to the edge of a darkness I won't come back from. The exact same darkness so many vampires live in: kill or die. The cliff crumbles beneath my feet, and I must scramble back or be lost.

I break free onto the stage. The crowd of magicians before me is as silent as a predator as they stare at me, hungry for blood. I doubt they even care who wins as long as someone dies.

My lip curls in disgust. I turn to Lucius, standing on my right, and then look around him to Ethan on the other side.

Lucius begins talking, explaining the final task, no doubt. No need. Everyone knows, it seems.

Ethan's hand rests on his gun. His smile winds up as he stares at me. He knows too. He will not hesitate. He's been trained for this, and he already stepped over the edge of that cliff.

Lucius leaves the stage. The crowd is yelling at us now. Xander and his troupe are in the front. I think my name is on his lips again, and I don't even care. Whatever they shout doesn't concern me.

I turn to Ethan because I should go down with my dignity. I don't want the last thing I see to be Xander's green hair. I don't want my last thought to be of kissing Roman. There's a particular hurt to the loss of something that might have been. I'd rather think of Parker laughing with Jacob. The sound gave me so much pain once, but now it gives me comfort. He will be okay if I never come back.

Ethan draws his gun, cocks it, and points it in my direction.

Confusion mars his determined look for single moment.

He probably thinks I have a plan or reason for not drawing my own weapon.

I don't. All I have left is me, and I am determined to hold on to her.

But as Ethan's finger twitches on the trigger, my heartbeat spikes. The magic in my blood awakens like it's been called. I try to push it away from me, try to keep still and face death head-on, but as his finger moves—

I dodge.

CHAPTER 34

My chains clink as I hit the ground and roll. They tangle around my knees, locking me in place as I scramble. I thought Lucius wanted me to win, but this dress seems designed for me to fail. *I* want me to fail, but magic unravels inside me, burning away the rational, moral part of me. I am an animal. I am pure instinct. I will survive. I make it up to my knees.

A boot connects with my collarbone. It snaps and heals, and the pain is there and gone before I can even register it. My basic instinct commands my magic. I shouldn't be able to heal that fast, and I don't know if I should let go of my last bit of control or try to regain it.

I snarl, on my back, belly-up like a beaten animal.

A hunter looms above me, and there is only kill or be killed.

His gun points at my face. He shifts its aim to my belly. "Natasha told me to make you bleed a lot, and I already know that you're not so good at healing from stomach wounds. But you did better than I thought you would," he gives me. "Thanks for making it fun."

He's pleased I've put up a little fight. He's a true performer.

But the show's not over.

My magic roars, and another little bar on its cage shatters. The pressure in my fingers grows until I'm panting. Ethan frowns. He might think I'm crying. I might be. But it's only because there's too much inside me, and something has to come out.

Control, I try to tell myself, but it's too late. The magic bursts out of me before I can focus on what I want it to do, like it's reading every thought in the deepest recesses of my mind and acting on it.

Ethan's eyes widen. The gun in his hands begins to shake as his magic fights against mine.

It goes off.

Splinters from the shattered floor sting my cheek.

He doesn't get another shot. The gun flies from his hands, soaring above the heads of the crowd. Their cheering matches the roar in my blood.

Ethan pulls at the gun in his other holster, but it won't budge. His eyes narrow on me. He's going to strangle me with his own two hands if he has to. And I don't know if I can control him the same way I can control metal.

The push of my magic fades the tiniest bit, reading my doubt in it.

But it also helps me focus. I'm *wearing* metal.

Perhaps this dress wasn't meant to be a curse at all. Lucius knows metal is easy for me to control. He dressed me in a weapon.

My magic is still one step ahead of me. The chains slide around Ethan's ankles, yanking his feet out from under him as I push myself to mine. My knives pull themselves from their sheaths without my touch until all of them hover above him as he lies on his back, still struggling to yank his other gun out. I stand over him and watch.

Finally he stops moving and stares up at me with a rage I find too relatable.

My knives don't plunge into him, though, because even with the magic reading my thoughts and acting without my commands, deep down, I don't want to kill him. As vicious as the power in me feels, it knows that.

And I *am* in control.

My knives clatter to the ground.

"Ava." It's Lucius's voice. There's disappointment in it.

I've never been prouder.

I turn toward him, willing my face to be neutral, to not give away how much I want to pick those knives back up and send them flying through his heart. Maybe it would work. Roman doesn't think so. But right now I need him to let both of us live.

Lucius's face is impassive when I meet his stare until his eyes flick past my shoulder, and his brows draw together just a fraction.

I spin just in time to grab Ethan's wrist as he tackles me with my own blade gripped in his hand. I barely stop it from plunging into my heart as I crash backward with him on top of me. My head hits the ground so hard that vomit rises in my throat. My vision wavers on the edge of blackness, and my magic fizzles as my mind refuses to focus.

"Weak." Ethan straddles me, blade poised above my heart.

He jerks as if someone pushed him from behind. His eyes widen as he twitches again. His hand relaxes around the knife, and it slips free just as I drop his wrist to grab it by the blade. I barely register the sting of it slicing through my fingers. His expression shifts from confusion to shock, and I know it must mirror my own.

Ethan slumps on top of me.

The crowd rages as I struggle to break free.

I push against him, and his head lolls like his body is an empty husk.

He is too heavy. I raise my head above his shoulders and find two familiar pearl-handled knives protruding from his back. For a second, I think they're mine. That my magic called them to kill without my realizing it.

But then Roman strides onto the stage, a third knife in his hand.

I struggle to unpin myself as he kneels beside me.

"This was not your choice," I tell him. My throat is raw with the kind of grief I thought I was past feeling.

"I know," he says, "but I failed to do this once before. Sometimes no choice is a gift . . . and, sorry, but he has to bleed."

He yanks Ethan's head up by the hair and runs the final blade across his throat.

I become nothing but blood. It blinds me. I breathe it in. It slips into my mouth, open and screaming for him to stop.

My skin burns with it, boiling the blood that keeps on coming. I can't find air. I'm not sure I need it anymore. There is only blood and the thirsty magic inside me, calling it, licking it from my skin. Magic rips through me, hot and cold, tingling and numbing all at once. I close my eyes, afraid the pressure will blow them from my skull. Before I do, someone rips Roman away from me. Was he holding my hand? My fingernails cut through the skin of my palms. My bones buck, trying to escape my own skin as the power threads into them, tying them down, taming them, making promises as it sings its soothing, violent song.

Finally, it ends, and I am left a throbbing ball of magic.

My heart stutters under the weight of power, and the power forces it to continue on.

Lucius rocks back on his heels where he's crouched beside me. I notice the black band that's tight around my stinging wrist. I blink at the red jewel at its center puncturing my skin, feeding my blood with the power it soaks from the garden.

There's not a drop of blood on me. The spell swallowed it all.

I gag and push Ethan from me like he is nothing. His head thuds on the floor, and I wince. Pulling myself to my knees, I look up at Lucius, who stands above me now like an angel of frost in cold white. His eyes glitter like ice as he watches me with a mixture of anger and disappointment. Finally, he bares his teeth in something that might be called a smile but isn't.

This was supposed to be the moment I proved myself as his heir. Instead, I hesitated. I showed compassion. I showed I'm *not* him.

"Welcome, Ava, to the Society of True Magicians. You are one of us now. You will be forever." His last sentence rings with a threat.

A few in the crowd clap. They do love a good show, and Roman gave them a twist they didn't see coming. More grumble until Lucius holds his hand up for silence. "Rules are rules, and she is the last one standing." His lip curls as he turns away from me to Roman, and my skin goes cold despite the barely contained inferno of magic raging inside me. "You, however, will be punished."

Roman keeps his chin dipped to his chest, so I can't see his face as Lucius makes a dramatic circle around him before focusing on me.

He holds my stare as he gives the judgment. "Interfering with the competition carries a death sentence. It seems fair our newest member should be the one to carry it out. After all, she benefited from his actions."

Roman's head finally shoots up and he stares at me. He wants me to do it. I can read it all over his face. When did I learn to read his few expressions? I shake my head slightly in answer.

I may be angry with him right now, in this moment, but I still recognize what he did for me and why he did it. I'd have done the same for him. But killing Roman would make me the very thing he tried to save me from.

Lucius watches our silent exchange and then claps his hands once.

"The execution will take place tomorrow at dawn. Decapitation works best for us immortals. Can't tell your body to heal when your brain's not attached anymore. Fun too." He gives me a sick grin. "Until then." He spins and strides into the hallway.

Lucius wants me to be like him—wants to push me until I can't look back, until I can't judge him because the blood on my hands will be just as thick. He's going to try again and again until one day I break.

I burst into the hallway after him. "You can't make me do this."

He doesn't even bother to turn around. His black boots click away from me down a hallway of glossy black tiles that turn to icy silver each time his foot touches one. He thinks he's a god. I want to show him he's not. I want to make him bleed.

Almost more than anything else in the world.

Except saving Roman. I'd let him live if it meant Roman would be safe. I'd bow to him. I'd play his little games if only he'd give me Roman back. The realization shocks me so much I stumble a bit and glance down at my feet. Gold blooms under my foot, erasing the trail of silver that Lucius leaves behind. I know he's the one making it change silver, but I'm not making it go gold. It's the magic itself, pressing against the cage it's been trapped in. It wants to be free.

I think it wants me to be the one to free it. I look back up at Lucius's retreating form.

"*You* killed my mother." I shouldn't say it. I shouldn't show just how much I hate him—that I'll *never* be his. Not yet. But I can't stand the thought of him not knowing for one more second. It's one illusion I just can't do.

The words stop him cold. He turns. I don't know what I expect to see on his face. Part of me wants to see shock. I want him to deny it, to give me an explanation, something that will let me look at him like a father and not the cruel person who ripped my entire life from me.

For a moment I imagine him opening his arms to me so we can both grieve what was taken from us. But he did the taking. And now he wants to take more.

I get nothing from him. No emotion. "How did you find out?"

My chest squeezes so tightly that it feels like my ribs will cave in. He doesn't even care enough to put on a show for me—to pretend like he didn't have anything to do with it.

"I found her stuff in your rooms."

"Ahhh, I thought it was you. I knew someone had been in, and it would take so much power to break through my security spells." A gleam lights his eyes. "How'd you do it? Never mind. Doesn't matter. We're on the same side now. I was going to leave you alone in your humdrum little life, but that was silly of me. You're full of power. My power."

This is a test—one last chance to bow to him.

"My *mother's* power," I spit.

He looks like he wants to hit me, but he rocks back on his heels. "Either way, it's mine now."

"Why?" It's the question that's been haunting me for years.

He shrugs. "She left me. Nobody gets to leave me." His voice goes hard. "Ever."

I know what he means: I'm not leaving either—not unless I want to end up like her.

"But she had too many allies here to kill her outright. I made sure our mutual enemies found her."

He got everything he wanted: revenge on my mother for leaving and more proof that vampires are a threat to magicians.

"I regret that part, though. I shouldn't have given the bloodsucker the honor of your mother's blood. It should have been *my* hands." He pauses, the corners of his mouth tilting up like he's reminiscing. "Like it was for Joseph."

His grin widens at the shock on my face, and he holds up his hand. Thin blades of ice sprout from the tips of his fingers, and even though he makes no move toward me, I can feel them tearing into me with the truth. Dad died in a mugging, they said. He died from multiple stab wounds.

"Of course"—he leans forward like he's going to tell me a secret—"I have you to thank for that."

I stare at him with my questions stuck in my throat. I thought I wanted all the answers, but maybe I was better with colorful puzzle pieces. I never should've tried to see the whole gruesome picture. But Lucius isn't going to let me off without knowing, without seeing how everything comes back to me.

He holds out his icicle fingers and then twists his palm up and open, setting free a handful of sapphire butterflies that float up and up until they explode like confetti. Torn wings sprinkle my arms, and my hands shake as I brush them off.

No. That night on the stage with the butterflies . . .

He watches me, smile still splitting his face. "That was quite the display of power for someone so young. Of course, you lacked control, just as you do now. You expended a lot more power than you needed for such a simple trick. You were like a little beacon—a lighthouse bringing me home." He takes a step toward me. "You've been on my side this whole time. Leading me to that hack that stole your mother and then later forcing her to use her magic to reveal herself? I couldn't have asked for a better daughter."

I stumble back, my throat burning.

I'm the link to everything bad that's happened to me.

Everything bad that's happened to Parker.

But there's one thing left I can do. Live. Get back to Parker. Make sure I'm not the reason he loses again.

Something's shattering in me—no, multiple things. My heart's one of them, but the other is the cage I've been keeping my magic locked in. It's escaping bit by bit, pooling in me like bubbling lava. I feel like I could take him right now.

I look at my feet so he can't tell what I'm thinking.

His eyes follow my stare.

The tiles aren't just gold beneath my feet anymore. The magic has spun a pattern of golden roses against the black, and I'm standing in the center of the largest bloom.

We both look back up at each other. His eyes grow sharp and cold, like the blades still on his fingers.

He knows the magic's with me. That I'm not something he can control, a weapon he can wield. Just like that, I'm a threat.

I know that whatever stopped him from having me killed all those years ago—it won't stop him now.

I square my shoulders, and he smiles. He leans toward me again just enough to be threatening, but he won't do it here.

He'll want it to be a spectacle.

He turns on his heel and walks away. My knives burn at my wrists, but I ignore the magic that seems to be asking me to kill him.

Not yet.

I wait until he's disappeared before turning as well, but as soon as I shift to the left, a black door has already materialized. I twist the gold doorknob and step into a boxy passageway made of gray stones that go from the floor to the ceiling. Winter-cold air wafts from the cracks between the stones. I let some of my magic burn against my skin, warming me like I'm holding a mug of cocoa while a storm rages around me.

The passageway goes on for so long that for a second I doubt the magic and wonder if it led me astray—perhaps Lucius's hold on it is stronger than I thought—but then the path ends, and I step into a cavernous circular room with giant cages lining the walls.

Only one cage has someone in it. He has his knees pulled up to his chest and his head resting on them. It's such a childish pose it makes my chest ache. I move toward him, but he doesn't look up.

His white shirt is ripped and bloody. He's probably already healed, of course, but they had their fun dragging him here.

I walk all the way to the bars of his cage before he lifts his head. His eyes are hard, and the beginning of a snarl pulls at his lips before he realizes it's me.

"Ava." He stumbles to his feet. "I wasn't sure . . ." His voice cracks. "I wasn't sure you'd come."

"I didn't want Ethan dead." I don't tell him it's okay. It's not.

He glances away before meeting my eyes again. "He was going to kill you."

"I know."

"I couldn't let that happen."

"I know," I say again, softer.

His eyes search my face. Of course I understand why he did it, but I don't want him to have one more death on his hands to save someone he loves. I should have been strong enough to do it myself—to live with Ethan's death on *my* hands.

I'm torn between anger and gratefulness.

Roman reaches out a hand through the bars, and I hesitate, but then I take it and watch as he squeezes his fingers around mine. His grip is too hard. It hurts, but I don't pull away. It calms me. The tiny bit of pain gives me focus.

I step up to the bars and put my other hand against the metal. It's so cold it bites me. I pull back with a yelp.

"Ava," Roman warns.

But I'm not listening. This is *my* plan now.

The magic bubbles in me, anxious to be used. I let it flow to my palm, heating my skin so that when I grip the metal again it doesn't sting. Manipulating metal is what I'm best at, and I know I can bend these bars. I push, but it holds, and I call on the magic in me, begging it. It roars in answer, and I push it against the bars, but something else pushes back—the same magic, but whereas mine feels like roses blooming from my hands, this one feels like vines of thorns, ripping my magic apart.

I stop. I'm panting. Roman's still holding my hand. His other hand is pressed against the bar just above mine—our pinkies touching. I didn't even know he was using magic too.

A bead of sweat trails down his face.

"This is one of the strongest spells I've ever felt," he says. "He's been feeding it for years."

"It's okay," I say. "He has to take you out to kill you, right? He promised everyone a show."

"I don't believe that's a positive," he says calmly.

"We'll strike him then."

Roman grabs my other hand so he holds both through the bars. "I want you to run."

"You said drinking magician blood makes you stronger. That's how you can perform better than anyone else here?"

Roman tugs my hands until my shoulders bump against the freezing bars. "Ava, you need to listen. Running is your best option now."

The wheels are turning in my brain, but I stop to look up at him. "You said running's *not* an option."

"That's when I thought we could just bide our time after you won. Figure things out from the inside, but we can't now." He swallows. "I won't be here to help you now. Your father clearly wants you dead."

"Shut up. I'm thinking." I shake my hands out of his.

His fingers latch around my throat so quickly I don't even see it coming, but there's no violence in it. They're soft and firm. "Ava," he growls. "You need to go." His fangs drop below his lip, and he parts his mouth so I can see them, but I don't even flinch. My brain doesn't scream *vampire*. All it says is, *this is Roman*. This is the boy whose lips I want on my own. It doesn't matter if there are fangs behind them. I lean forward, pressing my neck more firmly into his grip. His eyes widen and then melt.

Relief rushes into them, maybe happiness, but also grief. He thinks he's losing me.

Not without a fight.

"You need to drink my blood." I try to state it matter-of-factly. Like it's no big deal to me. But even as I say the words, I feel a weird mix of disgust and desire.

I thought his eyes were wide before, but I don't think I've seen such a strong expression on his face as now.

"My blood's the strongest around. If you drink it, you'll be stronger. Both of us can take him."

His hand is still around my neck. I'm not sure he even realizes it, but his thumb's running up and down my windpipe.

"Not from my neck," I clarify. I don't know if I'll ever be okay with that.

He drops his hand immediately. "Of course."

"Do you think this will work?"

There's a hungry glaze over his eyes that makes my stomach twist in weird ways. He seems to force himself to snap out of it.

"I know it will make me more powerful. I don't know if it will be enough. I still think you should—"

"Don't you dare tell me to run again."

He stops talking and watches me silently, waiting to see if I really want this. I hold my arm out through the bars, and we both stare down at the blue veins showing against my pale skin.

"Don't keep a girl waiting," I say. I try to joke, make things lighter, but he knows I do that in uncomfortable situations. His frown deepens.

"Roman," I say softly. "I want you to. I *need* you to."

That's enough. His long, cool fingers wrap around my arm just below my elbow. His other hand cradles mine, and his fingers press into my palm as he slowly bends toward my wrist. He pauses with his lips barely touching my skin, and I shiver. I know he feels it because his gaze darts to the side to watch me.

I nod.

He keeps watching me as his lips press harder into my wrist. His tongue darts across my skin, and it takes everything in me not to move. I keep my eyes on him. His mouth widens a fraction more, and I feel the tiny scrape of his fangs, and then the pinch of them sinking in and out again.

I can't stop myself from flinching, and he looks like he wants to stop, so I squeeze the hand that's cradling mine.

"I'm fine," I say, but my voice is hoarse. I'm not scared, though.

He relaxes slightly, and his eyes close as he drinks.

I don't feel his fangs anymore, just his lips on my skin and the faint pain from the wound underneath them, almost like he's kissing it and making it better. And then there's the magic. It bubbles out of me and into him, and I can feel the spell that makes him a vampire lapping it up in desperation, and I wonder if that's how Roman always feels: desperate and hungry.

My magic wants to help him, to heal him.

I started down this path wanting to make all vampires bleed, but now here I am—bleeding for one. I feel a tiny sting of shame. It's still hard to totally shake free of my past. But based on Mom's journals, I think she'd be proud of where I am. I discovered the same things that she did. She might not have had the power to change those things, but I do.

His thumb trails up and down my arm just above where he feeds, and it's almost too much sensation. My nerves spark from the magic and the pain and desire. I want more. I wish there weren't bars between us.

His eyes are open again, bright with more hunger than was there before, a different kind.

And then he pulls away. He breathes heavily as he stares at me, like he wants me through the bars of the cage too. His lips are red with my blood.

For a second it causes a sharp jolt of panic.

He sees it and turns his head. When he looks back, he seems closed off. The cold, practical Roman.

"Sorry," I tell him. "It's just . . ." I'm feeling too many conflicting things at once. What I want in the moment is warring with my past.

"Please don't apologize," he says. "I understand."

He runs a thumb across my wound, even though I don't need him to heal me now. My skin stitches itself back together, and then he pulls a handkerchief from his pocket and wipes my wrist. He hesitates for a moment before placing a small kiss against my pulse.

I clear my throat. "I'm going to need my hand back so I can focus."

He nods, and I can tell he's trying to keep his face serious, but the corners of his mouth tug up as he says, "Whatever you need."

CHAPTER 35

I wish the magic would play with me and delay my destination a little bit, but when I leave Roman's cell, it takes me straight to the place I need to go. It's definitely not where I *want* to go.

I knock on Diantha and Reina's sea-green door. Aristelle opens it. Her face gives away nothing as she steps back and lets me in. Everyone except the twins sits around the coffee table in the overstuffed chairs and couches in front of the television I've watched *Tomb Raider* on one too many times. It hurts to stand here in a room I felt safe in, knowing none of it was real.

But I need their help.

Reina's on her feet, reaching for me, but I hold a hand out to stop her. She blinks and stands frozen for a second, like I'm going to change my mind.

"We're sorry, Ava," Diantha says from the couch.

Reina sits back down beside her. "We only did it because—"

"I know why you did it."

"Then you understand why I'm not sorry." Aristelle's expression is hard.

We stare at each other in silence for a moment.

"Ava," Xander begins.

It turn my glare on Xander before he can say anything else. "I told you to stop saying my name."

He leans back in his chair like he wants to sink into it.

I glance around at all of them. Reina and Diantha both look wounded, like I've hurt them and not the other way around, Aristelle looks ready for a fight, and Xander just looks sad. His usual buoyancy is deflated. I've only ever seen him charming or fierce, and I wonder if I ever really saw him. I thought he was the fairy-tale knight I needed, but he was the trapped damsel that was desperate for rescue, even if the rescuer got hurt in the process.

But now we all need to rescue one another.

I need them to be the people who had my back.

I swallow, and it's hard and painful. "I need to know if you can be on my side again."

Aristelle and Xander share a look. Diantha bites her lower lip with worry in her eyes.

"Of course," Reina says at the same time Aristelle says, "It depends."

That hurts. They were willing to do anything to make sure nothing happened to their little family, and Aristelle's words just confirm that I'm not part of that. I was never part of that. They got what they wanted from me.

I can't stop the little well of tears in my eyes. I turn away and blink, and I'm not sure if I can bear to look at them anymore. This was a mistake. I start to leave when a familiar hand grips mine. I hate how right it feels, warm and secure, but not in a romantic way—that easy way you can grab a friend's hand and tug them along with you.

So I turn back to Xander. I let him see the tears in my eyes.

"You hurt me," I say. "All of you." Because I'm tired of hiding my hurt. I wish I could go back in time to that day with James and June. They hugged us like they were just saying bye for a little while. Parker cried. I kept my tears from falling, though, but I wish I'd told them that it hurt, that they had come into my life just to leave a gaping wound, but they weren't going to stick around to see it. They certainly weren't going to stick around to heal it.

Reina grabs my other hand. "We always wanted you, Ava. We were just so, so scared." Her voice sounds small and broken, but then she forces a smile onto her face. "Plus, you always side with me on Angelina being the best Lara Croft, and that is very important."

Diantha rolls her eyes. "No taste."

Reina lets out a tiny, fragile laugh, and I almost laugh too. It gets caught in my throat behind the pain, but it's there.

I know right then that I could laugh with them again.

They might have scarred me, but they want to stick around and help that scar heal, and that's what makes someone family—the willingness to stay when everything hurts.

I have to get back to Parker. I was hurt, and I left because I didn't want to put the burden of healing me on them. But maybe, when it's really your family, helping someone heal *isn't* a burden at all. It's just a sign of love. I get that now.

Aristelle sighs. "What do you need?"

"I need help saving Roman."

Xander drops my hand, and Reina squeezes my other one tighter.

"Let him go," Xander says. "He's the reason we lost Sarah."

"And you're the reason he lost his sister."

"She had the same chance as . . ." Xander fades off.

The same chance as me. But she didn't. Not if what Roman says is true.

"Be honest. Did you train her as well?"

There's guilt on all their faces. They didn't let me hunt vampires because they felt ashamed for dragging Beatrice into that world and not doing enough to train her to win. Plus, they wanted to manipulate me—to keep stringing me along without giving me what they thought I really wanted.

It's going to take a long time to heal. I force my rising anger down.

"You both owe each other," I say. "And this isn't just about saving Roman. We want to save everyone."

That gets their attention.

CHAPTER 36

I follow two of Lucius's goons through the garden of roses and hedges to the garden of death that feeds and waters everything about this place. Of course he would want Roman's death to happen here. Of course he would want one more reveal to shake me. Maybe he hopes to scare me into my place. But I already know all about his personal horror show.

When we reach the shore of the lake, I freeze. Lights bob in the thick fog like tiny trapped moons, and for second, all I see are the lights. They remind me of the ones Willow hung on the beach, but these are attached to the helms of rowboats. As the fog ebbs and flows, I can barely make out the faces of magicians in each one, and even though I can't see them clearly, I can feel heads turn and eyes follow me as I step onto the sinking planks and attempt to make my way across.

The heavy cloak I wear soaks up too much water. It was waiting for me this morning, bright white with icicles stitched around the hem. I turned it black with roses embroidered in the deepest red.

I step onto the bloody stones of the island and make my way to where Lucius waits in a perfect white suit. The hem of his pants is red. He looks like a bored angel of death with the hilt of a sword in his hand as he lazily grinds the tip into the stones. My eyes dart to Willow behind him, strands of her hair billowing in the breeze. Of course he would choose this spot. He raises his eyebrows at my cloak. I let it drop from my shoulders. Underneath I wear my regular clothes: faded black jeans and a ribbed white tank. I need to be able to move.

Roman kneels between us with his eyes closed.

"Ava." Roman's voice is soft. He says my name like a plea.

I don't look at him.

"Please," he says, and I know he's not asking me to spare him. He's asking me to do it. He doesn't like my plan. He wants me to take the way out that ends with him dead and me alive. But he didn't see the look in Lucius's eyes. I wouldn't be alive for long. This isn't just Roman's best shot. It's my best shot too.

I swallow and step toward Lucius, holding my hand out for the sword.

I'm not going to use it on Roman. I'm guessing Lucius would die by decapitation too.

Lucius's grin looks downright giddy as he passes me the hilt, like he knows I'll take a swing at his neck instead of Roman's. It'd give him the perfect excuse to murder me. My gut twists. My heart pounds like it will rip right out of my throat.

I want to think of Parker, but I also don't want to think of Parker. I try to picture him and push him away at the same time.

My vision blurs.

"Come on," Lucius invites me.

I know exactly what I need to do. I lift the blade. The magic's screaming at me to do it. End it. Set it free. Lucius isn't looking at the sword at all. He's looking at me like I'm a daughter who disappointed him.

I hesitate. My troupe's supposed to be backup, but they're in a boat out on the water. How are they going to reach us to help? I swing anyway.

He grins. His arm darts forward, and he grabs my hands, clasping the hilt, stopping my swing. His other hand closes around my throat, squeezing so tightly I can't even feel the magic in me anymore. Only pain. My fingers loosen, and Lucius rips the hilt from my grip. My vision blackens, and I start to look for Roman, but he's already there, behind Lucius's shoulder, ripping into Lucius's neck with his fangs. Blood sprays me in the face. Lucius's fingers lose their grip on my neck, and I stumble back.

Gasps and yells sound from the boats. Lucius had tried to keep help from reaching me, but it stopped his allies too—at least for a moment.

For a second, all I can do is stand there, watching a vampire kill him the same way he arranged for one to kill my mom. It's poetic in a way that makes me want to vomit.

But it won't be that easy. Lucius reaches behind him and grabs Roman, flipping him over his shoulder so he lands sprawled at our feet. He places a boot on Roman's neck, and I know he's powerful enough to crush his throat in an instant.

I crash into Lucius, and it's just enough to make him stumble.

Roman darts to his feet, and we both face him.

"Well," Lucius drawls as he turns to Roman. "I knew there was a reason I didn't like you. It seems you've been waiting for this."

Roman gives him a slow nod, and then his knives are flying. I don't even see them, but I recognize the flick of his wrists.

Metal clanks against metal, and Lucius stands, sword in front of him, Roman's knives at his feet. Except one. One is buried in his stomach. Blood blooms on his white vest like an unfolding rose petal.

It's a beautiful sight.

He glances from the knife to Roman, confusion on his face, like Roman should never have been able to land that shot, and maybe he wouldn't have without my blood and what he just drank from Lucius.

For a second, the wound looks serious, but then he plucks out the knife and sends it into Roman's stomach. Roman doubles over. "You know, I've decided not to kill you outright. I'll plant you in the garden next to your sister." He jerks his head toward me. "But I'm going to make you watch her die first."

His sword swings in a high arc. It would've been faster to just run me through, but he clearly wants the drama of cleaving me straight down the middle.

He's stronger than me. But I have something else: the desire to get revenge. My own for my mom's death, and the magic's for his abuse. We're both going to get it.

I raise my hands, and I finally let go of everything inside me—the pain, the rage, the longing—and the magic latches on to it, interprets it as a command, and burns through my veins and into my fingertips. I gasp as the blade bites the tender spot between my thumb and fingers on both hands. But it doesn't cleave through. The magic heals me as fast as the blade can cut. Rivulets of blood trail down my skin, coating my wrists, and my arms shake, but I'm holding strong.

Roman's blade sinks into his neck, and Lucius stumbles back, but it's not enough. I'm worried nothing will be enough, and my troupe hasn't come, and I don't know if it's because they abandoned me or if they just can't reach me.

Lucius tosses Roman to the side and raises the sword again, and the glint in his eye is sharper than the blade. Something tells me I won't stop it this time.

"Lucius." The voice is calm and quiet, but somehow it's enough to freeze Lucius. He lowers his sword, and there's tension in the easy smile he plasters on his face. He's scared.

Relief flutters in my chest.

A cold hand wraps around my wrist, but I don't jump. It's not the icy bite of Lucius's touch. It's the soothing balm of Roman's. He runs a thumb over the spot he drank from earlier, and I shiver. I can feel my own power in his touch.

"It's okay," Roman says. "They're here."

CHAPTER 37

*A*t least one part of our plan is going right.

I took down the barrier again this morning. After a lot of convincing, my troupe delivered a message to Roman's vampire connection in town to be here before dawn. Xander and Aristelle both refused to deal with vampires at first, but these are people Roman trusts, and I trust Roman, and my troupe trusts me because despite everything, I fought for them. I'm still fighting for them. The hope of freeing Sarah from the garden was the last straw to get them on my side. I'm not positive they won't try to stake Roman when this is over, though.

The vampire steps closer. His skin is pale, and his hair is straight and honey-brown, just long enough to tuck behind his ears. His features are delicate and unassuming. He wears dark-washed jeans and a black button-up shirt, and he looks like he might be heading to a casual office for a day of work. He moves slowly, and something about it seems off.

"Numerius." Lucius says the name like a curse.

I shoot Roman a surprised look, but he seems just as shocked. The other vampires he'd been dealing with must not have told him everything. That can't be good. But we don't really have any other choice except to go along and hope Numerius will keep the same promises.

Numerius raises his hands. "I come in peace."

That wasn't the plan.

"You killed my sister," Lucius states. For a second there's a flash of grief in his eyes, and I can see what that moment must have been like for him, finding her. And yet he did that to me. What kind of person can feel that loss and inflict it on someone else? Only a monster.

"And you killed mine in return."

There are murmurs from the water.

Numerius looks around. "Oh, they didn't know? Are you still spinning that same old tale of heroic sacrifice?" He raises his voice. "My sister was no saint. She didn't give her life to make your little trinkets. She helped Lucius kill a magician to make each and every one of your cursed stones. And then he killed her to keep it quiet and spun a tale of sacrifice being worth more than blood."

I glance at the fog-hidden boats, anxious to see how the other magicians are taking this. The fog thins, hugging the water. Most of them stare uneasily, glancing between Lucius and Numerius.

"And now . . ." He lets out a deep chuckle. "Now you kill a fellow magician each time you make a new one immortal, do you not? You all have blood on your hands. Are you any better than us?"

"One life to save hundreds," someone shouts.

"Just one, is it?" Numerius waves a hand at the bodies dangling in vines. "Looks like you all deserve the sharp end of a stake."

And then I see it, the stakes, sliding and blinking into the hands of the magicians in the boats closest to us. Even if there's truth to what he says, these are not people who will sit idly by for a slaughter. They have all been in a kill-or-be-killed situation.

They all chose to kill.

There's so much blood on everyone's hands. I look around at their faces. Some are hungry for more. Some love this life, but others just look tired and grim. They'll keep fighting because they think there's no other choice.

"Wait!" I shout. "They're not here to hurt us. All they want is Lucius. All they want is to end this."

"And then what?" The voice is loud enough to match mine and angrier. I know it. Natasha's pink hair is easy enough to spot in a boat near the shore. "We won't have immortality anymore. How do you know that we won't die?" She jumps off the boat, boots splashing into the water. "You don't care, do you?"

"I don't know what will happen, but do you really want to keep living like this?" I gesture behind me at all the pain and death. They feel trapped. Mom must have spent years feeling that way, but there's always a choice—sometimes it's just a dangerous one. I point at Numerius. "He's a way out. We don't need to fight. We just need to give him my father." I turn to Lucius. It's the first time I've called him that to his face, and I never thought I would, but I want him to know that I recognize what he is to me, and that because of all he's done, it means nothing.

Voices ripple across the lake. I'm willing to stand against my own father. That has to mean something.

A gleam shines in Numerius's eyes. "*Father*, did you say? How interesting . . ."

"I thought you were weak, not a fool." Lucius glares at me, then shifts his gaze back to Numerius.

A slow smile spreads across Numerius's face, and it reminds me so much of Lucius that I can picture them together, all those years ago, plotting for more power, their smiles slipping more and more from the joy of curiosity to something hungry and wicked. Something that turned them both into true vampires: not creatures who drink blood, but creatures who drink power.

I see my mistake: thinking for even a moment that one of them was better than the other, that something in Numerius had changed over the years.

Being immortal doesn't let you grow.

All it does is let you lose pieces of yourself.

We've led him to a blood bank, and all he has to do is take it.

Screams sound from the boats around the lake as shadowy figures climb from the water and sink their teeth into the vulnerable magicians. Lucius set up this execution in a way that made it impossible to interfere with, and now they're sitting ducks.

Numerius takes in the murky battle with a calm expression before his eyes settle on me. He's in front of me before I can register his movement. Fingers close around my neck. My feet fly off the ground, and I'm dangling, kicking as my hands dig into his wrists, acting like a girl without magic. Each breath struggles through my restricted throat, and I worry for a second that he's squeezed the magic right out of me, but it's there, buzzing and faint. He's dampening it like throwing a wet blanket over a fire.

It feels as if the fog of this place has woven into my mind, and I can't think of what I need my magic to do. I can't think of anything at all.

"Do you want to watch this time, Lucius, as I take away another thing that belongs to you?" Numerius asks.

My eyes sting, but I find Lucius. He's backing away. He's almost to the edge of the vines. I just tried to decapitate him, but it still stings that he'd leave me to die like this. Numerius pulls me closer to him, and all I can focus on are the fangs dipping below his open mouth.

And then I'm falling. Stones cut into me when I hit the ground, and I can't tell if the warm blood I feel is mine or from the streams that flow here. My vision swims as someone pulls me away. My magic comes rushing back, and I heave as I push myself to my knees. Roman's beside me. All his knives and stakes are suspended in the air around Numerius.

The weapons turn slowly in the air toward us.

They fly forward but halt halfway. I stand in front of them, staring them down, but they start to quiver. Sweat drips down my temples. Roman stands next to me, the veins in his neck straining. He's helping. I can't take Numerius alone, and the way the blades and stakes wobble as they inch toward us, I know the second I move, the second I let my focus slip, they'll tear us both to pieces.

"Move," I say to Roman through clenched teeth.

I feel it the moment Roman stops using his magic. Mine flares as it struggles to keep the knives at bay, but Roman's not moving out of the line of fire. He steps right in front of me, looking down at me with sad resolve.

My focus snaps. His eyes widen, and his hands clench my biceps as he jerks into me, but he doesn't fall. He looks as surprised as I am.

Someone else crashes to the ground behind him, and I jerk free of his grip and kneel down at their side.

Julia's wide eyes stare up at me. All the knives and stakes rise from her chest and stomach. I reach for one, plucking it out and pressing my hand into her cut, telling the blood to heal her.

The crunch of Numerius stepping toward us pulls my stare to him. I can't heal her and fight him. Roman faces Numerius, but all his weapons are gone. He can't call them to him while they're buried in Julia. I could never heal her that fast.

"Julia," Numerius says as if he's just bumped into her at the grocery store. "I'm surprised to see you here. I thought Lucius would have done away with you by now."

"Not for lack of trying." Blood bubbles at her lips.

Numerius gives a cool smile. "But here you are."

"You always did like doing his dirty work." She gives him a bloody, fierce smile.

Numerius frowns. "I always do my own."

He flicks his hand and the knives dig deeper.

I let go of her wound and send the knife I pulled from her into his stomach. He plucks it out and tosses it to the side with the ease of someone swatting a mosquito. Blood runs freely from her lips now.

She's no longer staring down Numerius leaning toward us. She focuses on me. I hate the way her eyes look, like the fog is seeping into them.

"You need your father."

I cringe at the words.

"Or maybe just his crown."

I search for Lucius. He's standing on the edge of the garden, watching as if waiting to see where the tides will turn. When he catches me staring, he takes a step into the bramble, past Willow's dangling body.

He's going to run.

"Go," Julia says. I squeeze her hand.

But I can't leave Roman. Numerius takes another slow step closer before a line of fire darts between us. The blood on the ground sizzles as the blaze grows high enough to make Numerius raise his eyebrows a fraction.

I follow the flames to Aristelle, crouching with her hands on the ground of the shoreline. She stands as Xander, Diantha, and Reina jump from the boat. They stride toward us in soaking-wet clothes with black streaks of ash on their arms and faces from however many vampires they killed to reach the shore. More magicians approach on the other side of Numerius. I never thought I'd be happy to see Natasha's snarling face, but she's there with her hulking brother and a wall of magicians behind them. I recognize the hypnotist with the lip rings. Cecily swings a wooden club covered with stakes. Her wet blue hair clings to her cheeks, and a wild grin stretches her face. She looks more like Harley Quinn than ever.

Julia squeezes my hand again, and when I glance down at her, I know she can't speak anymore. I don't hesitate. I need to act and trust that my friends, and kind-of-enemies, can take down our bigger enemy.

I launch myself through the wall of flames, past the confused stares of my troupe, and toward the vines Lucius has slipped into. I'm about to step into the garden when a hand grabs my elbow. Twisting, I ready my power, only to call it off when I meet Annalise's gray eyes. Fierceness flickers in them, and I can see the woman she used to be—the person who attracted the toxic interest of Lucius. Raising her trembling hands, she fumbles with the tie of my mother's necklace, and my heart feels like it pounds a million times in the second it takes her to undo it. We don't have time. Who's already dead? Xander? Reina? I don't look back to see.

The necklace falls from her neck and crunches into the stones.

I grab it. Ignoring the way my fingers slip on the blood, I slide it around my neck as I move past the first row of dripping bodies. The five jewels pierce my skin in a ring around my throat, and it's like the last barrier between me and the magic in this place has been obliterated. It roars through me like a lion let out of its cage, pushing and clawing at my skin. I stumble, catching myself on a vine weaving in and out of a girl's arm. Lucy. I barely look at her, but as I propel myself forward I make her a promise that I'll get her out.

I'm moving fast enough that the thorns rip me to pieces, drinking me in like the rest of the people here, but it doesn't slow me. I'm paying the tithe. I'm using the magic I want to end, so it seems fitting.

His white suit is easy enough to spot. He turns to face me just as I send a vine bursting from the ground to wrap around both his legs. I send other vines too, the ones already growing through flesh. I make them reach out to him, running along his arms and tying him to the very people he doomed. One of the vines curves around his throat, and a red rose blooms on the end. I want to smile at him, taunt him just a little. I'm not the only one taking my revenge. My mom's with me, Annalise is with me, my troupe, Roman, everyone trapped in this forsaken garden, and not to mention the magic itself.

He strains, and his eyes widen and then land on the necklace at my throat.

"Ahh." His brow furrows. "I didn't know she had anything left in her to betray me with." He looks almost impressed.

I worry for a moment about Annalise. If I can't end this, she'll suffer even more.

She'll meet the same fate as my mother.

"Couldn't do it on your own?" he asks.

"Neither could you." I shift my gaze to his crown.

His power bucks against mine, but I struck first. I have the upper hand.

Still, I wobble as I step toward him. He sees it.

"Numerius is the one who killed your mother."

"What?"

His arm breaks free, and I focus on trapping it again before he can strike, but he did what he intended. He distracted me.

"You're lying."

"Not this time. Let me help you kill him. All I did was tell them where to find her. I never would have done it myself. Never."

A lie. He said he wished he'd done it himself.

"I can kill him without you," I state calmly, even though my heart stutters under the strength of the power I'm using as the vines churn around him. What if I steal his crown and all that extra power breaks me?

"Maybe," he says.

That word slows me. It's not a lie. There might even be a small trace of worry on his face. I don't know if it's worry that I'll die or worry that Numerius will win. My guess is on the latter. But it's genuine.

He senses my hesitation.

"We can get vengeance for your mother together. Not a day goes by that I don't regret telling him where she was. I tried to take it back. I tried. I left hiding just to stop it, but when I got there, all I found was you, crying over her body."

The vines wrapping around him halt.

He smiles. "We can avenge her together."

"You watched me cry."

His smile falters.

"You left me alone in that moment." I don't know why it surprises me, this new, particular coldness, but my veins turn to ice thinking about him standing there, watching me in the worst moment of my life and not reaching out to me. And he didn't just watch me. He left me in the woods while he went inside and stole her things.

"It made you stronger," he says.

The words are a slap. It didn't make me stronger. It made me harder. I'm beginning to learn that those are two different things.

"It made you mine."

He turned me as cold and hard as the ice his power wields. Hard enough to do what needs to be done to win. Because Lucius isn't the only threat.

And he's not the one who drained my mother to the brink of death.

The vines peel away from him. Dots of blood cover his white suit where the thorns split skin.

It's a more appropriate outfit for him.

I don't wait to see if he follows as I spin around and shove through the tangled garden. He could run again, but he wants this. I can tell. He sees us as a team, especially with the extra power around my neck. He actually thinks giving me the man who bit my mother will make me forget who set it in motion.

I break through onto the shore again. Most of the action has made its way from the boats to here. Fighting bodies churn in front of me. The screaming and the shouting and the sounds of death blows push in on me, and I shake my head like I can get rid of the awful, screeching music of it. I don't want to kill another vampire. Even these ones. Aren't they here because we've been hunting them?

But I'm not going to sit back and die either.

A woman with startling blue eyes and blood dripping from her blond hair lunges for us with her teeth bared.

I'm quicker. My stake is in and out of her chest before her teeth can clamp together.

I snarl. I can be the predator if I have to be.

Lucius brushes a hand down his vest and strolls straight into the mayhem like he's taking a walk in the park. For a second, it's like they're parting for him. Until a group of vampires forms a semicircle around him. He moves in a blur of white and red and blond and flashing metal, and I hear the *thump thump thump* before I can even register what happened. When he stills, there are no more vampires in his path, only heads detached from bodies that are already withering to nothing. He props the sword on his shoulder and strolls onward.

They don't part for me the same way.

I crouch and slide deeper in, weaving around vampires with stakes protruding from missed shots and magicians pulling knives from their own bodies. I stub my toe on what I discover is a severed head and decide not to look down ever again. Keep moving. Keep moving.

Fangs latch on to my arm, and I scream, slashing my weapon toward the pain without looking. My stake jerks out of my hand, and the teeth release me. I spin and face a tall, thin boy with curly blond hair. Blood drips from his mouth and down his neck, and I try not to gag, but it's not the blood that gets me. My stake pokes out of his cheek. He smiles, and it bobs with the movement before he reaches up and pulls it out, tossing it over his shoulder. He keeps smiling as the wound stitches itself back together, and I should move and run, but I can't look away. It's like I never touched him.

The magic in me is snapping for the chance to do something, but I'm afraid to let it out. It doesn't want to demolish just this vampire. It wants to turn this place to rubble. I feel like I'm holding the leash of a rabid animal.

The vamp jumps and suddenly I'm on the ground, and he's on top of me with his full, sharp set of teeth snapping toward my neck. I barely have time to pull my arms up between us and push against his chest. He flies backward, and I blink, shocked.

Xander stands above me, grinning down like Batman's Joker, the perfect counterpart to Cecily. He holds the vampire out by his collar as he twists and snaps. "You're welcome," he says to me with a wink, then plunges his stake into the vampire's chest and drops him before he can even begin turning to dust. My hands are still in front of me, and he leans down and grabs one, yanking me to my feet. Xander stares after Lucius, cleaving his way through the battle. "He's still alive."

"I need him to kill Numerius," I grit out.

"Good," Xander says. Whatever he thinks about Lucius, I know he thinks Numerius is worse. He hasn't had time to know a vampire.

Regardless of what I've said, everyone here is just someone who killed his brother.

"Why aren't you with the others?"

"Roman sent me after you."

I give him a skeptical look.

"Don't worry—that's the first and last time I take orders from him." He stakes another vamp, and I'm fairly positive he's picturing Roman while he does.

And then we're there, on the edge of the circle that surrounds Numerius.

He is a mess of burning flesh and scratches that heal almost as fast as Aristelle and Reina can inflict them. Piles of vines trap one of his arms, but his other arm holds Natasha by her throat. Her hands claw at his. Her eyes bulge. Beneath her flailing feet lies a pile of magicians. The pink hair of her brother sticks out from the bottom of the pile.

Knives protrude from Numerius's body, and I do a quick count. It's all of them. Roman doesn't have any left. And Roman—he's pulling himself off the ground. One of his arms dangles limply by his side. His leg seems bent at an odd angle, but he pulls himself to his feet, and it snaps itself back into place as he moves. Numerius doesn't even see him. His eyes land on Lucius standing on the fringe.

"Are you going to participate this time?" Numerius asks.

"Do something!" I scream at Lucius. I didn't let him live so he could pop some popcorn and watch, but that's what he's doing, and Numerius looks as calm as an actor playing pretend.

Roman creeps up behind Numerius, who still doesn't see him. He *does* see me pull one of Roman's knives from my right wrist. I throw. He jerks to the side, and even with all his wounds, he spares me a smile for my missed shot.

But I wasn't aiming for him.

Roman catches my knife and plunges it into Numerius's neck. It's not enough to kill him, but it is enough for him to drop Natasha, who lands on the pile containing her dead brother. Numerius turns toward Roman, blade still bobbing in his throat. The total calm and slowness in his movement are more terrifying than anything. He doesn't need to use all his speed and strength. He's just picking us off like we're small nuisances. Not threats.

My magic feels endless, but it also feels as if it's leaking from my seams, and I'm barely strong enough to keep it focused. I need control.

Roman meets my eyes. *Breathe*, he mouths.

Cecily launches herself onto Numerius's back, swinging her club, which freezes in midair as she tugs on it. His legs flame and extinguish again and again. Numerius lunges for Roman at the same moment that Natasha rises from the pile of the dead, aiming two stakes at Numerius's back. He grabs Roman's throat with one hand and twists, shoving him into Natasha's stakes.

I dart toward their tangled bodies and pull Roman off her as she snarls at me like she's going to forget we're on the same side and rip my heart out right now. I ignore her and yank the stakes from Roman's stomach as he cringes. The wounds heal almost instantly. And Numerius's wounds heal faster.

"Ava." Roman's grabbing me, pulling me to my feet, and I know Numerius is there, but I close my eyes and imagine Roman's cool hands pressing against me, his mouth on my ear telling me to breathe.

I have to believe in myself.

I let out my breath and open my eyes to meet Numerius's. I smile and let go. The magic springs from me, and it feels like a thousand vines sprouting from my pores, and there's no need to tell each and every one what to do because my intent is clear. Real vines lurch from the ground, winding around Numerius's legs and arms, but he's breaking them as fast as I can grow them. I feel Diantha's power tangled in there too, but it's still not enough.

Until ice starts growing along the vines.

Numerius's eyes widen slightly as he realizes Lucius's power has joined mine. Together, we trap him in something that's half rosebush and half ice sculpture, and I hate the sight of our powers combined, but together we are unstoppable. Numerius's calm finally breaks, and he roars. Bits of ice flake away, but the structure holds. Stepping forward, I force the ice to shatter around his heart and the vines to part, leaving a perfect path. He stills. He looks confused, like this shouldn't be possible.

"This is for my mom." It feels like what I should say, but it also feels wrong, now that I know how hard she tried to keep me from this life, to stop me from coating my hands in blood and ash.

I don't get the chance to plant my stake. His head slips off and falls at my feet. It still has that vaguely alarmed expression on it, like he can't quite believe he lost.

Lucius stands with his sword still in the air.

Silence falls as the last bit of Numerius's head turns into dust and dissipates into the blood on the ground.

Lucius breaks that silence with a laugh as he flexes his fingers. All that power went to him.

One side of his mouth curves as he watches me. I'm not a threat to him anymore—at least not right now.

Even with my troupe at my back. Not all the magicians were with me.

"Ava." Roman chokes on my name, and I spin. I forget about killing my father when I see fresh blood dripping from Roman's mouth, and for a second I think he's killed someone, but his hands are on his neck. Blood leaks through his fingers. He drops to his knees.

I'm with him in an instant, sinking next to him, ignoring the bite of the gravel. "Who did this?" I snarl, twisting, bracing for an attack.

But other vampires are dropping too—not all of them, though. It must only be the ones whose curse traces back to Numerius. And apparently Roman was one of them.

"A shame," Lucius says as he comes to stand over my shoulder.

"Did you know this would happen?"

He shrugs. "It was a possibility, but magic is unpredictable." He eyes Roman with the clinical detachment of a surgeon. "It appears his original wound that made him a vampire is opening up."

Roman's hands drop from his neck as blood trails down onto the very ground he never wanted to feed. I press my hand into his neck, pushing my magic, demanding it to heal him.

Nothing happens. I'm not strong enough to stop the collapsing curse that's pushing the blood from his body.

"Nononono." The words run together.

Roman's mouth moves, but no words come out, only more blood.

His eyes close. His breath is shallow.

I look up at Lucius. "Help him." He has more power. Maybe he has enough.

"He was a traitor anyway. He's the one that led you astray." He kicks at Roman's leg, making it slide across the gravel.

The rage that builds in my throat almost makes me vomit. My magic pushes against me so hard it feels like my skin will peel away just to let it out, and I give it a command: hide. I can't let him think I'm a threat. I rise up from my knees and step toward Lucius.

I'm not a match for him now. Not with Numerius's power freshly stolen.

We both know I'll have to play pretend if I want to live. Be an illusion.

"You're right," I say. "He convinced me they were good." I try not to look down at Roman's face—I don't succeed. It's softer and more boyish with his eyes closed. I will myself to look regretful, and it's not hard. I regret a lot.

I helped kill the vampire I've wanted dead for more than half my life, and now I'm losing the one I might love.

I know Lucius doesn't believe my act, but I only need him to believe I'm doing it to save my own skin—that I'm the survivor he made me.

Lucius reaches out a hand to me; victory lights his eyes. There's actual joy in them and surprise, like he didn't know he could feel this way. He got the revenge he spent centuries pining for, but I know that joy isn't going to last. I can already see the way his pupils constrict as he looks at me, as he assesses how best to handle me. "Daughter," he says, his hand still open.

Everyone around us watches, waiting.

I put my hand in his. One side of his mouth curves upward, and I think I catch a glimmer of hope in his eyes, but I don't let it stop me. He got his revenge, but I only got half of mine, and I guess in this one way, I am my father's daughter.

This time, I don't hesitate.

He starts to say my name, but I don't let the second syllable leave his mouth. I step closer, like I'm going to pull him into an embrace—

And bury my knife in his heart.

"I don't belong to you," I whisper, and then I pull back, but I keep his hand in mine. Part of me always thought my revenge would be like this—a dramatic movie moment where I win—but I stare at the shocked expression on his face, like *I* betrayed *him*, and it just feels like I've lost all over again. He tries to rip his hand away from me as he attempts to lift his other hand to remove the knife, to heal, but I beg the magic to stop him, and it pulls him down. He sinks to his knees, mouth floundering, but I don't need to hear his last words.

I didn't get that luxury with my parents.

And then it's over. He falls backward, crunching into the gravel and the blood he spent years collecting. I focus on the bloom of red beneath my knife. It reminds me of a wilting rose.

I don't want to look into his vacant eyes. I don't want that memory. He doesn't deserve to be something that haunts me.

I glance around at all the magicians watching me, and then at the garden—the tangle of vines and flesh and blood. Nothing seems broken by his death, but these spells have been fed for years by more than just him. I'm not done yet.

I look for Xander. He's standing close to me. All my troupe is. Except for Reina. She holds Roman like she knows I need someone to stay with him. That I can't do what I have to do otherwise.

Xander steps up to me and kneels, running a hand over Lucius's eyes, and then I finally look down, but not at his face. I reach and pluck the crown from his head. I'm afraid to put it on. I'm afraid that if I let in one more sliver of power, I'll combust.

But I have to.

I take a deep breath and think of Nadine and Willow. Their magic is in me now too, tied to this sick place. But I also have the strength of their friendship.

And that's the thing that makes me put the crown on my head.

Instantly, my blood *boils*. Something warm and wet drips down my nose, and I lift a trembling hand. It comes back red. The magic wants out of all the places Lucius trapped it—every stone, every nook and cranny of this haunted place—and I can finally let it loose. But I need to hold on to it for just a little bit longer.

I turn to the hungry vines behind me. *Let go.*

Petals start to fall like red rain. Leaves brown and curl, and finally the vines begin to wither and retract, pulling from the wounds they caused. I run for Willow as the vines release her and her body sags closer to the ground. Her eyelids flutter and then pinch closed as she whimpers. Blood pours from her where the magic releases her but refuses to heal the bites it caused.

The last of the vines collapses to the dirt, and the stillness is filled with magicians and apprentices crying out in pain, gurgling on their own blood. I press my hands into Willow's wounds and start to heal them as I shout to the watching magicians, "Help them!"

Only some of them move.

Not enough to heal them all.

Willow's stopped bleeding, but her eyes are still closed.

I need to find Nadine.

I stand and try to weave through the groans and the hands, because I won't be able to save everyone. There are at least five people bleeding out for every magician here.

"Nadine!" I yell.

Maybe it's too late.

I slip, and my hands sink into the stones, slick with red. So much blood.

Blood magic.

Vampire magic.

Healing magic.

I close my eyes and think of Roman and everything he taught me. I think of wounds and healing, and how this place has cut me deeply but also stitched some parts of me back together again, and when I push that thought into the blood, I tell it to do the same. The magic leaving my body feels gentler, a steady hum. The blood beneath my fingers bubbles and hisses, but I keep my eyes closed, and my only thought is of mending broken things.

And then it stops. I glance down at my clean, dry hands.

The boy I fell next to sits up and holds a hand to his throat where a purple bruise spreads, but there's no blood. His hands search through the stones before he lifts a pair of glasses to his face. He squints at me like he recognizes me. Barry.

I stand on shaky feet and make my way back toward the shore.

I'm not done yet. Some of the magic's still here, in the stones that are hungry for more blood, and I know someone will feed them again unless I really end this.

I give the magic one more command: break free.

And it's ready.

Every cell in my body hums a different song—a soft lullaby, a grief-stricken ballad, a melancholy love song, a raging anthem.

I let it all pour out of me and rip through this place, tearing apart every spell binding the magic. Dead roses collapse into dust at my feet and sprouts of spring-green grass shoot from the ground like nature can't wait to reclaim what the magic stole. I can only imagine what the mansion must look like.

"Stop her!" Natasha takes a step toward me before crying out and bending at the waist. Others join her. And then I feel it. It's like all the new power inside of me is boiling away and turning into steam that's leaking out my pores. The pain of it is so intense that I fall to my hands and knees. And then, just as quickly, it's gone. The stone in the cuff on my wrist shatters and crumbles to the ground. Then the jewels in the crown on my head and finally those around my throat explode, the tiny fragments nicking my skin.

Almost everyone else is on the ground too.

The loss of so much power makes me feel hollowed out and empty, and I'd known it for only a moment. I look around at my friends. Reina's feeling her chest as if there's a hole there. Aristelle retches.

I pull myself to my feet. It's over. Some of the magicians are testing their powers. Aristelle sparks a small flame on the tip of her finger. She squints at it like she's trying to make it grow, but nothing happens. I can feel that familiar buzz—that promise of a hint of magic without all the horror.

I don't care about the power, though.

I turn toward Roman's tattered, blood-splattered shirt. It's all I can focus on. It feels like there are fangs in my neck, tearing me apart as I pick my way over to him. His eyes are open, and, bracing for the emptiness, I force myself to look into them. I'll let the memory haunt me if it means seeing him one more time.

He blinks. His brown eyes focus on my face.

Tears break from me with the same force the magic did. I begin to sob as he pushes himself to his knees and wraps his arms around me. I can't stop. I'm used to things not being okay, and he squeezes me so I know it's real.

"You're not dead," I choke out.

"No." I'm pressed against him so tightly, I feel the rumble of his voice in his chest. "It would appear like I'm not dead at all."

This makes me stop crying. I pull back and stare up at his face. He widens his mouth and shows me his teeth like he's going to make his fangs drop.

Nothing.

He closes his mouth.

"You're not a vampire?"

"I think I stopped being one when Numerius died, and then I would have died as well, but I felt your magic in me, healing me."

I glance around. It looks like I healed more people than I thought.

But not everyone. I didn't bring people back from the dead.

My eyes land on Julia.

And then the heap of magicians where Numerius fought and died.

"It's not fair." Natasha's voice rings out. "You didn't have a right to take that from us."

I push away from Roman and stand to face her as she strides toward me. Some other magicians shift around, like they might back her if she decides to attack.

Roman rises and steps slightly in front of me. His hands are curved like claws, and I don't know where his knives are, but his body tenses like he doesn't need them or his fangs.

"Don't," I say—both to him and her.

Roman turns to look at me, his eyes still wild and distant, like he's not quite registering my words. I put a hand on his bicep and squeeze until I feel some of his tension relax—not completely, though. He'll rip her head off before she can lay a finger on me. But I don't want more blood to spill.

"So this is about the immortality?" I'm gathering the magic inside of me, but I'm tired. I don't know what I'll do with it.

"Among other things," she says.

Ethan's expression sliding from living to dead fills my mind, and I remember him brushing Natasha's arm before the last fight.

I nod, and she frowns at me like she didn't expect me to acknowledge it.

"I really didn't want him to die," I say softly. "I didn't. I'm sorry."

She stops for a second, and the anger in her eyes gets overshadowed with hurt. I know how closely those two emotions are tied, but I'm not the person who can help her past that.

She takes another step, but it's not Roman who blocks her path. Aristelle stands in front of her. "You know I'll put you down with or without magic."

Natasha hesitates.

The rest of Aristelle's troupe—*my* troupe—shifts to close in around me. Even the twins step up in sync on either side of Aristelle, and normal little girls or not now, I'm sure they're just as terrifying as always.

"Another time, perhaps," Natasha says. Her eyes fall and scan the ground, landing on her brother's pink hair. "I have other things to do."

I wish we weren't enemies. I wish I could help her as she shuffles over and starts to dig him out of the pile of bodies, but I'm not that person for her. Some of the other magicians move to help her.

"Ava," a soft voice whispers behind me. It lacks its usual buoyancy, but I'd still recognize it anywhere.

Turning, I almost teeter over, but I make it the couple of steps into the arms of Willow, and Nadine behind her. I'm not a hugger, but embracing the two of them is more than that. They hold me up, and I do the same for them.

I'm afraid to pull back and look at them.

Dead leaves cling to their clothes, and violent bruises cover their skin.

"Are you okay?" It's such a horrible question, and I should know better than to ask it.

"Yes," Willow says brightly at the same moment Nadine says, "No."

Nadine shakes her head at Willow's obvious lie. "But we will be," she adds. "All of us." Nadine looks over her shoulder at a girl with hollow eyes that dart around. She must be Samantha.

And that's what I need to hear. We'll be fine. Eventually. Eventually is what matters.

Diantha and Reina smother a small blond girl between them. Aristelle and Xander watch with tired faces, like they've been trying to be strong for a long, long time, and now they're done.

Roman makes a small, wounded sound, and I jerk toward him, my leftover adrenaline kicking in, but he's fine. He's just staring at the young girl walking toward us. Her tangle of brown hair falls all the way past her hips. She blinks like she can't quite believe what she's seeing, and then Roman has her in his arms, pressed into his chest, but it looks like she's holding him upright, not the other way around, like he's finally given himself permission to stop being strong. I wonder who he'll be without his grief.

I wonder who I'll be without my revenge.

Soft crying pulls my attention. An older man leans over Julia, holding one of her hands gently between his. I step over to him.

"Edgar?"

He looks up, squinting at me for a second.

"I know you. Cassia's daughter." He glances over his shoulder at Lucius's body. "You?"

I nod.

"I'm sorry you had to do that. I'm sorry none of us tried sooner." He sighs as he looks down at Julia. "It's not that we didn't consider it. You'd think it would get easier to die the longer you've lived, but it gets harder. You've had too much time to think about what comes next."

"I'm sorry I had to take that from you."

"It was time. It's *been* time for way too long." He pats Julia's hand.

"She died saving me."

His genuine smile at that surprises me.

"I'm proud of her." He lets go of her and rises to his feet, staring out at the forest beyond with a blank expression.

"Are you going to be okay?"

His lips quirk a little, and he snaps his fingers, and a quarter appears in them. I feel the tiniest hum of his magic—pure and faint, the way it should be.

"The world still needs a little bit of wonder, I think. I'd like to give it that." He nods at me before turning back to Julia.

Aristelle comes up beside me and grabs my elbow.

We stare at each other for a moment. I don't fool myself into thinking she'll apologize. I wouldn't. She was doing what she thought she had to do to protect her family. That, I can understand.

She clears her throat. "None of us can stay here," she says, nodding around the garden. Some magicians happily embrace people covered with blood and leaves, but others watch us with hard, hating eyes. If our little group hadn't just taken down the ruling magician, they'd probably have us by the throats already.

I nod.

She looks away and then back. Aristelle never hesitates, so part of me is afraid of what's coming next.

"Our troupe has lots of hideaways," she says. "And when I say 'our,' I mean you, too. You should come with us."

"Please come," Reina chirps beside me like a little bird perched on my shoulder. I didn't even hear her come up.

I don't know how to feel. I'm still hurt, but underneath the wounds, I feel a little bit fuller. They really do want me. I might not want them right at this moment, but something tells me I'll always be able to run to them and fit right in in a way that can only be described as family. Family can hurt you, but they'll also show up when you need to topple an evil dictator.

I give them both a smile. It's the best I can do. It feels like a lot. "I actually want to go back home."

"We can help with that," Willow says behind me. I turn around, and she grins. "Girls' road trip, anyone?"

I sigh. Only she can pretend everything's fine two seconds after waking up in a garden of the living dead. "I'm going to take a rain check on that. I need to do something myself first."

CHAPTER 38

Everything is dead here without the magic. Some things were real, like the water surrounding the garden of death. The hedges were real, but without the magic they're a mass of dead sticks. There's a mansion, but it's an old, crumbling thing with rotting vines climbing the walls and shutters hanging by a single nail. The door creaks when I open it. Everything inside is gray and dingy—peeling wallpaper, stairs that creak when I take them, a rusted banister I don't dare touch.

Even without the magic taking me wherever I desire, it's not too hard to find what I'm looking for: a hallway of shattered pictures. I pick away at the glass, pulling free each photo, ripping the ones with Lucius in them until I have only pictures of my mom and the rest of her troupe, and then I step into the bedroom. The sofa's worn down with springs ripping through the fabric, and the glass coffee table is in shards, but the golden box still shines even though it's broken open, like he put Mom's journals in the one thing in this place that was real.

I take back those pieces of Mom that were stolen from me and hug them against my chest.

I almost drop them when I turn around.

He's awfully quiet for someone who's not a vampire anymore.

"Where's Beatrice?" I ask Roman. I thought he'd want to be with her—at least for a little while. She's his family.

Roman stares down at his foot, scuffing half circles in the dust. "She . . . has decided to leave with your troupe."

"What?"

He shrugs. I didn't think he was capable of looking sheepish. "Apparently she didn't hold it against them. She was the one who was begging to go hunting all the time." He chuckles. "She always had a vicious streak. She's shocked that I was vampire."

"And you're here," I say. "You didn't go with them."

He stares at me. And then walks slowly over, hands in his slacks, looking more like a vampire than ever in his red-splattered shirt. "I want to be with you." His face is solemn as he watches me. His eyes shift back and forth like he's hoping to read something on my face.

I set down the journals and take a step closer to him, then another. Each one feels like I'm crossing a bridge and lighting it on fire behind me because I don't want to go back to who I was before I met him.

I take the last step so that I'm standing right in front of him. He tracks the movement of my hand as I reach up between us and place it on his chest, above his now-beating heart.

My hand drifts higher, up to his tattered collar. I curl my fingers into it and pull him down gently. Even as I tug him closer, his eyes bore into me, like he's unsure what we are to each other now that it's over.

"Kiss me," I say, because I want it to be that simple.

He lets out a little sigh like he was holding his breath, and then his hands are against my neck, thumbs tilting my chin upward. His lips press into mine, and we both shiver, mouths moving slowly, like we're each exploring a new home. When we break away, I wind my fingers into his. I stare up into his wide, hungry eyes, but it's a different type of hunger than I saw in them before. It makes me want to pull him to me again. Maybe bite his lip just for fun. I can feel my cheeks heat at the thought, and he raises an eyebrow like he wants to know exactly what I'm thinking.

I shake my head as I smile up at him. There's something more important that we have to do. "I have people I want you to meet."

It hasn't been that long since I stood in front of this red door, but it feels like I've lived an entire year or maybe even an entire lifetime in the meanwhile. Roman stands beside me looking like a guy about to pick up a girl for his first date ever, but we're way past that.

I reach out a hand to knock and let it drop. It's the second time I've done that. Guilt needles into me sharper than any vampire fangs or knives. I was never leaving Parker for good, but I can't help worrying there will be hurt on his face when he sees me. And all I ever wanted was to be the one person who *never* hurt him.

Roman clears his throat. "Are you sure you want me here?"

"That's not the problem," I say. "I want you to meet my . . ." "Family" teeters on the edge of my tongue, and I want to say the word, but my heart squeezes as if it might burst if I do. Deb asked me to be part of the family, and I left. What if it was a onetime offer? She told me to come home anytime, but people say a lot of things they don't mean.

I try to start again. "I want you to meet everyone. I just . . . I left them."

Roman doesn't tell me it's okay. Instead, he reaches out for my hand and weaves his fingers between mine, squeezing tight enough that it feels like nothing in this world could break his grip on me.

I panic for a second. My body leans away from him. My instinct is still to pull away from that type of security before it can be taken from me. But that's what I did with Deb.

And of course I wanted security with Xander and his troupe, but it was something I had to fight for. I thought earning it myself would make it unbreakable. I was wrong. Having it given without any demands, like Deb had offered, is what makes it lasting. At least, I hope.

I can feel in Roman's grip and the way he stands there beside me, not saying a word, that he'd stand here for an eternity if I needed it.

We don't have an eternity anymore.

And deep down, I know Deb will welcome me back.

I knock.

The door creaks open, and Parker's and Jacob's laughter drifting through almost makes me cry.

"Ava?" Deb's voice is shocked as she pulls open the door. For a second, she just stares at me, and then tears well up in her eyes, and she pulls me in for a tight hug. After a brief hesitation, my arms encircle her as well, and we stand there tangled together for several long breaths, neither of us wanting to be the one to break the moment. Finally, Deb draws back but keeps hold of both my shoulders as she looks me over. When her eyes meet mine again, she unleashes her wide smile. "I didn't expect you home so soon. We've . . . we've all really missed you, Ava."

Her words startle me, the way she calls this my home without hesitation, the way she says that *they*—not just Parker, but all of them—have missed me. . . . But if I'm being honest, Deb's always been telling me that they want me, that this is my home. I just couldn't quite hear it before.

"I hope it's okay . . . ," I start.

"You know it's more than okay." She turns around. "Parker! Jacob! Ava's home!"

There it is again. So easy. It kills me a bit to realize it was always that easy, but I wasn't ready to let it be. I can fix that, though. In more ways than one.

I'm ready now.

I look up at Roman as I take his hand again. He gives me a small smile.

I don't get a chance to return it. Parker slams into me so hard that we almost topple down the steps.

I wrap one arm around him as he leans back with a grin. Roman starts to drop my hand, but I hang on to him. I don't want to let go of anything.

"Missed you so much, Ava," Parker says as he steps back.

I'm surprised when Jacob moves in next and gives me a hesitant side-hug. We've *never* hugged before, and it feels awkward but in a kinda perfect way.

Jacob turns to Roman. "Aren't you that knife guy?"

"I suppose I am," Roman says.

"Prove it," Parker says, grinning at me. He looks at our entwined hands and wiggles his eyebrows. I shake my head and groan, but I can feel the smile spreading across my face, and it puts every other smile to shame—every fake one or real one I've given in years—because this one is for everyone in front of me. This one is for my family.

Roman casually pulls a knife from his wrist and twirls it in one hand like a baton thrower in a marching band. Some skills aren't magic.

I snort, and he gives me a little look out of the corner of his eye. His lip twitches into half a smile because he knows what I'm thinking.

It's good to know he'll stoop to showmanship for my brother.

I look at Parker's wide eyes and then Jacob's.

Brothers. The *s* on the end feels weird but right. Something I'll have to get used to but won't regret.

Deb raises her eyebrows and gives me a look, and I can't tell if she's impressed or if it's something like parental concern. "Well," she says, "I guess we know who's carving the turkey on Thanksgiving."

Roman tucks his knife away. "It would be my pleasure."

Deb gives me a look like she's trying not to laugh.

I shrug my shoulders.

Deb steps back from the door. "Lucky for us, we're having pizza tonight, and it's already cut. Come on in."

This time I don't hesitate. I walk inside and pull Roman with me.

"I didn't catch your name last time," Deb says as Roman stands awkwardly next to me in the little foyer.

"This is Roman," I say. I wave a hand at the rest of them. "This is Deb, Parker, and Jacob. My family." I let the word fall this time, but it doesn't crash, because everyone's widening smiles catch the word and make it feel at home.

My throat feels tight, but it's the good kind—where you're so full of love that you might burst.

"Kitchen's this way," Deb says.

The boys are already running back to the pizza and probably planning the mound of cookies they'll smuggle to their room afterward for their gaming session.

"I'm just going to go up to my room for a minute," I say. I want to unload my knives. Now doesn't seem like the best time to show off my new hobby.

Deb hesitates, and I wonder if she's going to give me an awkward lecture about boys in my room, which would definitely be more than I could handle on the parenting front, but she just nods and lets me go.

The creaking stairs welcome me back.

I open my door and freeze.

The dresser and end tables are gone, and so are the flower paintings.

The bedspread is now plain white, and so are the walls. Everything's been stripped away. It never felt like mine to begin with, but it still hurts. Why would she change it so quickly? Had all her smiles since I'd gotten home been fake? Had she really written me off that fast?

Deb clears her throat behind me, and I jump, but I don't turn around because I don't want her to see the look on my face.

I focus on Roman's fingers supporting every one of mine.

"It's not what you think. I wanted you to feel comfortable making it yours when you got home."

I take a deep, shaky breath and look again at all the emptiness and see it for what it really is. A blank canvas. Something to be mine from this point on. Sometimes painting over walls means staying, not leaving.

"I want this to be your home, Ava."

My name is not a question this time. It almost feels like a command. Like this *is* my home whether I want it to be or not.

"I want to do whatever I can to make you feel comfortable here."

"I want to paint the front door," I blurt as I finally turn to face her.

Deb looks surprised, but she doesn't hesitate. "Sure. What color were you thinking?"

I'm tempted to say black just to test her, but I don't feel like she needs any more tests. I shrug. "Turquoise, maybe."

"That'd be nice." She smiles. "We can look at paint tomorrow. Now let's go before those animals downstairs scarf all the pizza up."

We all spend the evening together watching *The NeverEnding Story*, which, to the amazement of everyone, Roman has never seen. We all stare at him when Artax dies, and he wipes his eyes just once, but it's enough for Parker to make fun of him as if *he's* never cried watching it. But for most of the movie, Roman's smiling, not at the movie though—at me. When the movie ends, Deb asks him if she should make up the couch, but he declines, and I walk him to the door.

I fold my hand into his again as he steps outside, holding him with me just a moment longer. "Where are you going to stay?"

He leans in and hesitates with his lips just over mine. "I'll be back in the morning," he says softly, and then he kisses me while our fingers are still intertwined, and it's brief and firm—the kind of kiss that says it's okay to part for a moment because there will be many other times together. So when he pulls away, I let go of him, and I don't watch him leave.

I go back inside with my family.

ACKNOWLEDGMENTS

I've been making up stories forever, but this idea was the first one I ever took seriously. I didn't tackle it for a long time, though. I didn't even start writing novels for years after this idea took root, so seeing it become a book I absolutely love is particularly wonderful, and I have a lot of people to thank for that.

Rebecca Podos, you're amazing, and I know I can always count on you to encourage me with any of my odd story ideas, especially when there are vampires involved. Thank you.

Sarah McCabe, my favorite scenes in this book wouldn't be here without you. You helped me make this wild story exactly what I wanted it to be. Thank you.

To the teams at McElderry Books and Hodder & Stoughton: thank you for giving this book the best homes I could ask for.

Marcela Bolívar and Greg Stadnyk, this book has the cover of my dreams. Thank you for creating it. I stare at it every day.

Portia Hopkins, thank you for reading the first draft of this. Your encouragement made me truly believe I could do this.

Cameron Wilson, I know you've heard me talk about this book a million times between our classes, and our craft talks always left me inspired. Thank you.

Christy Cooper, thank you for always knowing just when I need you to call me. And thank you to your husband, Matt, for being one of my first readers and really understanding the book when he said, "Margie must really like blood." That's still my favorite feedback.

Bailey Gillespie, thank you for all our talks about writing and the trips we take that never fail to inspire. I can't wait to go back to Santa Cruz with you again and visit the place that inspired this book.

Jess Creaden, I wouldn't survive publishing without you. Thank you for all your wisdom and support. I can always count on you.

Savanah Cortino, thank you for all the laughter and fun times we shared in grad school. It was one of the best times of my life.

Stephanie Garber, thank you for always being willing to give me guidance when I need it. And thank you for the amazing blurb.

Angela Montoya and Sana Muttalib, I love you both endlessly, and I can't wait to be reading your acknowledgments one day.

Thank you to all my Pitch Wars friends. Dawn Ius and Kimberly Gabriel, I'll love you forever.

To my writing critique group: many of you read pieces of this book and encouraged me from the start. Thank you Jeff Wooten, Eliza Langhans, Emily Thiede, Ryan Van Loan, Brook Kuhn, Emily Taylor, and Brighton Rose. Special thank-you to Melody Steiner who gave me some of my earliest feedback on the full manuscript.

Thank you to my professors who made me believe I had what it took to make it.

To my former students: there's nothing I miss more than being your professor. Thank you for giving me some of my favorite moments. This is another book that many of you saw me working on, and I hope you're still pursuing your own projects.

And last but definitely not least, thank you to my parents for supporting me while I went through all the versions of who I thought I wanted to be before I finally, finally admitted I wanted to write. And thank you to all my family for your endless love. Lucas, Liam, Gabriel: I love you more than anything.